W9-ACL-291

ABSOLUTELY

NOTHING

TO GET

ALARMED

ABOUT

ABSOLUTELY NOTHING TO GET ALARMED ABOUT

THE COMPLETE NOVELS OF

CHARLES WRIGHT

THE MESSENGER

THE WIG

ABSOLUTELY NOTHING TO GET ALARMED ABOUT

HarperPerennial
A Division of HarperCollinsPublishers

HarperCollins books may be purchased for educational, business, or sales promotional use. For information please write: Special Markets Department, HarperCollins Publishers, Inc., 10 East 53rd Street, New York, NY 10022.

First HarperPerennial edition published 1993.

Designed by George J. McKeon

Library of Congress Cataloging-in-Publication Data

Wright, Charles, 1932–
    Absolutely nothing to get alarmed about: the complete novels of Charles Wright.—1st ed.
    p.   cm.
    Contents: The messenger—The wig—Absolutely nothing to get alarmed about.
    ISBN 0-06-096958-X (paper)
    1. Afro-Americans—New York (N.Y.)—fiction.   I. Title.
PS3573.R532A15   1993
813'.54—dc20   92-53418

93 94 95 96 97 ❖/HC 10 9 8 7 6 5 4 3 2 1

To My Lady of the Hats, Midge McKenzie

CONTENTS

THE MESSENGER

....

In memory of Billie Holiday and Richard Wright

....

I AM ON THE STOOP these spring nights. The whoring, thieving gypsies, my next door neighbors, are out also. Their clientele is exclusively male. Mama, with her ochre-lined face, gold earrings, hip-
swinging beaded money pouch, flowing silk skirts, is sitting on her
throne, the top step. She went to jail the other day, made the *Daily
News*. She had clipped a detective and tried to bribe him with ten
bucks. The gypsy kids are out also. The girl is five, the boy six.
They sell paper flowers. Some moron walking with his girl gives the
boy a dime and tells him to keep the flower. He takes his girl's arm
and they go off laughing, doing the slumming act. The sweet-faced
little gypsy boy looks up at me and mutters, "Cheap c————." The
gypsy girl, when her face is clean, looks as if she had been born to
wear a confirmation dress. She works men with her sad angel's
face; tears fall like soft rain from her eyes. Most men are not
deceived and then she jumps up and slaps them on the buttocks,
always the wallet pocket.

This street is a pretty spring night's dream, Forty-ninth Street
between Sixth and Seventh Avenues, with its frantic mixed bag of
colors. Chinese and French restaurants, the Gray Line sightseeing
buses, jukebox bars catering to soldiers and sailors and lesbian
prostitutes, parking lots and garages filled with people returning
from the theatre. And tourist hotels.

Later in my apartment, five stories up, nothing obscures the brooding night sky laced with orange-red neon. A haze hangs low over the buildings. The Empire State Building looms a giant obelisk; the rest is a misty El Greco painting. In the mist the low buildings are angular, surrealistic.

Here in this semi-dark room, I become frightened. Am I in America? The objects, chairs, tables, sofa are not specifically American. They, this room, have no recognizable country. I have always liked to believe that I am not too far removed from the heart of America (I have a twenty-five dollar U. S. Savings Bond) and I am proud of almost everything American. Yet I'm drowning in this green cornfield. The acres stretch to infinity. I dare not move. This country has split open my head with a golden eagle's beak. Regardless of how I try, the parts won't come together. And this old midtown brownstone is waiting mutely for the demolition crew, these two-and-a-half rooms which have sheltered me for two years. A room with a view: the magical Manhattan skyline, and all for five dollars a week because I have connections.

But the super just came in. I looked up. From the top of his cranium an unbroken hairless line runs straight down to the hollow of his neck like the bold stripe of a zebra.

"Charlie, why the hell you sitting in the dark like this? You drunk or something?"

"Want a beer?" I ask.

The super was standing motionless with his hand on the doorknob. All I could see was his steel-rimmed glasses. I had a feeling that he was staring hard at me.

Finally he blurted out, "Charlie, you gotta move. Somebody keeps ratting to the landlord. And it puts me on the spot."

"It must be those people next door. They wanted this place."

"Yeah," the super agreed. "But the Housing Authority said this place couldn't be rented again unless the violations were fixed. So a man from the office is coming round tomorrow and you do what you always do."

"Okay," I said. "Sure you don't want a beer?"

"Nope," the super said.

So tomorrow I must pack all of my things and store them with the people in number seven and with Maxine's mother, who lives on the second floor. I will sprinkle dust on the floor, close the shutters tight, scatter cigarette butts and old newspapers around, and take the mattress off the bed.

Nothing lasts forever, I remember telling Shirley. She had called to wish me a belated happy birthday. It had simply slipped her mind. Oh, she was fine. When she felt the need to come over, she'd let me know. "Well, you just do that, cupcake," I had said. "I'll keep you waiting on the stoop five hours like Easter." She hung up without a good-bye. We have been fighting and making up for more than two years now. This always happens when people are unwilling to give up even the carcass of an affair.

I must remember not to flush the cigarette butts down the can in the hall. I'll need them to make this place look unlived in. I'll sweep up and move back in when the Housing man has come and gone.

MAY DAY: Loyalty and Communist Front celebrations. I work for a messenger service in Rockefeller Center and it's just another day for this worker. A hop, skip, delivery, and I net exactly nine dollars and twenty cents a day. (The minimum wage has increased fifteen cents an hour, but prices rose and not my standard of living.) The other messengers, especially the elderly men, talk labor. A few of them are retired businessmen who work because they can't stand the yacketyyack of the wife. One has ten thousand dollars in the bank; another owns nine houses. They are fanatical collectors and readers of newspapers, and they take their messenger jobs seriously. During slack periods they sit on a long wooden bench in an odd-shaped room on the concourse floor of Rockefeller Plaza, talking together. They can drive you nuts, but I have learned from them and, on the whole, they're remarkable. They are still very much alive despite their various ailments.

One is eighty years old and has a prosperous goose step. His wife is ill and often he has to go home. When he speaks of her, his eyes light up and his voice is tender. Al, the messenger boss, sits in an old-fashioned swivel chair, puffing a cigar. This patriarch, referee of messenger disputes, dispatches deliveries all over the city. Miss Mary, the sixty-year-old telephone girl, is pert as a daisy. She has the gay voice of a schoolgirl. And on this first day of May, everyone is talking labor. I am silent. I have just delivered several boxes of dresses to the garment district. How I hate that place. Laura Vee models in that gilded Buchenwald.

Later Pepe, Tommy and I—fellow messengers—are in the subway john drinking Gypsy Rose wine, the champagne of winos. We are killing time. It has begun to rain.

"Shit," Pepe says. "I've gotta move. We just moved into the projects and we still ain't got enough room. My folks are fighting worse than usual. You can't shit straight in the projects."

"I'm saving my money to buy a pick-up truck," Tommy says. He is eighteen, a Tenth Avenue Irish lad. "I wanna go into business for myself. I've saved up almost two hundred dollars. Everytime the boss tells me to ride I walk and pocket the thirty cents."

"Shit," Pepe says. He's Puerto Rican and speaks with a Southern Negro accent. He lives in Harlem. "That's no bread. I'm gonna get me a whore or something. Right, Charlie?"

"Oh, yeah," I assured him. "You've gotta have something working for you."

"My old man hasn't worked in over a year," Tommy tells us. "I've gotta help Mama. I really want that truck. Hell, I don't know if I'm coming or going."

"Shit," Pepe says. "I give my old lady fifteen bucks a week and send my baby sister five a week. She has TB and lives in Puerto Rico with my aunt. The climate is good for her. I'm buying a guitar on time. I don't have five bucks left when it's all over. Shit!"

"Let's drink up, boys," I say. "Let's get this show on the road."

That afternoon, as I walked through the concourse of the RCA building, sneezing and reading Lawrence Durrell, dead drunk from the explosion of his words, I suddenly looked up and encountered the long face of Steven Rockefeller. He seemed startled. Doesn't he think poor people read?

SATURDAY MORNING I was walking in the East Fifties, going over to the river to find a bench and sit and reread Hemingway's short stories. A middle-aged man, with homburg, British raincoat, whiskey-ad face, jostled against me. He says, "Excuse me, sonny." His expression is guarded, his smile buttery. "All young men should read Hemingway." And: "I remember when I first read Hemingway."

Does he really like Hemingway? Or is this a front?

"I have a large collection of books, mostly rare. Mostly first editions. Would you care . . ."

I sighed inwardly and said Yes, what the hell.

His name is Mr. Bennett. We stand in front of his teakwood door. Picasso drawings in the foyer. *The Wall Street Journal* on the telephone table. A Marc Chagall over the English down sofa. A Vuillard above the fireplace. Pornographic Japanese prints in the bathroom. I drink a double scotch from a Swedish crystal glass. I once delivered a dozen glasses of the same design to a woman who had just moved to Sutton Place South. She looked as if she would have been happier in the Bronx. Nevertheless, she lived in a co-op on Sutton Place South.

Mr. Bennett was offering me imported Dutch cocktail biscuits and saying I must try this aged twenty-year-old brandy. I smile, teeth and all. I never get drunk and pass out. Alcohol is merely a brace for my spine, the fine oil for my reflex gears.

If I could only be alone with that wall of books! But Mr. Bennett said, "I think I'll return to North Africa. So simple. The Arab boys will do anything—for a price, of course."

He sat down on the sofa beside me like a careful old maid. His voice was fatherly. Sweat trickled down my armpits. My heart rose or fell a little, as it does at times like this. I bet I can't get an erection, I told myself. That seemed funny. I laughed secretly, and then I felt his hand on my buttocks. This queer would get nothing but his feelings hurt.

So I rose, smiling, and made my exit. I didn't even take a last, hungry look at that wall of books.

WE BLOW OUR OWN TRUMPETS though we always swear the music is coming from another horn. Some of my friends say I am cocky, arrogant. But I have always been alone and have developed what they see as arrogance for my protection.

Last evening Shirley came over. Once I dreamed of quitting the messenger service, get a better job, save money, put a down payment on a house, and marry Shirley.

She sat very demurely in my sagging canvas chair, her dark eyes staring at nothing. There was something fresh and lovely about her, like a single rose in a vase. Her hair was brushed back carefully. She had on a tailored white blouse, dark skirt, and French-heeled, black pumps.

We sat facing each other like proud enemies, silent, engulfed in the poignancy of a city Saturday night and our own thoughts. There was no light in the room, save for the bright slice of moon cutting through the window. The room glowed in this light, shadows springing lifelike.

"I thought this was going to be a special night," Shirley complained. "A celebration. I thought we'd go out and have a little fun. I didn't come all the way over here just to sit in your apartment."

"All right," I said rising. "Wait until I get dressed. We'll go down to the Village. But I thought we'd spend a quiet evening together. I've a bottle of champagne on ice."

"You and your quiet evenings," Shirley cried. "I don't like quiet evenings. Not anymore. I'm twenty-two years old. I want a little fun out of life."

I started to say, "Get the hell out of here then. Go on the town with your rich doctor." Instead, I finished my cheap port silently.

"You're nothing but a wino," she said, and she wasn't joking.

"So what?"

"I bet you don't even write anymore."

"Is that any sweat off your Goddamn back?"

"I told you about cursing at me."

"I'm sorry. But what the hell are you trying to do to me?"

"And what are you trying to do with me?" Shirley shot back, her voice fighting one of her terrible whimpers.

I poured another glass of port, thinking, I'm through with the Village, the intellectuals. I know the Village and now it is merely a place *not* to go. I want quiet evenings alone with you. My face is bright, I have a youthful stride, but I am getting old. I ought to stop wearing sneakers. My hair is getting gray at twenty-nine and there is nothing distinguished about that. The lines on my forehead are more or less permanent. My energy has been sucked up; I have given, traded my youth for both good and bad values and what mind I had has been ground fine as chopped meat.

I said none of these things. The moon has disappeared. The room was dark. I got up and put my arms around Shirley. She pulled away quickly, as though I were a leper.

Roughly, and with one quick movement, I grabbed her face in my hands and kissed her hard on the mouth.

Shirley broke away. "For God's sake, stop it! You don't own me."

She left angrily; off to her rich doctor. Well, I could sit on the fence and watch love freeze too. Actually I felt like a sea lion land-locked. I sat alone listening to the noises drifting up from the street.

THURSDAY EVENING Troy Lamb called and said he would be right over with his wife, Susan, and his three-year-old son Skipper. This was quite a shock. I met Troy four years ago at the White Horse Tavern. Those were lean, desperate days, and if Troy had a dollar, I certainly had half of it. Often we shared the same cigarette, divided a hard, buttered roll, split a container of black coffee. Neither of us had a steady job, though Troy received a spasmodic pittance from home. He was studying at N.Y.U., philosophy and anthropology. Ah, those days! Sometimes we rode the subway with the work-bound passengers. Troy would read a French or Chinese newspaper; I'd read the *Jewish Daily Forward*. It really upset the passengers; perhaps they thought they were still in bed, having nightmares. Once Laura Vee took me to the Dali show at the Carstairs Gallery on East Fifty-seventh Street, where I met a lot of rich kids. They thought I was very swinging, and came down to my place the following Sunday with hero sandwiches, three bottles of Dubonnet, and an inexhaustible supply of cigarettes. Troy dropped in. I introduced him to Susan Mantle, a freckled, doll-like girl. In the green spring of that year, Troy and Susan said they were going to get married.

Troy received a fellowship to study anthropology. Later they were married and honeymooned in Paris and went to Africa because of Troy's studies. Skipper was born there. Now they were back in New York and were coming over to see me right away.

I went out and bought two fifths of scotch for us, milk and oranges for the baby.

The bell rang. I heard Troy's gravelly voice coming up the stairs.

Susan, brown as a berry, all smiles, was wearing what appeared to be a camel-colored Berber's robe. She ran to embrace me. "Oh, Charles. It's so good to see you!"

"I've missed you kids," I said, releasing Susan.

Troy came up to me. He had on blue jeans, sweatshirt, and a floppy safari hat. Three-year-old Skipper was glued on his back, Indian fashion. Troy dropped Skipper to the floor, and gave me a man-killing slap on the back.

"Charlie, old man," he said. There was warmth in his voice and smile.

"Jesus Christ," I exclaimed, stunned.

"We got in this morning," Susan said. "You're the first person we've seen."

"Yeah," Troy added. "Had to see you. Had to find out what's been happening."

"Oh," Susan moaned, looking at her son. "We almost forgot the baby!"

"Skipper," Troy commanded, like a stern, proud father, "Say hello to Uncle Charles."

Three-year-old, tow-headed, Troy Mantle Lamb pouted and played with his fingers. He wore a little striped suit with matching cap, mischief-like lights sparkled in his blue eyes.

I am very fond of children. The neighborhood kids get all my spare change. "Hello, fellow," I said, picking Skipper up. "Did you kill any tigers in Africa?"

Skipper gave me a long serious look, which in an adult might have meant, "I know you, I know your kind."

"Nigger," Skipper said in a clear, small voice.

For a brief second, human breath was suspended.

Then Troy said angrily: "Shut your trap, you little bastard."

"Oh, Charles," Susan said, shaking her head sadly. "I'm sorry. Honestly, I don't *know* where Skipper heard that."

MY FRIEND NICK has spasms over my body. He thinks it is something to worship, to sing wordless hymns about. He must tell his well-connected friends about it. I must enter the rich world of queerdom.

So tonight, I have on my one-and-only good dark suit. There's a scent of pine about me. I'm using my boyish mannerisms. I've had three double scotches and the lights are in my eyes. I smile quietly, a diplomat in a new and perilous country. Nick, the eunuch guide, is in his glory. There is the proper, white-coated oriental houseman, razor-eyed, smelling of hothouse roses. The host, tanned with gray hair clipped like an oarsman, the face sexless and set like stone. I don't think it's possible for him to move a muscle of it, but he smiles faintly at me, a flicker of interest.

I take in this large room, covered in pale green damask. Empire paintings in gilt frames; the fruit-wood furniture with simple lines; masses of carefully arranged white tulips.

There are exactly twelve men in the room, talking quietly over drinks, their quick eyes darting around the room. They have little of the aura one associates with piss-elegant faggots; these men are well-to-do, not phonies. Still, I keep thinking if they're so unreal in real life, how is it possible for their sex lives to have any meaning? And the answer is: perhaps it doesn't.

"Writer? How interesting!" They knew slews of writers. It

might be fruitful if I came to cocktails next week. I need to get away to the Cape, or Fire Island. A writer needs solitude. I don't look like a messenger. (What does a messenger look like?) They're all round me, talking in their prissy, cultured voices and I'm thinking, Jesus, Jesus, the latest hunk of meat to be tossed into the arena.

Dinner in a shimmering black and white dining room. Real linen napkins, candlelight, three wines. Polite small talk. And now, shall we retire to the den?

We're all good and drunk now. To hell with good breeding, we're for real. Several of the men have suddenly become their favorite actresses. Gradually, the lights are lowered, one by one. Men are lounging in chairs, on sofas, the floor, in various poses. Shirts open or at least unbuttoned. Trousers: open or down. Most of them went about their business silently, except for a few who whispered in tense voices, cooing of love. It was a grotesque scene with wild, quick body movements, groans, great murmuring sounds.

No one had touched me. I have a feeling that they are waiting for the main show, *me*. When it came, it was the little man who had sat next to me at dinner, a jolly man who told amusing stories. But now he was like a man stumbling through the dark and afraid.

Nick and I left at three a.m. I wanted a drink. We stopped in a neighborhood bar.

"Oh, you were sensational!" Nick beamed. He seemed very pleased, like a mother when baby takes his first steps alone. "You're going places, Charles. Didn't I tell you, didn't I?"

I didn't answer him. I drank my drink, his drink, and four more.

It was an experience, nothing more. And if I felt like it, I'd do it again. It was as simple as that.

But Nick talked on. My anger rose. With a rock-and-roll singer on the jukebox yelling, "What is the price of happiness, what is the price of love?" I leaned over and tried to crack Nick's head with my glass.

SOMETIMES I FEEL as if I'm being strangled by the sophisticate scum of New York, by those millions of feet making it toward Mr. Greenbacks and what it takes to be a "smaht" New Yorker. And me, what does this sophisticate scum want from me? The understanding ear, the priest in blue jeans.

I hear the breathless, girlish voice of Mrs. Lee coming upstairs. "Now Pike . . . now Tike. Babies! One at a time, one at a time."

Her heels clicked on the tiled steps and she stage-called, "Charles, darling! You have visitors."

I opened the door and Mrs. Lee came toward me puffing, her short, plump body cleverly concealed in a black suit. She was weighed down with garlands of oriental pearls, a large garnet-pearl brooch, and exactly eleven gold bangle bracelets. A sable scarf dropped seven skins carelessly from her shoulders; a garnet velvet skullcap was perched on her thin, red-gold hair, fluffed wild. Her hair was not unlike that of Tike and Pike, her two miniature French poodles. She had the face of a warmhearted cherub.

"Whew," Mrs. Lee sighed. "These steps. Charles, you need an elevator."

I stood by the door and watched her. "You're looking wonderful," I said.

"Naughty boy," she tut-tutted. "I brought you a little present—champagne."

I put the champagne in the ice box and waited for the soliloquy. Mrs. Lee was posed grandly on the sofa bed.

"I was thinking of you, Charles darling, of something you once said, 'You are not defeated until you are defeated.' Remember Adolf? . . . Where he got that German name I'll never know. Oh dear, I was wild with grief, stayed in bed two days. I couldn't eat a thing, darling. But on the third day I was starved. I went to Schrafft's and had a feast. Over dessert I said to myself, 'Lee, dear, let's face it. Adolf was a first-class son-of-a-bitch!' Well he was, darling. And these two little sweethearts knew it all along." She paused to look lovingly at Tike and Pike. "Adolf would sit on the sofa beside me, and Tike and Pike would jump on the sofa *facing* us. Never once did they sit on *our* sofa. That's how I smell out rats. With Tike and Pike, the dears."

On cue, like guards of honor, Tike and Pike pranced over and sat elegantly at their mistress's feet.

"I had a little party last night, Charles, and I called you. Where were you, darling? It was only half-past-eight, and Chico had left. . . ." At this Mrs. Lee paused and tears began to play hell with the three layers of makeup. "*Left*, darling. Saying the most impossible things. Oh, dear."

Mrs. Lee has had a succession of lovers and suffers no illusions. Her heartbreak is only on the surface—the same act played with a different male lead. Mrs. Lee, an aging, ageless coquette, dressed in gold and lavender tea gowns, matching ribbon in her hair, dancing through an army of Puerto Rican gigolos, small pretty young men, manicured like dolls. Or Mrs. Lee, her face powdered chalk white, a headache band around her hair, yards and yards of black chiffon, screaming, "Go! This very moment! Back to your Goddamn island!" Or Mrs. Lee, motherly, chiding, "Your English hasn't improved. What are you going to night school for? No more pointed Florsheim shoes. No suede jackets and those tight pants. *Understand?*"

"Oh dear," Mrs. Lee was saying, "I need someone like you, Charles."

"Chico will come back," I tried to reassure her.

"Of course," she said coldly. "They all come back, the rats. But Charles, *do* you think I'll have another lovely, lovely affair? Like last summer?"

Remembering the champagne, knowing what she had come to hear, I nodded and said in a soothing voice, "As sure as the sun rises."

MITCH CAME OVER this afternoon with a mysterious bottle. He offered it to me, his tiny, glass-bead eyes never leaving my face. I screwed the top off the bottle and took a whiff. The smell was too sweet, sickening.

"Go on, man. It's cough syrup. Take a swig," Mitch invited. "You can buy it at any drugstore. Just go in and cough like mad. I never have any trouble. I'm so skinny they think I have TB."

"I thought pot was your speed."

Mitch gave me a long hard stare. "Have you got anything? It just so happens this boy is busted. I've got to get my nerves together and make a score. Real bad."

I knew what was coming. "I need some money myself," I said. "I don't get paid till Tuesday."

"Oh, that's right," Mitch said thoughtfully. "You ought to give up that messenger job. You've lost a fortune with that body of yours."

"Never in your stall, daddy," I shook my head, remembering what Alice had once told me: "I gave away a million dollars' worth before I discovered I could sell it. Pussy will sell when cotton won't."

"With me, it's morals," Mitch was saying, eyeing the brown bottle. "Are you gonna drink that shit?"

I took a short nip and it tasted like sugared glue. Mitch took the bottle. "Man, I got so high that I walked all the way down. From West Seventy-second Street."

I took another drink of the cough syrup and after a few seconds, my head was slightly light. I wanted a drink but I wouldn't stand Mitch a drink. A shot wouldn't do him any good. On moneyless days, we used to boil water and make a cup of tea, throw in a generous amount of cinnamon, inhale the fumes and drink the scalding tea down in a gulp. Today, I can't stand the smell of cinnamon.

"Mitch, have you ever drunk lemon extract?" I asked.

"What? Come again."

"Lemon extract. It's got eighty percent alcohol in it."

"Take me to thy vat," Mitch hammed.

We went into the closet kitchenette. I opened up a bottle of Seven-up, got a tray of ice and a ten-ounce reserve bottle of lemon extract, and poured them into a water pitcher. I stirred until the tangy mixture was chilled.

"This is something a cook in the army taught me," I said, giving Mitch a sample glass.

Mitch took a careful sip, his beady eyes pointed dead on me. He licked out his fox tongue and took a long drink.

"Ba-bee," he exclaimed, "this is a fucking groove. Man, we can bottle this shit and sell it!"

"Oh, sure," I agreed, pouring a glass. "We'll call it lemon juice."

"Yeah," Mitch hee-hawed. "Lemon juice."

We downed our lemon juice, poured another round, went into the living room, and exhausted the possibilities of lemon extract, joking about the crazy Bronx-Brooklyn kids who get high on marijuana mixed with store-bought oregano and catnip. Mitch used to push that stuff. The kick came from following the leader and because it was the fashionable thing to do.

"Awright," Mitch said. "Awright. With this codeine and lemon juice I can't help but score tonight."

"Do you mind if I have some more of this shit?" Mitch asked.

"Knock yourself out, baby."

Mitch returned from the kitchenette, a deep, one-track expression on his face. He fished in his pocket for a cigarette and out fell his red plastic toothbrush.

The toothbrush fell to the floor dully. I didn't say anything.

Mitch crinkled up the corners of his lips and I saw his teeth. But it wasn't a smile. He shook his head sadly. "I'm travelling light," he said. "Those whores are down at The Tombs. I ain't got any bread. I can't bail'm out. In fact, I got locked out of my pad. I have on my one-and-only wardrobe."

"That's tough," I said, feeling as foolish as I sounded. "Why don't you work the eastside?"

"Don't dig those pissy faggots," Mitch frowned. "And you know I got morals. I got to dig a fag."

"You're roofless, baby," I told him.

"But I'm gonna be one old clip-artist tonight. You just watch this kid operate. Awright!"

"You'll be all right," I tried to assure him. He was never sure of himself.

"I'm getting my nerves settled down," he said. "I got a feeling it's gonna be real nice."

"Well," I said slowly, "if you don't have a place to flop, come on back up here."

Mitch was smiling this time and wishing like hell that he wasn't. He gave me a warm buddy-buddy wink. "Charlie, you are a jewel."

TODAY I WALKED and walked through the rainy New York streets. I had deliveries downtown, uptown, westside, eastside. I walked until my feet were soaking wet and I could feel water coming through my raincoat, sweater, and shirt. I made my way through hordes of New Yorkers, and commuters, all walking, running, shoving, cursing. Finally the last delivery was over, and at 7 P.M. I climbed up my five flights and locked the door. I didn't even bother to take off my wet clothes, just lay down on the bed and asked myself what I was doing in this city. I knew some answers. After my grandmother's death there was nothing to keep me in Missouri. I had always been a travelling lad, and so I came to New York.

But I cannot connect the fragments of my life. These dirty, white-walled rooms, the mixed cheap furniture, the decayed scent of this old midtown brownstone, the constant hum of voices, music, and impatient traffic which comes up from the street— what do they have to do with me? The Chinese say that the first step is the beginning of a ten-thousand-mile journey. But what is the first step?

With my head burrowed in the pillow, I try to think of beginnings; my past.

"*One of these days, you gonna die, pretty baby,*" a voice sings mockingly from the jukebox of the bar on the ground floor.

With enormous effort, I go back through the bowels of memory, back to Missouri. It is death that carries me back, my mother's death in that four-year-old world.

She had only been sick two hot August days.

Death was a crowded cottage with paint peeling from the exterior.

"Poor thing. Ain't he sweet?"

"Come and give cousin Mary a great big kiss."

"He don't know what it is all about."

"Poor thing. Ain't he sweet?"

Death was my father, standing around looking lost, although he didn't live with us anymore. And Grandpa, a big tall man with handlebar mustache, in a black deacon's suit.

"Come here, Sonny," he said, picking me up, playfully rubbing his big brown hands through my hair. He gave me a bowl of raspberry ice cream. After the ice cream melted, I stuck my finger in it and the raspberries went round and round in circles.

Most of all, there was my grandmother, standing in front of the casket and looking down at the last of her four daughters. Her mouth was set tight and she clenched a handkerchief in her hand. But she did not cry. I did not cry either because they had already told me death was a long, long sleep and you did not wake until you got to heaven. Afterwards, I looked up at the sky and in my child's mind, I did not believe that that was true.

Then there was the fun of living with Grandpa and Grandma. Cookies and cakes, licking the big cooking spoons. Fishing with Grandpa. Walking through the courthouse square with him, listening to his old cronies and their tales of the muddy Missouri River.

School starts and I am very shy. I do not know the children. But the teacher likes me. My marks are good. There are fights with the kids.

"Teacher's pet."

"You think you is cute."

"You is a nigger like all the rest of us."

"Yeah. You ain't nothing but a shit-colored nigger."

"Half-white bastard."

Ella Mae was a pretty, dark little girl with merry eyes. She was skinny with long braids. She smiled at me during recess. I gave her my apple.

Years go quickly. I become the best-liked boy in the community. "I think it's simply wonderful the way you are raising that boy." This is said to Grandpa and Grandma.

I'm thirteen now and teaching Sunday school. I become a man in the sexual sense.

Mary Ann's grandmother was a sewing-circle crony of my grandmother. One hot, summer afternoon they went out, leaving Mary Ann and me alone. We drank lemonade and had a couple of half-hearted games of blackjack. Finally the card game petered out. Sixteen-year-old Mary Ann began telling ghost stories. The setting was perfect. An old Victorian house filled with dark, heavy furniture, stiff, dusty drapes at the windows and between the doorways, the odor of hothouse flowers. Very little sunlight entered. I was always fascinated by Mary Ann's house; it was like suffocating in a delicious dream.

Suddenly, Mary Ann became sleepy. I began to leave, believing she was trying to get rid of me. On the contrary, she wanted me to stay. If I wasn't sleepy, at least I could stay until she fell asleep. I could usually be talked into things which did not interest me. Not really talked into, but still I'd go along like a good sport. Already I had discovered that it caused me less worry, less arguing and explaining.

So I went into the bedroom and carefully turned my head while Mary Ann undressed. I caught a view of her buttocks and legs as she deliberately pranced in front of me, talking a mile a minute. Her naked body aroused my thirteen-year-old mind. I would have liked to ask Mary Ann to stand still so I could take a good full view. But I was too well brought up.

Mary Ann got into bed; I sat in a slipper chair, very uncomfortable, digging my nails into the palm of my hand.

"Come and get into the bed with me," Mary Ann giggled.

"I don't want to get into bed," I argued. "I don't take naps anymore."

"You know this old house is full of ghosts," Mary Ann said, sitting up in bed. "Remember my Aunt Sarah died in this very room. If you don't get in bed with me why she just might come wandering in here. Honest, Sonny."

I did not really believe in ghosts. But I wasn't going to take a chance. I jumped into Mary Ann's bed and pulled the covers tight over my head.

Mary Ann giggled, her nervous, long hands probing my body like cold snakes. And then it dawned on me why we were playing this game on a hot, summer afternoon. I let Mary Ann undress me, got on top of her, moved my body as she instructed, though I did feel a little foolish humping up and down like a dog. I was tense with fear, wondering what would happen if Mary Ann's grandmother walked in. The climax came and I stiffened my body and put my arms around Mary Ann. It felt as if I could press farther, but the distance was too great. And though I was still a little skeptical of this new act, I was certainly going to try it again.

Afterwards, there was a whole string of little girls and, of course, Mary Ann. She kept me supplied with contraceptives which I hid in my winter boots.

One cloudy afternoon that summer, the middle-aged minister of our church invited me into his small study in back of the church.

"Sonny, how old are you?"

"Past thirteen, Sir."

"You are getting to be a little man," the minister said. "I've watched you in Sunday school. Some day you'll make a fine disciple for the Lord. You have got the qualities and you act very grown up. That's what it takes. Now I don't want you to think I'm trying to force you into becoming a man of God. But I want you to think about it. You'd make a fine one and you could do a lot for our people."

"Yes, sir."

"You are getting to be a little man," the minister grinned. "Yes, sir, a little man, and I bet all the little girls are crazy about you."

He came and stood by my chair and patted my head, looking at me with a laughing expression in his eyes. "Yes, sir, you have all the little girls following you around. You must have a whopper."

As the summer evenings grew longer, more languid, Grandpa would constantly repeat, "This world is not my home." He had stopped reading the local paper, the *National Geographic,* and the almanac. I was surprised and slightly embarrassed. But I did not mention this to Grandma. We were very close but kept our secrets locked in our hearts. At the time, the great Why of everything had not formed in my adolescent mind. I knew Grandpa was not the

man of fishing, ice cream days. I was getting older, almost fourteen.

Grandpa's mind drifted as he felt that this world was not his
home. People began to talk. They were very decent about it; everyone knew my grandparents. We were a quiet, respectable, church-
going family.

We used to sit on the big front porch during the Missouri summer evenings. One night Grandpa tried to fight with Grandma. In
the past she had always been able to outwit him or at least calm
him down. But that night she was powerless. Two neighbor men
came over and put him to bed. The doctor arrived and was going
to give him an injection. But sleep had overtaken him, sleep that
turned into death by eight the following morning.

Then Grandma and I were alone in the paint-peeling, white
frame house during the long days and short nights of that fourteen-year-old summer. We became very close.

I began to be aware of something at this time, something perhaps I had been born with, and which was never to leave me.
Loneliness.

And this consciousness is here with me now, in this small, dark
room in New York. I get up and look out the window. It is still
raining.

I WALK THROUGH the early morning streets saddled with a numb, self-centered despair. The bars are closing, and a terrible, indefinable magic cuts the cool air. Early Sunday morning has that subtle, quiet quality in New York. Lonely people everywhere know that time of morning. Slow, uncertain footsteps, your own distorted reflection in darkened store windows. The shameful, envious, eyes-lowered glances at passing couples. You recognize other solitary fellow travelers. Both of you go separate ways, moving with the knowledge of Sunday papers, endless cigarettes, tap water, the hoarded half-pint, and the feeling of having missed out on Saturday night's jackpot prize. You give up the Waterloo, mount the steps, unlock the door, turn on the light, undress. You pace the floor and finally try to sleep, comforted with nothing but the prospect of another sunrise.

You pay for everything you get in this world. Glitter and polish, sophistication, the ejaculations delivered to a sterile country. Everything.

You are alone now, buried in your own morality. I have got to leave New York. I am saving my nickels, dimes, dollars, and this winter I will go away.

Now the Sunday sky is serene and pale blue. Toward the east a ballet of soft, white clouds. The rising sun breaks through shafts of gold. It was as if God had suddenly opened His powerful hand on the world. My heart bows its head in the presence of this force. I am suddenly at peace in this early morning. The sun comforts me; I am swaddled in the folds of those wonderful clouds. Let the rays of the sun touch your body and you will be made holy. Shirley used to say I was saintly, I had missed my calling, I should become a preacher. *You've got the makings, boy. Why did you stray so far from home?*

FRIDAY. Faded blue sky. Ninety-three-degree noonday heat. Jammed traffic and the smooth grind of the crosstown bus.

Maxine the pixie, honey-colored seven-year-old, bounces in. She lives on the second floor and has the mind of a twelve-year-old.

"Did I scare you, Charles?" Maxine throws her arms around me. "I've got a present for you. One of my fantastic pictures. Look!"

I look up slowly and smile. Maxine loves the word "fantastic." Now she is studying me closely, taking in the red-yellow eyes and the fat bags under them and the two-day beard.

Maxine has given up conventional children's drawing. She is on an abstract kick. The lines are firm; the colors blend. I took her once to the Museum of Modern Art, but she was very hostile to the gods of Modern Art. She prefers her own abstractions.

Maxine's picture has squares, circles, crisscrossing lines of lime green, yellow, black, and brown.

I try to show interest. I feel despondent. "What is it, cookie? I give up."

"Oh, goodness. You don't know anything. It's the Tip Top parking lot with the sun shining down on it."

"And it's beautiful," I say, taking another quick glance at the picture. "I'll put it in the kitchen."

"No, Charles, here. You don't have any light in the kitchen."

Evening arrives with the sudden press of a familiar inky stamp. I look out the window at the soot-caked, blank, brick wall of Tip Top parking and the grim, red-brick façade of the Elmwood Hotel. TV and mistily yellow lights glow in Elmwood windows. An unreal face appears at a gold-curtained window and withdraws, a shy ghost.

I grow old in the terrible heart of America. I am dying the American-money death. "There's plenty of money out there, Charlie," Al, my messenger boss says, waving his expensive cigar. "You only have to figure out a way to get it."

Why doesn't America let me die quietly? No. This country smiles on; the smile is a stationary sun. The sin is believing, hoping. But I am too tired, too afraid now to commit this sin.

AFTER THE BIGGEST DROP since the Twenty-nine hari-kari, the stock market is rallying. Tuesday, May 30, 1962 at exactly a quarter of six in the evening.

Three young and one gruff middle-aged brokers are quite publicly picking their noses. Nervousness? Relief from tension? Only one broker has the sanitary turn-of-mind to use his handkerchief. This is the Park Avenue branch office of a Wall Street firm. I am here waiting to take stocks and bonds downtown. But the ticker-tape hasn't closed yet. Everyone is tensely excited. All I want to do is deliver the stuff and go home. The sudden change of fortune has no effect on me.

As the Italian elevator operator named Smitty says, "The big boys are fucking up but good. Somebody's getting the gravy, you can bet your bottom dollar on that." Another elevator operator has lost four hundred dollars in the drop. He has six children and three hundred and fifty dollars in a joint account. He lives in a five-room, Second Avenue walk-up. He is not getting on with his wife. The second daughter is eight and just had a serious operation. The drop isn't helping things. He doesn't want to visit his father's grave tomorrow and he is debating if he should go to church Sunday, that is, if he doesn't get on a rip-roaring drunk Saturday night. He is a moderate drinker. Thirty-three years old, slender, with the jerky movements of a backward child. He has the pallid looks of a man who spends eight hours a day in an automatic tomb with his thoughts, his eyes straight ahead.

But here, fourteen stories above Park Avenue, the air is jubilant. If the voices, the laughter, are slightly on edge, the feeling nevertheless is that we've made the day. One of the brokers cracked: "Well I won't have to go to the blood bank after all." This is followed by lusty, breathtaking ha-ha's.

Now picture, if you will, a room about sixteen by twenty feet: ivory walls, deep gray wall-to-wall carpeting, reproductions of English antiques, steel filing cabinets painted pale green, Chinese-style lamp bases, and silk shades covered with clear plastic. The east wall has a large, plate-glass picture window. This is the operating room where the wheeling and dealing is done. There is God, or his earthly counterpart, the ticker tape. Phones ring. Brokers pick their noses and watch the vice-president as the ticker tape glides through his smooth, firm fingers. The brokers doodle with pencils, make notes. Now and then there's slight disagreement. The voices become angry. Warriors after an uncertain truce.

"I feel sorry for the girls downtown," the vice-president says, "printing the stuff. They must be really boiled. Every now and then they print the wrong number."

The lights in the glass-enclosed room are fluorescent and under that naked glare, I discover that all of the younger brokers need a shave. The older brokers are clean shaven.

The vice-president is the star, with ruddy good looks, a full flowing crop of white hair. He is wearing a black suit with matching vest and gold watch chain. He resembles a magnificent Irish actor. His black eyes are polished like marble and they are quick, too quick. His manner is friendly, even with me, the messenger. Perhaps that is why he is a vice-president. But there are moments when his nerves give and he overplays his role.

"Jesus!" he says, "six o'clock, and it's still coming in. Can you beat that! My wife and I, Jesus. Whiskey and soda all night long."

One young broker wants to cut out. I don't like his looks. I doubt if I would have him working for me. He looks like an overgrown prep school boy who will soon have a prominent stomach. He has been fucking around, walking in and out of the glass astronomer's cage. He wants to leave. Who will phone him on the outcome of the market? No one says anything. So he takes off his straw brimmer and starts fucking around again.

Then there were the phone calls, as everything was ticking off nicely, as the market would soon close, as suicide left the air, as the brokers began to inhale the fickle scent of money again.

And I know how upper-class men talk to their wives. It is very similar to that of middle-class, minor executives of oil and insurance companies.

For example: a young man, thirtyish, medium build, thrush-brown hair thinning at the temples, very good nose and mouth, round horn-rimmed glasses, blue-and-white pin striped shirt (very wrinkled, sleeves rolled back), maroon tie loosened at the collar, and charcoal gray trousers.

Here he is, talking happily, though he seems to be having trouble getting the words out, as if saliva was clogged in his throat.

"Hello, Bunny.

"Yes, no rush. I'll shave here and then we'll get a bite to eat. I'll have to come back here. Yes, hon. We'll go to the party from here. About eight. No rush. Come when you can. Be careful."

He laughs. Must be a private joke or, since everything is fine, he thinks his wife has a sense of humor. Perhaps she has. He signs off with a mouth-smacking "Bye-bye, Bunny."

The overgrown prep school boy passes again. To hell with it—he is cutting out this time. He casts an over-the-shoulder glance at the cage and then looks at me and drops his big, hazel cow eyes.

I pick up a finance magazine and read the slogan: all the news of the hire of the dollar. The broker with the thrush-brown hair and the round horn-rimmed glasses smiles at me, shaking his head. "Hectic day," he says.

Another phone call. This broker is tall and blond, cold and sad. He has a long face and a longer neck which, with his hunched shoulders, distracts from the rich aura of the suntan, the navy silk suit, the sea-green eyes. He took first prize in the nose-picking contest. The phone is cradled on his neck and he is playing with his gold wedding band.

"Hello, honey." (Like a slow, painful breath.)

"Yes, hon.

"Well, you go ahead. Yes, hon.

"No. Taxi. Yes. I'll catch the 6:25 or the 6:48."

He hangs up without a good-bye and goes into the cage.

Already he has the slow relaxed stride of an old man. I am certain he is around my age, twenty-nine.

Then the vice-president steps smartly from the cage. He smiles, rubbing his hands together which I know are never cold.

"Sorry to keep you waiting, sonny. Do you know how to get down there? Fine. Take it to the seventh floor. They're waiting on you. Thanks again, sonny."

I take the stocks and make it. And so that is how it was on May 30, 1962, at the Park Avenue branch office of one Wall Street firm. Earlier I had heard the vice-president exclaim, "We're making history." So in a very, very, vague way, I too helped bring this historic day to a close. And me, I don't have a Goddamn dollar.

ONE AFTERNOON, Al sent me to Esso Research in Florham Park, New Jersey. It's a good three-mile hike after you get off the train.

I started back to the station about five-thirty. The trains leave for New York on the hour.

The sky was dark with the promise of rain. A middle-aged man and woman in a dusty, beat-up station wagon stopped and asked if I wanted a lift. I said yes and started to climb into the backseat. The man said to sit up front with him and the missus. So I did. The woman turned and smiled at me in a motherly way.

"Thanks for the ride," I said, trying to make conversation.

"Think nothing of it," the man said. He held the steering wheel with one hand and bit into a plug of chewing tobacco. "Glad to oblige you."

"Pa and I always pick up hitchhikers," the woman said. "We got a boy in the service. He wrote and told us how hard it was to get a ride, even in uniform."

"You in the army?" the man asked.

"Out." I smiled.

We rode along in silence until I said, "It looks like we might have a storm."

"Yeah," the man said, taking another chew of tobacco. "What are you, Puerto Rican or Filipino?"

"Neither," I said. "I'm colored."

"I see," said the man thoughtfully. "Would you like a woman?"

The woman started crying before I could answer.

"Alfonzo," she moaned.

"Boy, I asked you if you wanted a woman."

"I don't know," I replied weakly.

The man turned off the highway and went down a road lined with tall green trees. It was a dead end. There were the ruins of a decayed farm. The man left the motor running. It made a whining noise.

The man put his arms around his wife. "Hold still, Elvira," he said.

"Oh! The things you do to me," the woman cried, trying to escape from her husband's grip. "The things I have to go through."

Then the woman turned toward me. I sat rigid, listening to the raspy sound of the motor and feeling as if a ball of fire had dropped between the woman and myself.

"What you do to me," the woman wheezed mournfully, pressing her body against mine.

She made a drooling noise like a baby who hasn't learned to talk. I felt her soft, fleshy leg.

"Let go of me, Alfonzo," the woman said. "He's got me. Take your hands off of me. Take'm off, Alfonzo."

The man released his wife and did not say anything. He did not look at his wife when she embraced me. He rested his head against the steering wheel. Toward the end, when his wife screamed joyfully, the man put his hands over his ears.

I straightened up in the seat. "I have to go," I said. "I have to catch a train."

"All right," the man said.

"No," the woman said forcefully, grabbing the steering wheel.

"Elvira, the boy has to go," the man tried to explain.

"You ruin everything for me," the woman said.

They let me off at the highway and I thanked them. I watched the car disappear into the darkness. It was drizzling now. I thought of the expression on the man's face. It was like something terrible had happened to him once long ago that had destroyed his sense of being a man, but it didn't matter much anymore. Whatever it was, resignation had settled in the creases of the pale, puffy face and under the tear-filled, forlorn eyes.

I walked to the station under the black sky, smelling the fresh earth.

I WAS IN Claudia's pad today. Claudia, the Grand Duchess, is a fabulous Negro drag queen who lives down the street from me. He is my friend and is nothing much to speak of as a man, but he makes a swinging broad. Often, after getting dolled up in female attire, Claudia cruises the street, rides the subways and buses, getting picked up by straight men who, after the shock subsides, often accompany him home. He is forever asking policemen for directions. By the time Claudia has made up his face and gotten high, he has gone through a mental transformation as well: he is a woman.

Today, when I entered, he was on the phone, in semi-drag. That is to say he had made up his great doe eyes, and Joan Crawford had nothing on him. He had on a simple, red lace hostess gown, a string of pearls. But he wasn't wearing his "piece," an expensive wig which originally belonged to a Hollywood studio. Without the wig, he looks like a very feminine dyke.

Claudia was off on a blasting high, laughing madly into the jeweled, white phone. I poured a glass of grappa (a gift from an Italian sailor), and sat down. He might talk for an hour.

Claudia patted his pomaded curls lovingly and bared his bold, white teeth. "Oh honey. Let me tell you. I brought this number home, and . . . Miss Thing! I had to put him through, put him through in the name. What? Oh please, Miss Thing. Built. Great,

Greek muscles. Muscles, just gushing. Oh honey, quite facial. We had one old ball. I was so unlovely when I woke up. Not a curl in my head. Miss Bobby tried to get him and couldn't. Greedy bitch. Miss Thing, I gotta hang up. Charlie. Yeah. Miss Thing, I've gotta hang up, child. Press, honey. Get something to grace my bed. Okay, child. Good-bye."

"Oh, honey," Claudia sighed, banging down the receiver. He trotted over and sat down at his concert-size electric organ. There was also a large gold harp in front of the bay window.

"Let's sing 'Nearer My God to Thee'," Claudia said with great dignity.

"Baby, what turned you on?" I asked.

Claudia threw back his head and displayed the evil giveaway, his prominent Adam's apple. "Child, your mother is stoned. The Queen's head is tore up. But I must pray for those poor bastards."

"What the hell are you talking about?"

"Didn't you read the paper? Didn't you read about those children at the UN?"

Claudia gave me a stick of pot. I lit up, taking a deep drag, and held it in my head. "Oh, yeah. You mean those Africans at the UN. I did glance at the headlines."

"Child. Those were no Africans. Those were BM's from uptown. Harlem, child."

"You kidding?"

The Grand Duchess struck a heavy trembling chord, blinking his great eyes. The bold, red mouth bordered on a big laugh. The jeweled hands waltzed over the keys. "Nearer my God to Thee. . . . Amen."

"Carry on, girl," I said.

"Jesus!" Claudia shouted. "I caught the BM's on the eleven o'clock news. They were fighting like crazy. It took two guards to handle one child."

Claudia paused and shook his head, banging down on the organ. "I hope they show those damn fools on the Late Late Show. Jesus. Give me a drag. I've got more in the vault."

"What did the NAACP have to say?"

"Child, those were Muslims or something. They're not connected with the NAACP."

"That's right," I said, reaching for the pot. "Those NAACP

bastards are too busy sucking ass in Washington. I wonder who's blowing who in the Capitol?"

"Oh, honey," Claudia said with great drama, "I'd love to trip through the Pentagon in heavy drag and get myself a lovely general!"

"That would be a test of *real* democracy."

Claudia and I turned on again and I left.

Back to my own place, to my white-walled, dark room.

TO SCORE ON THE SMART EASTSIDE without good connections, you have to know the right bartenders in the right bars who will set Johns up for a cut. But male and female hustlers are always telling me in sad voices, "Gee, kid, you should have been around during World War II. Or even the early fifties. Things jumped then. All you had to do was just walk down Third Avenue. You could even afford to be grand. Turn down tricks."

Now the scene has changed. Big new office and apartment buildings, bright new street lights, the cops clamping down like the great purge. Johns are also not as easy to come by. This is an age of elegance, stupidity, and fakery. Fags giving off an aura of wealth are often nothing more than glorified office boys, struggling like hell for the privilege of living in a walk-up on the East side. And those Harvard tones give under three martinis.

Still, Third Avenue has a little seedy, fashionable charm and sometimes I wander over, step through all that rich dog shit which peppers the sidewalk like a mosaic and peer into antique shops, knowing that some freaklina will accost me. I'll be picked up for ten-plus-drinks, or by a Vassar-type of girl who will want to discuss jazz.

But that evening I had been walking around about an hour, and nothing was happening. I was getting fed up with freaklinas baiting me like a bitch in heat. I was certain two bulls had spotted me. They were in a blue-convertible at First Avenue and Forty-ninth Street. I saw them again at Third and Fifty-fourth. Two well-built young men, trying to strike the cool pose of the athlete, newspaper reporter, or gangster flunkie. They couldn't make up their minds which was the more successful pose.

I made it into a dimly lit Third Avenue bar, an expensive repro-duction of an Irish saloon, pungent with the smell of advertising, tweeds, poodles, fashion-magazine women. The ratty denizens of that special small world: the overdeveloped cage of smart New Yorkers.

I went to the bar and sat down next to a handsome woman with silver-blue hair, ordered a double scotch on the rocks. I would nurse this one and leave if nothing turned up.

The woman and I were the only people alone. I sensed she knew this too, for shortly she turned her elegant face toward me. She had eyes like a half-closed rose. The simple black dress, the single strand of pearls, and the tired, bored expression on her face interested me. She looked swinging and damn sure of herself; most important, she seemed to be herself.

Presently a white-haired old queen with a lined, sunlamp face minced up and boldly stated that I was the cutest little thing and could he buy me a drink? I shook my head, though I was damn careful to be charming.

After the plucked queen left, the woman turned toward me again with the same, noncommital smile. Then she ordered another daiquiri, fumbled for a light. This was my cue.

"Thank you," she said after I had lit her cigarette. She returned to her private reserve of chilled rum and lime juice.

Later the woman asked if I cared to go for a spin.

The bar closed and we left together. The woman steered her big Chrysler like a man, making all the stoplights, going across the Queensboro bridge, going on until we were on Long Island. Far out. There was a chill in the air. I could smell the sea.

Niki—that was the name she used on the fifth drink; on the sec-ond she had said: Mrs. Sally Overton Wythe—Niki lived in a stone ranch house as elegantly turned out as herself. As we entered a mar-ble foyer, I thought how out of place I appeared in the Venetian gilt mirror above a Chinese console. I needed a haircut and was wearing a soiled, button-down shirt, and rumpled khaki trousers.

We made small talk for an hour amid the cool tones of a harp-sichord playing on an old Atwater Kent phonograph. Niki had expertly sidestepped my flirtations. The only thing she had done was caress my face in the foyer. Her soft hands sought out my face like a blind man groping for his favorite chair.

"How smooth your skin is. Like baked bread. You remind me of my son, Robin. He was killed at prep school."

That had been all and finally I came on with, "It's getting late. Let's turn in."

Niki sat primly in her black Empire chair with both hands fin-gering a scotch. She closed her eyes like a woman who has never seen the dawn or the early morning light of peace. Perhaps she didn't want to see.

I couldn't stand the silence. I took off my shirt, walked drunk-enly bare chested and stood in front of Niki. I tilted her head back with my hand. She turned angrily. She cringed. I felt her body stiffen.

"Don't be so ladylike," I taunted.

I leaned over and put my hand on her shoulder. She held her breath, let it out in deep, spasmodic gasps.

"Say the word, baby. It's getting late."

Then I jerked her up from her chair and held her in my arms. With the hate people vomit up in moments of weakness I said, "Look at me, white woman. Look at what you want and what you don't want. I know you'd pass me like the plague on the street. I know my looks got me through that front door. Otherwise back door, Boy! So, just say the word."

"Please," Niki moaned, "please try to understand. . . ." She broke off. Her lips grazed my neck. Her tears ran down my bare chest.

We went into her bedroom. A beautiful, cold, gray and white room. She was crying softly as we got into bed. I tried to comfort her grief and tears. I held her gently in my arms and stroked her silver hair until she went to sleep. If I knew or understood nothing else, I knew and understood loss and loneliness. It's like having all your breath sucked up in a balloon or like when you are in a dark room alone and you are certain your heart is beating for the last time and it doesn't matter. Anything is better than being aware of your own breathing.

IT IS FIVE O'CLOCK. I look out my window at a Tiepolo sky above the towering buildings, solid, and unreal as death. Tiepolo's mauve, pearl-white and soft blue clouds do not belong here in New York. Here where a pleasant breeze arrives and leaves as suddenly as if it had breathed on the wrong, maimed city. Even the policeman's coffee-colored horse's tail is stiff as a hairbrush.

And there they go, there they go, those quick-stepping, laughing goons, the office workers. They have found their niche in this world and they are going to make damned sure that you know it and that you will not attempt anything foolish that threatens to destroy their world. Bourgeois right down to their underwear and there go my people too, like dark dots in a white field, black and white, shrill and coarse voices like mad hungry children. Clogged traffic groans from the city's nausea. No, no, I do not belong down there.

One of the monkeys from Tip Top parking is staring over at me. They all wear ill-fitting green uniforms. Why do you persist in staring? Is your life that empty?

The diners at the *Steak de Paris* have a wonderful vignette: a gypsy baby standing on the elegant rear of a Cadillac, stark naked, eating an orange. The baby's mother does a little hop and skipping dance, laughing, her huge, cat-shaped eyes zero in on an approaching sailor. The sailor in stiff white passes, placing his right hand over his crotch.

There is no air. I watch the paralysis of mummified Americans waiting for their cars to take them back to suburbia.

Now the sky is an evaporating pearl gray with watery mauve patterns. Evening is here like a heavy, hot, dusty, velvet curtain. The Grand Duchess, Claudia, is leaving with Lady P, his tiny Egyptian dog.

Later, Shirley called and we quarreled as usual. "Sometimes I feel so close to you," she once said. "And then at other times, I don't feel anything. You're here. I can see you. Oh, I just don't know."

And then I heard the super call me. I did not answer. An oppressive stillness which I cannot break.

I DO A LOT of messenger work for the theatrical world. It is very pleasant to hear the famous, husky voice of Tallulah Bankhead chiding her dogs. Irene Manning looks as lovely with pincurls in her hair as she does over footlights, and she certainly brews a fine cup of coffee. Julie Harris is understanding about the long walk crosstown on a bitter, snowy night. Eli Wallach and his wife, Anne Jackson, are always excited upon receiving scripts. But not all theatrical deliveries are to the famous. Sometimes the delivery will be to a young actor or actress on the way up.

Such a delivery was my job the other afternoon to a young actor on the lower east side, on a side street in the bargain capital of Delancey and Orchard.

It was a tenement. Plaster peeped through the dirty crayon, butterscotch-colored hallways. It was a sunny day but it was like dusk in this hall. I had to strike a match to read the names on the mailboxes. The actor's name was not listed, or the name of the super. I would have to ask the tenants.

I knocked on several doors and, getting no answer, walked up a flight of shaky stairs. A door was half-open and I heard a strange, painful noise.

I knocked on the tin-covered door and stuck my head in. "Excuse me," I said. A PR woman sat on the edge of a pink-covered bed. She looked up at me and then bowed her head as if in prayer. The painful noise was coming from her.

There were two other PR women in the room in black dresses and black cotton stockings. They had fine mustaches and carefully braided white hair. They eyed me curiously.

"Yes?" the woman on the bed asked. She folded her hands and bit her lips. "Police?"

I couldn't make head or tail of what had happened. The room smelled as if a thousand people had lived and died in it, although the window was open and the room was cheerful with starched, white curtains and green plants growing on the window ledge.

"*Media, media,*" one of the old women said.

I turned and saw that she was pointing at a small bundle lying in a corner of the room near an unpainted chest of drawers. The bundle lay on the glossy blue linoleum floor as if waiting to be picked up and taken away.

I went over and examined the bundle. Inside lay a dead P.R. baby about a month old. He was naked and his head was turned on his left side. A circle of blood had dried and was caked around his mouth, and his little chubby hands were high above his head. There was a blue-black mark on his right cheek, as if he had fallen against something or had been hit or kicked.

I re-covered the bundle and looked over at the woman sitting on the bed. Her whole body shook but she had stopped making that strange noise. She rubbed her hands together and looked at the two old women but she did not look at me.

I held out a pack of cigarettes to her. She took one but her hand was shaking badly and I had to put the cigarette in her mouth. It fell from her lips. She put her hands over her mouth, trying to hold in that strange noise. I put my arms around her. She fell against my chest like a dead weight.

One of the old women went into the kitchen and the other came over and stood and looked at me. Then the old woman returned from the kitchen with a cup of milk-coffee. I forced myself to drink it because it seemed the thing to do.

Gradually the noise ceased and the woman asked for a cigarette. This time she could hold it. She took long, deep drags and said that her husband had come in drunk, demanding money. She would not give him money and so he beat her. In a final show of revenge, he had picked up the sleeping baby and had thrown him clear across the room.

That had been last night. After he had left, the woman had

called her two aunts who lived down the street. They had been sitting silently ever since, unable to move. It was funny, the woman said, sniffing, staring at the smoke billowing up toward the low ceiling, that no one had come to see her. Neighbors were always dropping in for coffee. But not today.

I said I would go and call the police. The woman thanked me. The two old women followed me to the door, smiling. Later, I learned that the young actor had left the building ten days before for Brattleboro, Vermont.

IT IS ONLY June and I am drunk with dreams of leaving New York, of going to Europe, going any place. I have always been a traveler. I remember the first time I left home. I was eight years old and Grandma had just bought me a pair of brown and white shoes. That summer afternoon I squeezed a couple of peanut butter-and-jelly sandwiches into the shoe box and started out walking to my great-grandmother's house. She lived in another town, thirty miles away. I had gotten three miles when a family friend spotted me on the highway.

At fourteen I hitchhiked to Kansas City and St. Louis every weekend. It alarmed Grandma, but I had to move. What would a fourteen-year-old boy do alone in a city? Well, I walked and walked, met all types of people. I went to movies, museums, the library. I remember a little old lady in a Queen Mary hat who went around the library in Kansas City giving notes to young boys.

"Are you lonely? Very well then. Come with me. I will feed you and cheer you up," was scrawled on pink, scented stationery.

I followed her one hot Saturday afternoon to a cluttered walk-up above a secondhand book store at Twelfth and Vine. Miss Sally lived with two dozen white pigeons which flew around the taupe-colored room. The roller piano tinkled merrily with barrel house music and Miss Sally danced around the room, a hop and skip, cooing like a drunken scarecrow. I refused to take off my shirt and refused the cup of hot chocolate, and later at the library, Miss Sally cut me dead, waltzed past my table humming "Little Black Sambo."

I remember arriving in Kansas City at four in the morning. I went to the bus station and parked out on a bench and had intended to go to sleep. A man came up and started a conversation. "Would I like to go to his place and sleep after a good breakfast?" I followed him home and, as I emerged from the shower, he put his arms around me and said, "Son, your eyes are closing. Get into bed." I was too shy to ask what had happened to the heavy breakfast. I fell asleep and then, in the half-world of sleep and consciousness, I discovered something was happening to the lower part of my body. I was too afraid to scream, but I twisted and turned on that large bed, a Hollywood bed with an imitation ivory-and-leather headboard and with brass nails. I felt as though I were dying. Silently I prayed to God to let whatever was happening end. And then it was over. The man said, "Here, kid, take this two dollars and get the hell out of here. My wife will be home soon."

By the time I met Mr. X, as I named him, I was no neophyte. It was a rainy Saturday night and I was sitting in front of Jones' Department Store. Mr. X sauntered up like an elegant giant in his pin-striped suit. His gold cufflinks gleamed in the darkness. He looked down at me, took the carnation from his lapel, threw it at my feet, and shot an explosion of French at me. He took my hand and we walked off in the rain, and this mad madman talked and talked. I wanted to leave. But he was more than six feet tall and I was a beanpole fifteen-year-old. We went to his beautiful, small pied à terre, as he called it. There were many paintings and books. Mr. X talked and talked and never once did he touch me. I remember that he said he was at the "menopause" of his life. I have often wondered if Mr. X killed himself.

And then there was a Negro blues singer. I never asked her if she knew my cousin, Ruby. She might have. I used to go and see her at four o'clock on Saturday afternoons. She would be getting up then and would be terribly cross. "Hey, you little son-of-a-bitch. Get me a black coffee, will you? Go down and get me some gin. And if you take one sip— one sip—I'll tan your hide. Do you hear me? Where in the hell do you come from? If the cops ever come here looking for you, and sweetcakes, I know plenty of cops, they'll put your little ass under the jail. Do you hear me?" She had many boyfriends and gave them all hell, throwing cups of coffee or empty gin bottles at them—"Yes, Goddamn it, I made a mess, but I pay the freight here, and that's why I have a cleaning woman,"—But once we were in her pink convertible and started for the club, the bitchy woman vanished. "Sweetcakes, you're gonna sit ringside tonight. At the best table in the joint. And if you want a whore, just say the word. Don't blush. You're a sassy little tomcat. . . ."

In my sophomore year at school in Missouri I began to read everything that I could lay my hands on. I was the best customer at the Sedalia Missouri Public Library. I shall never forget those wonderful women at the library. They even allowed me to read the so-called adult books.

But, after a while, Sedalia, St. Louis, and Kansas City weekends were not enough. The undiscovered world beckoned and one Sunday night, three months before graduation, I climbed out my bedroom window and with a carefully saved seventy-five dollars, I headed for California.

I caught a ride with a pleasant truck driver who was going as far as Albuquerque, New Mexico. I remember passing through countless grim, quiet, small towns, and I remember when we swung into the wide open, sunny, dusty face of Texas. There wasn't that "grand sweep" that I had read about. The landscape was a land of plains and rivers frozen over. Too many trees had been cut down and the towns all looked as if the hands of time had stopped. I remember driving down the short main street of one Texas town and reading a sign: "Nigger Don't Let The Sun Set On You In This Town." I closed my eyes, fell asleep, and when I awoke, it was the end of the line, Albuquerque.

I got out of the truck and discovered that it was morning again. There was a brilliant, turquoise-blue sky, serene Rocky Mountains; a red-pink sun was coming up behind the mountains. A heavy wind rose and then a sandstorm. I thumbed vigorously at the speeding cars and trucks. No one stopped, not even Negroes. I stood there all day and toward evening two young guys in a beat-up coupe stopped. They were California-bound, searching for work. Things were bad all over, they said. However, California, the exception, was the land of milk and honey.

But I remember Los Angeles as a version of hell.

I checked my bag at the bus station and walked all the way along Sunset Boulevard that first day and on into Beverly Hills. A slick young man with a pockmarked face picked me up in a drug-store. I thought he was queer, but discovered later that he was junkie-prone. (It was in Korea that I realized that my large, brown, dazed eyes gave me that junkie look.) Pimps would point their slender fingers at me and ask what my kick was. This young man lived in an apartment house high above Sunset Strip with his sister, Maria, a vague girl with waist-length hair. We made love during those cool afternoons, while her brother was out. He took a liking to me, saying, "Dad, you're a sensitive kid. My sister needs someone like you. Hell, I'll give you a salary just to be with her."

And thus the country boy began to move through the subter-ranean junkie world where there is no day or night but an endless golden dusk if you are "on." Without that saving fix, you did not even have the leftovers of dreams; black night of the soul when you tried to scale walls. You could buy two sticks of marijuana for the price of one as an introductory offer. I remember a teenage girl lying in an alley behind a jazz club screaming, "Hit me! Hit me! Won't somebody please hit me. I can't stand this pain." And a sev-enty-five-year-old news hack folding five "caps" of heroin inside an early edition and passing it to a waiting taxi.

California. Sleek-haired Mexican boys with loud sports shirts waiting for their rich keepers to come from Pasadena and Santa Monica—women paying for what they couldn't get free at home. Old men and women sitting in parks, talking about home in drawling Midwestern accents. The incredible blue of the Pacific Ocean and the grotesque, candy-colored buildings and houses. Stark white, store-front Negro churches with holy roller music. An old Lincoln cabriolet in front of the Mocambo night club; the chauffeur spitting on his shoes, taking a handkerchief out of his breast pocket and wiping off his shoe, then saying, "Boy, would you like to make thirty bucks fucking an old white-haired woman?"

I remember finally a bearded man with a tarnished silver crown who said he was the son of Jesus and a woman in a man-tailored suit, built like a boxer, saying: "Come unto me, son. This is the day of your salvation." And in a sense she was right. I discovered Maria was pregnant, and my cousin, Ruby, came for me from Missouri. We rode back to Missouri on the Greyhound bus and didn't say one hundred words to each other. I never knew whether or not Maria had the baby.

Back home, I worked on and off, hitchhiking back to Kansas City on weekends. I read a great deal and tried to avoid the kids I had grown up with. At eighteen, I had had my first slice of life and I wanted more.

I was searching for something, I would tell Ruby. What? She would ask. I don't know, I would say. But I'll know when I find it. Shit, Ruby would say.

RUBY STONEWALL, my cousin, used to say, "The blues ain't nothing but just sitting and rocking and feeling too miserable to get out of that chair."

I remember the first time I saw Ruby. She came to visit me and Grandma in Missouri that lonely summer after my grandfather died. She came in late August to visit, and stayed.

I can see her now, sitting in the hot, small living room, rocking in Grandpa's cane-backed, oak rocking chair. She was a cigarette addict, and I thought she was the most beautiful woman I had ever seen. Her light brown skin was smooth and the aquiline nose was a surprise in her Negro face. Her wide, red mouth always seemed to be on the verge of a smile that never appeared. She wore her blue-black hair page boy, and it fell softly to her shoulders. She had bags under her gunpowder eyes that never seemed to give off any warmth. She gave people a quick, seemingly cruel glance. I heard neighbor women say, "That Ruby is one mean woman. She don't give or take nothing from nobody. Why, them eyes of hers could look a hole through you."

"I'm played out, Grandma," Ruby said that summer, in a voice that was not bitter but cold and impersonal, as if she were reciting from an old newspaper. "My baby had the summer flu and died. Some bitching husband left me, and I got into a mess with a white man in Kansas City."

"Sonny, you'd better go outside," Grandma interrupted.

"Let him stay," Ruby said, blowing smoke rings. "It's no good hiding things from kids. They'll only get the dope from the streets."

Ruby had been a singer up in Kansas City and now her voice was shot. She couldn't make twenty-five a week in a ginmill unless she hustled on the side, and she wasn't ready for that. Grandma suggested she sing at the Hughes Chapel Methodist Church until she got her voice back in shape. No. Ruby would get a domestic's job and if her voice came back, fine and dandy. She had had a good voice; she no longer had a voice. Everything with Ruby was black and white, no buts and ifs.

The next day, Ruby and I both looked for jobs. Ruby found a job in a hotel as a chambermaid. I would need money as school was nearing. I saw an ad in the paper: busboy. I went to the back door wearing my white-folks smile and was told the job had been taken.

The ad continued for another week. I returned to the café, thinking the new busboy had quit. The man met me at the back door again and bellowed, "Boy, can't you get it through your thick skull, we don't hire niggers." It was like being slapped hard across the face or dashed with a bucket of ice water. I was standing on the back stoop of the café and the man was looking down at me. He slammed the door in my face because I couldn't move. It was a heavy, old-fashioned screen door and slammed shut like a giant mousetrap.

Next stop was a large store, the nearest thing to a department store in that Missouri town. I got the runaround there too.

So I made it to the hotel where Ruby was working. She was in the linen room, sitting on a pile of dirty sheets. She counted sheets and she listened to my tale of woe.

Finally I became furious and jumped up from the box where I had been sitting.

"The sons-of-bitches. I'd like to kill'm all!"

"Kill'm?" Ruby asked. "There ain't enough time."

"Yes, kill'm," I sneered. "Kill'm, line'm up. All the white bastards. I'd go BANG BANG BANG until I couldn't see another living white face."

"Oh. Talk that talk," Ruby mocked.

"Well, that's just the way I feel."

Ruby continued counting sheets, a cigarette in the corner of her mouth. Finally she tossed the sheets aside frowning and looked up at me with her cold eyes and began talking in that ice-water voice.

"You make me sick. You go to that department store and ask to be interviewed and they tell you to wait outside. So you wait and wait and then some white boy comes along and gets the job. And you get hurt and mad as hell. Start hating the white people again. If you had gotten the job, the white folks would be just fine. Now you're feeling sorry for yourself because you're black. No, not black, but black just the same. Nobody has the tough luck that us colored people have. And you're too Goddamn miserable feeling sorry for yourself to get up out of the gutter."

"Since when did you hit the big time?" I snapped.

"Since I stopped feeling sorry for myself. Since I learned there ain't nothing really bad. There ain't nothing that can really hurt you. Like the other night when I was waiting for a taxi. A bunch of white boys drove past me and threw a beer bottle on the curb. They yelled, 'Hey, a black bitch! Jump for joy 'cause we want some of that black poontang.' Did I want to kill those boys? Did I call them white bastards? No. I gave them my best toothpaste smile and said, 'Sorry, boys, you got the wrong bitch.'"

I kicked at the pile of dirty sheets and said bitterly, "Can it. You know you love white folks."

"I don't love anybody," Ruby replied quickly. "White or black."

"What about that white man in KC?"

"Oh, him," Ruby said indifferently. "That was nothing. A one-night stand that went sour after a week. Only I didn't know it at the time. Black men, white men, they're alike in the dark. I'm a good-looking black woman and I know it. But there ain't nothing the whole lot can do for me. I've had enough black and white men pawing me. How old are you?"

"Almost fifteen," I lied.

"Your father is a louse. I know Grandma hasn't told you anything. But she could, believe me. You're a good-looking kid. Women are going to be after you. White, black, all kinds. They're going to be dying to get into your pants. But if you take the advice of an old fool, you'll play it cool. When you get into the prime of life, you'll be a played-out tomcat. I've spent thirty-five years discovering how rotten life is if you waste it on nothing. Never be bitter, Sonny. Only people who can't face life and hate themselves are bitter. Maybe I was born black and lost my voice to teach me a lesson. Well, kid, I learned. I know damn well I learned something being born black that I could never have learned being born white."

I looked at her in wonder, listening to the clear flow of words, turning them over in my mind, which was not a boy's mind, nor a man's mind, but something in between.

Ruby lit another cigarette with the butt of one that was only half gone. I saw the wrinkles on her forehead and her eyes which now gave off a light, warm and small as a candle.

"Being black taught me humility," Ruby said, beginning to sound tired. The fire had gone out of her voice. "Another thing I learned was the meaning of compassion. I sang at the Blue Room in KC. We had so many white country-club folk coming in that we had to turn them away. Can you imagine? Rich white folk, wanting to hear colored blues. They weren't slumming. I know that kind. I asked Finkelstein who owned the joint. He said, 'Ruby, you know true blues is about suffering. Troubles. They know about these things too. That's what true blues have, compassion. Ruby gal, you reach the people.' And Sonny, I started watching those white faces out front. They were like the faces of you and me. Anybody."

I am brought back to the present by a neon light shining in on the seven-by-nine photograph tacked above my fireplace. It shows a boy, aged one-and-a-half, in a white knitted suit with matching knitted beret and white shoes and socks. He is standing in a peeling wicker chair. He's a cute, fat, healthy-looking kid. A golden teddy bear. But the eyes, large, too beautiful, are strangely adult. They seem to be staring beyond the photographer. Great, sad eyes. I would like them to tell me what they see, but they are silent.

BRUCE, THE DIVINITY STUDENT of soothing tones and quiet beliefs, stormed into my place at four this morning, dead drunk. "I'm pie-eyed," he blurted out and fell flat on his healthy, hairless face, knifed between the subway kitchenette and the living room. I managed to drag him to the sofa and shut my ears to his pleading, "No, no, no."

Half of his twenty-three-year-old body was still on the floor; the other half was resting uncomfortably in my arms. Long, drawn-out sobs shook his body. Tears slithered down my bare chest. Gone was the Ivy-League charm, the young Episcopalian grace. I hoped God heard his painful cries which keyed my taut nerves. The cries of men are almost like dying. I sat there silently, lit a cigarette, and tried not to think.

I began to doze, then jerked up again suddenly as Bruce moved slightly in my arms. He blinked his eyes and lapsed back into what appeared to be a troubled sleep. The cigarette had gone out in my hand and I relit it, watching the black sky turn to electric blue, solid as stone. The air was moist, the day would be a scorcher. There was no sound from the street. There was nothing to do but sit and try not to think and wait for the dawn.

Bruce, turning fitfully, came to life the following afternoon. He sat up groggily on the sofa and shook his head. "Boy," he said, like a sad announcement, running his pale hand through his mushroom-colored hair.

I had the bromo, orange juice, and black coffee ready. He wanted none of it. He wanted a drink.

So I gave the former teetotaler a water glass of gin straight and he put it down nicely, wincing slightly.

"The bastards," Bruce said with finality.

"Who?" I asked.

"My family," Bruce said, eyeing me steadily. "Give me another drink." He nursed his second straight gin bent over, resting his arms on his legs. He had the somnolence of a frog basking in the sun.

The afternoon was cloudless and humid, with the promise of rain; the room had a murky gloom.

"The bastards," Bruce said again, rising, and saying no more except, "Thanks, and I'll see you later."

THE GREAT DROUGHT has arrived. Dusty pollen falls like snow over this city; the skies are a washed-out blue. Listless, suspended days, baked streets. An insane jungle of voices day and night. It is never quiet here, not even in the soft hours before dawn. I do not go out unless I have to. We tenants leave our doors open, ears pricked, alert to footsteps on the stairs: "Are you going to the store? Walking the dog? How soon will it be before you return?"

I have an urge to stay in this white-walled room until the summer is ended, and then march out, leave the city and, unlike Lot's wife, never look back. The messenger service during the day, and at night I stagger back here, sweaty, exhausted, my Achilles feet throbbing like an inflated heart. I ask, what is wrong with me? I'm one of the boys, I'm as American as apple pie. But no. I cannot, simply cannot, don a mask and suck the c—of that sweet, secure bitch, middle-class American life.

Sometimes I sit in my fifth-floor window and watch the young Americans out on the town, healthy, laughing, contented as mother hens. Their faces indistinguishable as blades of grass. Look how happy they are! They are united and one. Yes, I could become one of the horde, despite the fact that I am Negro. (Remember the black dots on the great white field?) I could stop worrying about writing, about the corruption of this city, the world, and the fate of mankind. I could get a soft, safe, white-collar job, save the coins, marry, and all in the name of middle-class sanctity.

I remember one Monday I played hookey from the messenger service. I shaved very close that morning, glued on my average, boyish, American smile. This smile is no different from the average, boyish, white-American smile. After all, the Negro has been fucked through the years and in many different positions in this country. He has been the faithful, unpampered watchdog of the whites. Above all, he knows that white is right. Witness skin lighteners and all those magical oils, lotions, creams. They will not only take away blackheads and pimples, but your dark skin as well. Hence, the average, boyish, American smile. I donned my only good suit, white shirt, dark silk tie, picked up the Sunday *New York Times* classified section, and made it.

There were twenty or more men around, waiting for the fifty-seven-dollar-a-week midtown mailroom flunky job. All types, races, ages, backgrounds. It was a cross section of America. Several looked extremely intelligent and several were very well-dressed.

I filled out the application and middle-aged Mr. Personnel called me first. Twenty-three envious faces were on me. How did I rate? Nowhere, baby. I knew nothing about mail rates and they wanted someone experienced. Personnel was sorry. He would have liked to take me on; I seemed bright, on the ball. Personnel and I exchanged shitty grins. I exited and went down to Wall Street and applied for a brokerage house trainee. Seventy dollars every Thursday. The company paid the agency fee. Before reporting to Personnel, I dug the sorry-looking jokers in the "cage," sorting stocks and bonds like so many automatic monkeys with their white shirts, sleeves rolled up, and wearing impossible ties. They were the kind of young men who went bowling and, after four beers, became "cards," the kind of young men who took their girlfriends to Chinese restaurants on Saturday nights, the kind of young men who would say, "Let's get a couple of beers and pick up some dames." The only thing they could pick was their noses. I have double-dated with them and their vague pigs, and I know.

If I worked with these slobs, I would be stoned from nine to five, I thought. The average jerk, going along like a cog, questioning nothing, seeking nothing. I've heard tell that these young men are the beefsteak on tomorrow's menu.

But the new leaf; I could be wrong about them. The only way to find out would be to work with these young men.

Personnel was a woman this time. A sweet voice, charm herself. She put me at ease, glanced at my application, and then looked up, all smiles, and asked me if I was a black or white Puerto Rican.

"Neither," I said, rising, and making my exit. "I'm Filipino. You'll hear from my ambassador."

That afternoon, I returned to the messenger service like a prodigal son begging forgiveness.

AT EIGHT O'CLOCK Monday morning, Shirley walked in as casually as if she lived here. She put her beach bag on the bookcase and smiled roguishly. Her eyes were bright.

"Don't look at me like that," she said. "Surprised?"

"Are you working today?"

"No. I had my schedule changed. I worked yesterday. Channing said you didn't go to the beach because it was too crowded."

"Who said I was going to the beach today? I've got to work."

"Charles," Shirley warned, "don't be difficult. We won't have to borrow Tony's radio. My *friend,* the doctor, bought me a transistor radio."

"That's nice."

"Isn't it? Oh, Charles, he's such a wonderful person. He is all I ever wanted in a man. We're getting married in the fall."

"Congratulations."

"At least you don't have to be so dry about it."

"All right, I'll try to show a little emotion in my voice: Congratulations!"

"Goddamn it. Get dressed."

And now we lay under the boardwalk at Coney Island on an old army blanket, sheltered from the hot sun, staring out at the sea. Low clouds with the brilliance of a cold snow seem to bank at the edge of the sea. The small, black radio plays muted jazz. I began to doze and then Shirley's delicate, long hands clawed up and down my back like a bow on a taut cello. Would this warm, generous friendship always float on a beachhead of love? Pride and the cold technician have always kept my heart in check. Yet something goes out to this beautiful, honey-colored girl as easily as my breath.

The dazzling, red sky faded. Dusk arrived like a shy-dark child. Giant white waves broke on the sparsely populated beach. Nearby, a group of Puerto Rican boys played bongos. The air grew chilly. Silently, Shirley nestled in my arms.

"Want to go?" I asked.

"Do you want to go?"

"Not yet."

"All right then," Shirley said, squeezing my hand. We lay there silently until an army of cleanup men attacked the beach, shortly after ten p.m.

WHAT IS WRONG WITH ME? Yesterday, I got drunk. Al said I'd better take a week off. Now I am jobless and broke because I blew the works last night. I have a talent for getting too involved with people. One crisis follows another like the second hand of a smooth-running watch and this great republic might blaze with prosperity under fair skies, but each time I make a lunge for the dollar, the eagle flies in the opposite direction. The Negro Bernard Baruchs have a fence around their park benches.

I tell you, I've got to get out of this city, this city which will accept victory or defeat with the same marvelous indifference.

And my friends: a twenty-one gun salute to madness. Laura Vee, spitting icicles. Claudia, chained to the organ, composing his first drunken opera in English, singing at the top of his voice, "Oh, my most noble love, return. . . ." Bruce is having a financial tumor. Channing is not very warm these days because I said he was not a square but an octagonal fool. Last night, I swallowed my pride and phoned Shirley, begging forgiveness. But she was mesmerized by melancholia.

This pad looks as if the devil just stormed through and I've got exactly sixty-five cents. That ain't nowhere.

I left my place at eleven-thirty this morning and looked around for a fast hustle. Tee-shirted with faded, tight Levis, which is the equivalent of the ad man's gray flannel suit. I've scored fairly easily with men and women, though the competition is great. You'd be surprised how my color helps business. Though I've missed out several times because, of course, I just wasn't dark enough.

The siren blows noon. I can't make it up at Forty-second Street. Too many cheap hustlers. The one-dollar bed partners—those drawling, southern boys, the Brooklyn and New Jersey blades doing what comes naturally for a meal and a pad to sleep. Cigarette and coffee money for Grant's or Bickford's the next morning. Thirty cents for the waiting-in-line nine a.m. movie. That's where you catch up on your sleep and shop around. At noon the going gets rough. Too much happening and the cops are around.

I decided on Wall Street. Some stock or investment queer, itching for something somewhat brown and young. Never rough trade or a swish. Boyish, a connection with what happened at prep school eons ago.

Lexington IRT local to Brooklyn Bridge, change to express. Get off at Fulton Street.

Start hustling, kid. Fall in on the scene fast. The cops! Look blank like a diddy bop, fake a cat walk, a sort of bounce on the balls of your feet.

Now, down the steps. Quick! Here comes an old queen with a peaked, powdered face. Shabby suit. Two, five or nothing. Not worth the hassle today.

Young executive with attaché case at newsstand. About thirty, looks married. Yeah, he's married. Gave you the eye twice. Third time around, give him a come-on smile.

Saunter over by the Coke machine. No! The candy or chewing-gum machine. They have mirrors and you can watch the cat.

Don't look now, baby. But here he comes. Grinning like a lion. A live wire. Hope he hasn't got any weird ideas.

"Hi. What's happening?" Grinning, giving me the once-over politely. Pleasant, cultured voice. Appears swinging. Puts me at ease. One of the boys.

A full smile this time. Looking directly into his foreign, gray eyes, shrugging my shoulders, slinging my hands into the buckle of my belt.

"Nothing," I said. "Lousy day."

"What's wrong?"

"Oh. Everything" (this with a sly smirk). "The heat."

"How old are you?"

"Old enough."

A wise smile lit his face. "You're cute . . . Don't blush."

"What time is it?" I asked.

"One o'clock. Are you in a hurry?"

"No. Why?"

"You know why. Have you got a girl?"

"Yeah."

"Are you good to her?"

"I hope so."

"I know you are."

The punch line made me feel as if I were about to be raped in Rockefeller Center.

"Would you excuse me for a minute?" he asked, looking up. "I have to make a call."

The cops? He's going after his gumshoe partner. You had a crazy feeling all morning. Should have worked the Village.

Cool it, baby. The voice. No cop could bring off that voice. Cool it, now. Don't queer the deal.

Here he comes. All smiles, strutting jauntily, swinging his attaché case. Portrait of a successful, young businessman.

"Want to take a ride down to the next station? The first car. It will put us off at Exchange Place."

The train pulls in. I linger back. The stupid joker is motioning toward me. As if I wasn't going to make it.

I stand against the door nonchalantly. He is sitting on the opposite side of the car, watching me.

Exchange Place filled with people on lunch. There is tension in the air and on the brooding faces. People are walking fast like ants scurrying from rain. I remember this is where the money is.

We go up a side street to a small sandstone building. "Give me ten minutes," my boy said, patting my shoulder. "Get off at the ninth floor. The elevators are automatic."

"Okay. If somebody stops me, I'll say I'm a messenger."

"Fine," he nodded.

The ninth floor has been freshly painted. Not a stick of furniture. "Our main office is in midtown. We're getting our furniture wholesale. All good things take time." The last sentence with a leer.

Now he was facing me and I could see his Adam's apple working like mad.

"Sorry I can't offer you a drink."

"That's okay," I said. I could have used a drink. That old bitch, depression, coming on. Wonder what his wife looks like?

Then he stood directly in front of me. His gray eyes were misty. He stared coldly at me. I was reminded of gangster movies with tall, blond killers.

He pushed me against the wall roughly. I stared up at the ivory ceiling and stiffened and it was over.

"My name is Keith," he said. "What's your name?"

"Charlie," I replied.

"Do you have a phone?"

"Yes," I said, reaching in my wallet and gave him my number.

"Could I call you sometimes?"

"Oh, sure."

"Your parents wouldn't mind?"

"Just say you're from the Diamonds. That's a softball team I play with sometimes."

"I see," Keith said slowly. "I'll give you a ring. You're a nice kid."

"My folks worry a lot, though," I came on with. "They're saving their money so they can get us kids out of the city."

"You wouldn't miss the city?"

"Would you?"

Keith laughed and very smoothly greased my palm with a twenty. "Now be a good boy. And watch that little girl."

"Sure thing, dad," I said, and left.

Keith was all right. Didn't give me any phony jazz. I don't give a damn what people do. If they're real, and meet you face-to-face.

And me? Hard-working mother and father. Jesus! The lies you have to tell. To hell with it—people are people and I'm here to tell you. If you don't believe me, just go to bed with them.

Milkshake on Fulton Street. Take "A" train to West Fourth Street. Clams on MacDougal. A quick bourbon in San Remo's. Nothing happening.

The Billie Holiday Story album. Lovely, sad, bitter, Baltimore songbird. Singing a timeless song. I had to have it.

Milk, bacon, eggs, and French bread. Cheese, apples, and strawberries. A carton of cigarettes, six beers, a fifth of white port wine and, Jack, that's it.

TONIGHT I FINISHED taking my shower at eight o'clock, stepped from the bathroom nude, singing happily, and encountered a freckled, baby-faced sailor who was lumbering up the stairs. He had the dumb expression of a forlorn pup.

He walked up, took in my nudity, and grinned. "Hiya, sport."

I smiled faintly and nodded.

"Is number fourteen on this floor?" he asked.

"This is the top floor," I said. "The highest number is eleven. And that's my pad."

"Well, where are the whores?" the sailor asked. A look of alarm covered his face.

"Well, dad," I said, putting my towel over my shoulder, "there are no whores in this house."

And if it is possible for such a dumb face to sink deeper into the pit of confusion, the sailor's did. He fumbled in his white middy shirt and pulled out a piece of cardboard about the size of a book of matches. The sailor studied the cardboard intensely.

I took a deep breath and thought: How do you tell a man he is a sucker when he is not a friend?

Finally I blurted out, "Baby, you have been taken."

The sailor looked up quickly. His shoulders seem to rise as if they were suspended from balloons. His hazel eyes were moist, on the edge of heartbreak.

"You'd better ask to see the broad before you put out your

coins," I advised. "And then you can't be too damned sure. Anyway, now you know the score. How much did it cost you?"

"Twenty bucks," he said, kicking his foot against the steps. "Twenty fucking dollars. Jesus! I should have known better."

"We all make mistakes," I said in a gentle, fatherly tone.

"Yeah," the sailor agreed.

I started for my pad.

The sailor lumbered back down the stairs slowly, a perfect victim of the Murphy Game.

The Murphy Game is played every night in my neighborhood. A year-round sport, played overtime during the spring and summer. An expert and successful Murphy Game player is a smooth talker and generally very well dressed.

I understand from the incident with the sailor that Shuffle Along was working the neighborhood this season.

Shuffle Along is a master of the Murphy Game. He is a Negro of indeterminate age—somewhere on the other side of forty—with the bright enthusiasm of a twenty-year-old. He has the jolly confidential manner of Santa Claus and dresses in very good sports clothes. Despite his thirty-five-dollar alligator shoes, he shuffles along like he had a team of mules in front of him or as though a ball and chain had once been attached to his feet. Perhaps that is why the Murphy Game is his profession.

The Murphy Game is nothing but standing on a street corner or sitting in a bar, observing a man with a hungry look, a man who, you decide, is less intelligent than yourself. You strike up a conversation with him and in a few carefully chosen words, which must sound casual, you inform the man that you can get him a good whore for a certain fee. First he must hand over the money— "you know how these whores are." You tell the man to wait until you return. And you don't return. Or you say, "Just go into that hotel and tell the clerk you'd like a room on the fifth floor with a west front window." The man will think you're a cool pimp with a private code.

My friend, Mitch, can't play the Murphy Game unless he has smoked at least four sticks of pot. He's tall and good looking, but has no guts. Shuffle Along is something else again. He has nerves of steel. Before our front door was locked, I once leaned over the landing and saw Shuffle Along talking with a man. Shuffle Along held out his hand. The man opened his wallet and gave Shuffle Along three ten-dollar bills. Shuffle Along said, "Daddy, I'm the house man. What are you gonna give me?" So the man forks over five and one single. Shuffle Along departed slowly. Once he reached the street, he would take wings of the morning. The man started knocking on doors, seeking his nonexistent woman. In most cases, these men are not drunk. They simply have sex on the brain.

The young boys pose a problem. If you are a professional Murphy player like Shuffle Along, you know that some of the college boys think they can get a woman for two dollars. Shuffle Along has solved this problem magnificently. He will say in his confiding Uncle Tom's voice, "Now, boss. Ya know we been having trouble with the cops. And you look so young. Do you have any ID?"

The young man hands Shuffle Along his wallet.

Shuffle Along will give the ID card a quick glance, checking the money.

If the money is substantial, Shuffle Along will say, "Boss, I is sorry. You is straight. But like I say: we can't take no chance. Now what kind of woman do you want. I can get you a young one, old one, fat, skinny, black, or white."

The young man gives Shuffle Along fifteen or twenty dollars. Shuffle Along takes a piece of cardboard from his jacket. There are two identical numbers written on the cardboard with red pencil and Shuffle Along tears the cardboard in half and gives one half to the young man. The other half goes in his pocket and he says, "This goes to the big boss. He don't take no fuckin' around. Now you jest take this number next door and ring bell four."

The young man departs eagerly with his number and Shuffle Along scampers up the stairs and out through the trapdoor leading to the roof.

My messenger job allows me encounters with all kinds of people and I admire Shuffle Along and the men and women of the Murphy Society. All they do is tell you a story and hold out their hand. The Murphy Game is flourishing in June of this year. The hayseed tourist has arrived; the ships are in. And, of course, there are always the sports from Jersey and the Bronx.

TONIGHT, I AM COOLING IT. Balling in the East Sixties. Sitting in the beige, brown, and green living room of a town house. Big Daddy, my Korean pal, brought me. There are three other men and four girls. Everyone is under forty and the lights are low.

Barry, the host, looks about thirty-two and his healthy face goes with the Daks slacks, the silk sport shirt, and the black and white shoes. He is in the novelty business which he inherited from his uncle, and plays the stock market.

I was helping myself to another scotch when he came out with a dozen sticks of pot. Everyone was restrained, but their greedy eyes never left the pot lying on the coffee table.

Big Daddy reaches over and picks up two sticks of pot. "Let's get this show on the road," he says.

"Cool it," a pretty, pink blonde laughs and takes a stick from Big Daddy.

The guy sitting next to me refused the pot. He had a face like the pale, desperate junkies who hang around Sixth Avenue after midnight.

"You know what he wants," the pretty blonde giggled.

"Keep it up," the pale junkie said. "Keep it up. I'm going up side your head."

"Oh, shut up," the blond snapped. "You're a kook. You're getting too damn careless. How many times have I told you about leaving the Goddamn needle under the soapdish in the bath-room?"

I looked at Barry. He was blushing.

"This is good shit," I said.

"Panamanian pot, baby," Big Daddy added.

"I don't want any of that shit," the pale junkie said scornfully. He got up and Barry ushered him upstairs.

Another guy, who hadn't said a word since I had arrived about an hour ago, followed them quickly.

A girl, a typical Village type with long stringy hair, man's shirt, and paint-splattered blue jeans, bolted up and yelled, "Wait for me, you greedy bastards. You think you're going to get all the goodies."

Then Jelly Roll struts in like a proud rooster. He was a Korean War buddy of mine and Big Daddy's. Round chocolate bear, nuts for ballet. He makes his living now playing drums in a rock-and-roll band.

Jelly stands in the middle of the living room grinning, jerking his shoulders, rubbing his fat hands together as if for warmth.

"Charlie, my man, Big D," he said, "what's the haps?"

"Everything, baby," Big Daddy mumbled. "I've got to ration myself on this stuff."

"Ah, come on," Jelly laughed. "Man, I want some H. Some horse."

"Talk that trash," a girl named Louise said. She put her bour-bon down and gave Jelly the eye.

"Yeah," Jelly amended. "Take me to thy keeper."

"Come on, Charlie," Big Daddy says, getting up. "Let's get this show on the road."

Jelly turned to me. "Baby, I knew you'd finally get hooked."

"Hell," I grinned, "I just wanna see the orgy."

"Tell me more," Louise said. She came over and took my hand and we followed Jelly and Big Daddy up the carpeted stairs. A group of landscape prints decorated the stair wall and there was a chandelier of frosted glass. And because of the quiet, it reminded me of a funeral home.

Barry and the pale junkie were in the bedroom sitting on the floor. They reminded me of guys down at Wall Street with Big Deals brewing. Stoned junkies have that same cocky air.

They are the top dog because they feel that they are the world.

There was a girl sitting on the bed who hadn't been downstairs. She stared at nothing or perhaps she was seeing her thoughts like photographs on the jungly wallpaper. Her eyes were glazed like a cat's. The bedside radio was playing early morning jazz and she kept time with the music, snapping her fingers.

Louise went over and joined Barry and the pale guy who had his eyes closed, nodding his head.

"Who's gonna turn me on?" Big Daddy asked. He had a foolish expression on his face now.

"Yeah," Jelly echoed in a desperate voice.

Barry looked up. "Ellie. Turn the boys on."

Ellie was the girl sitting on the bed. "What?" she asked, frowning.

"Turn the boys on."

"Oh sure," Ellie mumbled, leaving her dream world.

Ellie got up from the bed in a very businesslike manner, went over to the mirror-topped dresser.

Jelly gave her a hard, cold stare, but Big Daddy was already rolling up his sleeves.

"Easy doll, easy does it," Big Daddy grinned. "Watch out for my veins. I got it bad once in the arm and they had to shoot me in the feet."

Ellie did not look up or crack a smile. She picked up the heroin spoon, and struck a match, and prepared the injection. She had the same bored manner of army doctors giving shots.

Ellie plunged the needle in Big Daddy's arm and quickly, expertly, swabbed his arm with cotton.

Big Daddy exhaled as if he had suddenly been relieved of a great weight.

Ellie glared expectantly at Jelly.

He eased up to her with a frozen grin. His mouth trembling as if he were on the verge of a scream.

Ellie shot him. He moaned, "Oh, bitch, suck my blood."

I left the white brick town house at about four p.m. the following afternoon and walked down the quiet, expensive, residential street. I doddered like an old man. My energy had been sucked up. But I didn't care and took the crosstown bus home.

MRS. LEE CALLS: "Charles, pet. Are you alive? Fine, fine. Listen, Charles, I have a most delightful idea. We'll round up a party and go to Jones Beach in a rented limousine. What mad fun we'll have. I bought a portable beach tent—yellow, green, and red. Oh, it's *too* much, pet. Cleo going down the Nile. Now, there will be Diego—you haven't met him, have you? What charm! Like taffy melting in the sun. He wants to be a cabinetmaker. Laura thinks he's adorable. She's coming. She has the most marvelous French bathing suit. A bikini. All red knit. A scream, Charles! I thought we'd ask Sade, too. Oh, sorry, pet. I forgot you were not on friendly terms. But I could ask that sweet little Jewish boy . . . what's his name. Oh, you know who I mean. And Lena. She's such fun. I hear she's out again—have you seen her? And what do you think of this pet? I've got champagne for you. Just for you, darling."

"Oh, Jesus," I moaned, on the verge of tears, and hung up.

Then Claudia, the Grand Duchess, dashes in like a mad potentate. His eyebrows are plucked. The makeup is wearing off and he resembles a spotted wild animal. He's giddy from the aftereffects of an all-night sexual drinking bout.

"Gimme a cigarette," Claudia said, swooping down in the chair like an exhausted bird. "Oh, child, I really had a ball last night. I really enjoyed myself. Those children carried on. Let me tell you: they carried on like there was no tomorrow."

And then Lady P comes in, wagging her tiny Egyptian tail like a shy debutante.

"Mama's love," Claudia croons. "Let's go for a walky-walky. And if you help me cruise a lovely man, we'll have chopped steak for dinner. That's what baby will have."

Claudia picks up the petite, silent Lady P and they exit, grand-opera style.

WORKED LATE AGAIN TODAY: seven p.m. There was nothing waiting for me at home and I walked over to Amsterdam Avenue for a drink. This was poor Alice's turf, and I thought of her and felt like saying a prayer. She got such a bang out of just living; the prostitution and drugs had nothing to do with it.

I remember Alice once leaning out the window and tossing a handful of coins down to the kids who lived in my block. "That's right, ya little bastards! Get'm! That's what you'll be after the rest of your life. Bastards!" This was followed by a great peal of laughter which could scald a sensitive heart. Bruce tried to convert Alice. "If St. Peter opens them pearly gates for you," Alice would tell him, "I think he'll open them for me. Yeah. That's right, baby."

About a year ago she got syphilis. A month later Alice was nearly nuts. Then, one windless, pale, March afternoon, she made crazy designs on a man's face with a beer bottle in her West Eighty-fifth Street room. She called me, her voice giddy. I thought she was back on heroin. "Charlie, come up quick. I think I killed somebody," Alice giggled.

"Who?" I asked. "Alice, are you high or something?"

"Yes, baby," Alice said. "I got a jolt this time. Some bastard is conked out on the bed, bleeding. Come on up, baby."

I arrived an hour later, and there were only blood stains on

Alice's filthy bed. There was one sole window in the room, the frame painted PR blue. The window was open and the pink, plastic curtains crackled. I looked out the window. But there was no trace of Alice in the garbage-littered backyard.

"I nuw it, I jest nuw it," the super told me gleefully, displaying a fine set of rotten teeth.

"What makes you say that?" I asked sharply.

"Nuttin'," he frowned. "You hur pimp or sompin'?"

"No," I said slowly, trying to hold back my anger. "I'm her brother."

Pity seeped into the super's lined face. "Her rent is paid til Satta."

This was a year ago, and in this mood of dark remembrance, I entered the Step Down bar on Amsterdam Avenue. There were four men and one woman in the place with the intimate, neighborly air of regulars. The bar was very clean and quiet. The television was sitting on its throne above the mirrored wall and the cowboys were shoot'n 'em up, but there was no sound.

I ordered a bourbon with beer chaser and took my usual spot near the door. If the street scene became dull I could watch the customers, provided that they weren't too inquisitive about me.

At the opposite end of the bar was a boy with a crew cut. He had a clean-cut, healthy appearance, with cold, deep blue eyes. He looked out of place with his madras sports coat, khaki trousers, white button-down shirt, and slim tie. I figured he must have come over from Central Park West.

From time to time he would stare up from his bottle beer at me. The stare was direct and cold like a shrewd housewife inspecting a leg of lamb at the butcher's. But I wouldn't let him shake my nerve. I wondered why he wasn't watching TV. The cowboy movie had changed to a cartoon of monkeys decked out like chorus girls. The single woman, a redhead, was drinking a Tom Collins. She looked like a clothed Rubens nude in her polka dot dress, cut low. Her voluptuous, creamy tits almost spilled out on the bar. The bartender was very busy with his wet cloth, adjusting the redhead's coaster. His eyes stayed down and his face was flushed. The redhead joked with a few healthy, four-letter words.

In the meantime, this joker with the crew cut was beginning to bug me. Here I was putting away my second bourbon, feeling

cool, grateful that tomorrow was a holiday, and trying to collect
my thoughts. My hair is cut just as short as his, though the quality
is different. I am clean shaven. I don't look in the least unusual. At
least that's what the reflected, mirrored image says.

I go to the jukebox and play a couple of Lady Day sides. "*Yes-
terdays*" and "*Ain't Nobody's Business If I Do.*"

Crew cut is drinking his bottle beer like there was no tomorrow. Well, I decide, I'm going to stare the bastard down. These
eyes are going to the market; appraise and set a judgment, look
right through him.

Okay. Now set your drink down with lowered eyes and then
look up. "Aw right," as Mitch would say, "you've shook him."
Now he's got a mean frown on the ruddy face, and he's knocking
ashes from his cigarette. He won't look at you.

Now he's smiling with his eyes as well as his mouth. I half
expected to see caps on his fine white teeth. What the hell is so
Goddamn funny? He must be nuts, lonely, has a problem, or is
queer. It might be interesting to find out his story.

Have another bourbon. He'd got his Goddamn blue eyes on
you. I'd like to put a good solid one on that firm, proud mouth.
He's looking up again. A bold smirk on that Ivy League mug.
There is nothing to do but stare him down.

The bartender ambles down to me and sets up a bottle of beer.
He has a bright, wise look on his owlish face.

"It's for you," he says knowingly.

Crew cut raises his bottle beer in mock salute, buddy-buddy
fashion.

I nod and give my boy a shit-eating grin.

Then he got up and walked toward me, and I discovered that
his left foot was a club foot. He had on a pair of highly polished,
cordovan brogues; the bottle of beer in his large hand like a flag.
Now his smile was warm, boyish. But I had my doubts.

"Hi," he said, brightly, by way of introduction. "You have
crazy eyes. Did you know that?"

I downed the last of the bourbon and started on Crew cut's
beer. I certainly wasn't going to make conversation after that
opening.

"What was the Mets' score?" he asked.

"I don't know," I replied, without looking up.

"The Mets really took a beating from the Pirates."

"Yes," I agreed. "The Mets were crucified."

Crew cut laughed easily and said: "Did you watch the Yankee-Tiger game last Sunday? Man. Twenty-two innings. I must have drunk a case of beer with that one."

"I never expected the Yankees to go that far," I said.

"I take it that you're a Yankee fan."

"Yeah. But in forty-five, the Tigers and the Athletics played almost five hours," I said, springing my baseball knowledge.

"No kidding," Crew cut said in an astonished voice, and then looked out at the stalled, horn-honking traffic. "Would you like to go to my place? It's around the corner. I've got some hard stuff there."

"Okay," I replied slowly, without thinking. I was certain Crew cut required no thinking.

Peter, that was the club-footed young man's name, lived high above Central Park West, in a mellow, woodsy apartment with a high, vaulted ceiling. An old hunting sideboard cleverly concealed a bar and stereo equipment. Peter was a proud host. He laughingly said that he would soon have to get a job; his rent was two-fifty a month. Now his eyes rarely met mine; the deep blue eyes expressed the fear and pain of a shy, young animal. I wasn't making much effort with him—I had met too many condescending, rich brats before, non-thinking jerks. The best education that money could buy, travel; but all of this did them very little good. I remember Mark who had gone to Harvard, and then to Cambridge, and who never had an opinion of his own. Take Channing—with all that money floating in the family background, he has never been to Europe. Poor little Elizabeth. She has lived abroad for the past seven years, mostly in Paris, yet she knows less about Paris than I do.

"You're the first colored person I've known," Peter said, groping for a cigarette. "That is, except my maid."

"I'm not surprised," I said sweetly.

"Why?"

"It's obvious, isn't it?"

"I suppose so," Peter agreed slowly.

I was drinking a gin and tonic; Peter was drinking beer out of a silver-engraved mug.

"Do you like tennis?"

"No."

"Opera?"

"No."

"Interested in politics?"

"No."

Peter set down his silver mug carefully and smiled. "I bet you like to screw."

Oh Jesus, I thought, depression settling in. I wish for once that I'd meet someone who would surprise me. I've been studying people closely for twenty-nine years and it is agonizing to be able to put them in slots like coins in a cigarette machine. Was Crew cut queer? You see the queer kids in the eastside bars lapping up beer, only beer. It is only the less affluent homosexuals who buy mixed drinks. I'm rather free sexually, but I'm a little sick of the queer scene. The queers are not really honest and their fear has nothing to do with it. With the straight squares and the police, the whole business is made up of fear, hate, money-making. The greatest problem of the American male is proving his masculinity. I myself find that I do not have to lift weights, wear heels with clicks, to assert my maleness. Claudia, the Grand Duchess, once said, "Oh child, one of these days we'll have a faggot for President. In high drag. Won't that be a bitch?"

Crew cut's voice cut in on my thoughts. "You know, I don't like niggers." He was sitting on the sofa, his feet propped up on the slate-topped coffee table.

I sipped my gin and tonic, looked over at Peter, and smiled.

His blue eyes flamed with hatred and his face was very red. "Well, what are you going to do about it, nigger?" he asked, his voice quivering.

I burst out laughing and shook my head sadly. "'Drown in my own tears,' Ray Charles sings. What do you want me to do? Beat the living shit out of you?"

"I like to be hurt a little," Peter said. "I like to have my hands tied behind my head. Then I'll do anything you want."

NINE-THIRTY A.M. A lustreless pearl sky, soft summer rain. The click-click, tap-tap, and shuffle of feet pressing jobward. The truck driver's four-letter morning song, "Get ya fuckin' ass in ge-aar." The somnolent, suburban drivers creeping into Tip Top Parking. I look out the window at the bumper-to-bumper traffic blocked to Fifth Avenue. The cars are like a hem in the great cape of Rockefeller Center. The slender trees lining the street look like cheap corsages. Through the veil of rain, the Empire State building looks very lovely this morning. No sign of life at the Elmwood Hotel except the fourth-floor ash blonde making up her face with a hand mirror.

Afternoon. The staccato tone of rain. Indistinct street voices. The cool air has a touch of autumn. A neighbor comes in to tell me there's been a police raid. It doesn't interest me. At five o'clock, the darkening sky is like the early dusk of winter. The blaze of neon cuts the approaching darkness. I long for the end of summer, and going away.

Maxine suddenly pops in from art school decked out with slick yellow raincoat and matching hat. She stands in the doorway, her merry eyes sharp observers of the semi-dark room. Then she runs over and sits down beside me on the sofabed. "Charles, the police were here," whispering her big secret. "They were here this afternoon. A raid."

"Yes, cookie," I said. "I heard them. Must've been a false alarm."

"False alarm," Maxine reflected. "Then it was a mistake, wasn't it?"

"That's right, cookie. How was the art class?"

"All right, I guess. Clay."

I have an idea of Maxine's prima-donna, natural-born-leader attitude at the Museum of Modern Art's children's classes.

"They're such babies over there," Maxine sighs. "We worked in clay this afternoon."

"I loved working in clay," I said. "You can make a lot of fantastic things with clay. I had a lot of fun when I was a kid."

Maxine looks up solemnly. "Did you, Charles?"

"Yes. It's a lot of fun. But you have to be very careful. It takes time and it's something new for you."

Maxine removes her coat and hat and folds them neatly over a chair. "I like clay. But I don't like to make boys and girls and dogs and houses. I like to make fantastic things. But the teacher says no, make boys and girls and dogs and houses."

"Well, if you're a good girl. . . ."

"Good?" Maxine laughs. "You know I'm always good, Charles."

Then Mitch calls me to the phone and when I return, Maxine asks, "Who was it?"

"Shirley."

"Oh, her. Is she coming over?"

"No."

"You like her, don't you?"

"Oh, I don't know, Miss Fancy Pants."

"Charles! There you go again. You'd better stop that. I mean it."

"Shall we have tea, Miss Fancy Pants?"

"Have you got any cookies? I don't like tea without cookies. But I like iced tea."

"You know I've got loads and loads of cookies. Mucho cookies."

"Mucho cookies." Maxine laughed and then added, looking me straight in the eyes, "It's been a long time since we've had tea and cookies. You don't even buy Ritz crackers anymore."

"They don't go good with vermouth," I joked.

The deep sigh and the I-know-that-Charles expression Maxine gives me . . . adds another notch to the guilt scoreboard.

"Come on, Miss Fancy Pants," I said, bolting up and taking Maxine's hand. "Let's have tea."

"I'll make the tea," Maxine told me. "I've grown very tall this year. I can even light the back burner on your stove."

"You're right, cookie," I said. "You're getting to be a big girl."

"Yes," Maxine exclaimed, taking the teapot from the cupboard, and quoting a litany, "I drink plenty of fresh milk and I have strong teeth and bones."

Maxine gives a dazzling smile and lights the stove. I have another vermouth.

"You really drink a lot," Maxine said. "Mama said the garbage you take down is all beer cans and whiskey bottles."

"Is that true, Miss Fancy Pants?"

"Yes it is, and stop calling me Miss Fancy Pants."

"What shall I call you?"

"Miss Fancy Pants, you jerk."

I decided to take a walk. Going out, I encounter Maxine returning from the hall bathroom.

"Charles, where are you going?"

"Out," I said sharply.

"Well, baby," Maxine slanged, "don't blow your cool."

"That's right, cookie," I grinned and counted the stairs as I went down.

TODAY I HAD a delivery in the serene, green world of Manhasset, Long Island. A group of nursery school children were playing in front of a large Tudor-style house. One little boy, with space helmet and Davy Crockett tee-shirt, aimed his yellow plastic water pistol at me and shouted, "Hey you! Chinese boy!"

I ducked the spray of water and reflected that this was the first time I had ever been mistaken for a Chinese. I had a sudden impulse to set the record straight. But then I thought that the kid *had* the right tone of voice, if the wrong nationality.

I have always known what I was—if I might have had a brief lapse of consciousness, there was always a sign, gesture, or word from the outside world to help me bear in mind my race. Even with my closest friends among the whites, there are these little reminders. Even Troy Lamb, of Scotch-German parentage with a trickle of Jewish blood, reveals now and then that his feelings are mixed on color. Yet I must be at the hospital at the birth of his second child and meet his in-laws. Laura Vee, the model, with new coiffure, Paris dress, takes my arm proudly and defiantly as we emerge from my building to encounter a sightseeing bus of southerners. But too, Laura Vee can angrily shout, "By God, you treat me like I'm white." I bow, because Laura has bowed often before my black throne.

I have moved like an uncertain ghost through the white world.

The wounds of my Missouri childhood were no worse than a sudden, sharp pain. As a six-year-old playmate of the twins whose father (a lawyer) my grandfather worked for, I used to go to her birthday parties, though they never came to mine. White Penelope Browne and I played as brother and sister, until we arrived at the acute age of twelve. Afterwards, very polite and formal.

I remember one white boy named Bobby. He was a cripple and a stammerer. His house was the first white house across the tracks. Daily, he would be at his white picket fence. He always greeted me with "Neigaaar." I always laughed and imitated his crude shuffle. Sometimes I would do a quick somersault on the sidewalk in front of his house. Then I'd jump up and say, "All right, crip. You try that." We balanced the score.

At the local movie, I had to sit in the balcony on hard wooden seats. Downstairs, the seats were upholstered with maroon leatherette. But it was very dark up there in the balcony, and us little colored boys would sneak smokes and pet with the little colored girls. That was something the white kids downstairs couldn't do. The lights were too bright.

The first time I spent a weekend exclusively with white people, I was fourteen, very shy, and late for dinner. They were waiting for me and I delayed coming down. I gave my shoes an extra shine, brushed my hair again. Despite the fact that I had just bathed, I checked my armpits. At the time the notion that Negroes smell was still alive; I didn't really believe it, but white people said it was true and they were always right. And as I came down the carpeted staircase, I heard my fifteen-year-old host's uncle, a Missouri state senator, say, "Maybe he won't come down because we ain't got no watermelon."

The senator laughed heartily at his own wit, but there was no other laughter.

The last word in Negro arguments of my childhood was always "yellow" or "shit-colored bastard." Sometimes us yellow, shit-colored kids stuck together as a means of protection. The varying light-brown colors of our skin didn't go to our heads; we were colored. Though a few of my fair-colored, childhood classmates changed in this respect when they grew older.

When I was sixteen, I got a job as a pinboy at Harry O'Malley's Fair Lanes bowling alley.

"Hey, Harry. See you have a coon back there."

Harry O'Malley made no reply. He merely looked away.

"Take a shot at the nigger, baby."

"Oh, honey." (This with giggles.)

"Look at that nigger go. Fast as lightning."

I was nicknamed 'Lightning' because I was fast. I worked there a week, frightened, and overly conscious that I must do a good job. This had been pounded into me in my colored neighborhood.

"Sonny, now you act right. Be the best."

"Yes. That's what white folks expect of you."

"Say 'yes ma'm' and 'no ma'm' and 'sir'."

"Get the lead out of your ass, boy."

"You should be proud. The first colored pinboy up there."

I did work hard and fast, and the second night I was handling two alleys. The next League night, Harry gave me the slow teams (which a pinboy accepts as a honor and a burden). This became a custom. A fast pinboy speeds up slow bowlers. The compliments of Harry, the envious glances of the white pinboys, and the egging on of other Negroes did very little for my ego. I knew I had done a good job. I was tired. That was that.

I often took the long way home from the alley, passing the courthouse square and going up a neat, white, residential street that gave onto a bridge, the railroad tracks, and home. I liked the old, crumbling, Victorian houses up that way.

One night the police stopped me.

"Nigger, where you going?"

"What?"

"I said, where are you going?"

"Home."

"Do you live up this way?"

"No. . . . I. . . ."

"Get in."

The police station. I remember standing in the center of an empty-looking room thinking, What will I tell Grandma? Above me was a harsh, unshaded light, just like the movies I thought. But I was frightened, surrounded by four policemen. My heart thumped like crazy and my eyes darted from man to man and then at the wall behind the rolltop desk. A portrait of Lincoln, the American flag, and a nude, calendar girl decorated the cream-colored wall.

Finally the policeman at the desk looked up. "What were you doing up there?"

"I work at O'Malley's bowling alley and I like to take the long way home. It's very quiet and I like to walk."

"Is that so?"

"Yes, sir. I'm pretty fast too. I'm on the track team at school."

The policeman at the desk nodded and smiled faintly.

"Take your hands out of your pockets," he ordered. "Search'm, boys."

The searching policemen found: a sweaty handkerchief, pocket comb, Zippo lighter, and a wallet containing four one-dollar bills, a fifty-cent piece, three quarters, one dime, one penny.

The policeman at the desk puckered up his lips and ran a pale, blue-veined hand through his close-cropped, gray hair. "No knife, uh? Never been arrested? Like to take hikes . . . and you're on the track team. Is that right?"

"Yes, sir," I said brightly in the moment of truth and salvation.

"WELL, GODDAMMIT. START RUNNING AROUND THIS ROOM!"

I began running. Head held high, arms arched at my waist, taking it slow and easy like a good trotting horse.

"Faster," a policeman yelled.

"He sure can go," another added.

"By God, jest like a rabbit."

"Faster, boy!"

I picked up speed. The room held heat like an overbaked oven. Sweat popped out on my face and ran in little streams down my face. My tee shirt was wet and clung to my body like a new layer of skin. Each time I swallowed, my throat seemed to contract. I closed my eyes once. The room seemed to spin like a top.

"Faster."

I could hardly get my breath but I continued taking long strides. About half an hour later, my legs began to give. A pain throbbed in my leg muscles. The room did not seem like a room to my blurred, dazed eyes: rather like a giant, faded cloth that was being doused in a washing machine. Strange, too; my feet felt as light as cotton.

"Okay, boy," the policeman at the desk said rising, "that's enough."

I slumped against the desk exhausted and wiped my face with the back of my hand.

"That was damn good," the close-cropped, gray-haired policeman said. He reached in his pocket and threw a nickel on the
floor. "That was a miteee fine show."

The nickel hit the floor dully, rolled, and fell on its tail as if on
cue. I kept my eyes focused on that nickel. (I still remember that
nickel. An old Indian-head nickel.)

Then I knelt down and picked up the nickel because that was
the only thing to do.

"You sure can run fast," another policeman said, handing me
my wallet.

"Never saw a nigger who couldn't," another policeman
reflected.

"Yeah," the gray-haired policeman agreed. "But stay across
the tracks. Do you hear me?"

"Yes, sir," I replied firmly, quickly, and walked out of the
Sedalia, Missouri, police station, trying not to think of anything.

It was a quiet summer night. The small town street was
deserted and the crumbling, Victorian houses faded like the night
from my dreams.

As I grew older, the white world beckoned. They wanted me. Now
I began to wonder what they wanted from me. I certainly didn't
have money. Were they trying to prove something to themselves,
using me as a reassuring springboard? Only a few of the young
white women I became friendly with wanted to sleep with me.

Young Negroes were another matter; the type of young men I
met at liberal white parties and chic black parties. Quiet, turned
out in Ivy League garb, usually with a pipe and mustache. Perfect
gentlemen: sophisticated Uncle Toms. I certainly don't go for most
Negro girls who have gone to a good college. They are usually
phony intellectuals. The swinging Negro girls were more likely to
be those who had gone to secretarial school—waitresses, maids,
promising singers. They knew the racial score; they had paid their
dues.

If you disagree on race relations with another Negro, well,
you're asking for a fight. I remember the fights at school about
Lincoln. What did he *really* do for the Negro? The fights would
take place around election time, the man's birthday, or when we
were studying a particular period in American history.

Born black, not actually without color, brightness, or evil.

Black, nevertheless. Rather, the fashionable café au lait. Half and half. Black. My family is almost equally divided between the shades of light and dark. I am tan, a yellowish-brown, exposed to the sun the moment I emerged from my mother's womb. Beige. I am a man of color. La Ronde began after my ancestors sailed in from Africa. I curse the day of their lust. I wish them many seasons in a syphilitic hell.

Their curdled semen . . . why couldn't they have stayed in their race! They make me an outsider. A minority within a minority. They called me dago as a child, before my curls turned to kinks. That sun again! But these kinks form my proud crown. Negro, Negroid, Nigger. Black, brown, and beige. Yellow, shit-colored. Buck, boy. I am the result of generations of bastard Anglo Saxon, African, Black Creek, and Choctaw Indian blood.

Me, the last of the Negro, southwestern, Missouri Stevensons.

LENA IS BACK on the scene. I am at Bobby's apartment in a small West Side hotel.

"Ah! There's my daddy," Lena says, grinning from ear to ear. "There's my sweet little motherfucker."

Lena then bounced over in a yellow, baggy, Italian sweater and form-fitting blue slacks, her buttocks quivering evilly. She planted a mouth-smacking kiss square on the top of my head.

"Hiya, doll," I said, bringing on a happy smile. "When did you get out?"

"Tuesday morning," Lena said, patting her tight spit curls which were geometrically arranged on her head like a careful bird's nest. "Yes. I'm operating again. Clipped a joker for two hundred bucks last night."

Lena threw back her head and cackled; her teeth were a miniature Fort Knox. Then she started jazzing me—huddling close, her long thief's hand lunging for my head as if trying to pull out a hunk of hair. Then she bends down, licks my arm with her sharp witch's tongue, and sinks in her gold teeth savagely.

I squirm and give her another painful grin. "Take it easy, baby."

"Miss Lena," Bobby says, pursing up his lips like a dried peach. "Child. You're trying to eat that boy alive."

Lena bolts up. "You're just a jealous bitch. Faggot."

Bobby tilts his head grandly. "Miss Thing, you are a freak."

A sardonic smile lights up Lena's amber face. "Yes, a freak. And a good one."

"I wish they'd kept your ass in jail," Bobby chides, handing Lena a beer.

"Trying to put the bad mouth on me, bitch?" Lena yells, and then in a very businesslike way pulled a roll of bills from her sweater.

"Child," Bobby exclaims, popping his butter-bean eyes, "that is enough to choke a mule."

Lena counts out one hundred and eighty dollars, puts a twenty back inside her sweater, and gives me the rest.

"Here, daddy. Take a twenty for yourself. I'll be over tomorrow to pick it up."

"Miss Lena, you love that boy," Bobby said.

"Yes," Lena said diffidently. "I can trust him, too. Can't trust any of you c———."

"Oh please, Miss One," Bobby tut-tutted. "You've got plenty of friends."

"Yes. As long as I'm hustling these streets and making a fat score. You Goddamn right."

Lena sinks into my lap and tickles my chin. "What's on your mind, baby? Thinking about Shirley?"

"We're not speaking."

"Oh, that again. Why don't you two get married?"

"I suppose you'd be the bridesmaid at their wedding," Bobby said sweetly.

Lena bolted up. "Yes, bitch. I'll be the bridesmaid and I'll baby-sit for them. What Goddamn business is it of yours?"

Bobby was alarmed and threw up his hands. "Oh please, child, I was only kidding. You don't have to get up in the air about it. Mercy me."

"Here, bitch," Lena said. "Here's five bucks. Go out in the kitchen and fix me something to eat."

Bobby was insulted. "Miss Thing," he said, "I don't need your money. And you know you're always welcome to eat at my house. Besides, I haven't forgotten the time you paid my rent when I was in the hospital."

"Not hospital, baby, jail. When you got busted for turning a trick in the subway. Don't try to be piss-elegant because Charlie is here. I know you from way back when. Now get out in the kitchen and fix me some food. And a plate for Charles, too."

"Lena, I don't want anything," I said.

"Oh, make that faggot work. You need to put some meat on those bones anyway."

Bobby blinked his eyes and stepped gingerly into the kitchen. Lena flopped back down into my lap and sighed heavily. I massaged her shoulders, and soon the heavy breathing stopped.

"That feels good," Lena groaned, closing her eyes outlined with navy blue mascara. The beat lines showed through her pancake makeup.

"Are you going to move into a pad or hotel?" I asked.

"Pad? Hotel? I wish I knew, Charles," Lena said without opening her eyes. "I'm so tired. Think I'll save my loot and move to California. I wanna make a new start with my old man. He gets out of Sing Sing next year."

"That's a good idea," I said. "But then, you'd better be careful."

"Don't I know it," Lena said. "I can't afford to get busted again. Hustling up by the Park Sheraton is out. But if I'm a good girl, will you help me?"

"Oh sure, doll," I said.

Last summer, Lena and I lived in a place off Third Avenue in the Fifties. I didn't work because Lena liked to have me around the house. She was out a great deal and there were many phone calls. Lena is a prostitute and a professional thief. Like the Murphy Game players, she works best in the summer. She'll meet a John in a bar, talk some trash. Once the John leaves the air-conditioned bar and hits the humid streets, he's Lena gravy.

The first score only whets her appetite. She used to come home, say at two a.m., hand over the first take, change clothes, have a drink, and hit the streets again. She would still be hustling after the sun had come up. Lena had discovered that there were good scores to be made in broad daylight between six and nine a.m. But this was usually on Saturdays. But it was on an early Sunday morning that Lena got busted in the doorway of a Fifth Avenue dress shop. The John said that Lena had cleaned him for a hundred and seventy dollars. Yet when the cops took her down, she only had ninety in her stockings. Lena never said what happened to the other eighty-five.

Bobby knew a lawyer. We had a fund-raising drive among Lena's friends. Even Bruce kicked in ten bucks. A week later, Lena was out on a five-hundred-dollar bail. The John was from out of town, didn't want a scandal, and the case was dropped.

Then Lena got busted again. I went to the trial and Lena cried in my arms, saying I was against her, everyone was against her. She was going back to Philly. Back to her middle-class, respectable family of social workers, teachers, post office clerks, and railroad conductors. Lena had studied dress design for two years.

Now she lay in my arms, breathing hard, catnapping.

Bobby came in with a whopping plate of fried chicken, greens, and buttered rolls. "Wake up, Miss Lena, and eat," he said.

Lena stretched and smiled up at me. "Look at this dumb bitch. Waking me up for some Goddamn food."

"Child," Bobby exclaimed. "You sent me to all this trouble. Mercy me."

Lena sat up and rubbed her eyes. "Have you got anything to drink in this house?" she demanded. "I've gotta go out and see what's on the log for the lizard."

"Miss Lena," Bobby said, "It's *only* five."

Lena glared at Bobby and shook her head sadly. "Listen to him, will you?" she said, her eyes dancing merrily as her work plan developed in her mind. "I'm going to do my eyes, freshen up my makeup. There's this new bar that I'm dying to work. It's cozy as a womb. Soft lights, deep rugs on the floor. I'm going in very grand, my dear. Like those whores in Miami. I'll spend ten or fifteen bucks across the bar. But I'll come out with a hundred dollar trick. Now what do you bet, bitch? Miss Subway Queen?"

Just then, Claudia swept in grandly with the ever-present, silent Lady P. "The queen's head is tore up," Claudia cackled.

Bobby closed the door and glared at him. "Miss Claudia, you are too much."

"She's a grand bitch," Lena said. "Have *you* been in drag lately?"

"Oh, child," Claudia sighed. He gestured haughtily as if dismissing an invisible royal court. "Let me tell you, Miss one—"

But Bobby interrupted: "Really? I don't see how you go in drag. You're not femme. You have buck teeth."

Claudia threw back his head and snapped his fingers. "Ain't no man asked me for teeth yet."

"The kind of men you have," Bobby huffed. "Butch sissies."

"And when have *you* had a man?" Claudia asked. His large, doe eyes seemed to be larger.

"Why my boyfriend, Hank—" Bobby began.

"You stupid faggots make me sick," Claudia said. "You wouldn't know a man if you saw one. You don't think a real man would sleep with a hard-ass faggot like you?"

"I don't have to take that," Bobby cried.

"Oh, please, Miss Thing," Claudia laughed. "There's only one real man in this room. It's Lady P."

EVENING FINDS ME on the stoop with a beer. Vapor holds the air. You would expect the neon signs to melt like multicolored candles. Standing in front of the hotels and restaurants like wilted sentries are the people who live on this block. It is too hot to sleep. The lights of the tall buildings gleam down like ghosts and create a nightmare haze. The smell of fresh baked bread wars with the garbage smells from the litter baskets. I see a wet, burned sofa cushion, rotten bananas (the gypsies), a head of crushed Iceburg lettuce, and a half-moon of hamburger on toasted bun. Broken soda bottles and a gin bottle, a pink paper napkin smeared with lipstick. A drunk knocks over the litter basket which usually sits in front of our stoop like a piece of cheap, abstract, garden sculpture. I refuse to go down and pick it up. The owners of the bars do not care. Nor does the haughty, homeless cat strutting by, cursing. And then, all this suddenly is drowned out by the crude, imploring voice of a nightclub singer from down the street: "*I wanna be loved. . . .*" A terrible proclamation.

Miss Roberta trips up like a shy gazelle. She is dressed in white from head to foot, her dyed strawberry-blond hair has been freshly set. She offers me a swig of brandy from a silver purse flask. Her Thunderbird is in the repair shop and she has to walk her beat; the twenty-five-dollar I. Miller's are giving her hell. Miss Roberta spots a likely prospect and moves on.

Two more prostitutes. This begins to seem like a union meeting. They're Negro and do a land office business downtown. Sally and Sue. Sally is very dark, with short slick hair and a great body. She looks like some rich jungle fruit that has been carefully preserved in waxed paper. Sue is delicate, light-skinned, very ladylike. Sometimes Sally and Sue use me as a front and turn an occasional trick at my place.

Sue and Sally came rushing up, breathing hard, and shaking like jelly on those spike heels. The cops have run them off Broadway. They have to rest and get their bearings.

"I don't feel like working tonight, anyway," Sally says hoarsely, chewing gum avidly. "And, baby, I can't afford to get busted. Went to the can last Wednesday night and was picked up again Saturday night. I'm trying to talk those cops into letting me go. Maybe give'm a little free pussy." She laughs. "Anyway, baby, so they take the doll to the West Fifty-fourth Street station. Way up on the top floor. And then, in the squad room, all hell breaks loose. The cops run out. Baby, they shouldn't have done that. Leaving me there all by my lonesome. I took off my heels and crawled down those four flights and pressed."

We laughed. A young rookie cop is suddenly on the scene, swinging his nightstick, walking stiffly like he had a board up his ass. He comes up to the stoop and demands, "What're you girls doing here?"

Sally, cracking her gum, looks over the cop's shoulder at a crowded station wagon pulling out of Tip Top Parking. She swings her fine brown legs and begins humming "John Brown's Body."

"You girls ain't talking, huh? I bet if I took you in, you'd talk plenty. Didn't I see you about an hour ago on Broadway?"

"Officer, we ain't doing nothin'," Sally drawled. "We just trying to cool off."

"Cool off at home."

I decided to speak. "These girls are friends of mine," I said firmly, looking the cop straight in the eye. "And we're sitting here cooling off. We are planning to sit here as long as we feel like it."

The cop was stunned. "Oh. Is that so? Who the hell are you, their pimp? I can take you in too, you know."

"I've lived on this block for five years," I said, rising. "I know you have enough to keep you busy without bothering people who are trying to cool off."

I have very little respect for policemen, because I've walked the streets enough to know that if the cops really worked hard, the jails would overflow.

After my remark, the cop turned quickly and headed for Sixth Avenue. He still moved as if he had a board up his ass.

"A tough cop-shitter," Sally said.

Finally Sally and Sue start off, ready to sign in for the early morning shift.

I go up to my place, and Maxine pops in, wanting to know why I haven't gone to bed.

"I'm goin' to the country," Maxine said. "Not with those fresh air kids. I'm going to Virginia with my *grandmother*, and then we're going to Canada. You've never been to Canada, have you, Charles?"

"No, Cookie," I said, "lots of places, but never to Canada. You're a lucky girl."

SAW MY OLD ARMY BUDDY, JELLY, on Sixth Avenue this morning, standing at the subway entrance, wolfing down a bag of French pastry. His brown face seemed paralyzed with terror.

"Charlie, my man," he whined. The day was pleasant, about sixty-five degrees, but sweat poured down Jelly's face. Jelly gave me a panicky grin and said, "Where you going? Let's get a beer."

"Sure," I said.

We started off and were almost at the corner when Jelly stopped. "Wow," Jelly exclaimed, the panicky grin still glued on his sweaty face. "Look, Dad. I don't want any beer. I've gotta have a fix and I know where I can get a twenty-dollar fix for fifteen dollars and it's real good shit and Charlie, my man, I don't wanna hit you like this but I swear I'm dying, my guts feel like they're coming loose. Oh baby, I gotta have that fix or I'll go nuts and it only costs fifteen dollars fifteen bucks. . . ."

"I can let you have five," I said.

Jelly threw his arms around me and, for a moment, I thought he was going to kiss me. His fat, trembling hands clung to my shirt and his eyes had a worshipful gleam. "Daddy," he said, "you are a doll. A real living doll. You've been a swinging stud ever since Korea."

I remember the Korean Jelly. He'd tip into the tent at four in the morning, treading lightly, his voice high and tremulous, like a woman's. Sometime's he'd do a couple of graceful ballet turns and yell "On guard!" or get tangled up in the mosquito bar. I would have to help. I'd get up, trying to keep him quiet so he wouldn't wake the other guys. All of them knew the score: several were novice junkies.

It wouldn't be long before reveille and I never tried to undress Jelly. But he would always ask, breathing hard like a man with heart trouble, "Charlie, my boy, take off my boots, please." After unlacing Jelly's boots, I'd light a cigarette and sit on the footlocker beside his bunk. I'd do most of the talking. Jelly either giggled or let out a heavy, "Yeah man!" Silently we'd listen to the changing of the guards, cursing up at the motor pool, and the peasants singing down the hill, starting for the Seoul markets before the hot sun and heavy frontline GI traffic blocked the dusty roads. The peasants padded along barefooted as if they were moving through a valley of sand. Moonlight made their white muslin clothes seem more white. It was like watching a carvan of ghosts.

Finally Jelly and I would doze off. A couple of hours later, he would awake cursing in that high and tremulous woman's voice, snapping his eyes angrily around the tent, jerking the mosquito bar and frame from the bunk and, as always, moan: "I don't feel well this morning. I think I'll go on sick call." Then he would give orders to the silent, moon-faced Korean houseboy to go into Seoul and get his drugs and his deep "Yeah man" voice back.

The memory of the United States Army begins for me with the exuberant spirit in which I took basic training. I really enjoyed the hikes on cold, rainy mornings with full field pack, the infiltration course, bivouac. There were guys who went through training because they were afraid of their superiors and guys who trained diligently because it seemed to them that it was the right thing to do. Then there were guys, and these were the great majority, who constantly fucked off during those first six weeks of basic training. Most of us were young—18, 22—and away from home for the first time. There were days and nights when things happened, when the army outdid itself and surpassed the tales of toughness we had heard all our lives.

As novice soldiers we talked very little of the fighting in Korea. After basic training I waited eagerly for my overseas orders, which never came. The mess sergeant took a liking to my buddy and me, and we were farmed out as cooks, though I had never fried an egg in my life. Then one weekend, I got on a roaring drunk and went AWOL. Upon my return I was shipped out to another company filled with green trainees and manned by a company predominantly of white southerners.

My color, as always because of GI records, had preceded me. I came into the new barracks and was unpacking my duffle bag when the platoon sergeant walked in. We exchanged a few short comments. The trainees had gathered around us like a group of excited fans in the last round.

Then the platoon sergeant said, "You think you are a smart nigger, doncha?"

I looked up at him and said: "No. I don't think I'm smart. But I do think I'm intelligent."

There was nothing much left for the man to do but walk away. But after that, pressure was put on me from all sides, in a hundred ways, and my nightly prayer was to be sent overseas. I went AWOL about three times during this assignment, because I had heard a rumor that if you took off you would be sent to Korea without orders. The last time I was picked up AWOL I was marched to the stockade with a guard punching a loaded carbine into my back. Later, after my court-martial, I heard that the officers of my company celebrated the fact that they had put me away for six months.

The second day I was in the stockade, I received permission from the chaplain to visit the library. My court-martial had been swift. I was certain that they had put the screws on me. I read up on court-martial procedure and discovered that within seventy-two hours after he has been sentenced a soldier may have the proceedings reviewed.

The reviewing colonel was very understanding. I had had a good record and he was going to suspend the six-month sentence. How could a nice, intelligent young man like me get into such trouble?

But what about overseas, I wanted to know? There was plenty of time, the colonel said.

I walked into the mess hall that noon and a silence fell. I had conquered the company. After that, I had no more trouble. I spent a year at Fort Leonard Wood, only one hundred and twenty miles from home.

Finally, though, it was the boat for Korea. Our Korean ship docked at San Francisco at nine on a fine Saturday morning. We were not allowed to get off and had to console ourselves with a view of the city.

Then the ship was at sea, and the lights of the city became nothing more than tiny, earthbound stars. We settled in our bunks and the card and dice games began. Then they were over, along with the bull sessions, except for the all-night drinking sports like myself. Shortly after midnight, I stumbled down those tiers of bunks and was horrified to hear the muffled weeping, the cries of hundreds of young men. This unashamed weeping engulfed the whole ship.

After a very long crossing, twenty-two days, we sailed into the port of Sasebo, Japan. We went ashore, were given lectures in Far East soldiery, and it was here that I gave away civilian clothing, toothpaste, soap, candy, cigarettes, books, money. Later this innocent Missouri boy was to learn that these *poor* Japanese met every ship; a very profitable activity of their existence.

Next came the steep, dusty hills of Korea, riding in a two-ton truck, and suddenly hearing from far off the explosion of a bomb. GIs fell over each other getting out of the truck and scrambling into the nearby trenches, and Big Daddy yelled: "Where are the fucking gooks?" Everyone cut him hostile glances. But soon the others adopted Big Daddy's bravo spirit. We were combat construction engineers. There were occasional skirmishes, but the fighting was already petering out by the time we got to Korea and in July the truce came.

Now that the war, the Korean police action was over, military life became routine, petty. I grew bored and difficult. I was shipped off to fire-fighting school. Graduating from that, I was transferred to another engineering company and there I told myself to shape up.

Part of my family were carpenters and I took easily to the back-breaking work of helping to rebuild Korea. I watched promotions and favors go to gold bricks, and seeing this happen taught me things it was good to know. The fire marshal, a corporal of our company, was soon to be transferred to Japan. His bunk was next to mine and he appointed me fire marshal. With the new job I had only about two days' work a month and there were favors and a promotion, which I promptly lost because of the platoon sergeant. The platoon sergeant was a southern white, had spent ten years in a federal prison, and could not read or write. He disliked Headquarters tent of his platoon and he disliked Negroes.

But there were many things to turn my mind away from company politics. The Korean people I ran across were wonderful, and I like to believe that my money and the country my uniform represented had nothing to do with the way they felt towards me. The ROK soldiers, the elite of the Korean army (the KATUSAS were the peasants) were better dressed than most of us GIs. (I'll not soon forget trying to evade my houseboy's question as to why I didn't have new boots. He had taken my boots to the village shoemaker to try to have them repaired even though they were ready for the trash barrel.) On the Sunday afternoon when the ROK soldiers received word that they were no longer attached to American military units, they all got very drunk and tore up tents and equipment, shooting wildly with their weapons.

The Korean children used to line up, hungry-eyed, at the fence, to watch all our rich food being dumped into the garbage cans. I remember being invited to a Korean home and, after the tea ceremony, each member of the family came over to me shyly and rubbed their hands through my hair.

In September of 1953, Korea was shaking on her post-war legs in the changing world of East and West. The uncertain peace hovered over everything; at each loud noise our eyes scanned the sky.

I came back home, to Missouri—to Grandma, my friends, with thousands of GIs for whom Korea had been pretty meaningless. It was as if they had never left this country.

Before I went into the army, my feeling about it, about the war in Korea, was that of a boy who loved playing soldier. I looked forward to the United States Army and Korea with glee; it was to be another adventure, another experience, and, when I received my draft notice shortly after my nineteenth birthday, it was like Christmas. I looked forward to fighting, perhaps even to dying.

The night before I left for the army, Grandma and I were sitting on the vine-covered front porch in Missouri. It was a soft, summer night and you could smell the honeysuckle vines which grew up the sides of the porch.

"Sonny, do you still say your prayers?" Grandma asked.

"Yes, ma'am," I replied quickly and lit a cigarette.

"You're not lying to your old Granny, are you?"

"No, ma'am."

"All right. I'll take you at your word. Now you go on out and see your friends. Go on. We don't have to sit here like someone has died. But first, before you go—pray with me, Sonny."

Grandma and I got down on our knees and put our elbows in the swing seat and bowed our heads.

Grandma prayed first and her voice was like a peaceful hymn: "Dear Heavenly Father, again you've spared one of your humble servants to bend on their knees before thee. Father, I thank you for carrying me through this blessed day and giving me strength to live from minute to minute, hour to hour, on this blessed summer day."

Grandma's voice rose slightly. I looked up out of the corner of my eye and saw Grandma rubbing her hands together. She was looking at the faded, flower-printed back of the porch swing. Even in the darkness her eyes sparkled and I knew tears were in them. "Father, I want you to have mercy upon my grandson, that he may see the light and come over on your side before it's too late. Father, dear, sweet Jesus, I want you to throw your strong arms around him as he goes off to war. Guide him . . . he's only a child. Guide him, and bring him home safely to me. Help him and all the other young men and women in this wicked world."

My clasped hands were sweaty; I dug my nails hard into the palms of my hands as I continued to listen to Grandma's low chant: "Father, Father, there is so little time left. Children are born into this world of sin, and before you know it, they are grown. They drift away from home and from the church. They stumble along the byways of life. Blessed Jesus, let your light shine that my boy might see it and come unto you before it is too late and that he may have life everlasting. I ask this in your name, through Jesus Christ Our Lord. Amen."

Grandma paused briefly and said, "Your turn, Sonny."

I turned my head and stared out at the dark night. There was nothing out there. Darkness. Fireflies. Street lights beaming through the trees, and against the shadowy houses.

"Your turn, Sonny," Grandma repeated. Then she turned toward me. "My child, have you forgot how to pray?"

I did not say anything. I looked at Grandma and blessed the darkness so I would not have to meet her tear-filled eyes.

"Sonny," Grandma said. "Pray."

I bowed my head again and opened my mouth. The words would not come. I looked up at the porch ceiling. It seemed as if the ceiling was between me and God.

"Well," Grandma said finally, rising, "You might as well get up. I'll pray for you and you try to pray yourself and then it will be all right. If you *believe*, it will be all right."

I got up and kissed Grandma on the forehead. "Goodnight, Grandma," I said.

"Goodnight, Sonny. Don't stay out too late. You'll have to get up early. . . ."

I heard her cry for the first time in my life as I walked off the porch.

I am glad for Grandma that I returned safe from Korea. I was all that she had in this world and I knew what the loss of me would mean to her.

Korea did not turn out to be my personal salvation as a man, nor a field of glorious exploits and adventures. It was simply and deeply my first rude lesson that most men and women suffer unbearably.

THE VIEW FROM the fifth-floor window is very fine. The temperature is a balmy seventy-nine degrees; the sky black, starless. There are tiers of lights beaming from the Empire State building, the revolving search lights, Pizza House, rainbow-hued neon, Hertz car rental, Tip Top Parking, and the hotel's blue-white signature. My FM radio plays respectable cool jazz. Bellowing above the jazz is the cry of the jukebox bars, and the aching churn and clunk of the garbage truck.

Three sailors pass, doing the Jersey bounce in their tight, white suits. A six-foot, grayhaired whore walks by like a white, proud, Viennese horse. The Amazon whore slaps one of the sailors on the back heartily. They move off down the street.

Next on view is little Miss Dumpty-Dump with her great rouged cheeks, working the midnight shift. I see her each morning getting off the BMT subway with her cannister in a brown paper bag or under the folds of her flaring raincoat. She solicits for every known and unknown charity, and I know she has been with her chapter seven years. She is one of those old, sweet-voiced, motherly women, all of whom have a profitable con game. Their organization is a strict and exclusive one, run on the lines of the D.A.R. Not just anyone can get in. Their meetings are held in Horn and Hardart over tea and rolls, once a week, between two and four p.m.

L. C., the Tip Top attendant, has just bought a Pepsi Cola from the machine in the garage, and is staring intently at a seven-year-old boy who is walking hand and hand with his parents, ogling that mirage, Rockefeller Center.

I wonder about Tip Top. There is an open doorway between Pizza House and Tip Top Parking. It is deep and dark, almost the width of my narrow room. Men enter this dark, brooding tomb to urinate or to take long nips from a hip-pocket pint. The brilliant neon signs and streetlights create only a gray haze there; it's a kind of island in evening fog. If you are not too particular and don't mind standing up, it is a fine place to have sex, and quite a number of people do just that. The people passing are locked in a dream world, their eyes focused elsewhere. The island is a safe and secret place.

For example: A Negro night-cleaning woman passes the doorway, weighed down with two large packages wrapped carelessly with white tissue paper, like two giant white roses. The Negro woman has the left foot up, right foot down, flat-footed stride of a duck. She seems very tired and looks neither to the right nor left. The knowledge of more work at home clings to her body like sweat. More shirts to iron? Is Junior off the streets? Tomorrow is Saturday, but she cannot afford to sleep late.

As she passed the doorway, the man within stands back from the woman. He stretches out his long arms and fondles the woman's breasts. He is smiling, talking, very sure of himself. I can't see the woman's face, but she is short.

Four young men amble by. They are tourists: All of them wear colorful, short-sleeved summer shirts and blue jeans. There are deep cuffs in their blue jeans. Suddenly, one of the young men raises his arm and points at the tall buildings.

Now the man in the open doorway has his body pointed tight against the woman. His hands are clasped on her buttocks like a vise. The woman doesn't move. The man lowers his head and plants a kiss on her forehead.

Ah! The woman has sprung to life. Her skirt is pushed up around her hips. I can see where her stockings end. The man is in her but his trousers are not down. The woman flings her arms around the man, but her movements are delicate, as if the hormones in her body were frozen.

And then the man and woman came to a jerking halt and it is over. He releases himself from her very quickly, reaches in his pocket, and pulls out a handkerchief. Then, he lights a cigarette and, like a gentleman, offers it to the woman. She refuses. He looks away as she arranges herself.

The man and woman emerge out of the darkened doorway and into the light. He takes her arm and kisses that forehead again. He is a big man with gray, curly hair and ruddy face. His olive drab suit fits him well. The woman is very young with short, clipped hair, a pleasant face, devoid of makeup. She is staggering slightly. She has the look of a model for petite fashions and she wears short white gloves.

I look out at the wonders of the sky's black face. A sharp, autumnal breeze circles through this stone Hades, this island on the Hudson. Those tired old tramps, those neon signs! Even when I close the shutters, I can see them blinking on and off like a pretty bitch who likes to tease.

The lunatic music continues to scream from the bars. In a country noted for its wealth, the mass music is not even hybrid corn. Why can't I live in Forest Hills or Fairfield County where, I suppose, all is quiet and ordered. I don't really know. There I would be lulled to sleep by the whisper of leaves, the sprinkler jetting on the green lawn. Why am I here, why New York?

After the two years in the army, I went to St. Louis. I wanted to try to write, and set up shop in that city on the Mississippi. It was the spring of 1956 and for a season I was the darling of a heterogeneous group of the arty and the literary. I moved among them in a state of spectral wonder. In time, they tired of me and I of them.

There was nothing to do but move on to New York. I arrived in August of 1957. A visit only, I had told myself, but there was something that held me powerless. The pace, the variety, the anonymity, the sense of walking on glittering glass eggs, walking in a city like a big-time prostitute with her legs cocked open. A challenging, wondrous city, fit for a wide-eyed country boy. But do I really belong here?

TONIGHT I CAUGHT the A train, went up to Harlem. Kenya, the Iron Curtain, I thought. When I first got off the train at 125th Street, there seemed to be nothing foreign or menacing about the Saturday night street. But after a while, I felt a certain violence hovering in the air, as if a great symphony of dark emotions was keyed, waiting for the maestro's exploding baton. The great black mass is restless. If you doubt this sense of imminent violence, watch the few uneasy whites who live in Washington Heights, upper Broadway, and the Bronx.

As I walk down 125th Street, I see young men, sharp as diamonds in suits that they can't afford, leaning against flashy cars that don't belong to them, or stepping smartly as if on their way to a very high-class hell. 125th Street is Forty-second Street, Broadway, Times Square, Fifth Avenue all combined in a jungle of buildings. It is a prayer meeting with a hand-clapping, tambourine "Yes Lawd." It's Blumstein's Department Store, the Harlemite's Macy's. It's the Apollo, with the only live stage show in Manhattan. It's the smart bars catering to Big Time wheeling and dealing Negroes and downtown whites, who want a swinging Harlem night.

I turned down a side street where children were playing hide-and-seek, with families gathered on the stoops, or leaning out of brightly lighted windows. Here the sense of violence was in abeyance. It was Saturday night and there was a happy peace about the block. Gone was the blue world of Monday morning and Mr. Boss Man. Gone were the loudmouthed, cigar-smoking Negro leaders who try to rouse the great black mass to glory at the meeting of the waters in America.

"That bitch scorched my head with them hot irons. And these curls have got to last me two weeks, honey," I heard a woman laugh to her friends, who were leaning out a second-floor window. The woman was unconcerned with the world at large. There was too much to think about, what with the lousy tenement where you lived, and that job where you worked too hard and were underpaid. Now a bitch used too-hot combs and tried to burn your scalp. This woman would listen to a black leader simply because he was black, but distrusting even him, knowing that he was really the white man's mouthpiece—and that he couldn't do a damn thing about the bitch with the red-hot straightening comb.

Nearby was a storefront church with a painted window resembling stained glass. There was a crudely printed legend that said: THE HOLINESS SUNDOWN CHURCH, and in small letters: *The right Rev. Stokes D. Masfield, Pastor. This house of worship is open twenty-four hours a day like the eyes of God.*

A bold, large, black and white eye emblazoned the door. I entered to find this congregation in a silent prayer. The pastor looked up, nodded, and I sat down in a folding chair near the door. There were about twenty adults in the church, more women than men, and about a dozen fidgeting children, and there was a sweet smell about the place but no flowers except a few gleaming, green leaves from the five-and-ten.

"Sis-tas and bro-thers! We prayed silently. . . ."

"Yes, now! Didn't we pray!" the congregation cried.

"Prayed to da LAWD, silently . . ."

"Silently! Praise da Lawd!"

"Praise da Lawd. He hears us when we don't hear ourselves."

"Yes," cried the refrain, "he hears me. Oh, yes he does!"

"Let us make a joyful noise unto da Lawd. Unto da almitey on high . . ."

A tall dark young woman rose and with head lifted high, hands clasped, and the most serene expression I had seen on a face in a long time, opened her mouth and began to sing, "Just a Closer Walk with Thee." It was a pure, powerful contralto, the words flowing as easily as a mother talking to a sick child. The woman sang the verse and then the rest of the congregation took up the chorus and the sweating fat man showed that the organ was meant not only for cathedrals.

I found myself singing in a small voice. Something stirred inside me. Perhaps it was remembering Wednesday prayer meeting and Grandma and Grandpa. Perhaps it was just a corny emotion; I don't know. I only know that something stirred, touched me, and for a few minutes, sitting in that whitewashed-walled, storefront church, listening to that beautiful voice, I had a feeling that all was not lost. Somewhere there was such a thing as peace of mind and goodness.

I didn't, couldn't, stay long; too many things would start playing hell with my mind. I went up, shook the pastor's hand, and gave him a dollar. He smiled and said, "God bless you, son," and then I left.

It was almost midnight now. Everything was alive on 125th Street. This was Saturday night, the time when the Negroes let their hair down, relax, get drunk, fight and grumble about Mr. White Man and the price of pork and eggs and the troubles of their cousins down south, knowing that, come Monday morning, it will all be the same.

I went into a bar, had a couple of two-for-one drinks, and then a couple more, and headed for the subway. The drinks were terrible and bucked uneasily in my stomach. As I was going down the steps a Jew in a pre-Warsaw suit was coming up, mopping his lined red face. He looked up at me and smiled: "Kinda hot tonight, ain't it, boy?"

"Yes, Lawd," I said, and suddenly and uncontrollably vomited all the way down the subway steps.

I DRIFTED THROUGH FRENZIED, hot days and nights, drunk much of the time, despondent. August is working itself out slowly; time is a miser with an eyedropper. Summer. Summer's end. Will the summer ever end? I look at the picture of me above the fireplace, the baby in the white-knitted suit, standing in the old wicker chair. At one-and-a-half years old, the child poised, alerted for the takeoff. The large, soft eyes are unblinking and locked as ever. The boy would grow, become shy, secretive, and later would stand at a distance from life.

I remember Grandpa's lament, "This world is not my home." I think: You are the last branch of the tree. As in a novel by Faulkner, except that the family is Negro. For me, at the end of the line, nothing to look forward to but my own death, which I do not fear. But this, this doomed air of the present; what will happen to me before I die? What could possibly happen after all that *has* happened?

In the fall of 1958, I had a dream about Grandma. She was riding a bicycle and had stopped at the one-room, redbrick schoolhouse where I had gone for eight years. Grandma wore a black chiffon dress and a large, wheat-colored straw hat. It was a very hot day and Grandma was smiling at me as if we shared a delicious secret. I woke up in a sweat and this dream haunted me for days. Her most recent letters, written in her neat small script, had not been cheerful, which was unlike her, for even when ill or depressed, she feigned an air of happiness.

I decided to go home.

I remember walking through the courthouse square as the clock tolled six a.m. and broke the small-town quiet. The street was deserted. I knew, without looking up toward the November hills, where the landscape of cottages and big Victorian houses rose to meet a soft dawn, that there would be no movement, no lights in the windows. But somewhere in the brown hills a rooster crowed, and the chill morning air revealed a column of smoke; an early riser burning leaves.

I crossed the gravelled square with its moldy, bronze statue of Captain Zimmerman, the town's founder. The old-fashioned bandstand had a fresh coat of blue-green paint and looked as if it had been abandoned by a touring tent show. (The Toby Ward tent shows of my childhood; the Midwest's summer Broadway.) The slat and iron benches had not changed. They formed a forlorn semicircle. I sat down wearily on one, which was damp with early morning frost, and I looked out across the wide muddy Missouri. My eyes followed the flat river-bottom lands and the thrush-brown jungle of trees, the sparsely populated farms with blue lines of smoke rising from the chimneys, the windmills turning gently in the river wind.

Home.

I was born here, two miles from town in a little valley surrounded by sloping dogwood and blackberry-covered ridges. Now the house where I was born is gone and there are only the wild orange tiger lilies. Cows graze in that cup of a valley. The red-brick schoolhouse and Bette Sue Estill, the little girl with the laughing black eyes, and Grandpa fishing and hunting rabbits when the cornfields were covered with sheets of frozen snow. The Red Dog Café, the Royal movie house, and the Hughes Chapel Methodist Church (named after a great-great-uncle who was a famous Missouri Negro preacher). The whites moved further out from town and the Negroes moved into the town together with the church.

Sitting in the open space of the courthouse square, I found myself suddenly murmuring a solemn, desperate "Oh Jesus." My life seemed like that of a tomcat who had slunk down too many alleys and had gotten nothing but a whore's bag of experience. I was on the run, and fatigued, played out. And now I wanted to turn around and flee the town. I didn't want to face Grandma, face the moment of recognition. We were too much alike—silent, reading each other's minds, a painful blessing. Somewhere across the railroad tracks was my father, sleeping, as Grandma would say, like a big dumb ox, and there also were the countless girls I had loved in another time when this town had been my world, except for dreams. I had lost whatever I had had in those days, a shy lonely boy, veteran of a small war at twenty-one, who had made the bohemian pilgrimage without finding a roosting place.

I got up from the bench slowly, yawned and stretched lazily, and summoned up a grin for Captain Zimmerman: "Good morning, Cap. The dead welcoming the dead."

I walked through the tranquil fir trees, saddled with two heavy leather bags which held everything I possessed, and on down Main Street. Already the sun was up, a warm buttery yellow. And there was the lusty, muddy song of my childhood, the Missouri River, rushing to join the Mississippi a hundred miles away in St. Louis. I felt strange and hollow being back, but I strode briskly, long-legged, a voyager in a fresh green land.

I saw it: East Cooper Street, house number four, a mound of weathered clapboard. A porch circled the house like a crazy horse-shoe; dried, frostbitten vines covered the porch like a cape. The windows of the second floor were shuttered and my eyes travelled down the first floor. Yellowed lace curtains framed the living room's bay window; the sill supported a group of potted plants and a tattered, pink-shaded lamp.

Nothing had changed and I mounted the porch steps slowly. An alley cat sprang out of the porch swing, hissed angrily, and disappeared. I started, then smiled, and raised a trembling hand to knock on the door.

There was no sound from within the house and I rapped again, then stood rigid with my hands hanging down at my sides. Finally I heard Grandma's soft voice: "All right, I'm a-comin."

The door opened and she stood facing me. I had a sense of falling. My heart, heavy as a log, dropped, just dropped. I bit my lower lip to hold back the tears.

"Sonny!"

"Grandma!"

We embraced, falling into each other's arms as if the ground under the sagging porch were giving way.

I held Grandma gently in my arms. She was seventy-nine years old. She had been a full-bodied woman, but I could feel the change in her. She was thin now, no more than a bundle of dried sticks. The round face was not even a mask of what it had been. Her cheeks had caved in and there were only her proud bones beneath a thin layer of wrinkled brown flesh. The waist-length hair, before always crowned in tight braids, had almost all gone. What was left was plastered against her skull like a baby's knitted cap. Her eyes were the same: warm, brown, laughing. They peered up at me questioningly.

"Grandma, Grandma," I crooned, rocking her in my arms, hoping she did not note a change on my smiling face.

"Surprised?" I asked, knowing there was nothing I could hide from her.

"Glory be . . . I can hardly get my breath." Grandma looked at me tenderly, there were tears in her eyes. Her voice was happy and lilting, like that of a young girl. "And you didn't even write to let me know you were coming. Shame on you."

We were not only connected by blood; we were friends. Whatever had happened to us, whatever thoughts crossed our minds that early November morning, could not destroy the love we bore each other.

"Let's go inside," Grandma said. I picked up my bags and followed Grandma inside, kicking the door shut.

The living room was not the cool, flowered room of sleepy summer afternoons or the warm crackling room of winter. I could not believe that I had played in this room as a child. Giant red roses in the grimy wallpaper overpowered the room. Hunks of plaster peeped through the wallpaper and paint peeled from the ceiling in fancy paper scallops. A web of dust framed the portrait of Grandpa, which hung above the closed-up fireplace. A horsehair sofa littered with shiny silk pillows was shoved against a wall and near it sat an oil burner, covered with dust. Two carved rosewood tables and four moth-eaten olive chairs occupied the space opposite the fireplace. A hard, rock-maple chair, as perky looking

as ever, and the old marble-covered table were on either side of the
bay window. A carpet, ravelling at the edges, covered the floor.

Fronting the window was Grandma's Pennsylvania Dutch bed
which had been given a coat of horrible, cheap, blue paint. The
scene of dry dampness, of medicine and flowers, hung in the room
like a sickening perfume.

From the corner of my eye, I saw Grandma sit down on the
edge of the bed and sigh. She resembled a wretched little doll. Her
thin, bloodless hands fumbled on the nightstand.

"I haven't been well," she said, "and the doctor has given me
all sorts of pills."

"You still look great to me," I said nervously, and removed my
jacket and unlaced my shoes.

Grandma's eyes never left my face. "You think so?"

"Same old gal," I joked.

Her laugh was unrestrained. But she choked slightly and
caught her breath. Only four years before, after the Korean discharge, she had played touch football with my younger cousin and
me. "The old mare ain't what she used to be," she said, smiling.

I carefully averted my eyes and sat down on the horsehair sofa.
I wanted to sleep, close my eyes, but awaken to what?

"You look tired, Sonny. How'd you come, by bus?"

"You know I'm a bug for buses," I lied. "Buses and fire
engines."

"My little Sonny," Grandma marveled. "I forgot to ask, are
you hungry? You'll find something in the kitchen."

"Think I'll make a cup of tea," I said, rising.

"I'm going to take a nap." Grandma said. "Got to watch
myself."

"You're still sweet sixteen and have a dozen beaux."

"Come and give Granny a kiss."

I went over and kissed her lightly on the cheek. Her trembling
hands sought out my face and the fingers moved slowly across my
face, and then her shrewd eyes met mine again.

"I've waited, prayed for this day . . . Still the same old Sonny?"

"Still the same," I mustered up, feebly.

"And I thank God, dear sweet blessed Jesus."

The first rays of the sun swept the room with a cruel light. I
closed the door noiselessly, leaving behind Grandma, already
stretched out on her bed, praying for me.

* * *

The languor of autumn diminished as the nights grew cold. The small-town life slowed down. There was little rain and the old people said that that was a sure sign of a cold, long winter. I loved those new days. I slept well and was up at dawn, chopping wood for the old woodburning stove that Grandma had refused to give up. I made breakfast for Grandma and then would get the morning paper, do some chores around the house, and some also for the neighbors, which made them buzz around me as if I were a saint.

I read a lot that winter, going to the library three times a week. I tried to avoid the kids I had grown up with. They all worked eight-to-five shifts and were carving out their future in this small-town Negro world. And in this quiet world for the first time in years, I relaxed; I drank very little and did not feel the need for sex. Gone was the fevered air of New York, gone the hipped-up, Freudian complications. These small-town folk had problems like people anywhere, but they faced them by looking them square in the eye, accepting them as they accepted changes in the weather.

I remember the first of December, 1958, in that Missouri town on the banks of the river. Snow fell softly through the bare trees and onto the old buildings and houses. Peace. There was almost no sound in the street night or day except for the laughing voices of children returning from school at three in the afternoon or the grinding whirr of a stalled car. Grandma had taken to bed and old Doctor Bess would creep in with his black bag and joke with Grandma and give out white, pink, orange, and yellow pills. Then he would talk with me. He had gone to Columbia in 1905 and we discussed the changes in New York City. Ruby came almost daily; she had married again but was still her same, solid, cold self. I never saw my father, although he lived only three blocks away.

The snow lasted well into the middle of December. Grandma was permanently bedridden, and had developed bedsores. Like most old people, she moved into what is called a second childhood, had lapses of memory. My own mind was on the edge of a cliff during those days; fear had settled inside me. Grandma and I were sometimes cross with each other, but then our eyes would meet.

I remember that clear winter Saturday, blue sky, white sun. The snow was melting and water dripped from the eaves of the house. I saw icicles drop noiselessly from the naked trees and a few birds chirped on the bare branches. I remember the little boy who lived down the street dragging his sled on the sidewalk, the screeching sound of steel on concrete in the wintry, mellow sun and the afternoon shadows like fine lacework.

I was sitting in the rocking chair with a black coffee and a cigarette, rocking peacefully. Grandma sat up in the bed and said in a slow gravelly voice: "Sonny, ain't that Mrs. Carter out there at her fence? What is she doing out there with a baby in this weather? Why, he has on only a diaper."

There was nothing out there but a wood rail fence with water dripping from a green hedge. The afternoon wore on and I became frightened and called Ruby. Soon the house was filled with neighbor women, church and sewing-circle friends of Grandma's. They all stood around quietly with their hands under their bib aprons. Doctor Bess arrived. Grandma began reminiscing about people that only the silent old women remembered. Doctor Bess got out a hypo and pricked her body here and there. Water sprang from her like from a fountain. Dropsy. Ruby and I changed the bed again and again. Grandma just lay there, moving her lips with closed eyes. Toward midnight, as I put a wet cloth to her lips, a cry rose from my stomach and I prayed: "Oh, dear Jesus, if she dies, please let there be nobody in the house but me."

But she did not die. I forced Ruby home toward morning. The little boy who lived down the street brought the Sunday paper. I sat in the rocking chair, reading the paper, and I remember hearing the church bell toll for morning worship and thinking: "Grandma is very quiet. She's been sleeping a long time. I had better put a wet cloth to her mouth like Doctor Bess said."

I went over and applied the wet cloth and she did not move. I went into the kitchen and made a cup of tea, returned to the living room, and sat down in the rocker. I smoked a half-dozen cigarettes and then went over to the bed. I felt Grandma's pulse and forehead. Then I lifted up her right arm which fell back down on the bed with a life of its own, and then I fell on my knees beside the bed and cried.

Memory withdraws. There is now only this cluttered, yellowing room on West Forty-ninth Street, in the heart of Manhattan. Here, there, again, and always, the Why of my life, the meanings. Terrible depression as I sit here watching darkness settle in the corners of this room. Aware of the muted, miscellaneous noises that drift up from the street, I am also aware of the loss of something. It is strange that I had never felt the suffocation of this small room before; as if shadows, objects, furniture were rising toward the ceiling and would explode into what had once been my life. Thinking of all I've ever done and not done. Thinking and feeling this terrible loss.

Where did it all begin? A small town on the banks of the Missouri River. Trees and the red-brick school. Grandpa and Grandma, dead. Grandma. Ruby and all the little girls with ribbons in their hair, and all the people I later met taking the long road through hell.

ALL MY DELIVERIES are over and it is late afternoon. The scene on my block is completely gypsy. A group of them have set up shop at the end of the street. They are what I call upper-middle-class gypsies. The women of this group do not practice the fortune-telling game, and their children are always clean as if each day were Sunday. The men all wear very good casual clothes. One of the women has a mink stole that must have cost at least $750. They do not speak to the gypsies who live in the building next to mine.

One day, a few weeks ago, I heard loud curses and looked out the window. The whole gypsy clan who live next door was rushing down the steps of their building, with a middle-aged man with thin brown hair, brown suit, brown shoes, in their midst.

One of the younger gypsies let him have a good one on the chin, yelling, "He beat up my sister! That's what the son-of-a-bitch did!"

A crowd quickly gathered. Several of the sages from Tip Top Parking came over and tried to calm the young gypsy man. Mama, the gypsy queen, was talking her unknown tongue a mile a minute, flashing her foxy eyes, one hand glued to her hip-swinging money pocket.

The argument between the gypsies and the middle-aged character in brown finally broke up, and he headed rapidly toward Sixth Avenue, wiping his forehead with his hand. The two younger gypsy men went and sat in their car, which was parked across the street. The rest of the clan trooped back into the house, except for Mama, who remained on the stoop, hands on her hips, a cigarette in the corner of her mouth. She had her sharp eyes fixed in the direction of Sixth Avenue.

The crowd of onlookers did not disperse. They were waiting for the second act of the drama. Grinning, discussing the incident, they continued to wait, sure that something more was going to happen. The gypsy queen thinks something might happen too, which is the reason she sent the young men to the car. If the cops or detectives arrive, they can drive off without being noticed. If the middle-aged man had called the police, Mama would have to deal with them.

The owner of the *Steak de Paris* was worried too. He paced up and down in front of his restaurant, arms folded. The gypsies are fine local color for his customers, but fights and cops are another story.

An hour went by, and finally Mama, giving her long braids a toss, sauntered back into her house like a defiant queen. And after the gypsy Mama had returned to her headquarters, a squad car drove by very slowly and I saw a cop point at the gypsies' house. But the squad car did not stop.

Now the question is, what caused a medium-sized, middle-aged man with thin brown hair to beat up a young woman who was telling his fortune? Whatever the reason, it must be a good one because now the gypsies have opened a smaller place almost directly across the street. The gypsy girls sit out in front on chrome-plated kitchen chairs and wooden soda crates and hustle fortunes. All the people passing our block believe that we have an open-air whore house.

It is now evening. I decide to take a shower. Returning from the hall bathroom, I hear many footsteps on the stairs, coming toward the top floor. It is the police.

A sergeant comes up. I am carefully holding a towel around me, the soap and washcloth clutched in my right hand.

"This is all residential here, isn't it?" the sergeant asks.

"Yes," I say.

The police sergeant's sharp eyes take in the corridor and he spots my garbage outside the door. "Do you have a phone?"

"Not anymore," I say, showing him my teeth.

"Okay. Thanks," the police sergeant said, and lumbered back down the stairs yelling, "Okay. This is all residential. Yeah. Residential."

I go into my apartment and have a beer. As I go into my living room, I discover a living gallery of portraits in the windows of the Elmwood Hotel. I look down at the street, and there is a crowd of about seventy-five people peering up at my building as if expecting a recluse king and queen suddenly to appear. Four squad cars are blocking crosstown traffic. But what is happening? Nothing! I shake my head and laugh, close my shutters and lie down.

But, more footsteps on the stairs. A defiant knock on the door. The police again.

"Are you sure this building is all residential?" the police sergeant asks. "What kind of business is going on here?"

"What kind of business do you mean?"

"Well . . . we got this alarm down at headquarters," the police sergeant says (he is not unlike those popular heroes on television). "Mind if I come in and look at your place?"

"Welcome," I answer gleefully.

The police sergeant takes one short glance at the cluttered living room and starts to leave.

"There is no legit or shady business going on in this building," I say. "It was a false alarm. And don't come knocking on my door again or I'll have you arrested for disturbing my peace."

The sergeant looks dumbfounded. "What?"

"That's what I said. Usually you know exactly where you are going. But last year you came into this building and broke the door down in number three looking for bookies. And you knew damn well what street the bookies were on. I suppose you'll go back to headquarters now and say nothing is happening in my building."

"I'm sorry to have disturbed you," the police sergeant says, and exits.

Feeling very, very self-righteous, I returned to bed and dreamed that I opened the door and asked a policeman what he wanted. He did not answer but came charging into my apartment followed by six other policemen. I protested angrily. Finally I gave in and started yelling, "Welcome! Come on in!" At last there were about forty policemen in my living room. They formed lines on each side of the room and I walked between the lines of policemen, naked, with my hands clasped behind my back, lecturing on the crime of disturbing innocent citizens' peace.

I knew the police in Sedalia, Missouri—remember?—and I don't like them.

MAXINE'S Virginia-Canada tour is off temporarily due to her grandmother's illness. This afternoon after I made a few deliveries, Maxine and I took a ride on the Staten Island ferry because, as Maxine said, without batting an eye, "Charles, you have been neglecting me."

It was a pleasant afternoon, cloudless, with the temperature an even seventy-five degrees. Maxine and I fought all the way down on the Seventh Avenue local to South Ferry. She loves me. It is not because I play with her and offer gifts. No. With Maxine one would get nowhere that way. Rather, it is because she knows I am for real. I don't play with her as an adult with a child, but as her equal. Somewhere between the shelter of childhood and the wide open adult world, we laugh together as friends. Shirley always used to be a little jealous of our relationship.

Maxine and I have taken this nickel voyage many times and so we sat on the starboard side of the ferry, passing the Statue of Liberty and saying as always that we must go there sometime. Then we begin telling jokes and making up riddles which never turn out right. Then, as the air grew cool, Maxine asked for her sweater and nestled in my arms. She began singing in a haunting, quivery, little girl's voice. "Doe-re deer, a female deer." When I did not join in, there were sharp jabs in my ribs. Soon Maxine fell asleep, and I held her quietly until the lovely evening façade of Manhattan came into view.

LAURA VEE ARRIVED in the heat of a gray afternoon. The sullen sky gives no promise of rain. The murmurous street voices drift up as if begging for something which escapes them in this elusive city. I am putting down my sixth beer and watching Laura's friend, Jim. He has problems, Laura has said.

Jim has the lanky, awkward grace of a basketball player, a hyperborean face, and unbelievably burnished red-gold hair. He is morosely opening his sixth beer.

Laura is in a gay mood. She has discovered that she is not the only human being with the ability to weep. "Give the lady a beer," she laughed, wiping her ringed hand across her smooth forehead. "I say, how about a cold one?"

"Wouldn't you like something stronger?" Jim asked.

Laura reflects on this. "All right. All right, Jim boy," she said slowly.

Jim went over to the sofa and took a fifth of whiskey from his beach bag. He placed it on the table with the air of a man planning an experiment. I was glad he was not a loud drunk, despite his problems.

"The glasses, Charles," Laura said, giving me a hard stare.

"You know where they are, love juice."

"All right, you kook. But get the ice. You haven't defrosted that thing in a year."

Laura followed me into the kitchen. "What's happening?" I asked.

"Nothing, dear," Laura whispered. "Jim's a little mixed up. I thought perhaps you'd talk to him. That's all."

"Are you two making it?"

"Not so loud," Laura warned.

We went back to the living room. Jim was opening another can of beer and looked up, frowning, as if we had invaded his privacy. It made me uncomfortable, but Laura smiled gaily. "Oh, we're going to have a wonderful party, aren't we, Charles?"

"Yeah," I mumbled, because in my world the word 'party' takes on many meanings.

"I'll have mine straight," Jim said. "With the beer. That's the way my fucking old man drinks. Bald-headed old lush."

Baby, I told myself, this isn't going to be a very cool afternoon. I'm sick of these emotional jerks. If Junior gets out of hand, we'll rumble.

"Charles, see if you can get a little decent jazz on the radio," Laura said.

"I like jazz," Jim said quickly. "Jazz is my speed."

I turned on the old, dependable, Zenith AM-FM just in time to catch Lady Day with "Fine and Mellow."

"This is a groove," I said happily. "Quick girl! Give me a shot of that man-killer." I've discovered that drinking and jazz go hand in hand. A wonderful tranquilizer. Problems do not get less, but I can see them more clearly, or think I can. I was thinking about this when Jim said, "Laura, why don't you and Charles dance?"

"I'm not much of a dancer," I threw in quickly.

"I'd much rather dance with you, Jim," Laura said smiling. "Charles is a wonderful audience."

"I like a slow dance," I said.

"That's a slow number," Jim said.

"I'll sit this one out."

"Shall we dance, Jim?" Laura said sweetly, offering her quick, vibrating hand.

Jim got up and took her hand carefully, diffidently, like a young man aware of the eyes of a chaperone. His dancing was nothing to write home about, but it was intense. I watched them dance without really moving across the floor.

The afternoon waned: three o'clock, a darkened sky, a faint warm breeze. The radio music is smooth now, sentimental, semi-classic in the popular vein. Music for those poignant American Saturday nights, for those quiet American Sunday afternoons, music something like a golden bell, promising that tomorrow will be better. Jazz, good jazz, tells no such lies.

These thoughts cross my mind as I put the whiskey down. Laura and Jim have gone into the bedroom. The whiskey will be of no use to them, so I pour myself another. If I have to be bothered with the tangled lives of others . . . well, let the bastards pay me for it.

"Charles," Laura calls. Her voice sounds tired. "Charles, come here." For some reason I freeze and call out nervously, "What do you want? Cigarettes?"

They are lying on the sturdy narrow bed, naked. Jim is nestled in the curve of Laura's arm, staring up at the ceiling: His eyes are glazed, reflecting, perhaps, his world of dreams. It is not a happy world, judging from his taut face. Laura looks up, sighing, a pleading expression on her face. "Light me a cigarette, will you, Charles?" she said in a polite voice.

I lit the cigarette and gave it to her and stood against the wall with my arms folded, waiting to see what would develop. But, to tell the truth, I'm bored with sex scenes.

"I should be punished," Jim said quietly.

"Why?" I asked.

Jim's voice bordered on a cry. "I can't make it with Laura, I can't make it with anyone, because I think it's dirty! I have all these feelings of guilt. I can't sleep at night."

"In that case, you shouldn't do these things," I said. "Then you could sleep."

Jim got up slowly and began to put on his clothes. "*You* make it with her," he said and went into the living room and closed the door.

I lay down fully clothed beside Laura and took the cigarette from her trembling hand and put it in the ashtray on the bedside table. Then I put my arms around her. She began to cry. There seemed nothing to say or do, so I just held her and let her cry. I could hear Jim typing in the living room.

Finally Laura went to sleep and I went into the living room.

Jim had gone. There was a sheet of paper in the typewriter and I
went over and read it.

"This is for Charles," it started out, and went on in a drunken,
mucked-up way, obscene and pitiful, for a dozen ill-typed lines or
so, and ended with a string of X's savagely punched almost
through the paper.

I don't know why, but that series of X's made me want to cry.
Something rose and fell in me like a dead weight. What did I know
or care about Jim, a lanky, twenty-two-year-old IBM tab operator
who liked good books, wanted to save the world, was fond of
jazz, no longer believed in God, but couldn't make the scene. He's
not your problem, I told myself. Nor is Laura, or Mitch, or Jelly,
or Lena. None of them. Not a fucking one of them. You are your
own problem, I said.

And if that wasn't enough, just then the super came barging in
and said that I would definitely have to move. The Housing people
meant business. There wouldn't be a stay of execution this time. I
would have to give up my plantation, this priceless midtown pad.

IT IS MORNING. I'm on the second cigarette and the first cup of coffee. It is a time of stocktaking, and what is there to see? A fairly young man with a tired boyish face, saddled with the knowledge of years and nothing gained, lacking a bird dog's sense of direction most of the time, without point or goal. "I am the future," I once wrote in a passionate schoolboy essay. Now, at twenty-nine, I am not expecting much from this world. Fitzgerald and his green light! I remember his rich, mad dream: "Tomorrow we will run faster, stretch out our arms farther." But where will this black boy run? To whom shall he stretch out his arms?

At the moment, I need not think of tomorrow. I've come to a decision. I am getting my possessions in order. Tonight there will be an auction in my pad. Everything will be sold, got rid of. And then I'll go away.

THEY'VE COME ABOARD the lifeboat, dragged themselves up to me, up the five flights of stairs, to say good-bye. The room is crowded and gray with smoke, and I begin to wonder if the liquor will hold out. The noise is terrific, and no one, including me, cares. I have a bus ticket in my pocket which will take me all the way to Mexico, and this morning I went to three pawnshops until I found a good leather bag cheap.

Claudia, the Grand Duchess, stoned to the gills, wearing skin-tight, pale blue slacks, belly dances to the strains of Ella Fitzgerald's "Smooth Sailing."

"Big Daddy," the Grand Duchess yells, "look what you get if you are lucky!"

Big Daddy smiles at him but makes no move. He is having a serious talk with Mrs. Lee, who has arrived poodle-less. Is she thinking of changing horses, I wondered. But Big Daddy is not Mrs. Lee's type. On the other hand, he is having hell supporting his habit. I know because yesterday he asked me if I wanted to buy some "hot" jazz albums.

"Charles, pet," Mrs. Lee crooned imploringly, and held up her empty champagne glass.

I gave her a warm smile and refilled it. She looked, I thought, rather like a withered toad in her white piqué and Byzantine costume jewelry.

"Darling, it's a shame you have to give up this wonderful studio. There's a most charming little *atelier* near Beekman Place. . . ."

I walked away without a word. Where the hell did she think I'd get the money? Unless . . . Oh no, not that. I touch the bus ticket in my pocket. No Mrs. Lee for me.

Troy and Susan were leaving for an intellectual gathering in the Village. They can't quite forgive me because their child once called me "Nigger," and to conceal the fact have been especially warm and friendly ever since.

Susan flings her arms around me. "Everything will turn out fine, Charles. I know it will. You are *not* to worry!"

Troy squeezes my arm hard. "You could always move in with us. You know we'd like to have you."

I nod and try not to look sad, and see them to the door. They mean well, but they fawn on me too much. There's such a thing as being too Goddamn sincere. I have a double scotch to counteract the champagne and to wash away the dust of Troy and Susan's leaving.

I wondered where Shirley was; she said she'd be over, and then I thought about the other times she'd come here and of how we had quarreled, and of the day—when? a few weeks ago?—we'd gone to Coney Island. And I remembered the time Lena had said, "Why don't you kids get married?" And why not? I asked myself, but I knew we never would.

I was brought out of my reverie by Lady P, trotting by me into the bedroom. At the same moment, Claudia screamed at Laura: "Miss One! That mirror belongs to *me*! And so do the couch and chair. Charlie gave them to me."

Laura stared at Claudia coldly for a moment and then marched over to me. "I thought you said you had *sold* the couch and chair," she said. "Charles, you are a lying son-of-a-bitch. You gave them to that faggot. And you know I wanted the mirror."

"You should have asked sooner," I said weakly.

"How was I to know you'd lie to me?" Laura shot back. "It's such a lovely little mirror and I wanted it. I remember when you bought it at the Salvation Army store."

"Oh shit, Miss One," Claudia said, suddenly bored as only Claudia can be, "you can have it."

Just then Big Daddy came in from the bathroom singing, "I

dreamed I had a reefer nine feet long," and he made for Mrs. Lee, still singing, "I could smoke it from the bedroom clear out into the hall."

"Marvelous, oh you are marvelous!" Mrs. Lee crooned.

Sometime later, I saw Mrs. Lee leave with Big Daddy, and at the same time Bruce came in with the super. They were both drunk. Ivy League and Caliban.

"Charlie," Bruce said, "look what I dug up. A good old son-of-a-bitch." Evidently Bruce was off his Episcopalian kick, at least for the evening.

The super put his arms around me and sprayed saliva on my neck. "You don't ever have to pay any rent here, Charlie. Fuck the Housing. Stay as long as you want. We're one big happy family. Gimme a drink."

"Sure," I grinned, trying to break away.

"Charlie," the super said, but his words were cut off in a rising tide and suddenly he vomited all over the floor.

Claudia, who had made no time with Big Daddy and had just finished tricking with Mitch in the bedroom, came out just in time to scream, "Oh Jesus!"

"I'm sorry," the super said, tears rolling from his red eyes. "Really I am."

"I'll clean it up," Bruce said, feeling guilty. "Don't worry about it."

"Forget it," I said. I went over to the window, got a breath of air, and looked at the sky. The pale, morning light was coming fast. Where was Shirley? The aroma of coffee drifted from Chris's delicatessen down the street. There was a touch of autumn in the air; summer was almost over and this country boy was ready to run. I turned from the window and glanced at my friends, looked out the window again. All day I had been drinking: wine, beer, gin, scotch, champagne. I ticked them off in my mind, maybe to prove to myself I was still sober. I had taken six bennies to ward off a high and smoked a little pot. It had done absolutely nothing for my head. I just was not with it. There was horror in the knowledge that nothing was going to happen to me, that I was stoned on that frightening, cold level where everything is crystal clear. It was like looking at yourself too closely in a magnifying mirror.

I heard the buzzer and bolted from the room and ran down the five flights of stairs. It was Shirley.

She kissed me warmly, but she seemed nervous.

"Guess what's in this box?" she said. "Your books. All the books you've lent me. I knew you'd want them. I took a taxi up here."

"What happened to you?" I said. "You were supposed to be here hours ago. Now almost everyone has gone."

"I know."

"Well?"

"Please, Charles," Shirley said softly, taking my hand.

"Fuck it," I said, jerking my hand away.

"I'm not going to marry that doctor," Shirley announced quietly. "I've changed my mind."

I didn't say anything. Suddenly I didn't care. All I wanted to do was sleep, but I knew I wouldn't sleep just yet. Tomorrow I'll sleep on the bus, but now Shirley and I will climb the stairs together, back to my drunken friends upstairs. The party had turned into a free-for-all; I could hear their voices wild above the music, searching for that crazy kick that would still the fears, confusion, and the pain of being alive on this early August morning.

"What's wrong?" Shirley asked. "Charles, what's wrong?"

"Nothing," I said. "Absolutely nothing."

We started up the stairs and then I heard Claudia's voice, as clear as day, scream, "C———!"

T H E   W I G

A MIRROR IMAGE

••••••••••••••••••••••••••••••

*For Charles Trabue Robb and
in memory of Lowney Turner Handy*

I

....

*"Every phenomenon has its
natural causes . . ."*

—JAMES JOYCE

O N E

I WAS A DESPERATE MAN. Quarterly, I got that crawly feeling in my wafer-thin stomach. During these fasting days, I had the temper of a Greek mountain dog. It was hard to maintain a smile; everyone seemed to jet toward the goal of The Great Society, while I remained in the outhouse, penniless, without "connections." Pretty girls, credit cards, charge accounts, Hart Schaffner & Marx suits, fine shoes, Dobbs hats, XK-E Jaguars, and more pretty girls cluttered my butterscotch-colored dreams. Lord—I'd work like a slave, but how to acquire an acquisitional gimmick? Mercy—something had to fall from the tree of fortune! Tom-toms were signaling to my frustrated brain; the message: I had to make it.

As a consequence, I was seized with a near epileptic fit early one Thursday morning. I stood in the center of my shabby though genteel furnished room, shivering and applauding vigorously. Sweet Jesus!—my King James-shaped head vaulted toward the fungus-covered ceiling pipes where cockroach acrobatics had already begun. The cockroaches seemed extraordinarily lively, as if they too were taking part in the earthshaking revelation. Even the late March sun was soft and sweet as moonlight, and the beautiful streets of Harlem were strangely quiet.

Smiling ecstatically, tears gushing from my Dutch-almond

eyes, I recalled what the man in the drugstore had said: "With this, you may become whatever you desire."

Indeed, I *did* have a Mongolian chance, perhaps even a brilliant future; the black clouds would soon recede. I had tried so hard. Masqueraded as a silent Arab waiter in an authentic North African coffeehouse in Greenwich Village. I'd been quite successful too. Tempting dreamers of Gide, Ivy League derelicts, and hungry pseudo-virgins. Barefoot, marijuana-eyed, fezzed, wearing nothing under my candy-striped djellaba, I was finally unmasked by two old-maid sisters, one club-footed, both with mushroom-colored mustaches, who had lived for a decade in Morocco. The sisters swooned at the deception, left a two-dollar tip and their hashish-scented calling card. Those sisters turned me on, and that night I had a mild attack of Napoleon fever and began insulting the customers. The Zen Buddhist owner was going to New Zealand anyway.

What happened after that? More of the crawly worms in the stomach. Misery. I tap-danced in front of the Empire State Building for a week and collected only one dollar and twenty-seven cents. I was refused unemployment insurance, maybe because I looked foreign and spoke almost perfect English. Naturally, I could have got on welfare, but who has the guts to stand on the stoop, hands in pockets, chewing on a toothpick ten hours a day, watching little kids pass by, their big eyes staring up at you like the eyes of extras in some war movie? There are some things a man can't do.

No, a man tries another gimmick. But what? For me a Spanish façade would be simple, but very uncool. Filipino? American Indian? I wondered. Eurasian might provide a fetish glamour. Was I capable of bringing off a Jewish exterior? I wondered. Becoming a nice little white Protestant was clearly impossible. Born with a vermeil question mark in my mouth, twenty-one years ago, I have been called the son of the Devil; my social-security card is silent on the point of whether or not I'm human. I suppose that's why I'm slightly schizophrenic.

Hump psyche reports! *I* was going to attack *my* future.

I rushed to the bathroom, the meeting place of exactly seventy-five Negroes of various racial origins. Standing rigidly, religiously, in the white-tiled room, my heart exploded in my eyes like the sea. My brain whirled.

Do not the auburn-haired gain a new sense of freedom as a blonde (see *Miss Clairol*)? Who can deny the madness of a redesigned nose (see *Miami Beach*)? The first conference of Juvenile Delinquents met in Riis Park and there was absolutely no violence: a resolution was passed to send Seconal, zip guns, airplane glue, and contraceptives to the Red Chinese (see *The Daily News*). The American Medical Association announced indignantly that U. S. abortion and syphilis quotas are far below the world average (see *Channel 2*). Modern gas stations have coin-operated air pumps in the ladies' room so the under-blessed may inflate their skimpy boobs (see *Dorothy Kilgallen*). Undercover homosexuals sneak into the local drugstores and receive plastic though workable instruments plus bonus Daisy trade stamps (see *Compliments of a newfound friend*). Schizo wisdom? Remember, I said to myself, you are living in the greatest age mankind has known. Whereupon, I went to the washbasin, picked up the Giant Economy jar of long-lasting Silky Smooth Hair Relaxer, with the Built-in Sweat-proof Base (*trademark registered*). Carefully, I read the directions. The red, white, and gold label guarantees that the user can go deep-sea diving, emerge from the water, and shake his head triumphantly like any white boy. This miracle with the scent of wild roses looks like vanilla ice cream and is capable of softening in sufficiently Negroid hands.

I took a handful of Silky Smooth and began massaging my scalp. Then, just to be on the safe side, I added Precautionary Oil, thick, odorless, indigenous to the Georgia swamps. Massaging deftly, I remembered that old-fashioned hair aids were mixed with yak dung and lye. They burned the scalp and if the stuff got in your eye you could go blind from it. One thing was certain: you combed out scabs of dried blood for a month. But a compassionate northern senator had the hair aids outlawed. Said he, in ringing historic words: "Mr. Chairman, I offer an amendment to this great Spade tragedy! These people are real Americans and we should outlaw all hair aids that makes them lose their vibrations and éclat." Silky Smooth (using a formula perfected by a Lapp tribe in Karasjok, Norway) posed no problems.

Yes indeed. A wild excitement engulfed me. My mirrored image reflected, in an occult fashion, a magnificent future. I hadn't felt so good since discovering last year that I actually disliked watermelon.

But the next step was the most difficult act of my life. I had to wait five minutes until the pomade penetrated, stiffened, evaporated. Five minutes of suffering. I stood tall like the great-great-grandson of slaves, sharecroppers, Old World royalty. Tall, like a storm trooper, like an Honor Scout. Yes! I'd stalk that druggist if the experiment failed. Lord—it couldn't fail! I'm Walter Mitty's target-colored stepson. Sweet dreams zipped through my mind. A politician had prophesied that it was extremely likely a Negro would be elected President of the United States in the year 2,000. Being realistic, I could just picture myself as Chairman of the Handyman's Union, addressing the Committee on Foreign Relations and then being castrated. At least I'd no longer have to phone Mr. Fishback, the necrophilic funeral director, each time I went downtown. What a relief that would be. The dimes I'd save!

While the stuff dried I thought of Mr. Fishback. Sweet Daddy Fish, Nonnie called him, but Nonnie liked to put the bad mouth on people. I owed Mr. Fishback for my latest (was it counterfeit?) Credit Card.

Beams of the morning sun danced through the ice-cube-size window as I began to wash the pomade out of my hair. I groaned powerfully. The texture of my hair *had* changed. Before reaching for a towel, I couldn't resist looking in the cracked mirror while milky-colored water ran down my flushed face.

Hail Caesar and all dead Cotton Queens! Who the hell ever said only a rake could get through those gossamer locks?

Indeed! I prayed. I laughed. I shook my head and watched each silky curl fall into place. I had only one regret: I wished there were a little wind blowing, one just strong enough to give me a windswept look; then I'd be able to toss a nonchalant lock from my forehead. I'd been practicing a week and had the bit down solid.

You could borrow an electric fan, I was telling myself, and just then I heard Nonnie Swift scream.

"Help! Won't somebody please help me?" The voice came from the hall.

Let the brandy bitch scream her head off, I thought. A Creole from New Orleans, indeed. If there's anyone in this building with Creole blood, it's me.

"I'm dying. Please help a dying widow . . ." the voice wailed from the hall.

I unwillingly turned from the mirror. The Wig was perfection. Four dollars and six cents' worth of sheer art. The sacrifice had been worth it. I was reborn, purified, anointed, beautified.

"I'm just a poor helpless widow . . ."

Would the bitch never shut up? With the majesty of a witch doctor, I went to Nonnie Swift's rescue.

She was sprawled on the rat-gnawed floorboards of the hall, clutching a spray of plastic violets, rhinestone Mother Hubbard robe spread out like a blanket under her aging, part-time-whore's body, which twitched rhythmically. Nonnie's blue-rinse bouffant was a wreck. It formed a sort of African halo. Tears sprang from her sea-green contact lenses. She jerked Victorian-braceleted arms toward the ceiling and whimpered pitifully.

"What's wrong?" I asked.

Nonnie folded her arms across her pancake stomach and moaned.

I knelt down beside her, peered at her contorted rouged face, and got a powerful whiff of brandy.

Like a blind thief's, Nonnie's trembling hands pawed at my chin, nose, forehead, and The Wig.

I wanted to break her goddamned hand. "Don't mess with the moss," I said. "What's wrong with you?"

"I'm in great pain, Les."

I tried to lift her into a sitting position. The lower part of her body seemed anchored to the floorboards.

"Feel it," Nonnie said, belching.

"Feel what?"

"Feel it," Nonnie repeated tersely.

"Don't you ever give up? You're old enough to be my mother."

She screamed again. Cracked lips showed through her American Lady lipstick, which is a deep, deep purple shade.

"Thank you, son," Nonnie sighed.

"Are you stoned?" I asked. I had a feeling she wasn't talking to me.

"Stoned?" Nonnie sneered. "I'm in *pain!*"

"Just try to sit up," I pleaded. "Then put your arm on the banister."

"What us poor women go through."

"Do you want me to call the doctor?"

"Yes! Call the doctor! Call the fire department! Call the militia!" Nonnie shouted. "It's coming. Two years overdue."

Disgusted, I stood up. "You're really loaded."

"I ain't no such thing. I've been trying to have this baby for a long time. I even said I'd have it on television. But they wouldn't let me. Of course *you* know why, don't you? I come from one of the oldest families in New Orleans, too. I'm only living among *you* people because of *him*. I want my son to see all the good and bad things in this world. Understand?"

I understood only too well. "Do you want me to help you to your pad?" I said. "I ain't got all day."

"You'd leave a pregnant woman flat on her back?"

Just then Mrs. Tucker opened her rusty tin-covered door. Resplendent in a pleated burlap sack dress, domed head, always sucking rotten gums, she stood and glared.

I glared right back. "Hey," I said (that's Carolina talk for "hello"). "Hey, you dried-up old midwife."

"Harlem riffraff," Mrs. Tucker spat. "A young punk and a common slut. You'd be lynched down home."

Nonnie raised up and said sweetly: "Mrs. Tucker, my baby is coming at last. Aren't you delighted?"

"A sin," Mrs. Tucker shuddered. She pulled her seventy-nine pounds up and slammed the tin-covered door.

"She just ain't friendly," Nonnie commented sadly.

"Don't let it get you down, cupcake."

"At least she could have offered to nurse my baby."

"Is the father a white man?"

"I hardly think so," Nonnie said slowly. "But you never can tell, can you?"

Suddenly, Nonnie was choked with sobs. Strong tears washed away the sea-green contact lenses, leaving only the true color of her sky-blue eyes. "No more pain, Les. I've paid the cost. But just think what he'll have to go through in Harlem. Leaving the warm prison of my womb. Born into unchained slavery."

I looked down at Nonnie. Perhaps she *was* Creole. "Things are getting better every day," I said.

"Oh. I hope so," Nonnie cried. "Things have got to change, or else I'll go back to my old mansion in the Garden District, where the weeds have grown and the Spanish moss just hangs and hangs, and the wind whistles through it like a mockingbird."

Does that chick read? I asked myself, can she? and decided probably not, she probably saw it and heard it all in the movies.

I had an urge to tell Nonnie she ought to be on the stage or in a zoo. I'd listened to all this fancy jazz for three years. I realize people have to have a little make-believe. It's like Mr. Fishback says: "Son, try it on for size because after you see me there'll be no more changes." Sooner or later, though, you have to step into the spotlight of reality. You've got to do your bit for yourself and society. I was trying for something real, concrete, with my Wig.

So I said to Nonnie, "I'm gonna make the big leap. I'm cutting out."

"You? Where the hell are you going?"

"Just you wait and see," I teased. "I'm gonna shake up this town."

"And just you wait and see," Nonnie mocked. "You curly-headed son of a bitch. You've conked your hair."

"Not conked," I corrected sharply. I wanted to give her a solid blow in the jaw and make her swallow those false teeth. "Just a little water and grease, Miss Swift."

"Conked."

"Do you want me to bash your face in?"

"I'm sorry, sweetcakes," Nonnie said.

"That's more like it. You're always putting the bad mouth on people. No wonder *you* people never get nowhere. You don't help each other. You people should stick together like the gypsies."

"It's a pity, ain't it?"

Although I was fuming mad, I managed to lower my voice and make a plea for sympathy. "I can't help it if I have good hair. You can't blame a man for trying to better his condition, can you? I'm not putting on or acting snotty."

"I didn't wanna hurt your feelings," Nonnie said tearfully. "Honest, Les. You look sort of cute."

"Screw, baby."

"I really mean it. I hope my son has good hair. God knows he'll need something to make it in this world."

"That's a fact," I agreed solemnly. "The Wig is gonna see me through these troubled times."

Nonnie questioned the plastic violets for confirmation. "It gives me a warm feeling to know that I can buy bread in my old age," she remarked with great dignity. "My baby boy will be a great something. I'm sure high-school diplomas and college degrees are on the way out, now you can get them through the mail for a dollar ninety-eight, plus postage. Look at the mess all those degrees have got us in. By the time he's a grown man success might depend on something else. Might well be a good head of hair."

"That's true," I agreed. Then, blushing, I couldn't help but add: "You know, Nonnie, I feel like a new person. I know my luck is changing. My ship is just around the bend."

"I suppose so," Nonnie said bitchily. "I suppose that's the way you feel when your hair is conked."

I turned and began walking away. Otherwise, I would have strangled Nonnie Swift.

Now, she began to cry, to plead. "Les—Lester Jefferson. Don't leave me flat on my back. Please. I'm all alone. Mrs. Tucker won't help me. You'll have to sub for the doctor."

"Screw."

I had no time for the drunken hag. How could a New Orleans tramp appreciate The Wig? That's the way people are. Always trying to block the road to progress. But let me tell you something: no one, absolutely no one—nothing—is gonna stop this boy. I've taken the first step. All the other steps will fall easily into place.

Who was I talking to? Myself. Feeling at peace with myself and proud of my clear reasoning, I decided to make it up to Miss Sandra Hanover's on the third floor, to what Miss Sandra called her pied-à-terre.

Miss Sandra Hanover was intelligent, understanding. A lady with class.

T W O

THE DOOR, HUNG with an antique glass-beaded French funeral wreath, was open. Hopefully, I entered and looked over at Miss Sandra Hanover and was chilled to the bone.

Miss Sandra Hanover, ex-Miss Rosie Lamont, ex-Mrs. Roger Wilson, nee Alvin Brown, needed a shave. The thick dark stubble was visible under two layers of female hormone powder. But she had plucked her eyebrows; they *v*'d up toward Chinese-style bangs like two frozen little black snakes. A Crown Princess, working toward a diva's cold perfection, she did not acknowledge my entrance. She looked silly as hell, sitting on a warped English down sofa, wearing a man's white shirt, green polka-dot tie, and blue serge trousers. Her eyes were closed and her Texas-cowboy sadist's boots morse-coded a lament. At home Miss Sandra Hanover normally wore a simple white hostess gown which she'd found in a thrift shop. So freakish, I thought, mustering up a smile.

Coming up, I'd decided not to comment on The Wig, realizing rhetoric would not be effective. The Wig would speak for itself, a prophet's message.

I went over to the warped sofa and said, "What's wrong?"

Miss Sandra Hanover clasped her two-inch fake-gold-finger-nailed hands. Then she opened her bovine eyes, but made no reply.

"Did you upset those faggots last night?" I coaxed.

Miss Sandra Hanover blew her nose with a workman's hand-kerchief. Her face was bright. Then it caved. A chalice of tears.

"Oh, Les. It was simply awful. Remember Miss Susan Hay-ward in *I Wanna Live*?" Her voice was so heavy with suffering that I immediately thought of Jell-O.

"Yeah. But why the waterworks?"

The Crown Princess masked a doubting stare. She bolted over to the gun cabinet and got a perfumed Lily cigarette.

Imitating a high-fashion model's coltish stride, Miss Sandra Hanover paraded around the nine-by-seven pied-à-terre, striking grand bitchy Bette Davis poses.

Sucking in her breath, she suddenly stopped and began speak-ing as if she had rehearsed her monologue diligently:

"Well, I went to this drag party on Central Park West last night. Mr. Fishback couldn't chauffeur me in the Caddie. A night-rider funeral. So, your mother taxied down. Ever so grand. I looked like Miss Scarlett O'Hara. Miss Vivien Leigh was simply wonderful, wasn't she? You should have seen how lovely I looked, Les. Peach-colored satin. I let my silver foxes drag the floor like Miss Rita Hayworth in *Gilda*. I'm maiding for this call girl on Sut-ton Place South. The sweetest little thing from Arkansas. She let me wear her diamond earrings like those Miss Audrey Hepburn wore in *Breakfast at Tiffany's*. She had this John glaze the foxes. The sweetest little furrier. I didn't even have to do him. I just told him that he really loved his mother. Like he wanted to sleep with her when he was four years old."

"Still up to your old tricks." I laughed.

"Now, Lester Jefferson," Miss Sandra Hanover said coyly. "Everybody's got *something* working for them. I bet you've got something working for you."

Smiling and silent, I went and sat down in a modern Danish chair which looked like a miniature ski lift.

Miss Sandra Hanover cleared her throat. "Remember Miss Gloria Swanson in *Sunset Boulevard*? Coming down that spacious staircase, mad with her own greatness, beauty? And all those com-mon reporters thinking she was touched in the head? She knew deep down in her own heart that she was a star of the first *multitude*! Well, love, that was me last night."

Greedily relishing her victory, Miss Sandra Hanover clucked her tongue, leaned back and struck a *Vogue* pose. Vigorous, in the American style, she wetted liver lips, exhaled, and continued: "Oh, did those faggots want to claw my eyes out! I acted like visiting royalty. Remember Miss Bette Davis in *Elizabeth and Essex*? I sat on that cockroach-infested sofa like it was a throne and didn't even *dance*! I just gave'm my great Miss Lena Horne smile . . ."

Drunk with dreams of glory, Miss Sandra Hanover's voice became a coquette's confidential whisper: "Later, things got out of hand. The lights were turned down low. Sex and pot time. Miss Sammie knocked over the buffet table, which was nothing but cold cuts anyway, and those half-assed juvenile delinquents started fighting. I pressed for the door.

"Three Alice Blue Gowns came running up the stoop. Naturally, they thought I was a woman. I flirted like Miss Ava Gardner in *The Barefoot Contessa*. Then this smart son-of-a-bitch starts feeling me up. You see, I was a nervous wreck dressing for the party. I couldn't find my falsies. I looked high and low for those girls! I had to stick a pair of socks in my bosom. And this smart-ass cop has a flashlight and pulls out my brand-new Argyle socks. Oh! I was fit to be tied. In high drag going to the can at two in the morning. Suffering like Miss Greta Garbo in *Camille*, and before you knew it: daylight . . ."

"And the doll was ready for breakfast in bed," I joked, craning my neck for a glimpse in the oval-shaped mirror above Miss Hanover's crew cut.

She cleared her throat again and slumped back on the sofa. "Breakfast? I couldn't eat a bit. Slop! I felt like Miss Barbara Stanwyck in *Sorry, Wrong Number*. But I did this lovely guard and he brought me two aspirins and a cup of tea."

Miss Hanover fell silent. I couldn't resist another glance at myself in the mirror, dreaming an honest young man's dream: to succeed where my father had failed. Six foot five, two hundred and seventy pounds, the exact color of an off-color Irishman, my father had learned to read and write extremely well at the age of thirty-six. He died while printing the letter Z for me. I was ten, and could offer my mother little comfort. I remember she sprayed the bread black. I remember the winter of my father's death as a period of black diamonds, for my mother and I had to hunt for coal that had fallen from trains along the railroad tracks. Like convicts hiding in an abandoned farmhouse, we sat huddled in our ramshackle one room. My mother read to me by candlelight. I vowed that I would learn to write and read, to become human in the name of my father. The Wig wasn't just for kicks. It was rooted in something deeper, in the sorrow of the winter when I was ten years old.

Remembering this now, I bit my lower lip and turned to Miss Hanover. "It's a good day, doll."

But Miss Sandra Hanover only saw the blood of suffering. "Les, they sent me to a headshrinker. Everyone knows I'm a clever woman. I am *not* about to go to no nut ward! I lied to this closet queen. I said I was from down South and they'd told me it was all right to go in drag in 'Nue Yawk cit-tee.' The closet queen nodded her bald head and said, 'That's interesting.' 'Yes,' I smiled back like a nice little water boy. 'Don't feel bad. This is quite common among Negro homosexuals who come North.' 'Let's get this straight,' I said. 'I am *not* a homosexual. I am a real Negro woman.' 'You don't understand,' Miss Headshrinker had the nerve to tell me. 'My name is Miss Sandra Hanover. Do you wanna see my ID card? You know. Blue is for boys and pink for girls.' Did Miss One turn red in the face! She excused herself and came back with two more closet queens. These bitches told me that I was a common Southern case. Ain't that a bitch? I was born and raised in Brooklyn. Now I got to take treatments twice a week because they think I is queer and come from the South. Why, everybody knows I'm a *white* woman from Georgia."

Miss Hanover leaned forward on the warped sofa and gestured like Mother Earth. Puckered liver lips. Her dark, aquiline nose quivered.

"Oh! I feel so bad. Remember how Miss Joan Crawford suffered so in *Mildred Pierce*? I could just die . . ."

A sharp intake of breath. A flurry of batting false eyelashes. A guttural sob, and Miss Sandra Hanover tumbled dramatically to the floor, very unladylike.

Dead she wasn't. No one like that ever dies. I got up, found a bottle of Chanel No. 5 and bathed Miss Hanover's forehead and temples with the perfume.

Counting to ten, I stared at Miss Hanover's carefully brushed crew cut. I missed her glamorous false wig. It was true; everyone had something working for them.

Presently, the great actress regained consciousness.

Sighing erotically, she looked up at me. "I must have fainted. Isn't that strange? And you look strange too, love juice."

Swallowing hard, I backed toward the door. "I'd better be going," I said.

"Now, Les," Miss Hanover chided.

"I'll see you later, doll."

The Crown Princess rose quickly. "Come here, honey," she pleaded. "I ain't gonna bite you. My, my. Those beautiful curls. Naked, you'd look like a Greek statue."

"Yeah," I mumbled and bolted out the door and down to my second-floor sanctum. Pleasure, I reflected, was not necessarily progress, and I had a campaign to map out. I had to get my nerves together.

T H R E E

WHISTLING "Onward, Christian Soldiers," I put the night latch on my door. I wanted no one coming in. I lit a cigarette, flopped down on the landlord's hallelujah prize, a fire-damaged sofa bed, crossed my legs, and exhaled deeply. I smiled lightly, like a young man in a four-color ad. I realized that nothing is perfect, but still, there was a possibility I might now be able to breathe easier. The Wig's sneak preview could be called successful, provided one knew human nature. Nonnie Swift's taunts: pure jealousy. Miss Sandra Hanover: simply a case of lust. I grinned and touched my nose.

Dear Dead Mother and Mother. Why do I have visions of guillotining you? Mother baked lemon pies. Father was a Pullman porter, a heroic man with a cat's gray eyes. Worthy colored serfs, good dry Methodists—they did not believe I had a future. How could they have possibly known? Otherwise, they'd have done something about my nose. No, it's not a Bob Hope nose, no one could slide down it, although it might make a plump backrest. If my parents had been farsighted, I would have gone to bed at night with a clothespin on my nose. At breakfast, Father would have peeped from behind the morning paper and lectured me on my bright future (I've seen those damn ads and motion pictures. I know how fathers act at the breakfast table).

Lord—just to think I could have had a sharp nose, a beak. —However, in the morning? Yes, I said in the morning. In the afternoon. Yes, after the sun goes down, and I wanna tell you—at the crack of dawn. In the heat of summer or on a cold rainy day in November, and we all know about those dark days—when the sun refuses to shine. Yes. Sometimes there's no light in our souls. Yes, I wanna tell you—I can sweat until Judgment Day and no grease will run down my face. No grease will congeal behind my ears. My hair will not go "back home," back to the hearth of kinks and burrs. Silky Smooth is magnificent! I am no longer afraid. At last, I have a dog's sense of security. Yes.

I've seen my young Negro comrades downtown. Sharp as a son-of-a-bitch with their slick Silky Smooth hair. *Esquire* and *Gentlemen's Quarterly* have nothing on them. But as they approach Grand Central or 42nd Street or Penn Station or Wall Street—they become as self-conscious as a sinner in church. Looking around the subway car nervously, clutching attaché cases. And just as the train approaches their station, out come the kinky-bur false wigs. And the others? The Buzz, Robin, Keith, Kipp, and Lance boys? The boys who can afford to be silky-smoothed twenty-four hours a day—Jim, you might as well forget it. These young men have "good" connections.

There is a very select shop in Harlem, on a side street. The building is very old; it emits dust the way a human does when breathing hard. Quite often bricks fall from its façade and clobber pedestrians. Still, matrons of "good" Harlem families call the building Mecca.

I have memorized the discreet ad in the window of that building.

We Are At Last Able To Provide You People With A Coat Of Arms! Done entirely by IBM on heavy, rat-proof antique paper. Your family name has been carefully researched from all the proper books in existence. Only good family names are available—400—including African families as well as the common names from the British Isles.

Bewigged I am. Brave, an idealist. But what can I do without a good family name, a sponsor, a solid connection? There's Mr. Fishback but I'm not sure about Mr. Fishback. I have a funny feeling that one day, if you let Mr. Fishback help you, you'll have to pay up. In what way I can't say. But there'll be no way out.

Dammit! The doorbell buzzed, a desperate animal-like clawing, funny little noises, like a half-assed drummer trying to keep
time.

Upset, I went and flung open the door.

Little Jimmie Wishbone stood there. A dusty felt hat pulled
down over his ears. Cracked dark glasses obscured his sultry eyes.
The ragged army poncho was dashing and faintly sinister, like a
CIA playboy.

"Brroudder! Ain't you cracket up yet?" Little Jimmie shouted.
"I thought I'd see you over thar."

I stiffened but gestured warmly. "Come in, man. When you get
out?"

"Yestiddy, 'bout two o'clock."

"Good to see you, man."

Grunting like a hot detective, Little Jimmie surveyed the room.
He flipped up the newspaper window shade and looked out on the
twenty feet of rubbish in the backyard. He jerked open the closet
curtains. Satisfied, he pulled a half gallon of Summertime wine
and Mr. Charlie's *Lucky Dream Book* from under the poncho and
put them on the orange-crate coffee table.

"You're looking good," I said, hoping I didn't sound as if I
were fishing for a compliment.

"Am I?" Little Jimmie wanted to know.

Sadly, I watched him ease down on the sofa bed, like a king in
exile.

Aged twenty-eight, Little Wishbone was a has-been, a former
movie star. *Adios* to fourteen Cadillacs, to an interest in a nation-
wide cathouse corporation. He had been the silent "fat" owner of
seven narcotic nightclubs, had dined at The White House. Honored at a Blue Room homecoming reception after successfully
touring the deep South *and* South Africa. At the cold cornbread
and molasses breakfast, Congressmen had sung "He's a Jolly
Good Nigger." Later, they had presented him with a medal, gold-
plated, the size of a silver dollar, carved with the figure of a naked
black man swinging from a pecan tree.

I had to hold back tears. Could that have been only two years
ago? I wondered. I got a couple of goblets from under the dripping
radiator. Mercy—depression multiplies like cockroaches.

I couldn't look at him, so I pretended to polish the goblets with a Kleenex, remembering.

The NAACP had accused Hollywood of deliberately presenting a false image of the American Negro. After the scandal subsided, Little Jimmie had the privilege of watching his own funeral. The government repossessed his assets. The Attorney General wanted him jailed for subversion but he pleaded insanity. Then his wife left him for a rock 'n' roll bass-baritone and that really did send him crazy. Little Jimmie had spent the past year commuting between Kings County Hospital and Harlem, but he had endured. The famed lamb's-wool hair had turned white. Little Jimmie's gold teeth had turned purple. He was slowly dying. Time and time again the doctors had explained to him that Negroes did not have bleeding ulcers nor did they need sleeping pills. American Negroes, they explained, were free as birds and animals in a rich green forest. Childlike creatures, their minds ran the gamut from Yes Sir to No Sir. There was simply no occasion for ulcers.

I poured a goblet of Summertime. Little Jimmie drank straight from the bottle.

"What's wrong?" he growled.

"Nothing, man."

"Something must be wrong," he insisted.

"What makes you say that?"

"'Cause something is wrong. You ain't never drunk out of no glass like that before."

I blushed. "Oh. You mean . . ."

"No. I don't mean. Hell. I got eyes. What you trying to prove?"

"You don't understand," I said sharply.

"Whacha trying to prove?"

"Whacha see? What's the impression? Slice the tater, slit the pea?"

In exactly one minute and three seconds, Little Jimmie had swallowed half of the wine. "Split the pea—I is with thee. What's the haps? Come clean. I is Little Jimmie Wishbone from Aukinsaw."

Brotherly love engulfed us. I drank from the bottle.

*   *   *

We had killed Summertime. Little Jimmie kept his eyes fastened on
the empty wine bottle. He looked like an angelic little boy who
had been kicked out of his orphanage for failing to take part in
group masturbation.

"You look down," I said. "You need some nooky."

Little Jimmie sighed. He looked very tired. "Nooky? Dem
white folk messed wit yo boy. Shot all dem currents through me.
Y'all took way my libin', I said. And they jest kept shooting
electricity. It was even popping out my ears. I took it like a
champ. Kinda scared dem, too. I heard one of dem say: 'He's
immune. It's the result of perpetual broilization. Nothing will
ever kill a Nigger like this.' I did my buck dance and the doctor
said, 'They got magic in their feet.' Man, I danced into the village. Now they can't figure out why those currents and saltpeter
make me so restless. They puzzled. I'm amused. But it's not like
my Hollywood days. All my fans and those lights and twenty-
seven Cadillacs."

"Fourteen Cadillacs," I corrected.

"Fourteen," Little Jimmie agreed. "But I traded them in every
year. Les, I just don't feel right. I just ain't me."

"I know what you mean."

"What am I gonna do?"

"You need another drink."

"Yeah. Some juice. Out there . . ."

"You didn't escape, did you?"

"Where could I escape to?" Little Jimmie exclaimed.

"Nowhere, man," I said, averting my eyes.

"I can't even get unemployment, though I was honorary president of the Screen Guild."

"You could always pick cotton in Jersey," I said.

"Pick cotton?" Little Jimmie sneered. "What would my fans
think? I think I'll appeal to the Supreme Court. I figure they owe me
an apology. I worked for the government, man. I kept one hundred
million colored people contented for years. And in turn, I made the
white people happy. Safe. Now I'm no longer useful in the scheme
of things. Nobody's got time for Little Jimmie Wishbone."

"What did you expect? Another medal? It's not profitable to
have you *Tom* . . . It's a very different scene."

"Well, what are you gonna do? Why the hell don't *you* pick cotton?"

"What the tell do you think I was doing last summer? *Where* do you think I got the money for the fried chicken I brought you on Sundays?"

War between friends is deadly. I mustered up a breathless laugh. "I'm gonna try something I never tried before. Dig The Wig."

Little Jimmie grunted scornfully. "Look at all those curly-haired Mexicans they import to pick berries and cabbage."

"But I'm an American," I protested.

"And I've got a million dollars."

"I *am* an American. That's an established fact. America's the land of elbow grease and hard work. Then—you've got it made. Little Jimmie, I'm gonna work like a son of a bitch. Do you hear me?"

"Yeah. I heard you. Now let's make it to the streets. My throat's dry."

F O U R

Little Jimmie and I moved out into the street under a volcanic
gray sky. A cold wind made a contradictory hissing like an over-
heated radiator, crept under heavy clothing with a shy but determined hand. Nothing could stifle our sense of adventure; Little
Jimmie was home again, and I always feel cocksure, Nazi-proud,
stepping smartly toward the heart of Harlem—125th Street.

125th Street has grandeur if you know how to look at it.
Harlem, the very name a part of New World History, is a ghetto
nuovo on the Hudson; it reeks with frustrations and an ounce of
job. Lonely, I often leave my airless room on Saturday night, wander up and down 125th Street, dreaming of making it, dreaming
of love. This is the magical hour. The desperate daytime has, for a
time, disappeared. The bitter saliva puddles of the poor are covered with sperm, dropped by slumming whites and their dark
friends who wallow in the nightclubs that go on to early morning.
These are people who can afford to escape the daytime fear of the
city. Envious, I watch their entrances and exits from the clubs. I
especially watch the Negroes, who pretend that the black-faced
poor do not exist.

I glanced at my misbegotten friend, a silent but bright-eyed
Little Jimmie Wishbone. In his heyday, he'd been unique: a real

person, an offbeat hero. Now he was only a confused shadow.

"Look where we are," I cried out as we swung onto East 125th Street.

Little Jimmie grunted. "What's playing at the Apollo? I once had a one-night stand at the Apollo and they held me over for six weeks."

"I remember. You were great. Man, listen to that wind!"

"The Apollo is show biz uptown."

"Yeah," I said quickly. "Man. The wind is a mother grabber. I really need some joy-juice."

"The Apollo is the last outpost. No other place like it in Manhattan."

I began whistling "Them There Eyes"—a nervous habit of mine. Diplomatic phrases refused to slide off my tongue. Presently, Little Jimmie would see the legendary Apollo Theater, its lobby a bower of plastic out-of-season flowers, shuttered and forlorn, due to the management's judgment (bad) in booking a string quartet from South Africa. This had shocked the entire city. The Mayor held a press conference. Harlemites stayed home in their photogenic tenements and watched television travelogues of Southern hospitality, while a group of near-naked white liberals picketed the Apollo. They mourned the loss of Negro music—so powerful that one felt it in the soles of one's feet (if one did not truly feel it, then one visited a chiropodist). The liberals prayed for a soul-shaking orgy. After three days, they marched back downtown, bewailing the Negroes' torpid attitude.

Gradually an aura of commerce, peace, splendor returned to 125th Street. Blumstein's Department Store announced in the *Amsterdam News* that polar-bear rugs were obsolete. Human-hair rugs were the latest rage. These rugs, clipped from live Negro traitors, had a lifetime guarantee. Blumstein's reported a remarkable sale. The Society of American Interior Decorators declared human-hair rugs "in." And the Du Pont Empire closely watched the proceedings. If human-hair rugs became a truly basic part of the American Home, perhaps they'd produce them in synthetics.

Strolling briskly with my friend, I felt pride seep into my pores. I was part of this world. The Great White Father had spoken. His white sons were carrying out his word. His black flunkies were falling in line. The opportunity for Negroes to *progress* was truly coming. I could hear a tinkling fountain sing: "I'll wash away your black misery—tum-tiddy-diddy-tum-tee-tee." Yes. Wigged and very much aware of the happenings, I knew my ship was just around the bend, even as I had informed Miss Nonnie Swift.

125th Street, with its residential parks, its quaint stinking alleys is a sea of music, Georgian chants, German lieder, Italian arias, Elizabethan ballads. Arabic lullabies, lusty hillbilly tunes. Negro music is banned except for progaganda purposes. "We'll let *them* borrow our music," a Negro politician remarked recently. "We'll *see* what it does for them. We'll see if *they* ride to glory on our music." I remember the Negro politician sailed a week later on a yacht, a sparkling-white yacht, complete with sauna, wine cellar, and a stereo record collection of Negro music second only to the Library of Congress's.

No one's perfect, I was thinking, when Little Jimmie elbowed me.

"I see *they're* still here," he said angrily.

"Of course, Little Jimmie," I said softly, mindful of his mental condition, his swift descent from Fame.

"You're nuts."

"Don't get yourself worked up," I said. "No one's gonna bother you."

"But they're still here," Little Jimmie protested.

"Naturally." I knew all along what had him bugged. It was the police.

New York's finest were on the scene, wearing custom-made Chipp uniforms, 1818 Brooks Brothers shirts, Doctor U space shoes (bought wholesale from a straw basket in Herald Square). A pacifistic honor guard, twelve policemen per block, ambitious nightsticks trimmed with lilies of the valley, WE ARE OUR BROTHER'S KEEPER buttons illuminating sharp-brimmed Fascist helmets—they bow to each fast-moving Harlemite from crummy Lenox to jet-bound Eighth Avenue.

Little Jimmie's fear was disgusting. The policemen were our protectors, knights of the Manhattan world. I wasn't afraid. I was goddam grateful.

"Are you ready?" I asked cheerfully.

Little Jimmie groaned deeply. "Lord. I might as well be back in Kings County's nut ward."

"It ain't that bad."

"That's your story, morning glory. It wasn't bad when I was riding through like Caesar in my bulletproof Caddie . . ."

"You have got to get used to the streets again. That's all. Doesn't it feel good to be home again?"

"I suppose so," Little Jimmie said slowly. "I guess I been away too long."

"Everything's still the same," I told him. "We're very fortunate to live in a ghetto that still honors traditional values."

Little Jimmie motioned across the street. "What's that funny-looking little green house over there?"

"That's an electronic snake pit. When things get too tough, you just hold this electronic cord until you can't stand it any longer. A gas. Almost like taking dope. Cheaper than the subway."

"It jest don't seem like Harlem anymore."

"But this is home, baby! This is the only place in the world where you can have the time of your life. You always could, and we still do."

"That's why I'm scared," Little Jimmie said.

"But it's different now," I tried to explain. "Even the cops are different."

"I don't hear a word you're saying."

I tried to reassure Little Jimmie, brushing back a curly lock that rose in the wind that whipped through the skeleton of an apartment house fringing a condemned residential park. "The cops are our friends."

"Then why do we have to run?"

"You'll never understand," I said, sighing. "Are you ready?"

"Give me a head start," Little Jimmie whined.

"Why do you want a head start?"

"Didn't they give you a medal last year 'cause the blood-hounds couldn't catch you?"

"Jesus. I'd almost forgotten. I guess I'm sort of an American hero."

"Yeah, and I've always been a movie star. But give me a head start. I've been taking the waters at Kings County."

"We gotta make it just to Eighth Avenue. It's not like a cross-country race."

"It's the same!" Little Jimmie cried. He pulled the felt hat down over his ears and started off.

I let him have a comfortable lead. Arching my arms, head held high, I bounded off graciously, the son of a desperate, dead runner.

Up ahead, a policeman sharpening a bowie knife snapped to attention as I dashed across Lenox Avenue.

Bowing, the policeman said, "Good morning, sir."

"Morning," I replied, gasping for breath. I'd never been frightened before, believe me. Little Jimmie's gloomy forecast, I told myself. He's a very sick has-been.

And soon I bypassed him, smoothly sprinting toward a photo finish. I galloped across the right side of Eighth Avenue, feeling my ego-oats. I was in good condition for the Spring Run-Nigger-Run track meet (the winner of this meet receives a dull black wrought-iron Davis Cup. There is always savage bribery; each borough president shills and makes a play for his favorite black son). Sunrise, sunset, winter, or summer—it had never been Succoth—the Promised Land, or the ingathering of the harvest for me. But with The Wig it might soon be.

I wiped my sweaty brow and saw three whores standing on the corner, adjusting white kid gloves.

"Little Jimmie," I called. "Look at our reward. Standing tall, sweet, and brown."

Little Jimmie eased up his pained physical-fitness smile. "Call the mojo man. Too bad Caddie number twenty is in the repair shop."

Stalking coolly, we approached the three whores.

I opened. "What you pretty girls doing out in this weather?"

The finely built group spokesman scanned the sky and giggled. "We're waiting on the Junior League pick-up truck. Those fine ladies, always so discriminating, have consented to see us. We're gonna add a little funky color to their jaded lives. Ain't that nice? They're planning a tea benefit for Harlem settlement houses. We're in charge of the entertainment. Ain't that nice?"

"It sure is," Little Jimmie guffawed boyishly.

"An honor," I agreed, eyeing the innocent, lyrically pretty

debutante. Tawny, a smasher, she toyed with short white gloves and averted her dark bacon-and-eggs eyes.

I remained worldly, indifferent, like Marcello Mastroianni. Then, to change the pace, I grinned a Humphrey Bogart grin.

Spongecake number two cleared her throat. "Well, well. I do declare."

"You look sort of familiar," the group spokesman said to Little Jimmie.

The rusty gates of glory creaked open; Little Jimmie cocked his hat on the back of his head and said in a resonant voice: "I jest might be. I is Little Jimmie Wishbone from Aukinsaw."

The group spokesman clutched a gloved hand over her right tit. "Little Jimmy Wishbone, the movie star? Oh, I feel faint!"

"I do declare," Spongecake said. "I heard you were on skid row."

"That was only for a proposed television series," Little Jimmie said modestly.

The whores feigned belief. Little Jimmie beamed. I blushed, watching three spotted horses trot toward the Harlem Premium Priceless meat factory. My stomach grumbled. I hadn't eaten in two days due to my extravagant Silky Smooth act.

"When you gonna make another picture like *Southern Sunset*?" the group spokesman asked in matronly tones.

"Well," Little Jimmie began grandly, "my old company, MGM, wants to sign me up for a Western epic. But my agent warned we'd better be incorporated in Switzerland first. I'm a hot property, you know."

The group spokesman gave her fellow travelers a firm didn't-I-tell-you-so expression. "A comeback, girls. A surefire sellout benefit première. I must inform our ticket scalpers."

"Hollywood is very excited over Little Jimmie's comeback," I said.

"I do declare," Spongecake said.

The calculating charm of the finely built, matronly spokesman began to show. "Which direction might you be headed, Mr. Wishbone?"

Little Jimmie shrugged, basking in the glow of the past. "Me and my boy jest out for a bit of fresh air."

"You and your valet?" Spongecake asked. "I read about your servants in *Screen Horror*."

"I got him in Hong Kong last year."

"I do declare."

I wanted to kill the dirty, wine-drinking son of a bitch. I bowed my beautiful head in shame, silently vowing to see Madame X, the reincarnation of Medusa, the smoldering rage of the Harlem firmament. A few incantations by her, and Little Jimmie's wagon would really be fixed.

"Orientals make the best servants," the spokesman commented.

"That's true," Little Jimmie was quick to agree. In Hollywood, he'd had a Finnish cook and a British gentleman's gentleman.

"We're servantless. Thursday, you know," the spokesman smiled sweetly. "And we're simply delighted to meet you, Mr. Wishbone, in the flesh. I think we should give those Junior League girls a rain check. Another day for dice and cards and chitchat and Bloody Marys. But I'd be delighted if you'd join me in my study for an informal lunch. I'm a follower of Dione Lucas and James Beard, you know. I'll try to whip up something simple. Kale and turnip greens cooked with juicy ham hocks. Yankee pot roast. German potato salad. Green beans soaked in fat back. And my specialty, cornbread and sweet-potato pie."

Little Jimmie made a dapper bow. Lordly he said, "Delighted. One gets tired of frozen frog legs, frozen cornish hen, instant wild rice, and pasteurized caviar."

"Well, just come along with us," Hostess spokesman smiled. "The Deb can stay with your valet and keep him company. 'Bout as close to royalty as she'll ever get."

Swooning, Spongecake said: "I do declare. Such a refreshing change from the round of parties and balls and dinners at the Bath Club where we're always encountering the same crowd."

The worms in my stomach were too hurt to cry over the great luncheon—they were resigned.

I watched spokesman and Spongecake proudly encircle Little Jimmie, saunter down Eighth Avenue.

"And you have twenty-five Caddies," Spongecake marveled.

"Forty-two," Little Jimmie lied. "And I'm getting a Rolls next week."

A loner, always on the outside, I looked at The Deb.

"You sure got pretty hair," she said.

"You really think so?" I asked, ready to assume my lover-boy role.

She nodded. I could see her body tremble under her battered tweed windbreaker. "My hair is so short and kinky. Nobody wants me."

Silly girl. Poor, innocent, and good—Lord, a piece of my lonely heart and hot hands telepathically grabbed her bosom. We were on the same wavelength.

"Everybody wants you," I said. "You're lovely."

"No," The Deb cried. "I've got bad hair. I've tried Madam C. J. Walker and Lady Clairol too. Oh, I don't know how I can go on living."

I went over and put my arms around her. She moaned and fell into them easily.

Yes. The touch of her flesh made lizards scale through my body as on sun-scorched rocks. I had never felt such sweet desire and I was grateful for the power and glory of The Wig.

"You're ever so kind," The Deb whispered. "All foreign men are real gentlemen."

Despite icy winds, sweat trickled down my armpits. It was the first time I'd been called a gentleman. "Oh, I wouldn't say that."

"It's true. Every time a Swedish ship comes to town I feel like the Queen of Sheba. And you're a man of quality. So sensitive. I can feel it."

"You're a sweet little thing," I murmured, feeling rather Swedish myself.

"You're ever so kind."

"Let's make it, baby. Some place that has a view, an open fire, soft lights, and sweet music."

"It sounds so romantic," The Deb cried, her lips brushing against my chin. "But how much you gonna pay me?"

"What?"

"How much you gonna pay me for my charms. You know: money. Loot. Bread. Greenback dollar bills."

"In Europe," I stammered, "we believe in free love . . ."

"This ain't Europe, honey. This is New York City. You gotta pay one way or the other. I'm a simple cash-and-carry girl."

She elbowed my chest and broke away.

"You American females are very strange. In Europe . . ."

"Sweetie, I dig you *and* your Wig. But they'd bar me from the union if I gave it away. The chairman said: 'No finance, no romance.' I hope you understand."

Sadly, I slumped against a litter basket. I'd had The Wig less than four hours and already I felt the black clouds gathering.

"I'll see you around, sweetie," The Deb smiled and walked away.

"Yeah," I mumbled, comforted with the knowledge that I was at least on the right side of Eighth Avenue.

F I V E

REJECTED, DEJECTED, I started walking east on 125th Street. The wind was dying and the sun had come out. Those cool knights, the cops, were dozing or filing their fingernails or reading newspapers. Negroes no longer raced across streets. They had slowed to a sensual stride. It was siesta time in Harlem. Everything was so quiet and peaceful that you wanted to take the mood home in a paper bag and sleep with it.

A candy store's loudspeaker played a Bach sonata— Landowska on the harpsichord. But the only music I heard was "no finance, no romance." The Deb, I sighed, feeling my whole body shake like thunder.

Up ahead loomed a great big fat bank, a foreign bank. Bracing my shoulders, I went into the bank and asked about a porter's job. I might as well try the dream of working my way up. Yes, there was an opening, I was informed by a very polite Negro girl with strawberry-blond hair. First, I had to fill out an application and take a six weeks' course in the art of being human, in the art of being white. The fee for the course would be one-five-o.

I thanked the girl with a weak smile, saying I'd return later in the afternoon or perhaps tomorrow. I'd have to place a long-distance call to Nassau.

"My father's in Nassau," I added, "hitting the golf balls right down the middle. He's dead set on Yale, but I like to build my own roads."

Outside, in the quiet street, I saw a crowd gathering and went over. A Negro Civil Service worker—he looked to be about forty-five—had dropped dead. His skin had turned purple blue-black.

"Oh, Lord," a woman cried, gesturing like a fishwife in an Italian movie. "I'm a widow and my husband is dead. All his life, he'd wanted to go to Florida in the wintertime, when the snow's on the ground in New York. All his life he'd wanted that. And we were going next week. Oh, Lord. He'd been having these heart attacks caused by terrible racial nightmares . . ."

A worldly looking young Negro couple next to me whispered: "It's a publicity stunt. The dead joker aped those Buddhist monks who used to set fire to themselves."

"Jesus," I shuddered and then began running, running home. Suddenly frightened, knowing if I didn't swing a secure gig, twenty years from now, I'd be flat on my own back, my chafed lips open as if to receive a slice of honeydew melon. Purple blue-black and dead, spotlighted by the early afternoon sun.

Darkness, symbol of life, arrived. I was naked and alone, clutching a patched gray sheet, lamenting The Wig's first encounters with destiny.

But there was the fatback sensation of meeting The Deb, and the glorification of what I had always referred to privately as "my thorny crown," The Wig itself. I turned uneasily on the sofa bed, wary of the night guard of cockroaches. "Happy Days Are Here Again," I whispered softly, thinking of The Wig and trying to make myself feel good and then, Lord—my own private motion picture flashed on: memory.

I remembered Abraham Lincoln, who had died for me. I remembered the Negro maid who had walked from Grapetree, Mississippi, to Cold Spring Harbor, Long Island, and was flogged for being too maidenly fair. I remembered the young man who, competing for the title "Blacker the Berry, Sweeter the Juice," was killed during an avant-garde happening in a Washington Mews carriage house. The killing did *not* take place during a Black Mass, as was first reported. The Negro youth had committed a sexual outrage, according to *Confidential Magazine* in its exclusive interview with the host and hostess, who were famous for their collection of Contemporary Stone Art. Their sexual safaris were legendary, too. Inspired by childhood tales of lynchings (ah, the gyrations, the moans, the sweat, the smell of fresh blood, the uncircumcised odor), the couple had explored Latin rice-and-bean delights, European around-the-world-scootee-roots, Near Eastern lamb, flip-flop, and it's-all-in-the-family.

Hoping to avoid the press, which arrived by helicopter, fifty miles from shore, exhausted, jaded, they returned to their native land on a luxury liner but in steerage class, with seventy pieces of Louis Vuitton luggage.

"It was off-season," the hostess had jokingly told reporters. The host added with great dignity: "We are returning to our native land, where fornication is pure and simple. We're returning to the womb of nature." They went into seclusion in their Greenwich Village carriage house until the night of the celebrated "happening," the night that was to reestablish their worldly reputation. The gleaming, white-toothed young Negro with the rough but carefully combed kinky hair (if one ran one's hand through his hair, one trembled and saw Venus and Mars) displayed a rosebud instead of a penis! The effrontery—a Negro and nipped in the bud! Certainly a shock that could drive anyone to murder, only it hadn't been murder, the courts decided. It was only a happening.

Sleepless still, I rolled over and scratched my stomach. I felt weak—a sure sign that happy days were here again and that I'd already opened a new door. As a child I'd always believed I could fly. One night, after sniffing The Big O in someone's bathroom, I *knew* it was possible. Until the countdown. Then I couldn't stand up, I was anchored to the floorboards. But the sensation, the idea of flight, the sensation of being free, that had been wonderful! I touched The Wig. Yes. Security had always eluded me, but it wouldn't much longer. American until the last breath, a true believer in The Great Society, I'd turn the other cheek, cheat, steal, take the fifth amendment, walk bare-assed up Mr. Jones's ladder, and state firmly that I was too human.

Lying in the quiet darkness, I decided to see Little Jimmie in the morning and work on a new big-time money-making deal. But first, we'd have an early morning seance with The Duke.

Yes! This was the land of hope and that was it! Sweet brown girl, I'll become a magician for you. Sweet brown girl. Bulldozing between your thighs, you with roses in your hair, I thought as my eyelids grew heavy.

No. No, no!

Sleep. Dream. Rest in peace. Until morning.

2

....

"If I could holler like a mountain jack . . ."

—FROM *JOE WILLIAMS SINGS*

S I X

WE KEPT OUR early morning séance with The Duke. He'd come a long way from his handyman-porter days in Chicago. A perfect specimen of the young man on the Amen train to success, the Duke had recently returned from his forty-seventh expedition into the Deep South and he had returned with a fantastic collection of antiques, a rare, historic collection. Sincere culture-prowling clubwomen were bursting out of their Edith Lances bras, trying to persuade The Duke to let his collection be included on their spring house tours.

The collection was extraordinary. It included the last word in expensive water hoses (nozzles intact, brassy but dented by human skulls); an enormous hunk of chestnut-colored hair from a Georgia policeman's gentle dog (The Duke planned to have this among his contemporary masterpieces); a hand-carved charred cross seven feet long; three dried Florida black snakes in a filigree shadow box; a lace handkerchief, reputed to be one of the oldest in America. These assorted objects were casually arranged in The Duke's mansion on the solid gilt edge of Central Park North and Fifth Avenue.

Little Jimmie and I swanked our way toward the Avenue. I saw people shield their eyes from The Wig.

"It's another world when the sun is shining," I remarked, but Little Jimmie made no answer.

Little Jimmie was in another world, very serious. Elegant: a twelve-foot cashmere striped old school scarf boaed his neck. Pigskin-gloved hands clutched a clear plastic attaché case bulging with ancient rock 'n' roll music he'd acquired at the Parke-Bernet galleries.

"What we gonna do first?" he asked solemnly.

"I don't know. Let's hope The Duke has some good stuff. Let's hope it inspires us. How's the lips?"

"I can't hang'm any lower, Les."

"At least you could try. This is very important, you know."

"No, I can't," Little Jimmie insisted. "Hollywood couldn't do anything with my patrician lips. The makeup man, and he was an artist to his fingertips, finally gave up."

"But we're rock 'n' roll singers," I tried to explain. "We've got to *dum-dee-dum*. You know, American kids are flipping over anything that has a jungle sound. It's their coming-of-age ritual."

Little Jimmie stopped suddenly. "Didn't have nothing like that when I was growing up. Didn't have nothing but misery and flog-gings."

"I know," I said, tugging gently at his arm. We were approaching the stark splendor of Central Park North, where green leaves were in embryo, and I wanted to get Little Jimmie to The Duke's.

"Kids got it too good now," he complained. "TV, bubble gum, plenty to eat. Nothing bad ever happens to them except they die from an overdose of heroin or else they go to jail for shooting a cop or a cop shoots them to an early grave. Yeah. Kids got it too good now."

"But their new way of life is our gravy. If they didn't dig rock 'n' roll and weren't so goddam queer we wouldn't be on our way to fame and fortune."

"That's right," Little Jimmie finally agreed. "Where's The Duke's pad?"

"See that manse on the left-hand side of the street?" I asked proudly. "The manse with the orange-tasseled canopy?"

"You mean the one that looks like that leaning tower in Italy?"

"That's it. Ain't that manse saying something? Something right out of *House and Garden*?"

"Oh, it's a mother-grabber. But I had thirty-five Caddies and I hear The Duke's only got one coupe de ville Caddy and that's almost a year old. I used to trade my Caddies in every four months."

Little Jimmie slowed, deep in past memories.

"Sure," I said, and tugging his arm, I led him gently across the street.

The Duke's soot-caked five-and-a-half-story limestone mansion did lean slightly out over the sidewalk, but, as he once remarked, that was part of its charm. It was a real conversation piece. Who else in Manhattan could boast that half of the fifth floor had fallen into the street by itself? The Duke didn't even have to call the demolition crew, though the Sanitation Department complained like hell when they had to clean up the bodies of three small children, all victims of rickets disease. A joyous Welfare Department sent The Duke a twenty-five-year-old quart of Scotch and officially axed the children from their list. The poor mother, The Duke had told me with tears in his eyes, was twenty-three and very frail and had seven other illegitimate children on welfare, including two sets of twins.

"It's a beauty," Little Jimmy exclaimed as we bounced up the gold-veined marble steps. "But in my Hollywood heyday I had a twenty-car garage. Miss Mary Pickford and Mr. Douglas Fairbanks, Senior, ruled Hollywood in the twenties and *I* ruled Hollywood after the Second World War. That is, until those devils sent me into exile . . ."

Little Jimmie shed one great tear, his trembling hand grasped the railing of the stoop.

"Now, don't go into that again," I said softly. "You'll get upset and be back in Kings County. Everything's cool. You're gonna reap fame and fortune in another field."

"But I was a star," Little Jimmie protested. "A movie star is the greatest thing in the world. A movie star lives forever."

I nodded and pressed the buzzer. The Wig would live forever, I thought. A monument to progress in the name of my dead parents.

Presently, the double-barred iron door swung open and we went into the bare white entrance hall.

Brandishing a genuine poison bow and arrow, The Duke emerged from behind a sackcloth curtain. Exactly five-feet-five, a dark version of Maximilian of Mexico, he carefully wrapped the bow and arrow in several back issues of *The National Review*. He wore bright Turkish trousers and a Hong Kong patchwork smoking jacket.

"Adds a little color to my life," he joked. "I was afraid you boys wouldn't show."

"What made you think that?" I asked. "After all, we got big deals brewing."

"Well," The Duke began, "you know how it is. People are discovering that marijuana is bad for the teeth."

"I've heard," Little Jimmie said sadly.

"However," I said, putting mountain air and clear running springs into my voice, "what pot does for the intellect and the soul! And you get high, too. Getting high is gonna see me through this world."

"I know," The Duke said, displaying a garland of black teeth stumps. "Marijuana is habit-forming, like hatred. It's being reclassified as a major drug by the government . . ." The Duke paused and rubbed his soft hands together. "What will it be today, boys?"

"I guess you heard," I said blushing.

"Oh. You mean . . . The Wig. It's great, man."

"Just a little experiment. Taking a public poll, you might say. And then I'll get down to the heart of the matter."

Little Jimmie grunted. "He looks like a goddam Christmas tree. Blinding everybody on the street. There was a terrific traffic jam at one hundred and twenty-fifth. Six people injured, but they was all white."

"Didn't I say I was going to shake up this town?" I laughed.

"Well," The Duke nodded in agreement, "I don't see how you can fail."

"I never needed a wig," Little Jimmie boasted. "But I was a movie star of the first rank. The late Louis B. Mayer said, 'Little Jimmie, you and I keep the lion roaring here at MGM.' And I said, 'That's a fact, Louis.'"

"I remember," The Duke said quickly. "Nobody could touch you with a ten-foot pole until you lost your place as America's favorite dark Mickey Rooney."

"I never lost my place in the American moviegoer's heart," Little Jimmie cried. He flung the plastic attaché case to the floor angrily. "It was those secret devils that double-crossed me . . ."

"What secret agents?" I scoffed, forgetting that he was touched in the head.

"How should I know?" Little Jimmie pleaded. "All I know is I'd jest been made an honorary member of the Arm Forces. This was wartime, mind you, but General Motors okayed a custom-built job for me. I was essential to the war effort. I made the people on the home front forget fear and tragedy."

Lies, insanity—I didn't care. "Peace on the home front? What the hell are you talking about? There was tragedy. My father learned to read and write and then died. My mother died grieving over him. That's how things were then. And I suppose you showed your teeth when the white folks said, 'Two more niggers gone.' I remember in the picture called *The Educated Man* there was a line that made the whole country laugh. 'No sur. Me caint weed nor wight to save muh name . . .'"

Little Jimmie came over and tried to console me. "That was just part of the script, Les."

"Then why did you always sign your name with a rubber stamp and put an X beside it?"

"That was a gimmick. I had a good public relations working for me."

"But do you really know how to read and write?" I asked, breaking away from his grasp.

"I know how to read the Gallup Poll, *Variety*, and *The Hollywood Reporter*. I placed first in *Photo Digest Magazine*'s popularity contest five years in a row. And then . . ."

Little Jimmie slumped against the wall and moaned, head hung low, large, ashy hands grasping at something that wasn't there.

The Duke sighed. I felt a quick pain, felt sweat splash down my armpits. I thought of The Wig and my own dazzling future, but that brought little comfort now.

Finally I forced myself to say loud and clear: "Yeah. Just about the time you were gonna get an Academy Award they kicked your ass out of Hollywood."

Little Jimmie raised his head slowly and looked over at me. "You didn't have to say it like that, Les."

"What else could I say? It's the truth. It wasn't my fault the white goat had horns."

The Duke broke in sweetly: "I've got some good stuff for you colored rock 'n' roll singers. Colored rock 'n' roll singers. That's a laugh. Sure you boys ain't trying to go white on me? Anyway, you're in my corner. I've got quality stuff. A five- or ten-dollar bag?"

"We'll have a couple of joints and turn on and see what happens. Okay, Little Jimmie?"

"I don't care. New gig shaping up and you guys trying to put me down." He smiled painfully.

"Go ahead, baby. Plough through the rye," I said, following The Duke into the next room.

It was an L-shaped room with what had once been a dumb-waiter converted into a drug bar. When The Duke moved in, he had discovered a dead, half Seal Point, half Abyssinian cat whose sky-blue eyes now floated in a Mason jar of alcohol. Functioning as a free-form shelf, a colonial pine packing case sagged under the weight of Chinese canisters (the pattern designs were the bonus of instant Australian tinned beef). A large, Danish cut-glass bowl was a rich sea of marijuana, finely chopped, heavily seeded, and blended for taste and its dried-leaf color.

"Everything's in marvelous taste," I said.

"Yeah," Little Jimmie agreed.

"Thank you," The Duke smiled, and let us on into his private sitting room, a mild gray room, bare except for the seven-foot charred cross opposite a modern sofa. The Duke did not want people to miss the significance of the cross. Posters of the Nazi epoch, the Spanish Civil War, four-color spreads of winters at Miami Beach, and one discreet calling card from a family in Newport surrounded the cross.

"Gentlemen," The Duke said graciously, "I am at your service."

Little Jimmie flopped down on the sofa. He seemed not to notice the cross.

I sat down on a hassock made from a four-gallon tin of Muddy Blue detergent, a souvenir of The Duke's handyman-porter days.

The Duke was a fine host. Calmly, he offered Little Jimmie a brimming Malacca pipe of pot.

I already had my hand out for the fat rolled joint. I lit up, inhaled deeply, and thought: Happy days. Little Jimmie and I will be rock 'n' roll sensations. Plus, I have The Wig; plus, there is still potency in the Little Jimmie Wishbone name. Plus, pot.

Feeling the pot and my bravado load, I went to the drug bar and flipped another joint into my golden lips and then looked over at Little Jimmie.

"Another pipe, man?"

Holding the pot in his head, riffling sheet music, Little Jimmie nodded gravely and I refilled his pipe.

Dry-heaving, The Duke clamped his hands over his mouth and turned toward the wall.

Two minutes later, he swung back around, breathing hard. "Fill my sax, Les. We'll make a session."

The Duke, a frustrated musician, always smoked pot out of a baby saxophone. A cute gimmick, like those coffeehouse musicians before Lily Law ended that scene. Smoke drifting out of the saxophone, a motif of cool music.

I filled the sax and joined The Duke, who now sat Indian fashion on the floor.

Three (pot-smoking) Wise Men, we silently savored the joy of marijuana, unmoved by the 10 A.M. foghorns signaling the first quarterly hour of radioactive dust.

The Duke elbowed me. "Are you feeling it?" he grinned.

"I am getting together," I replied. The image of The Deb floated into my mind. Boiling with inspiration, I added: "We could start off with a rock 'n' roll love song.

You upset me like the subway at night
Do, do, do uh a do . . . do
We'll hold hands in the first car
You and I and Oh . . .
Do, do, do, uh a do the policeman.
Do, do, do, uh a do, do

"What's the rest of it?" Little Jimmie asked.

"That's all. We jest keep repeating. Then let the sax and piano pick it up and, baby, we have at least two minutes. A record. A hit on our hands. By the time we make our first personal appearance on a TV show, we'll think of something freakish. You've gotta have something freakish about your personality or else the kids won't dig you. We gotta provide fantasy for their wet dreams."

The Duke exhaled and cleared his throat. "I think you're barking up the wrong tree. We're moving into a very *brotherly* racial era. And what's bringing the colored and white people together is real soul music. You know that, Les."

"Funky," Little Jimmie Wishbone shouted. "After the pot and whiskey, everything is jest like yesterday. And there's no real music. When I was a movie star . . ."

"But listen," The Duke interrupted. He knifed up from the floor. The sax rested easily under his arm. You could almost feel the gravel gritting in his throat as he said: "Folks, these are the blues. From way down home. In the southland of Brooklyn. They tell a story of sweat falling from people sitting on stoops on hot summer nights. Too hot for them in bed. They ain't got no money. Got nothing but the pain of fighting a lost cause. So what can they do? They sing, yes, they sing the blues . . ."

"Shit," Little Jimmie said.

"Let's have another joint," I said, "and get this show on the road."

"Yeah. We gotta see the man," Little Jimmie put in.

"The man?" The Duke asked, frowning.

"Yes," I said. "The A and R man at Paradise Records."

S E V E N

AFTER CLANSMEN GOOD-BYES, we were mellow. I wanna tell you: every muscle and vein in our bodies relaxed. We moved out onto the Avenue like crack athletes, briefly spotlighted by the fickle March sun. The Avenue was deserted and quiet except for the long-drawn-out cries of a hungry child. A rare cry. Normally, the Avenue's children were well fed, healthy, and happy.

"Terrible. Ain't it?" I said, looking up and down the Avenue.

A wave of old-star glory had washed over Little Jimmie. "It'll all be over soon. Remember when I was a star? Butter and biscuits and Smithfield ham every day. I was one of the big wheels in the machine. It'll be like the old days after we cut our first side."

"We can't miss," I said. "We've got too much going for us."

In an extravagant mood, I hailed a taxi, a sinister yellow taxi, festooned with leather straps and Bessemer steel rods. What looked like black blood caked the rear fender. The driver was a small pale man with an open face.

"Good morning," he said in a quavery voice. "I am at your service."

"Paradise," I snarled, easing into the taxi.

"That's Broadway and Fifty-second street," Little Jimmie said. "The musical capital of the world. We're part of the action."

"You're very fortunate," the pale taxi driver said.

Little Jimmie and I exchanged blasé-celebrity glances and laughed.

"Did I say something wrong?" the driver asked.

"Wrong," Little Jimmie exclaimed. "Listen to this turd."

Sweat showed on the driver's face. "Yes, sir. That's what I am. A turd. But you people are the greatest. You have so much soul. And how you can sing and dance. You must be the happiest people on the face of the earth."

"Cut the lip," I said. "Get this show on the road."

The perspiring driver swallowed hard and replied softly, "Yes, sir."

The sinister taxi started off smoothly enough and went down Fifth Avenue, leaving the upper Avenue's strong odor of decay. The denuded trees of Central Park formed a bleak bower, and, on the opposite side, glass fronts of apartment buildings gleamed. It was as if the architects had all worked from a single design.

Now the taxi was at 82nd and Fifth. Little Jimmie dozed. I watched the park side where gouty, snobbish mongrel dogs howled discontentedly. Infected infants sat in Rolls-Royce baby carriages guarded by gaunt nursemaids. Good Humor men equipped with transistor laughing machines hawked extrasensory and paranoiac ice-cream bars. The unemployed formed a sad sea in front of the apartment buildings: they jostled, spat, bit and hit each other in the stomach, their voices a medley of frustrated cries, while merry apartment wives peered from plate-glass windows, hiding smiles behind Fascisti silk fans.

The pot was surely working, I thought hazily.

I closed my eyes and saw my Deb behind her own plate-glass window, spoon-feeding Lester Jefferson II—Little Les, while twenty floors below, I polished the Mercedes with Mr. Clean. It could happen: rebirth in this land, or was such a birth only an exit from the womb, not a door to the future?

Life is one pot dream after another, I thought, and yawning, I turned to Little Jimmie. "We're on our way," I said.

"It's in the bag."

Suddenly the driver's chattering teeth caught our ears.

"What's wrong with him?" Little Jimmie asked.

"Guess he's got thin blood."

"He's a skinny little son of a bitch."

"It's a wonder the wind doesn't blow his ass away."

Little Jimmie chuckled, and leaned back in the seat like a king.

"I ain't cold," the pleasant-faced driver cried. "I'm scared to death. I know you gonna take my leather straps and chains and beat me up. I know you gonna make black-and-blue marks all over me and take my money. Ain't that right? Ain't that right?"

Sighing, Little Jimmie said, "Is he trying to get in on the act?"

"No, man. He's a masochist. Dig?"

"Come on," the driver shouted. "Beat me and get it over with. I can't stand the waiting."

"Don't blow your cool," I warned him.

"Ain't that right, ain't that right?" Little Jimmie laughed.

"Sounds like the title of our second solid-gold hit record."

Just then the taxi driver picked up speed, raced down Fifth Avenue to 62nd Street, where he slammed on the brakes quickly.

"All right," he sneered. "Shut your trap. I've had enough from you jokers."

"Dig this mother," I said.

"What was that?" the driver snapped.

"Lay off, man," Little Jimmie said.

The taxi zoomed through a blinking red light and came to the fountain fronting the Plaza.

"Boys," the pale taxi driver began clearly, "you ain't on home ground now. You had your chance. So now don't you blow your cool. This is my turf. We're *downtown*."

"I know, I know," I sighed.

"Yeah," Little Jimmie put in, "but we're the two new BB's from tin-pan alley. You wouldn't wanna do nothing that would fuck up the economy and cause an international incident, would you?"

"Jesus," the taxi driver exclaimed. "Wait until I tell the kids and my old lady. Jesus. You could have had a police escort all the way downtown. Get you away from the Harlem riffraff. I knew all along that you two gentlemen were something special. The riffraff is causing all the trouble. Making it bad for you colored people."

"I know, I know," I sighed again as we swung on to Central

Park South. I ran a moist hand through The Wig. It was still soft, luxurious, and together. Visions of fame and fortune bounced through the soul of The Wig: The Deb, the girl next door, the girl at the end of the double rainbow.

We turned on to Broadway. The driver said, "Oh, the way you boys can sing!" He paused, breathing hard. "Never knew a colored person that didn't have a fine singing voice."

Crossing Broadway and 57th Street, I was a one-man chorus. "I know, I know," I sang.

"You're the greatest, you're the tops," the pale driver said.

"Oh yes, oh yes," I sang.

Straight-faced, Little Jimmie Wishbone looked out the window.

"Now don't get me wrong," the driver chuckled pleasantly, slowing at Broadway and 52nd Street. "That'll be three-fifty even."

Like a late winter grasshopper, he jumped out and opened the rear door. "Its been a real pleasure and I wish you guys the best."

I got out of the sinister yellow taxi slowly, like an old man who knows his days are numbered. I did not look at the driver. I felt tired.

But Little Jimmie smiled warmly and said bitterly: "Keep the change." There was a ring of authority in his voice.

Paradise Records, Ltd., is located on the eighty-eighth floor of The League of Nations Pill Building. It straddles Broadway and 52nd Street like a chipped marble pyramid and is topped by a cone-shaped tower sporting five revolving neon crosses. Piped music echoes from the lobby to the tower: opera, symphonies, sweet ballads, American rock 'n' roll, and selected international hits.

We stepped smartly through the lobby to the strains of "Nearer My God to Thee," the number-one song on the nuclear hit parade.

"Next week it'll be us," I said, breaking into a wild grin.

"It's in the bag," Little Jimmie said brightly. Only eighty-eight floors and a new career. He'd recapture his public image. I watched him square the felt hat, flip the brim down over his left eye. There was even a glint of expectation in that eye.

"Gotta rent me a Caddie," he said. "Can't be seen making it through the streets in a taxi. My fans wouldn't like that."

I pressed the elevator button. "How do you feel?"

"Like being born again. I know how you feel too, on the first wave of fame."

The wide doors of the elevator swung outward like the doors of a saloon. Little Jimmie braced sloping shoulders and pushed past me.

"Let's go, boy," he said.

A sudden thought hit me. "We don't have a manager," I said.

"It doesn't matter at this stage of the game. Press the button. Eighty-eight. I'll do the talking. You know I'm an old hand at this type of thing. But in the past, people always came to me. Either to my Beverly Hills mansion or to my Manhattan penthouse. But we'll manage."

The elevator closed silently. We stood stiff and proud, our hot eyes focused on the walls of the elevator. The walls were eye-catching: mahogany, with carved musical scales and American dollar signs.

"Lucre, my ghost," Little Jimmie sighed.

"You're a swinging stud."

"Nothing to it, boy. I know what's happening. I've had too many gigs."

Exiting from the elevator, I prayed for ten thousand one-night stands, for a million six-week holdovers. Balloon images of The Deb burst inside my excited beautiful head. I was happy like a man when a particularly painful wound begins to heal. I was no longer jockeying for position: I was *in* position. I followed Little Jimmie through the great bronze doors of Paradise Records.

The receptionist was licking stamps, and a sequined sign on the desk said: MISS BELLADONNA.

"Yes?" Miss Belladonna said in a hoarse voice, without looking up.

"We're the two new BB's and we want a hearing," Little Jimmie said with great dignity.

"Yeah?"

"Yes, young lady."

Miss Belladonna yawned. "Well . . ."

Impatient, Little Jimmie drummed his fingers on the kidney-shaped glass desk.

"Look alive, young lady," he warned sternly.

Giggling, Miss Belladonna said, "I'm sorry. You know how things are in Paradise. All this *joie de vivre* jazz. We're ever so busy, too. One hit after another."

"I know," I said, "but we're gonna make an explosion in Paradise."

Miss Belladonna showed us her jaundiced eyes. Lips trembling, she pressed a gold button and seized a hand mike.

"Mr. Pingouin! Mr. Pingouin! Front and center," she sang.

Then, clasping hands over a flat chest, she cried: "Oh! This is so thrilling. I've seen the best of them walk through that door. Just walk right in and open their mouth and—cling-a-ling-a-ling—the coins literally roll off their tongues, and it's so thrilling!"

Little Jimmie beamed. "That's the way it goes. But you gotta have star quality."

"Yes," I said quickly. "Stars are always collected and cool." It was something I had read in a gossip column. I liked the sound: collected and cool.

"Cool?" Mr. Pingouin purred, minueting into the reception room.

A young man, dapper in banker's gray and wearing large, round, fashionable glasses. He looked like a happy Uncle Bunny Owl.

"Welcome to Paradise. The home of hits."

"Naturally, I am aware," the comeback star hee-hawed. "I is Little Jimmie Wishbone from Auk-in-saw."

"Little Jimmie Wishbone from Arkansas?" Mr. Pingouin asked, his round glasses skiing down his smooth nose.

"Little Jimmie Wishbone," Miss Belladonna gasped.

"The late-late show and the afternoon soap opera? My mother just loved *Southern Sunset*. She's seen it seven times."

"And no residuals," Little Jimmie added painfully.

"Forget it," Mr. Pingouin said with a wave of the hand. "I know you are money."

"Oh! It's so thrilling," Miss Belladonna cooed. "Shall I call Mr. Sunflower Ashley-Smithe?"

"Mr. Ashley-Smithe is our A and R man," Mr. Pingouin informed us.

"What about promotion?" Little Jimmie wanted to know.

"We have the networks and the press by the balls," Mr. Pingouin said, smiling shyly.

"I should say we have," Miss Belladonna said. She seized the hand mike. "Mr. Sunflower Ashley-Smithe. Front and center!"

Silence, a rich soft silence, enfolded the nonchalant future recording stars, the jaundiced receptionist, and the owl-eyed first assistant vice-president.

Presently, doleful Muzak came on with Napoleon's Funeral March. Little Jimmie stood at attention, Miss Belladonna seemed to doze, Mr. Pingouin bowed his head, and I counted to one hundred.

Then Mr. Sunflower Ashley-Smithe entered to the strains of "Home on the Range."

There was nothing unusual about Mr. Sunflower Ashley-Smithe. A thoroughbred American Negro, the color of bittersweet chocolate—chocolate that looked as if it had weathered many seasons of dust, rain, and darkness, chocolate that had not been eaten, but simply left to dehydrate. He was more than six feet tall, I guessed. And when he smiled at us, I knew my ship was docking at last.

"Gentlemen," he said and bowed sedately. "I know ours will be a perfect relationship. Now, will you please join me in the inner room."

"It's our pleasure," Little Jimmie bowed back.

"Oh! Goodness," Miss Belladonna squealed. "This is so exciting. It always is."

"Have a happy session," Mr. Pingouin said, "and please remember that you are in the hands of Paradise."

Despite an abundance of expensive flowering plants, the inner room had the serene masculinity of a GI sleeping bag. Facing the window wall were two baby-grand pianos with smooth brass finishes. Large lounge chairs formed a fat lime-green circle centered on a stainless-steel coffee table. It was a large pleasant room, ideal for music.

"Gentlemen," Mr. Sunflower Ashley-Smithe said, extending the pale pink palm of his dark hand, "please be seated. Everything is very informal here at Paradise. That is the key to our worldwide success."

Finger popping, Little Jimmie agreed. "That's the method. When I was making my last trilogy of flicks about homesteaders . . . Wow!

Remember? Everyone went ape over them. Took the Cannes, Venice, and Berlin film festivals by storm. Well, *my* method was always to have a relaxed set. Even on location."

"You were one of my heroes, Mr. Wishbone. Pity you couldn't bridge the changeover. Perhaps your new career will rectify the situation."

"Mr. Ashley-Smithe, you are a knight of humanity. The first star—the first *flower*, of deep emotions. The musical genius of this century."

"You're very kind, sir."

Lord, this was getting too much. Trembling, I broke in: "We're relaxed and ready to sing, Mr. Sunflower Ashley-Smithe."

"Fine, fine," the first flower of deep emotions said, rubbing his hands and executing a nimble ballet turn.

No music penetrated the cork-lined inner room. There was only a brush-fire silence until the graceful A & R man faced us.

"It's so soft . . . easy," he said. "Two groovy-colored studs. You've got everything in your favor. I know the countdown of this racket. I've worked hard to help my colored brethren and fortunately you've got what the white people want. What the *world* wants! I don't have a social life, nor do I indulge in sex. At night I go home and plot the future of my golden-voiced colored brethren. I keep a dozen milk bottles filled with lice so I won't be lonely. I never have a dull or idle moment with my happy family around me. And come morning, I'm ready to face this mother-grabbing racket again. Understand?"

"Certainly, Sunflower," Little Jimmie said.

"Certainly, Mr. Ashley-Smithe," I said.

"Fine, fine. Now please join me at the baby."

Riffling through the plastic attaché case, Little Jimmie said, "Let's run through 'Harlem Nights.' It has a simple gaiety. But keep the tempo down. We have to build on this one. Know what I mean, Sunflower?"

"Oh yes. Exactly."

Little Jimmie strode manfully over to the baby grand piano. "Let's take it from the top, Les."

"Yeah, baby. Let's go. I'm in excellent voice this morning."

Bowing again, Mr. Sunflower Ashley-Smithe rippled the keyboard expertly. "Wonderful. Your choice of an opener is great."

Little Jimmie cleared his throat and peered at the sheet music closely. "Now, I'll take the verse and you take the chorus, Les. Let's rip a gut. This must be spontaneous."

The musical genius of the century laughed vigorously. "Let's see if you're colored."

Camaraderie like sunlight filled the inner room. I really felt as if I *could* bust a gut. I wasn't embarking on a Madison Avenue or a Wall Street career. No, this gig was glamour, Broadway, night lights. Champagne supper clubs, call girls, paying off bellboys and the police. A million hysterical teenagers screaming, clamoring for your autograph, a strand of your curly hair, a snotty Kleenex, a toothpick, a bad cavity filling, a pawnshop diamond ring, and all because few parents are child-oriented. And now *I* was a part of the racket!

"Lester," Little Jimmie said sharply.

"I'm with you, baby."

"Ready?" Mr. Ashley-Smithe asked.

I watched Little Jimmie flex his muscles, clench his fist, and breathe deeply. So deep I could see the outline of his soul on his sweating face.

And then he began to sing as if he were alone in a splendid garden on a cool summer morning. Looking at his contorted face, I thought: what a magnificent actor. A Harlem-born great actor.

Mr. Ashley-Smithe was impressed too. He clasped his hands and closed his eyes.

"The rebirth of my hero," he whispered.

Gesturing, alone in the garden, Little Jimmie's voice filled the inner room.

Harlem nights are gloomy and long
A cold, cold landscape
Darkness, darkness.
Will I ever lift up my voice . . .
And sing, I falsettoed right on key.

"You curly-headed son of a bitch," Little Jimmie yelled, "you didn't bust a gut!"

"What?" I faltered.

The first flower of deep emotions moaned. "My brothers, my fellow countrymen. Please. Please, stop. Let's take a break."

The comeback lion was fuming. "Yes. Let's take a *long* break!"

Hurt, I silently vowed to go it on my own. Solo, baby. Who needed a washed-up movie star!

When I came out of my sulky reverie, I heard Mr. Ashley-Smithe's voice: "I work very hard, I am a good man. I do not practice black magic. I love my fellow man and that includes white people . . ." Mr. Ashley-Smithe paused. "So how could this happen to me?"

What was the mother-grabber talking about? I couldn't make it out, though Little Jimmie seemed to know. He looked like a freshly cast mummy. Hump him! I'd go it alone.

"I could try 'Limehouse Blues,' Mr. Sunflower," I enunciated clearly. "I think I could fake a Chinese accent. 'Limehouse Blues' is a particular favorite of mine, and an all-time classic, as you well know."

Mr. Sunflower Ashley-Smithe seemed to be trying to check a bathtub of tears. "That won't be necessary," he said. "Would you gentlemen kindly leave? Both of you. You are both a disgrace to your colored brethren *and* to this great republic! Why, you poor slobs can't even carry a tune."

The first flower of human emotions arose from the piano. His laughter was loud and frightening.

E I G H T

No LAUGHTER WELDED my shocked dark heart. I marched swiftly out of the inner room, past Miss Belladonna, who seeing my face screamed, "Goodness!"

Waiting impatiently for the elevator, I wanted to scream myself. The Wayward Four rocked, rolled, wallowed through the loud-speaker Muzak. *"Play-a simple melody, play-a simple melody,"* they sang. Off-key, no doubt spitting their puberty juice. "A racket," Sunflower Ashley-Smithe had said. Well, I wanted no part of it. Right then and there, I told myself, it had been an impulsive, foolish mistake. I was destined for a higher calling. Perhaps not Madison Avenue or Wall Street. No. A real man-sized job. A porter, a bus boy, a shoeshine boy, a swing on my father's old Pullman run. Young Abe by the twenty-watt bulb. Sweating, toiling, studying the map of The Great Society. One is not defeated until one is defeated. Hadn't the drugstore prophet said, "You may become whatever you desire?" Perhaps I'd even become a politician or a preacher—those wingless guards against tyranny and misery.

The saloon doors of the elevator opened. Piously, I entered. Muzak thundered with a gospel group singing:

This little Light of mine . . .
I'm gonna let it shine . . .

I ran my hand through The Wig and stamped my feet until the elevator reached the ground floor.

The lobby was teeming with the fabulous show-biz crowd, yak-yakking, hustling. Well, they could yak and hustle without me.

I decided, however, to wait for Little Jimmie. My anger had cooled and I wanted to talk with him quietly. Plus, I didn't want those earnest boys from Kings County to nab him on Broadway. I waited for what seemed a long time and then I spied him standing against a piece of blowtorch sculpture, looking like a confident young executive with big deals brewing.

"You were up there a long time. What happened?"

Little Jimmie hee-hawed. "Oh, you know how it is, Les. Show-biz talk. Putting out feelers. Sunflower said he thought we were too tense. Nerves."

"Is that what he said?"

"Yeah. Told him I'd meet him tonight. He suggested the Copa. But I said Jilly's. More intimate."

"That's great," I said.

"It's boss, man," Little Jimmie smiled.

And we didn't say another word until we emerged from the League of Nations Pill Building, blinking at the ferocious midday sun.

"Think we could go to Europe and gain some experience?" I asked.

"It's an idea," Little Jimmie said gravely. "I ain't been in Europe in a long time. They know me over there."

"Let's go for coffee," I suggested.

"No, Les."

"Then let's go some place. What about digging those Harlem society broads?"

"I don't wanna see no society chicks." Little Jimmie started walking off, walking up 52nd Street.

"Where you going?"

"I don't know. Just going."

"See you later," I said.

"Yeah. Later."

I watched my slow-shuffling friend disappear into the noonday crowd. The mambo strains of "Happy Days Are Here Again" drifted from a nearby record shop.

N I N E

THE SUN WAS very bright the following morning; there was something almost nice about the polluted air. I had my glass of lukewarm tap water, said my Christian prayers, recited a personal Koran, and kissed the rat-gnawed floorboards of my room. (Nonbelievers, please take note: I was definitely insane, an ambitious lunatic.) I had spent a sleepless night plotting and thinking. Impersonation is an act of courage, as well as an act of skill, for the impersonator must be coldhearted, aware of his limitations. I, however, suddenly realized I *had* no limitations. I felt good. The sun was shining. Bathed in its warm rays, I became Apollo's Saturday morning son. My new image had crystallized. An aristocratic image, I might add. The new image was based on The Wig, and was to be implemented by the forethought of Mr. Fishback. It took me a little while to accept the fact that I was going to act upon it, but I did.

Here is the timetable: 10 A.M., perspiring. 10:15, borrowed two cigarettes from Nonnie Swift. Three minutes of cheers; Nonnie had been barred from the Harlem Sewing Circle because of her Creole past. Quarter of eleven, a last status sip of lukewarm water. At two minutes to eleven I snatched Mr. Fishback's Christmas gift from under the sofa bed: an all-purpose, fake, forged Credit Card, guaranteed at five hundred hospitals in all fifty states. Honored

instantly by one thousand fine hotels and restaurants, plus major
service stations, and airlines. Car rental agencies also guaranteed.
With Mr. Fishback's dandy all-purpose card, I was going into orbit.

As a result, I found myself at 1 P.M. alighting from a chauffeur-
driven Silver Cloud Rolls-Royce on Sutton Place South. In my
14th Street-Saville Row suit (dark, synthetic, elegant) that I'd
bought from Mr. Fishback—I was truly *together*. And the six
joints of Haitian marijuana I'd smoked on the way down made me
feel powerful. Like Cassius Clay. Like Hitler. Like Fats Domino.
Like Dick Tracy. I dismissed the car and driver. They'd done their
work, I had my high, and I saw no reason to push my luck.

I walked through Ionic columns and onto the plastic-marbelite-
tiled courtyard of the Riverview Tower Apartment Residence (the
last stronghold of concentrated capitalists) to receive a sharp click-
ing of heels from the amazed doorman.

"*Bonjour,* Mac," I said, between clenched teeth.

The doorman saluted smartly. "Good afternoon, sir," he said
clearly, opening the entrance door. "Lovely weather for March,
isn't it, sir?"

"Smashing," I replied, scanning dark clouds. "Is the lift self-
service?"

"Yes, sir."

"Pity."

"Yes, sir."

"The modern world is going to hell."

"Quite right, sir. Would you like me to press the elevator button? They were made in Japan. Amazing little gadgets, and I'd be
honored if you'd grant me permission to push the button for you."

"Oh, yes. By all means. Jolly good of you."

There were tears in the doorman's eyes. "Thank you, sir."

"What's your name, old chap?"

"Abraham O'Reilly, sir."

"O'Reilly. A fine name. Must remember that."

"God bless you, sir."

Joyfully, I waltzed into the elevator and ascended upward,
heavenward.

The elevator did not quite reach the ramparts of heaven. It
stopped on the ninetieth floor, the penthouse floor.

I got out and felt my feet plowing into a deep shaggy Greek

carpet, a sensation not altogether pleasant, but I was determined to maintain my bored-rich-boy expression. I pressed a well-scrubbed finger against the doorbell and waited.

Tom Lacy opened the penthouse door. Tomming a wee bit, he bowed and rolled his eyes. He seemed not to recognize me. Was The Wig that effective?

"Ain't nobody home. They is in the country," he said. "Won't be back till late Monday morning."

"You're the man I wanna see."

Moaning, Tom Lacy looked away. "Mister, I ain't done nothing and I ain't buying nothing. Good day."

"Just one moment, please."

"Mister," Tom whined, "I done told you already. I ain't buying nothing. I gits plenty of good used clothing from the boss, and the mistress throws a few hand-me-downs to the old lady. I got plenty of insurance and a wristwatch that runs jest fine. I'm scared of cars. And as you can see, skin lightener will do me no good and I'm dead set against hair grease and don't try to sell me no back lot in Westchester, cause I ain't buying. But come back Monday. They'll be back then."

Yesterday at Paradise Records, Ltd., in a moment of panic, I tried like hell to bust a gut. Now staring hard at Tom Lacy, staring at his sweaty immobile face, I tried not to bust a gut.

Slightly envious of his brilliant impersonation, I said, "Shit."

"Mister. I didn't mean to offend you. I jest don't need nothing. I is way up to my ears in debt already."

"Okay, Tom. Can the cat. It's me. Your boy Les. Ask me in and fix a drink."

Tom Lacy stared hard at me. Gritting his alabaster-coated false teeth, he let the placid mask of his face change to that of a natural killer.

Just to be on the safe side, I took several steps backward.

"I ain't in the mood for no jokes. I had to work my ass off to get them bastards to the country."

"Man, you just ain't with the happenings. You're non-progressive."

"Youyouyou . . ." Tom Lacy shouted.

"Control yourself," I said. "You're sweating too hard and might catch a cold."

His eyes zeroed in on my Wig. Before I could open my mouth, he lunged like a besotted bull, rammed his kinky head into my stomach, and knocked me flat on my back.

"Tom!"

"A little louder."

"TOM!"

"That's more like it. Now, do you have any last-minute special requests?"

"Yes. Get your mother-grabbing hands from around my neck. I can hardly breathe."

"I only asked for last-minute requests, and I'm doing you a favor at that. You were once my friend."

Tom weighed only a hundred and seventy pounds but his grip was forceful. I could hardly breathe. His hands played a teasing, sadistic game on my neck.

"Tom, old buddy . . ."

"I don't wanna hear that jazz."

"Tom, please. I'm flat on my back. Let me up and I'll explain."

He groaned. I could see tears mixing with the sweat. His Adam's apple went up and down like a yo-yo.

"What's wrong with you?" he shouted.

"Nothing. Tom . . ."

"Have you gone crazy? This ain't Halloween."

"Please take your hands off my neck," I said, struggling for breath.

"You've lost your mind," Tom Lacy sobbed.

"I haven't lost my mind. Now will you please let me up? I'm getting full of goat's hair."

He bit his lower lip and let go. "Les, you've taken ten years off my life . . ."

Sobbing immodestly, he rose slowly. I felt like a jackass.

"I never thought you'd do something like this," Tom said.

"Do what?" I asked angrily. I got up and ran a cautious hand through The Wig. "You must be off your rocker."

"I've known you a long time, Les. I've known you since you were born. I was your godfather. I know you were orphaned at an early age and that your life has been nothing but trials and tribulations . . ."

"Tom, what are you getting at?"

"Shut up," my grieving friend commanded. "Don't interrupt. I'm trying to talk to you like a father. Yes, trials and tribulations. You were such a good boy. Your dear parents taught you to read and write. You had good manners and went to Sunday School. And you've got a sturdy head on your shoulders. I was always proud when I never found your name on the sports page of the *Daily News* listed among them juvenile delinquents."

"Tom. You're breaking my goddam heart."

"WHAT HAVE YOU DONE TO YOUR BEAUTIFUL HAIR?"

"Nothing," I said.

"Infidel!" Tom Lacy accused in a shaking voice and lunged at me again.

I jumped back quickly. "Listen to me. Please. I'm doing this for the sit-ins. Did you hear me? I'm doing this for the sit-ins."

"The sit-ins?" Tom Lacy's dawning smile was absolutely saintly. "Great day in the morning!"

"Yeah," I grinned. "What a morning."

"Man, you had me scared to death," Tom said.

"I was a little uneasy myself."

Tom wiped his sweaty brow. What would the hero like to drink? Champagne? A little Château Haut-Brion? Or could he whip me up a quick snack? Rossini steak? Creamed eggs in ramekins, slightly gratiné, floating in caviar?

"No. Double vodka on the rocks. Gotta work a picket line this afternoon."

"Okay, sport," Tom smiled. "I *knew* you'd never betray us!"

Settling back in a down-stuffed chair, I said, "How could I possibly betray you?"

"Your parents would be proud of you."

"How's the chart coming along?"

Tom frowned sadly. "Not too good, Les. According to this morning's *Times,* only a hundred and seventeen died."

"That isn't too bad," I said, accepting the vodka.

"There have been better days," Tom said, pulling up a comfortable chair, a kind of Chinese rocking chair.

"Of course," I agreed. "Still, you can't complain. Anyway, Easter is coming, and after that it will be vacation time all over America."

"I know. But I like New Year's Eve better."

"I heard on the radio this morning that a jet crashed and killed forty-five."

"Really?" Tom exclaimed. "That's wonderful. That tops the fire at the old-folks home in Jersey. Only nine of them burned."

"A woman was strangled in Philly yesterday."

"Usually there are more sex murders in the spring."

"That's true," I agreed.

Tom was very excited. "Let's toast to spring."

"To spring and to death," I said, raising my vodka glass.

"That's a great toast. Sure you don't want me to open a magnum of champagne? Thirty-four. A good year."

"No. I'll stick to vodka. Don't forget, I'll be out in the cold, picketing until sundown."

"You are a fine young man," Tom said quietly. "I'm proud of you."

"You're an earthly angel."

"You're Moses walking in the wilderness!" Tom said jumping up suddenly. The Waterford chandelier prisms tinkled merrily.

"To spring and to death," Tom announced rapturously. "We're making progress, Les. In fifty years there won't *be* any white people!"

"There'll always be white people," I told him.

Tom Lacy was a stunned Negro man. He seemed to age again. "You really think so?"

"Yes, Tom. They'll be having babies, you know."

"I always keep forgetting that," Tom said.

"But they'll be a minority by then," I assured him.

"Oh, that'll be the day," Tom Lacy cried. "I come from a long line of human beings, too. My people was Watusi. Cattle barons. I'm seven feet tall in my stocking feet, as you well know. Your folks never talked much about family background. Do you know where your folks came from?"

I polished off my drink and shook my head. "I don't know exactly. I don't know much about my family tree. Although I've heard we're descended from the Queen of Sheba, Marco Polo, and Pope Paul the Fifth."

"That's mighty impressive. Funny I never heard your ma and pa mention that, or any of your other relatives."

"We're very modest."

"If I were you, I wouldn't worry," Tom told me. "Family trees don't mean much these days."

"I'm sure happy to hear that."

Rocking, Tom looked as warm and shrewd as Harry Golden. "Yes. We're making progress. Finally things are looking up."

"You're right," I said. "Now the Puerto Ricans are getting shit from the fan."

Tom Lacy had a faraway look in his eyes, and they were misty. "No. It won't be long now."

A tugboat droned on the East River. I don't know why, but I suddenly thought of Abe Lincoln, and Thomas Jefferson too, and all the people who had made me believe in them. I leaned forward in my chair, dead serious, and listened to my godfather's wisdom.

My godfather shook his weary head. "Lord. I can hardly wait to act like a natural man. I've had to Tom so much that it's hard for me to knock it off. I even shuffle and keep my eyes on the floor when I'm talking to my own wife."

"I know what you mean. When I'm in a restaurant and leave a tip, I feel as if I'd committed a sin."

"That's a fact," Tom agreed. "It's like giving myself a tip somehow."

"By the way, godfather. Could you let me hold fifty?"

"What?"

"Fifty dollars."

"I ain't got no money," my godfather whined. "It takes every cent I get for those charts. I have to subscribe to every daily and weekly newspaper in the country."

"Have I ever failed to come through? Who went downtown with his little red wagon and got all those old newspapers when you were in bed with the flu last winter?"

"What you need it for?"

"Haven't I got to eat in all those segregated restaurants?"

"You're right," Tom Lacy agreed, reaching for his wallet. "Are you sure fifty will be enough?"

Strutting down Sutton, I perhaps looked like a happy citizen of Manhattan but my real roots were deep in the countryside that had produced people like my dead parents and, yes, Tom Lacy. One day, one fine day, Tom and Aunt Bessie would be proud of me.

"I'll shake up this town if it's the last thing I do," I vowed to the sky, serene and gray, watching a train of pigeons wing down on the balcony of an apartment building. Their drippings looked like some rare melting metal.

The wind was receding. I walked over to the parklike promenade of Sutton Place South. Freshly planted trees (each tree discreetly sporting a name tag) lined the promenade. I glanced at the expensive trees and then looked down at the sewer waters of the East River.

Lester Jefferson was at peace with himself.

Hadn't I been trying since day before yesterday? Goodness. Plotting and thinking, plotting and thinking. And hadn't every happening bounced right back in my face? Ding-dong-doom.

There had been one moment: The Deb. She had made me feel warm, alive, ambitious. She had taken a piece of my heart without knowing it. With the crisp fifty neatly stashed in my jacket pocket, I knew what I wanted most was to see her.

"Mister," I heard a voice behind me call.

I turned and saw an apathetic-looking middle-aged Negro, a man.

"Could you spare a cigarette, Mister?"

"What are you doing over here?" I said severely. "Don't you know beggars aren't allowed over here?"

"I ain't no beggar," the man said. "I'm a runaway slave."

"Don't give me that shit. You half-assed con man. Slavery was outlawed years ago. Centuries ago."

"You're wrong," the man said in a quiet voice. He unbuttoned his tattered trousers. "Look at this if you don't believe me."

Around the man's waist was a flexible chastity belt at least ten inches wide. Engraved letters on the belt read: "I paid good money for this sturdy black man. He belongs to me and not to God."

"No," I screamed and started running.

"Wait," the slave cried.

Frightened, I halted at the promenade's entrance. A bronze plaque marked the entrance:

Life is worthwhile, for it is full of dreams and peace, gentleness and ecstasy, and faith that burns like a clear white flame on a grim dark altar.

I got the fifty from my suit-coat pocket and gave it to the man—not because I was frightened or generous or worried about sleepless nights—I gave the man the fifty because he *looked* like a slave. I knew he was a slave. I have a genius for detecting slaves.

"Thank you and may God bless you," the slave said.

"You'd better get something to eat and a room," I said.

Then I turned off Sutton Place South and walked up 54th Street and up First Avenue toward home, toward Harlem.

T E N

It was Saturday night. The sky was starscaped, and homespun rib-tickling brotherly love had settled over the city. You felt it even at the frontier gate, above 96th Street, leading to the Badlands of Harlem. The air was different too, with a strange smell rather like mildewed bread. And I, too, managed to be happy (courtesy of Mr. Fishback's Christmas gift): at the end of the evening, The Deb had come home with me.

Now while Saturday night turned into cold Sunday, I copulated like crazy. My groin ached.

"You're too much," I said.

"Whee!" The Deb somersaulted and wiggled her toes. "You've made me extremely happy, Mr. Jefferson."

"Do Debs really like that?"

The gyrating Deb moaned.

I wiped my forehead, watching The Deb's rhythmic buttocks. "Wanna be a slave, baby?"

"Yes. Come on, lover. It really moves me."

"Take it easy, little woman."

"Please. It drives me out of my gardenia-picking mind."

"I've had enough," I sighed.

"Don't you wanna make me happy?"

"Yes," I said slowly, trying to play a cool hand.

"Ain't I been good to you?"

"Yes," I admitted, feeling clammy, feeling that I was playing a losing hand.

"Then move me, sweetie," The Deb teased. "I ain't dead. I can be moved."

"No," I said firmly.

The lyrically pretty Deb pouted. "Finky-foo. I'm just beginning to enjoy myself and you treat me like this. I can't help it 'cause I got kinky hair."

"Your hair has nothing to do with it."

"Yes, it does," The Deb cried. "You foreigners're always hot after us colored girls and then you throw shit into the game. Why don't you go to Africa and get the real thing? And as far as I'm concerned you can take your fine fine self right back across the sea."

For one quick, insane moment, I cursed the miracle sitting on top of my King James-shaped head.

The bitch. To hell with her. Tawny tiger smasher. I'd be as cool as Casanova.

Frowning, I jabbed a cigarette into the corner of my sensual thick lips.

"It's all the same to me, cupcake."

Stretching languidly, The Deb said, "Why do you treat me like this? I know you're kind and gentle. I can tell by your eyes. You look like one of those saint types I read about in grade school."

Clever, a cornucopia of cleverness. Supple, sweet. A young luxurious mountain.

I stalked over to the sofa bed. "Kiss me, baby," I said, the cigarette dangling out of the corners of my mouth.

"No."

"Broads," I spat.

"I'm like any girl. I like to be pleased."

I wanted to cry out against my own helplessness. "But, baby," I tried to explain, "didn't I show you a good time? Weren't you pampered all through dinner by the plus-ultra service way up on the sixty-fifth floor of the glittery Rainbow Room? And what about the fizzy discothèque . . . where we were mobbed by all those frug people who thought we were Egyptians, and later we breezed uptown in a Duesenberg from Buckingham livery. Jesus, woman."

"That's all very true," The Deb said, "but you didn't give me any money to get my hair fixed."

"Tomorrow, love. You'd only get it messed up in bed."

"You don't want me to have my hair fixed," The Deb protested.

"That's no way to talk. Tomorrow, love. Tomorrow I'll see personally that you get the works at Helena Rubinstein."

The Deb sulked. Her body was rigid on the sofa bed. "You foreigners are just like white people. You don't like to see Negroes with good hair. You're not just satisfied with getting your rocks off . . . you like to get an extra kick. By running your hand through kinky hair!"

"You don't understand," I said weakly.

"Oh, but I do! I got your number, sweetcakes."

"But you've got such wonderful hair. So natural. You want to be different, don't you?"

"I am different," The Deb informed me.

"Not if you have curly hair like me."

The Deb looked hard at me. "When I get my hair fixed tomorrow I will be like you. Almost, anyway. And pretty soon us colored people will be as white as Americans. They gonna make some pills that will turn you white overnight. Won't that be a bitch? *Everybody* will be up shit's creek then."

"You'll take all the excitement and drama out of being Negro," I laughed.

"Have you ever wanted to be a Negro? I'm not talking about daydreaming of being a Negro. I mean, have you really considered it?"

"No. I'm afraid not."

"Then why have you got that suntan?" The Deb asked.

"I suppose for the same reason that you want curly hair."

"According to the Bill of Rights, which I read in grade school, being black is a sin in this country. But I never heard of curly hair being a sin."

"You're right," I said. "Now come on and give daddy a kiss."

"You know what you can do for me."

"Are you gonna be discriminating, after all I've done for you?"

"I hadn't thought of that. I simply said no."

"You're a strange girl."

"You're pretty funny yourself," The Deb glared.

Feeling an acute sense of shame, I knelt reverently beside the sofa bed. "I'm sorry, love."

"You don't love me," The Deb pouted.

"Why do you wanna act this way?"

"You know why."

"Does that really move you?"

The Deb grazed a smooth, fine brown leg against my cheek. "Pretty please."

I thought I'd die. Racked with desire, I buried my head against the side of the sofa bed.

Lightly, with the most feminine of touches, The Deb caressed The Wig.

I stiffened. Buckets of anger clogged my blood. A rebellious rage engulfed me.

"If you touch my head . . ." I warned.

"Well. I do declare. If that's the way you feel."

"I'm sorry," I cried, biting my tongue, giving my hot hands orders to patrol The Deb's body.

Her flesh was warm. "Delicious," my hands radioed to my brain, and then returned to their reconnaissance patrol.

"I'll do anything for you, cupcake."

"Then do it."

I stood up. "You like it, don't you?"

"It sends me clear out of this world."

"You're just like a junkie," I teased. "Ordinary please doesn't move you."

I looked down at The Deb's face warped with pain. She closed her eyes and moaned. "Stop it! Stop torturing me. I can't stand it. Play the goddam record."

I went quickly over to the record player and put on "Rocking With It."

"Oh. You're so good to me. Come here, lover. I wanna give you the kiss-kiss of the year."

But I had to make a quick run to the bathroom, and when I returned, "Rocking With It" was almost over.

I went straight to the sofa bed. Driven by passion such as I had never known, I tried to ram my tongue down The Deb's throat.

She squirmed under my power and I understood the lust of the conquistadors.

"Daddy," she begged, "turn on the other side of 'Rocking With It.'"

"In a minute, cupcake."

"I'm gonna scream!"

"Scream," I laughed. "Scream your fucking head off. I've got you covered."

E L E V E N

MORNING CAME as I knew it would: gray with rain. Cooing
pigeons and doves. The smell of bacon grease and burnt toast and
powerful black Negro coffee, spiced with potents which would
enable you to face The White Man come Monday morning. The
sound of Mrs. Tucker's Carolina litany could be heard through the
wall. A typical Sunday morning.

Grateful, I reached up and touched something unfamiliar: The
Wig, silky and very much together. Then I began to doze, until I
felt The Deb's lips against my neck.

"Les, honey," she yawned. "Be a good boy. Don't be a finky-
foo."

"No," I mumbled. "Not the first goddam thing in the morning."

"I hate you!"

"Go back to sleep. It's early."

"Oh. You'll be sorry."

"Knock it off, cupcake."

"I hate you!"

I had to quiet the bitch. So I pinched one buttock and commanded: "Sleep or else I knock you out of bed."

"No, you won't," The Deb sneered. "I'm getting up. I'm cutting out. 'Go back to sleep, cupcake,'" The Deb mimicked.

She was up now, prowling around the room like an early-morning hag.

"Oh, you're one labrador retriever in the bed," she said angrily. "But ask a simple favor like turning on the record player for a little good music, and . . . finky-foo."

I covered my head with the sheet and presently there was no longer the lazy beat of raindrops, or the cooing of pigeons and doves.

Early morning had exploded. The Deb had "Rocking With It" on real loud.

Bolting up in bed, I shouted: "Are you satisfied?"

"Yes, thank you."

I watched her dress, each deft movement timed to the rocking music. I felt forlorn, for there is nothing worse than a lovers' quarrel on a rainy Sunday morning. I wanted to jump out of bed and hug and kiss The Deb and say: "Baby, if that's what you wanna hear, it's all right with me."

No, I'd hold out. After all, I was Bewigged and possessed a great future, that no one could deny.

"So you're cutting out," I said.

"Indeed."

Dammit! If I had had my own natural kinky hair, "my thorny crown" (a most powerful weapon, I suddenly realized), The Deb wouldn't be switching her tail around, acting so high and mighty. She would have known by the texture of my hair that I was a mean son of a bitch. I'd have made her eat dirt.

She stood in the center of the room giving me the evil eye with her legs spread apart like those butch fruit cowboys on television and tore the wrapper from a stick of chewing gum and threw it on the floor.

"I'm cutting, shithead," The Deb said. "When you get some loot, and that means money, drop around. I sorta like you, I do." And she left, giving the door a good bang.

I lay on that cold bed, twisting, turning. I wanted to go out and strangle every last one of those pigeons and doves in the name of love and then cook them for dinner. Suffering, I didn't feel romantic or noble about letting The Deb walk out on me. Why couldn't I have found a chick who was strictly a Wig lover? No, I like drama. I had to be someone else. I had such a celestial picture of being someone else, and a part of the picture was that my luck would change. But had it? No, life still seemed to have me by the balls, stuffing poison enemas up my ass.

"Oh, well, tomorrow's Monday," I said aloud to the cockroaches on the ceiling pipes.

Then, like the first trumpet of morning, piercingly alive, like the cello of death, Nonnie Swift screamed.

"No," I sighed. In a gesture of rejection, I crossed my hands over my penis.

"Help," Nonnie cried. "I mean it this time."

"That's what the would-be suicide said when he slipped accidently off the bridge," I thought happily.

"Help! Help!"

The voice was coming closer. A mad bat with a human voice was running amok in the hall.

A rattling rap on the door.

"Les!"

I felt as if the skin were peeling off my face.

"Do you want me to break the door down?" Nonnie shouted. "I know you're in there. I always thought you were a gentleman like those cotton planters who used to court me down in New Orleans. I never thought you'd let the rats eat me up!"

I wanna tell you: pins and needles pricked my body. Rising slowly to a lotus position, I felt the glow from The Wig. My Imperial lips quivered. Tremors shook my brain. Starry brain pellets finally exploded.

Rats. *Rats!* The Magic Word.

I jumped out of bed, slid into my pants, ran to the closet, and grabbed my spear gun.

Barechested, barefooted, I was sort of an urban Tarzan, a knight without a charger.

"Where are the rats?" I shouted, storming out the door.

"My hero," Nonnie sang. Her face set like stone. "They're in my room. Where the hell do you think they're at?"

"Lead the way, woman."

"Follow me," Nonnie said.

And I followed, hot with excitement, clutching my spear gun, ready for the kill. One hundred rat skins would make a fine fur coat for The Deb.

TWELVE

ONE MAGNIFICENT RAT, premium blue-gray, and at least twenty-five inches long, walked boldly into the center of Nonnie Swift's cluttered living room, its near-metallic claws making a kind of snare drum beat on the parquet floor.

"I started to call the ASPCA," Nonnie whispered.

"I'll handle this mother," I said.

"Please be careful."

"Sure thing." An old proverb crossed my mind: Bravery is a luxury; avoid it at all cost. "Take the gun," I said to Nonnie.

"Oh! Les . . ."

"Take it."

A terrified Nonnie reached for the spear gun. "I'm praying as fast as I can, Lester Jefferson."

"This is gonna be child's play," I said. "Hell. I thought he'd come on like a tiger," and just then, before I could get into a quarterback position, the rat bit my left big toe.

"The sneaky son of a bitch," I yelled, hopping on one foot.

"Are you wounded?" Nonnie cried.

"No. I got tough feet."

The rat moved back. He had a meek Quaker expression and the largest yellow-green eyes I've ever seen on a rat.

"He's the lily of the valley," Nonnie said, foolishly, I thought.

"Shut up," I warned and knelt down and held out my hand. "Here, rattie, rattie," I crooned. "Come here, you sweet little bastard. Let's be pals."

"Call him Rasputin. They love that," Nonnie advised.

"Rasputin, baby. Don't be shy. Let's be pals, Rasputin."

Rasputin lowered his head and inched forward slowly.

"That's a good boy, Rasputin," I said.

And the little bugger grazed my hand lovingly. Rasputin's fake chinchilla fur was warm, soft.

"That's a good little fellow," I smiled sweetly and clamped my hands so hard around Rasputin's throat that his yellow-green eyes popped out and rolled across the parquet like dice.

"Oh, my gracious," Nonnie exclaimed. "You killed him with your bare hands. Oh, my gracious!"

"It was a fair fight."

"Yes, it was, Lester Jefferson. You killed the white bastard with your hands."

"Yeah. He's a dead *gray* son of a bitch," I said happily.

"He's a dead *white* son of a bitch," Nonnie insisted. "White folks call you people coons, but never rat, 'cause that's *them*."

"I didn't know that."

"It's a fact. I should know. They got plenty of rats in New Orleans. But none in the Garden District, where I was born."

"Well, well," I said. "You never get too old to learn." Seizing my rusty Boy Scout knife from my patched hip pocket, I began skinning Rasputin I. "Do you think the others will be afraid to come out because they smell the odor of death?" I said.

A delighted cackle from Miss Swift. She lifted her skirt and displayed rosy, well-turned knees. "Let'm come. You can handle'm."

"You're right for once."

Nonnie walked over to me, like a fifty-year-old cheerleader. She touched my shoulder lightly. "Your true glory has flowered," she said. "Samson had his hair and, by god! you got your Wig."

Modesty forbade me to answer Miss Swift, but her voice rang sweetly in my ears. I would have kissed her, except my hands were soaked with blood.

"Are you ready, warrior?"

"At your service, Ma'am."

"That's the spirit," Nonnie said. "I'll get the coal shovel and bang against the wall. Then I'll close my eyes. I don't want my baby to be born with the sign of a rat on him."

Waiting for Nonnie's overture, I stood up and stretched. The blood had caked on my hands, making them itchy.

"This is gonna be more fun than a parade," Nonnie said. She spat on the coal shovel for luck.

"I'm ready when you are," I said, bracing my shoulders and sucking in my belly.

"Here we go," Nonnie cried, and banged the shovel against the wall three sharp whacks.

Lord! Eight rats bred from the best American bloodlines (and one queer little mouse) jumped from holes in the *chinoiserie* panels. Nonnie had her eyes tight shut and was humming "Reach Out for Me." Or were the rats humming? I couldn't quite tell.

Fearless, I didn't move an inch. Images of heroes marched through my Wigged head. I would hold the line. I would prove that America was still a land of heroes.

Widespread strong hands on taut hips, fuming, ready for action—I stomped my feet angrily. If I'd had a cape, I'd have waved it.

The rats advanced with ferocious cunning.

Perhaps for half a second, I trembled—slightly.

With heavy heart and nothing else, Nonnie Swift prayed. Through the thin wall, I heard Mrs. Tucker wheeze a doubtful, "Amen."

Then, suddenly feeling a more than human strength (every muscle in my body rippled), I shouted, "All right, ya dirty rats!"

My voice shook the room. Nonnie moaned, "Mercy on us." I could hear Mrs. Tucker's harvest hands applauding on the other side of the wall. The rats had stopped humming but continued to advance.

And I went to meet them, quiet as Seconal (this was not the moment for histrionics)—it would have been foolhardy of me to croon, "Rasputin, old buddy."

Arms outstretched, the latest thing in human crosses, I tilted my chin, lifted my left leg, and paused.

They came on at a slow pace, counting time. The mouse shrewdly remained near the wastebasket, just under the lavabo.

"Yes!" Nonnie cried out.

I didn't answer. The rats had halted, a squad in V-formation. Connoisseurs of choice morsels—of babies' satin cheeks, sucking thumbs, and tender colored buttocks—they neared the front for action.

"Come a little closer," I sneered.

"Oh, oh," Nonnie cried. "I can't wait to tell *him* about this moment! I am a *witness* of the principality!"

She was obviously nearly out of her mind, so I said only, "Patience, woman."

"Yes, my dear. But do hurry. He's beginning to kick. We're both excited."

I stood my ground. The rats seemed to be frozen in position, except for one glassy-eyed bastard, third from the end.

He broke ranks and came to meet me.

I flung my Dizzy Dean arms, made an effortless Jesse Owens leap, lunged like Johnny Unitas, and with my cleat-hard big toe kicked the rat clear across the room. He landed on Nonnie's caved-in sofa.

But I'll hand it to the others: they were brave little buggers, brilliantly poised for attack.

Strategy was extremely difficult. I had to map out a fast plan.

"Les, Les . . . are you all right?"

"Yeah," I breathed and started to close up ground.

One rat, a second-stringer, made a leap but I crotched him with my right knee. He nose-dived, his skull going crack on the floor. Another zeroed in on that famed big toe, but I was ready for him too. Kicking wildly—because four were sneaking from the left flank—I could only knock him unconscious.

Now the four and I waltzed. One-two-left. One-two-right. One-two-left, one-two-right. One-two-left, one-tworightone-twoleftonetwo—and then the biggest son of a bitch of all leaped as if he'd had airborne training.

I hunched down fast and he sailed right over my head. I spun around just in time to land a solid right in his submachine gun mouth.

Panting hard, I watched him go down slow, his head bobbing in a kind of ratty frug.

I felt good.

"They at war!" I heard Mrs. Tucker yell. I looked over at Nonnie. She was backed against the door, mesmerized with admiration.

When I turned to face the enemy again, two rats were retreating.

Pursuing as fast as I could, I slipped on the waxed floor and fell smack on the remaining three. But I fell easily and was careful not to damage the fur.

I lay there briefly, rolled over, and scouted for the deserters. Two were making a beeline for the wastebasket, which was brass and steel and filled with empty Fundador bottles.

I was decent. I waited until they thought they were safe, only to discover that they were actually ice-skating on the brandy bottles.

I knelt down and called, "Rasputin, Rasputin." They raised their exquisite heads and I put my hands in the wastebasket, grabbed both by the neck—I squeezed, squeezed until the fur around their neck flattened. It was easy.

"You can open your eyes, Nonnie," I said in a tired voice.

"A Good Man Is Hard to Find," the gal from Storyville sang.

I was tired. I made a V-for-victory sign, winked, and started skinning rats.

Someone knocked at the door.

Nonnie was excited. "Oh, Les. The welcoming committee has formed already!"

"Wanna sub for me, cupcake."

"Delighted."

Another knock. "It's Mrs. Tucker, your next-door neighbor, and I couldn't help but hear what was going on . . ."

"There ain't no action in this joint, bitch," said Nonnie.

"I just wanted to offer my heartfelt congratulations to young Master Jefferson."

"Is that all you wanna offer him?" said Nonnie bitchily.

"Now that's no way to talk, Miss Swift, and you a Southern-bred lady."

"You're licking your old salty gums," Nonnie taunted. "You smell fresh blood. If you're hungry, go back to yo' plantation in Carolina."

"I will in due time, thank you." Mrs. Tucker withdrew in a huff.

"Go! Go!" Nonnie said, and turned abruptly and walked over

to where I sat on the floor. "I guess you know those skins ain't tax-free," she said.

Engrossed in my job and thinking of The Deb, I did not answer.

"I could report you," Nonnie went on. "You don't have a license for rat killing."

"But *you* invited me over. You were afraid they'd kill you!"

"That's beside the point," Nonnie said sharply. "There are laws in this land that have to be obeyed."

"You didn't mention the law when you were trying to break down my door."

"Smart aleck! Ambitious little Romeo. I want a percentage on every perfect skin!"

"But I'm not gonna sell them," I said clearly.

"Listen, conkhead! You'll put nothing over on me."

"Never fear, cupcake."

"You try to outsmart me and I'll see your ass in jail if it's the last thing I do."

I looked up at Nonnie and laughed. Rat killing was a manly sport and there was always the warmth of good sportsmanship after the game. I split open the belly of Rasputin number nine. The rich blood gushed on the parquet and I thought of the long red streamers on a young girl's broad-brimmed summer hat.

"At least you could give me some for broth," Nonnie cried. "Don't be so mean and selfish. I'm only a poor widow and soon there'll be another mouth to feed."

I wasn't really listening to Nonnie; in my mind I saw the tawny face of The Deb, saw her rapture upon receiving the magnificent pelts. We would talk and laugh and later make love. My penis, which I have never measured, flipped snakewise to an honest Negro's estimate of seven and a half inches.

THIRTEEN

THREE HOURS LATER, I found myself with a slightly crushed Christian Dior box, jumping the sidewalk puddles, in which I saw the reflected solidity of Victorian brownstones. Despite the chilly drizzle, children seemed to be enjoying themselves on the fire escapes: laughing, singing, catching raindrops, telling dirty stories.

I walked along, blinking at the reflections in the pools, thinking of the children against the background of the harsh Harlem streets (but magical, all the same, stuffed with riches), and looking up now and then at the wet gray sky, only to be knocked out of my reveries by the sound of music.

It was blues, blues so real the'd make you hollow at five o'clock in the morning, no matter if you were alone or in the arms of your lover. These blues were coming out of a three-for-one bar and grill. I stopped for a moment and listened to Jimmie Witherspoon grind out "See-See Rider" on the jukebox. Through the steamy face of the grill, I saw hands working with the dexterity of an organ grinder, turning banquet-size slabs of barbecue spareribs on a spit. I could smell the spareribs, too. The crawlers in my stomach performed (Mr. Fishback's Credit Card carried no weight in three-for-one bar and grills), so I moved on down the street, past select pawnshops, fourth-hand boutiques, liquor stores. In a doorway, narrow as a telephone directory, I saw a group of young people sitting on the staircase, playing Charlie Mingus music. I didn't stop. Mingus always takes my energy away.

Nor did I stop a little farther on, hearing, from a storefront church, Gospel music. No, I didn't stop. I've been listening to Gospel music as far back as I can remember.

As I went on, I began to hear Spanish music. I was not far from Spanish Harlem, where no rose ever grows, but human and paper roses sometimes blossom in the street. The Deb's flat was here, in Harlem's International Zone.

She lived in a "real co-op," she had told me. The cooperation came from the police department; the commissioner had stationed bluecoats on split six-hour shifts at the entrance. Even so, a "society" murder had been committed in the entrance last Thanksgiving morning.

Walking up the flagstone path of the co-op, I recognized the Sunday afternoon bluecoat. He sported a frozen smile. Rumor said that a few of Harlem's more inventive citizens had (under the personal direction of Mr. Fishback) drained the blood from his body and that now 150-proof gin ran through his veins.

Offering a sunny, arctic smile, bluecoat eyed the Christian Dior box.

"Hi," I said, stepping smartly into the lobby. A hunk of dung-colored plaster fell from the ceiling, which was frosted like a cake, missing my head by inches.

An old stoop-shouldered crone was standing opposite the mailboxes, stuffing beeswax into cracks of the wall.

"Excuse me," I said, "are you the concierge?"

The crone looked up. Her face was buttermilk-yellow and granite-hard. "The who?"

"The super."

"No. I am not the super and I ain't his wife. I just happen to live here."

"I'm sorry. Do you know if The Deb's in?"

The crone seemed interested. "Which one, Sonny?"

"The one on the ninth floor."

"Oh, her. She's in. But I don't know if she's busy or not . . ."

I clicked my heels, walked away, and bounded up the shaky staircase.

The strains of "Muslim Da-Da, Mu-Mu" (the Faust of rock 'n' roll) drifted from The Deb's pad, but nothing could blanket my schoolboy joy as I knocked on the solid door.

The doorknob fell off. Rolled, spun like a top. I watched until it stopped and then turned, certain The Deb would be spying through the peephole.

"Oh. It's you," were her first words when she opened the door. She wore a yellow robe. "Come on in *if* you gonna."

"Thanks," I said nervously.

"You almost missed me. I was just getting ready to go to Radio City Music Hall. In a taxi, so as not to miss the newsreel."

"I thought perhaps we'd go to some quiet bistro . . ."

"You got any money?"

"Why must you *always* think of money?"

The Deb stared at me briefly. "You're a card," she said. "Did you know that?"

"Now, cupcake . . . Look. Here is a little something I thought you might like." I held the box out.

"Oh. A present. What is it . . . no, let me guess. The definite, collected rock 'n' roll records?"

"Guess again."

"It wouldn't be a blond Macy's wig, would it?"

"Women," I sighed. The most fascinating, hypnotic—the strangest creatures on the face of the earth.

"Give it to," The Deb said and lunged at the box.

"Easy, baby," I said, brushing her hand aside. I tossed the Dior box casually on her rumpled bed and sat down on a sick chair which was vomiting straw.

The Deb's hands tore the box open. I yawned.

"Oh! Oh Oh! Oh!"

Hot-eyed, I watched The Deb fling open her yellow robe and press the pelts against her naked body.

"Mr. Jefferson, you are *the* most thoughtful man!"

"Just a little token of my esteem."

The Deb switched over and gave me a wet smacking kiss on the forehead. It was a sugar-daddy kiss, but I was grateful to be in her alluring old-rose presence. Dimpled nipples brushed my chin; the scent of her body was fresh as dew. My hands prepared for travel.

"Now, Mr. Jefferson," The Deb warned.

"*Cup*cake . . ."

"Men," The Deb sneered, breaking away. "You want the world but don't wanna pay the price. You don't know the first thing about gentleness, and I don't care what country you come from."

"Shut your trap," I commanded. A masterly manner just might work.

The Deb veered away from me and then stopped. "*What* did you say?"

"You heard me," I told her and stood up.

"If that's the way you feel," The Deb said, "I'll just play me a little music."

"Don't you touch that goddamn machine!"

"It's mine," The Deb said, "and I meet the landlord coming up the stairs on the first day of each month."

"Don't give me that jazz," I said, and began to sulk.

"Your, your . . . Wig looks very glamorous this afternoon," she said in a let's-make-up tone. "I really mean it. It's so dark and rainy out, it brings kind of a glow into the room."

"To hell with The Wig," I said, not really meaning it, but I was interested in something more than sweet words.

"I love it. Really I do."

Without answering, but thinking clearly, I went up to the tawny smasher and gave a backhanded slap that threw her against the low bed.

"And I thought you came bearing gifts of love," she cried.

"But I did," I said, kneeling down and cradling her tear-stained face in my firm hands, thinking of that old cat Othello. But being only an average young man, living in a terrible age, cuffed by ambition, and now in love—I could only press her against me and hope.

"Les," she said softly.

It was a small triumph, a midget step past the gates of pain.

The Deb had an "important engagement" at eleven and I had to be up early for Monday-morning business, so I left promptly at 9 P.M. Just as I reached my own block, I saw white-uniformed men carrying a covered stretcher. The frame of the stretcher gleamed under the street light.

Nonnie and Miss Sandra Hanover were coming down the stoop. Miss Sandra Hanover was out of costume. She wore blue jeans and a man's raincoat.

"It's old Miz Tucker, Les. Poor old thing passed away about an hour ago."

"Yes," Nonnie said. "Thoughtless bitch. She had to kick off and me in the condition I'm in."

"That's too bad," I said.

"We're going to the funeral home and make arrangements," Miss Hanover said. "She's got no family, so we're shipping her back to her white folks in Carolina."

"Yes," Nonnie said vigorously. "That was her last wish. To have her remains sprinkled on the plantation's blue grass. She'll make excellent fertilizer, I'm sure."

"Where's Mr. Fishback?" I asked.

"Go up and look in your room," Nonnie said. "He stopped by after you so rudely walked out on me this afternoon. I saw you steal that fancy box off the garbage truck."

Fuming, I rushed up the stairs.

Two messages were stuck under my door. One was from Little Jimmie Wishbone and read:

URGENT. Must talk with you. Please call me at this number.

But there was no telephone number on the matchbox cover. I picked up Mr. Fishback's note. It was written on Mr. Fishback's usual fancy paper, a pale gray, with a border of asphodels and black bleeding hearts. It read:

Lester Jefferson, this will come as a surprise STOP I am leaving for the deep-sea diver's club STOP on Eleuthera Island which is in the Bahamas STOP From there I will go by chartered plane to Toledo, Spain STOP Will return in good time STOP

"—F— —," I said. Hump Mr. Fishback. But what did he mean: "Return in good time"?

FOURTEEN

THE FOLLOWING MORNING was, naturally, Monday, warm, windless, with a calendar-blue sky. I was up at the crack of dawn. I shaved, took a bath, borrowed a cup of day-old coffee grounds from Nonnie Swift from which I brewed a fine pot of java. Sitting at the kitchen table over coffee and cigarettes (it pays to rise early: first one in the john, where I found a pack of unopened filter-tip cigarettes), I began reading a small leatherette-bound volume, *The New York Times Directory of Employment Agencies*. "Whatever the job, depend on a private employment agent to help you find it," it said. "You'll find more employment-agency jobs in *The New York Times*"—a statement I was extremely glad to hear, for I was in desperate need of a job.

Before the first cup of java had cooled, I started to read a listing of the employment agencies.

CAREER BLAZERS—FLAME THROWERS & EXTINGUISHERS AGENCY
We Are Looking For Young Men On The Way Up!
We will find you any type of job that can be performed by a human being and not by computers. The fact that it sounds so ridiculous is what makes it so appealing and a step forward! Your very own human future! It wasn't too long ago that the idea of having humans in every major industry was thought to be a little "ridiculous." But now these dreams are realities. We must all look for new worlds to conquer.

Being realistic at heart, we invite you to pay us a call at your convenience. Special service for those on lunch hour or for those waiting on the first major afternoon attraction at a 42nd Street cinema.

RESERVATION AGENCY is proud to announce that it has immediate openings for men and women who want to work as a member of a closely knit research institute, located in Huntsville, Alabama. This is an opportunity to provide support for the U.S. Defense program. Activities involve analysis and evaluations of newly proposed weapons. In addition to a broad background, applicants must be thoroughly experienced or show some interest in the following: Discrimination, Simulation, Motivation, Meeting Head-on Aggressive Personalities.

To Arrange An Interview Kindly Call Our New York Office
RESERVATION AGENCY
—an equal opportunity employer—

BOYS! GIRLS! Take your Pick! Come see us! We never charge! The men who will play an important part in your future pay! We know you are tired of ads that say start in the mailroom or ads that say start selling homemade cookies! Here is a partial listing of our weekly "specials":

GIRLS—No experience if you are alert and looking for a dream future. But you must speak well, like to meet interesting people, and use telephone. Must be able to be accommodating. After a rotating program of three intensive weeks and, qualifying, you will be promoted fast—to men and boys and sporting buyers. Don't be afraid. No real speed. Our clients pay beginners $60, plus fast raises and high bonuses.

BOYS—BOYS—BOYS wanted by large active Queens organization. Attractive. Boys who are interested and willing to deliver and clean. Some weekend work. Routine. Boys must be strong. Willing to work for giants. Vets preferred but not required.

BOYS AND GIRLS! Procurement trainees. $55 as a starter. Seeking specialists. Only high-pressure sales types considered.
BOYS & GIRLS UNLIMITED OPPORTUNITY AGENCY

ART PROMOTION EMPLOYMENT AGENCY
Position available as face retoucher. Requires skill in white and black. Dyeing, bleaching, applying plastic. Light manufacturing. Mostly cold items in all areas. No pre-pack. Frozen over 200 years. Please do not solicit. Our employees know of this ad. They have the incentive to succeed. Bacon is their specialty. Your salary is open.

MISS NATIONAL SECRETARY EMPLOYMENT AGENCY
Famous company is seeking well-bred ladies to screen Ivy League grads. Terrific opty for real pro with understanding. No shorthand required but must be capable of setting up exhibits for out-of-town executives. If you are assigned to diversified secretarial duties—we pay

your medical expenses in confidence. We enjoy our employees and are liberal with them. Good salary plus low-cost lunch.

EXPORT EMPLOYEE SEEKERS

The Opportunity Of The Year!

If you could write your own ticket you'd probably leave out some of the things offered by our client. No children. Multi-million-dollar credit benefits. Tax-free and sugar white. Brains and fortitude—not required. Do you live in a slum area? Do you have the ability to sell? Fantastic response to our Negro sale. Acclaimed by top authorities.

If you think you qualify for this remarkable opportunity, please come to the East Side Air Terminal. Car necessary. Full transportation and monitoring. Paris. San Francisco. Hawaii. Take your pick. Our client asks us for men with vibrations. Men with a desire to succeed before 30! Men who are extremely active in extracurricular activities. Do you have the ability to reach top men and test, gas, debug, and interview? We are seeking safety maintenance men. Civil. Designing. No hand devices. This is a position entailing use of radar—malfunction performances as applied to manned space vehicles. No transients need apply. Our chief will be in New York. Liquidation is necessary.

ACT NOW!

When applying, please bring separation papers.

I closed *The New York Times Directory of Employment Agencies,* although there were still forty-six more pages of listings, lit a cigarette, and leaned back in my chair, thinking. You Are Not Defeated Until You Are Defeated, I thought. You must maintain a Healthy Outlook when seeking a job, I added.

So I threw the employment directory out of the window and made up my mind to see The King of Southern-Fried Chicken. I would become a chicken man. It wasn't work in the real sense of the word. The pay was $90 for five and a half days, plus all the chicken you could eat on your day off. Not many young men lasted long with the Fried Chicken King, but I'd stick it out until I could do better. At least, I consoled myself, the feathers were electrified.

For the truly ambitious, time truly flies. One hour later, I was crawling through the streets of Harlem on my hands and knees, wearing a snow-white, full-feathered chicken costume. The costume was very warm. The feathers were electrified to keep people from trying to pluck them out or kicking the wearer in the tail. So effective was the costume that I didn't even have to stop for traffic signals; traffic screeched to a halt for me. And, as I said, the pay was $90 per week. The Deb and I could have a ball! I planned to eat chicken only on my day off and that was free. I also figured that if I cackled hard and didn't quit, I was bound to get a raise. How many people are willing to crawl on their hands and knees, ten hours a day, five and a half days a week? For me that was not difficult: I was dreaming, not of a white Christmas, I was dreaming of becoming part of The Great Society. So I went through the March streets on my hands and knees and cried:

Cock-a-doodle-doo. Cock-a-doodle-do!
Eat me. Eat me. All over town.
Eat me at the King of
Southern Fried Chicken!

FIFTEEN

I DID NOT LET the first day get me down, although when I got home that night I could still hear the voices of pedestrians ringing in my ears.

"I bet he's tough."

"No, honey. He's a spring chicken if I ever saw one."

"Here chickie-chick!"

"Mama, can we take him home and put him on the roof so the dogs won't get to him?"

"He's white but I bet if you plucked those feathers off of him you'd find out he's black as coal."

"I bet he's the numbers man."

"No, baby. Probably pushing pot."

"You can't fool me. It's the police. I knew they'd crack down on all of these carryings-on. Just think. In broad daylight. On Times Square."

"Bill, he's just what we need for our next party."

"Wish I'd thought of that gimmick."

"I bet a quarter he's deaf and dumb. That ain't him talking. It's a machine inside of him."

"Think he can get us tickets for the ice-hockey game at the Garden?"

"I wouldn't be surprised. People in show biz have all kinds of connections."

"Why don't you ask him?"

"No. We'd have to slip him a fin or he'd be a smart aleck; that is, if the bastard can talk."

"I wonder if he's hot. Do you think he can see?"

"I think he's the one we saw on TV last night. Remember the one that was always clowning? 'You'll see me around town,' he said, and just when he was going to tell us where, that goddam commercial flashed on."

"Jesus! What some people won't do for money."

All in all, it had been a rather interesting day. Things were looking up. My ship was at last docking, and *I* was safely guiding her into port.

Feeling pretty good, around eight o'clock that night I joined the tenants of my building in the backyard. There a mandarin tree had taken root in a compost of garbage which we had been putting there for two years, trying to shame the landlord (we said) into a sense of responsibility.

It was like a holiday, a miracle in our backyard. I joined in the fun until I received a telephone call. Employed, a part of our national economy, I trotted into the building. Wait until Little Jimmie Wishbone hears about me, I thought happily.

But when I picked up the telephone I heard The Deb's voice: "I know what you are—you're a Nigger . . ."

She laughed, but there was no connection between this laughter and the laughter I remembered.

"Those curls are the most beautiful thing I've ever seen, and yes, I'm a businesswoman, but I sorta liked you. You always seemed to be walking a tightrope, smiling to beat the band 'cause you were happy. Talk about the numbers I meet! Baby, you really gave me a jolt. And you know what I'm gonna do now? I'm going out and get my short kinky head tore up. I'm gonna go out and get shot down. Stoned out of my ever-mother-loving head. I'm gonna hit every bar and nightclub in Harlem. And I want you to stand there and *hold that receiver* until you hear the next word from me. Ha! That'll be the day . . ."

I let the receiver drop from my hand, and started for my room.

I'd planned to touch up my hair with Silky Smooth because the hood of the chicken costume had pressed my curls against my skull. But for the moment Silky Smooth had lost its groove.

As I was going up the stairs, stunned and unhappy, I met the perky party girl, Miss Sandra Hanover. A male-femme in sundown antelope costume and matching boots.

"Les," she cried. "I thought I'd have to leave without saying good-bye."

"Leaving?"

"Yes, love. Your mother is going to Europe with the call girl. She just married this millionaire. Just like in the movies, and I'm here to tell you! I'm going along as her personal maid. I'll ride the high seas in full regalia. Talk about impersonation!"

"That's great," I managed to say.

Miss Sandra Hanover gestured, like the great soignée Baker from St. Louis, Mo. "Ain't it? I may even go into show biz in Europe. The truly smart-smart flicks always sport a dark face these days."

Ordinarily, the word "impersonation" would have interested me, would set me to thinking. But the only thought it brought me now was that my own impersonation had caused the death of a bright dream.

Finally, I managed to say, "That's great, doll. When you leaving?"

"Wednesday. At the stroke of midnight."

"Well, I'll see you later. I've gotta go to Madam X's."

"Madam X!" Miss Sandra Hanover exclaimed. "You must be off your rocker!"

"No," I said. "I'm not off my rocker. I wanna survive."

Madam X's is located in Harlem's high-rent district, in a real town house fronting the barrier of Morningside Heights and St. Nicholas Avenue. It looked faintly sinister to my eyes, so I stopped and hesitated. Quiet as a bird-watcher, I read the neat hand-painted black-and-gold sign:

WANT TO KICK THE LOVE HABIT?
Madam X guarantees that you will never fall in love again.
Low down payment. Easy terms can be arranged.
Open as long as there is love in this world.

Bleeding emotionally from The Deb's bullets, I wiped one long, slow tear from my left cheek, and I'm not a weeper. But something like dry ice had coated my heart. Was I brave enough to blot her out of my mind and life? Before I might decide I was not, I bounded up the stoop, went in through the marble arch (there was no door), and found myself in Madam X's presence. And it was as if we had known each other all our lives, as if we were mother and son.

Madam X was a very dark woman of undefinable age with a gentle clown's mask of a face. She wore a black, hooded cape which reached the floor, yet it did not seem to catch lint or dust. She proposed tea and I accepted.

"One or two lumps?" said Madam X.

"One lump, please."

"Lemon?"

"No, thank you. Lemon seems so artificial."

"That's what I've always said. I'm a very Oriental tea drinker. Adding lemon to tea defiles it, you might say."

"That's a fact, Madam."

"I thought you looked like a well-bred young man who'd appreciate the better things. The *true* things of life."

"Thank you, Madam X. You are the first lady of the land."

"Thank you, son. Ah, you're a lad after my heart."

"Your teapot *is* something!"

"Isn't it though? Faïence, from the Mediterranean. I always say, nothing is too good for my tea. Sometimes I use a brass pot, even a plain earthenware pot. It depends on my mood, the situation, you know."

"Oh. Yes, indeed."

"The tea ceremony is practically a lost art in the Western world."

"I understand it's dying in Boston. No one really observes the ritual."

"Pity. But I understand the Russians are quite fond of tea. I imagine it's sort of a crude affair, though."

Gingerly, I took a sip of tea. "This is great. The absolute end. Real boss."

"I'm glad you like it," Madam X smiled. "Horrid, horrid world. Everyone clamoring for cocktails. I suppose they drink themselves to death because they know they're hellbound."

She paused and said, "Do you feel it, son?"

I gulped tea and belched.

"Do you feel it, son?"

"It's a mother-grabber."

"You're much too kind."

"I wouldn't lie."

"I always try to brew the finest."

"What's the brand?" I asked.

"Brazilian marijuana," Madam X said grandly.

"It's too much, baby."

Laughing softly, Madam X said, "A lad after my own heart. But I've made a recent discovery. The state of Virginia, famed as it is for its tobacco, also grows the most wonderful marijuana. But please don't breathe it to a soul."

"On my word of honor."

"I understand Mr. Fishback is sponsoring you."

"Yes, and he's something else, too. He's in Europe now. Spain."

"Mr. Fishback is a very important man. But I don't quite cotton to his taste for deceased females. I might add, however, that we all have our own taste."

"That's true. I once collected stamps."

Madam X laughed merrily. "The things we think we want to be! I wanted to be the mad bomber, and then a city planner and an architect, so I could redesign Manhattan and make it beautiful and efficient. But that was before I became a saint."

"Manhattan is going to the dogs," I said. "I'm gonna move to Jersey."

Ignoring this statement, Madam X said, "Would you like another cup of tea, Lester?"

"In a moment, thank you."

"Yes," Madam X said. "The only way to appreciate marijuana is to brew it. Serve it hot and inhale the fumes, a custom in my family for many years." Pausing and smiling a stoned smile, she said, "Your bill has been taken care of. Mr. Fishback. You're very fortunate."

Fortunate? Suddenly I remembered The Deb. Forgetting myself, I shouted, "Fortunate, my ass! I'm in love and it's driving me crazy."

"Your troubles are over," Madam X said, proper and poised

and very gentry (there was even something bouncy and braying about her voice). "I have *never* failed. I *could* be the most famous woman who ever lived. I prefer *not* to be selfish. Human emotions are my one and only charity. If there wasn't love in this country, just think what would happen to the economy! Now Negroes are dirt poor. They haven't got time to worry about love. After they've received their papers, their Nationalization papers, then it will be time enough for them to think about love. Personally, I think love is ridiculous. A *bourgeois* sin. Something that the devil invented to make mankind *nervous*. The only passion that's worth suffering for is a passion for hard, cold cash."

Gripping my teacup, I leaned forward. Was I hearing right? Was my high wearing off?

"Madam, Madam . . ."

"Yes, Lester?"

"I, I, I . . ."

"Do I shock you?" Madam X asked sweetly. "You have *such* beautiful hair."

"Do you really think so?"

"I do indeed. It's a pity that you will have to get rid of it."

"What do you mean?" I asked. I was unexpectedly angry. I would have taken a swing at the old bat, except that she was a friend of Mr. Fishback's.

"Now, don't raise your voice at me. I am not hard of hearing. In fact, I hear everything. And you just do as I say."

Trembling, I managed to set my teacup down. "That ain't got nothing to do with love. My Wig, I mean, my Wig has nothing to do with it."

"Oh, but it does, lad," Madam X continued in the same sweet voice. "*All* vanity is fear. I bet you can't imagine that I once had hair as lovely as your Wig? Tresses worth a king's ransom, but there're precious few kings these days. Only humble saints, like myself, and Mr. Fishback."

"Your hair was never as beautiful as my Wig," I said boldly. "I don't care what color it was."

Madam X stiffened. She had the look of a Biblical figure. Crossing woodsy hands against her bosom, she smiled. The terrifying, disconcerting eyes were closed: Madam X had the innocent smile of a seven-year-old girl.

"You are the road to self-destruction," she chanted. "All is not lost, though. You may find the way, *despite* The Wig!"

I was really angry now. It was taking all my family training and self-control to remain calm.

"Don't try to put the bad mouth on me, old woman!"

"Never," Madam X intoned. She stood straight and tall. Then, with a great birdlike swoop, she sank to the floor.

Her head was bowed as if in prayer. The hood of her cape slid off, and her perfectly shaped bald head revealed one magnificent twelve-inch-long whorl of *golden* hair. It made me shiver.

"I'll see you later, Madam," I said.

"No, you won't see me," Madam X warned, without looking up. "You'll see the *portrait* of Lester Jefferson, and he'll be *without* The Wig."

3

....

". . .and one fine morning."

—SCOTT FITZGERALD

SIXTEEN

IT WAS NOW morning all over America. It was also morning in Harlem. The first of April in the year of my National Life Derby, there was a doubtful sky, laced with soft white clouds. And although it was not the day of reckoning, my Dutch-almond eyes were open at 7:30 A.M., E.S.T.

My, how the chicken days were flying! Three weeks of crawling around town on my hands and knees had made me a minor celebrity. Still, I didn't like some of the things the people said about me. My true i-dent was a guarded secret. I refused to appear on television (I was afraid The Deb might be watching). I was hopeful of a reconciliation, although, according to the gossip columns, she had become Café Society's darling. When she had gone out to get her "head tore up," she had evidently done it in the best places, I reflected sourly.

Harlem's new beauty is the girl with the short natural hair. She has fabulous style; she has never needed beads and bangles like some Cleopatra types, and she never will—Dorothy Kilgallen

Short-haired smasher making Broadway scene is The Deb. A swinging African princess incognito.—Walter Winchell

Everyone wants The Chicken cackling about town but he belongs to The

King of Southern-Fried Chicken. Last night a well-known television star was heard saying: He must be a fallen angel. He seems so lonely.
—Dorothy Kilgallen
    Gothamville's latest cackle and delight is from The Southern-Fried Chicken. —Walter Winchell

All that stuff in the papers and no one knew who I was. Impersonating a chicken, cackling, I was alone. I'd go on living by myself in my small airless room. I'd continue to be a trapped person, and if I ever got to heaven, I'd ask God one question: "Why?"

Meanwhile, I'd extol the delights of Southern-fried chicken. But not today; today, thank God, was my day off. I got out of bed and went slowly to the hall bathroom to prepare for a fiesta, a ball, a non-feathered swinging day.

Lord, Lord! Should I get down on my knees and pray, or kill myself? Was it a miraculous dividend, or another smart son-of-a-bitching trick of the white people, or Madam X or Mr. Fishback or Nonnie Swift and her Creole magic? All I'd done last night was touch up The Wig with a tablespoon of Silky Smooth and a teacup of lukewarm water. Then I'd masturbated and gone promptly to sleep. And the sons-a-bitching chemicals in the pomade had cooked, baked. The Wig gleamed, a burnished red gold, more fabulous than ever.

At least I was the first. But soon there'd be millions of red-headed Negroes. I'd start a new chapter in American Negro history.

Would *Time* magazine review this phenomenon under Medicine, Milestones, The Nation, Art, Show Business, or U. S. Business? Would the children of red-headed Silky Smooth parents have red- or kinky- or mixed-colored hair? Mixed, maybe, like a Yorkshire terrier? Would there be a new type of American Negro? Red-headed American Negroes, a minority within a minority? An off-color elite? And would that be a good thing? Maybe not. There'd be some Negroes (and *other* racially sick people) who'd be ready to beat the living hell out of red-headed Negroes just because they were not like other Negroes. One couldn't accuse red-headed Negroes of going white, or could one? Would white people hate or love red-headed Negroes more than they loved or hated other Negroes? Would white people find red-headed Negroes sexually attractive?

All these questions were pouring in on me. "Mother of God," I cried helplessly, gripping the edge of the washbasin with all my strength. No good. I made a mad leap over to the john just in time.

As the tensions left my naked body, exhaustion set in. I was in no condition to deal with the possible problems of my Wig. I listlessly heard the sweet cries of children in the hall, pleading not to be sent to school (an imposing red-brick structure that had split in half for some strange reason the week before, killing twenty children, all under the age of twelve). Nonnie Swift had cackled happily about it ever since. Her son, she said, would be tutored at home.

A New York mockingbird chirped in the mandarin tree.

I went back to my room but I couldn't stay there. I had to get out. Out and walk, walk and try not to think. I wanted to scream to anyone, to the sky: "But I didn't mean anything! All I wanted was to be happy. I didn't know to want to be happy was a crime, a *sin*. I thought sin was something you bought for ten dollars a major ounce and five dollars a minor ounce, both qualities highly recommended, and each wrapped in plain brown paper. I never bought any—not because I couldn't afford it. I just took pot for a dollar a stick . . ."

But why go on? Why try to explain? Was there anyone to hear me?

I dressed hurriedly and, magnificently Bewigged, went out, locked the door, and walked slowly down the steps, thankful that Nonnie Swift was not about.

Half of a neatly folded telegram stuck out of my mailbox. Filled with apprehension, I ripped the telegram open. It read:

I bet you can't guess where I am at. I wasn't doing nothing. These colored clubwomen wanted me for a benefit but the white clubwomen said I wasn't college. At least not Ivy and queer. The colored clubwomen agreed. I wished you could have heard the names they called me after the white clubwomen had left. I wasn't doing nothing but walking through the streets looking for my lavender Cadillac number three and the bluecoats arrested me for nothing at all. I only had a quart of Summertime wine and was just drinking. I paid for it, didn't I? So why can't I drink it on the street? So I'm back here. The white devils. I was getting ready to do a profile on TV, too, with Mr. Sunflower Ashley-Smithe. Don't worry none, though. They got a cell ready for you. Next to mine. How long you think the white devils gonna let you go through the streets with your hair looking like that? Why didn't you phone me? I left my number.

Little Mr. Jimmie Wishbone

Despite the springlike air, goose pimples peppered my body. The nut ward at Kings County! Lord—and all I'd wanted was to breathe easier.

I tore up the telegram, threw it into the air like confetti. The sky was clear and blue. A glazed sun highlighted the Harlem skyline. Looking at that skyline, I remembered what Mr. Fishback had once said to me. "Lester Jefferson," Mr. Fishback had said—it was on my sixteenth birthday—"you're almost a man. It's time you learned something. That Harlem skyline is the outline of your life. There is very little to discover by looking at the pavement."

I didn't know what he meant then, and I didn't know now. If I asked him—and I had asked—he'd just say, "You're on your own for now. *My presence won't be required until . . .*"

As if I wasn't aware that he was always, always around, hovering over me. He was a prime mover of people, a black magician. But it was the first of April, and too many things had happened, and Mr. Fishback was in Spain, or somewhere. Perhaps I didn't need him as yet.

I walked over to Lenox and 125th Street, where I joined a group of Black Muslims standing in front of the Theresa Hotel. The Muslims had flutes and flowers and were making joyous sounds. They were hawking chances on a specially built armored tank that was guaranteed to go from New York City to Georgia and back on one gallon of gas. The chances were only twenty-five cents.

"I ain't never going back to Georgia," one man exclaimed. "Why don't you have something that will take me to Biarritz or Cuernavaca? That's more like my speed."

Gradually, the crowd grew bored and drifted away. I moved on down the avenue to where a sneaker-shod young man, pink-jacketed with pink low boy trousers, sold French poodles. "Be like the fashionable common masses," he shrilled in a vaguely cultured voice. "Own a real French poodle sired by Chee of New Jersey and Dame Chowder of Staten Island. Poodles are the latest rage. Everyone has a smart French poodle. Why not you? Poodles should be clipped twice a week. You can use the leftover curls for your own head. The latest word in African hair styles. And these genuine French poodles are only thirty-nine dollars and ninety-nine cents, plus neighborhood, city, county, state, and federal sales tax."

But I needed no poodle curls; I was my own Samson, a Samson with Silky Smooth hair. My true glory had flowered, I thought bitterly, remembering Nonnie Swift's words.

"Poodles, poodles," the sneaker-shod young man called after me, but I crossed the street and went on my way.

"Look at him," a small boy cried, pointing his bony hand at me. "I bet *he* ain't going to school!"

Smiling, I said, "No, Sonny. Not today."

"But *he's* going to school," the boy's mother said to me, doubling a suède-gloved fist and slamming it against the boy's mouth.

"Jesus, he must be a very bad boy," I said.

"He is," the mother said vigorously.

I stared hard at the crying boy. "What did he do?"

"He doesn't want to go to a segregated school. I broke my broom handle on him a few minutes ago. That's what the NAACP and the Mayor and the Holy Peace-Making Brotherhood advised. You wouldn't have a pistol on you, would you?"

"No," I shuddered. A sudden pain hit me so hard that I felt faint.

My throat was dry. "Isn't there some other way you can make the boy understand?"

"No," the mother replied.

"Maaa," the boy moaned. "Please take me to the hospital. I ache all over. I think I'm gonna die, Mama."

"Shut your trap."

Just than a soothsayer wearing a dark policeman's uniform walked up twirling his nightstick.

"What's wrong, lady? Having trouble with your boys?"

"Only the little one," the mother laughed. "He doesn't want to go to a segregated school. I've got to beat some sense into the boy's head if it's the last thing I do."

"Wanna use my nightstick? I'm sorry I don't have my electric cow prod with me because that does the trick every time. That always makes them fall in line."

"Oh, officer," the mother said, "you're so kind and understanding."

"Think nothing of it. Just doing my duty. I've got kids of my own. I certainly wouldn't want them to go to an integrated school."

"Now, wait a minute," I said angrily. "This isn't fair!"

"Buster," the policeman said, "do you want me to knock that grease out of your hair? I'll get you thirty days in the workhouse. You're trying to obstruct justice."

Silently, I watched the mother slam the nightstick against the boy's head. The boy's mouth opened and he fell to the sidewalk. Blood flowed from his nostrils and lips. "Mama," he sighed, and closed his eyes.

"Get up from there, you nasty little thing," the mother cried. "Get up. Do you hear me? Just look at you, and I stayed up half the night getting your clothes clean and white for school."

"I think the boy's dead," I said.

"He ain't dead," the policeman said. "He's just pretending because he doesn't want to go to school."

The mother knelt down and shook the boy and then stood up. "He's dead," she commented in a clear voice. "I could never talk to him."

"It's not your fault," the policeman said. "Kids are getting out of hand these days."

I tottered off, knowing that I couldn't eat any free fried chicken even if it was my day. I hadn't been to a church in a very long time and I thought I might go to one, but then I remembered that all of the churches in Harlem were closed. The Minister's Union had declared April first to be a day of soul-searching, a day devoted to making money, a day of solitude for the ministers whose nerves had failed them.

So I veered on to Eighth Avenue and 116th Street, where all was quiet except for a rumble on the west side of the Avenue. Fourteen shoeshine boys were fighting savagely with a gleaming six-foot Negro man. The shoeshine boys were winning.

One ferocious shiner jumped me. "Are you a shiner?" he asked.

"Not today," I said.

"Where is it at?" the six-foot man asked. "I'll call the police on you little black bastards."

"Call'm," the shoeshine boys chorused. "We ain't done nothing against Lily Law."

"That's right," the ferocious shiner said. "We ain't done nothing. We just invented this dust machine to help our business downtown. The dust shoeshine boy stands on the corner with the machine in a shopping bag from Macy's, rolling his white eyeballs and sucking a slice of candied watermelon. You know. Like he's waiting on his mama. Every time a likely customer walks by, the dust shiner pulls the magic string. By the time the customer reaches the middle of the block he sure need a shine. He our gravy. And now this mother-grabber is gonna call Lily Law. He wants to suck white ass. He ain't thinking 'bout us little black boys."

The gleaming tall man broke away and ran inside a diner. "I'll fix you little devils."

"I'll go inside and see what I can do," I told the shoeshine boys. "Now you boys run like crazy."

I wasn't a hero and I've never aspired to be one (except in a private, loverly sense—ah, The Deb), but I've always, always, tried to help people. It's a kind of perverse hobby with me. Opening the diner door, I offered a diplomatic grin. The gleaming man was on the telephone.

"Mr. Police. This is Jackson Sam Nothingham. Yes, sir. The Black Disaster Diner. What do you mean . . . It's me, Mr. Police. Your sunny-side-up boy. That's right."

The diner owner hadn't noticed me. I eased over and deftly pulled the phone cord from the wall.

"What? I can't hear you. Say something, Mr. Police. I pays my dues . . . And what's more, I takes care of the Captain when he comes around . . ."

"Maybe they hung up on you, Mac," I said.

The bewildered owner swung around. "What you mean, boy? They hung up on me? Wait until the Captain gets a load of this. He knows I sell a little gin and whiskey in coffee cups after hours. All the Mister Polices on this beat says they don't know what they'd do without good old Jackson Sam Nothingham. My good down-home Southern cooking and a nip on a cold rainy day. I'm keeping up the morale of the police force and you try to say they hung up on me?"

"That's the way the cookie crumbles," I philosophized. "It doesn't have to be a Chinese fortune cookie either."

The angry tall man looked hard at The Wig. "You curly-

headed son-of-a-bitch. Git out of here. Git out of the Black Disaster Diner. I am the owner and I refuse to serve you. All you spicks
and niggers are the cause of my troubles."

"If that's the way you feel about it," I said.

"Git out," the tall man shouted. His whole body trembled.
"You people are ruining me. I've been in business twenty years
and the white people have loved me and I've been happy."

He slumped down into a cane-backed chair like a wounded
animal.

If that is how he feels, there's nothing for me to say, I thought,
and, lowering my eyes, I walked briskly out of the Black Disaster
Diner.

Now the sun was behind the clouds; there was the quiet of
mid-morning except for the sound of singing, coming from an
open window.

Singing was another world as far as I was concerned, although
I was capable of producing a rooster's resonant crow. And it felt a
little strange to be walking like a human being on the first of
April. Strutting around Manhattan on my hands and feet was
good exercise, I'd discovered.

By the time I reached Central Park and 96th Street, four Puerto
Ricans stopped me.

"*Español?*"

"No," I laughed, trying to break a gut string. I understood. It
was The Wig. I realized that many Puerto Ricans wanted to lose
their identity. Many of them pretended to be Brazilians. It was not
only safer, it was chic. Puerto Ricans had inherited the dog trough
vacated by the Negroes.

Burnished-red-golden-haired Puerto Ricans were extremely
rare, as were burnished-red-golden-haired Negroes, I sadly
reflected, crossing at 72nd Street and Central Park.

I walked along, magnificently Bewigged, shoulders erect, firm
hands jammed in my blue jeans, jingling nickels and pennies, calm
and a little lonely.

Suddenly I wanted to talk to someone; hoped someone would
say, "Good morning. What lovely weather we're having." "Yes.
Isn't it?" I'd reply. "I think we'll have an early spring." "I hope
so," the other party would say. "Of course, you never can tell."
"That's right," I'd say. Corny human stuff like that.

I was rehearsing the imaginary dialogue when I smiled at a middle-aged woman with a face that looked as if it had stared too long at the walls of too many furnished rooms. The middle-aged woman's tiny pink eyes went from my smiling face to The Wig. She leaned back on the bench, opened her mouth, and shut her eyes tight.

Well, I thought moving on, she is not accustomed to beauty.

An elderly couple were eying me. I heard the man mutter to his wife: "It's all right, Wilma. Times are changing. Remember the first automobile? World War One? We can't escape what we've never dreamed because we've always believed it was impossible. Wilma? Please don't cry. We'll be dying soon. *And then we won't have to look at such sights.*"

He meant me.

The sight went calmly on, smiling at a fat Negro who carried a shopping bag with Silky Smooth printed on the side. The fat Negro woman spat tobacco juice at my shoes, and a blond Alice-in-Wonderland type urinated in a plastic sand bucket and tried to splash me. Her mother applauded.

I was beginning to get a little sore. I felt like saying, "Nothing, nothing—do you hear me—nothing can stop me." Who the hell did they take me for? Was I the young man who had ground three hundred pounds of chopped meat out of the bodies of seventy blind people? Or the young man who had rescued a pregnant mother and her five children from their burning home, and then single-handed built them a ranch house overnight? Was I the champion rod who had respectively screwed wife, husband, mother-in-law, part-time maid, twelve-year-old daughter, fourteen-year-old son, white parrot, and family collie pup?

No! I was the celebrated chicken man, and none of them knew it. Ten hours a day, five and a half days a week, crawling on my hands and knees all over Manhattan. And I'd been a target for such a long time. Five-feet-ten, naked without shoes, normal weight one hundred and forty pounds. Boyish, with a rolling non-nautical gait, my face typically mixed: chamber-pot-simmered American, the result of at least five different pure races copulating in two's and three's like a game of musical chairs.

Following my own shadow, it seemed that I was taking a step in *some* direction and that The Wig was my guide. Progress is our most important product, General Electric says, and I had progressed to the front door of hell when all I had actually been striving for was a quiet purgatory. And I did not find it strange that hell had a soft blue sky, a springlike air, music, dust, laughter, curses.

I only wished I could see a friendly face.

Up ahead I saw a girl wearing what seemed to be a white mink coat. I checked my stride. A trick of nature or a goddam trick of my eyes? I neared the girl. My blood began to percolate. She was different. Blue-black shiny hair. Complexion: light brown, or did it have an Oriental cast, or was it a trick of the light? The girl's dark eyes were heavily lidded. The lips might have belonged to a beautiful woman of any race. But what was her actual nationality? Mulatto? American Indian? East Indian? Italian?—she had a mustache of moisture on her upper lip and I had been schooled in the folklore of Italian women by printed matter. There was a hint of warmth in her marvelous dark eyes; so it was extremely possible that she was a beauty from North Africa. She might even be Jewish, I thought, remembering that beautiful Jewish girl on West 87th Street.

I would die if the girl was simply a dark Gentile.

I was about ten paces from her, when the sun blazed forth. Traffic around the circle was jammed.

The girl said, "I've been waiting for you."

"And I've been waiting too," I found myself saying.

"I've been waiting for someone exactly like you."

"You're beautiful. You don't have to wait for anyone."

The girl smiled warmly. "No. You're wrong," she said. "Are you coming with me?"

I nodded doubtfully but I took the girl's arm. "All right. I'm game. Where are we going?"

"Just keep in step with me. I've been so lonely," she said, "I feel like I'm living in the desert, though actually I'm living in a great city with millions of people."

"I've often felt like a hermit, too," I said. Was this chick stoned? She didn't look it.

"I know. I know. Now it'll be different for us. I've got a lifetime of love to give and I couldn't give it to just anyone. Understand?"

"Yeah," I replied, beginning to relax. Man, The Wig was really working! "I know what you mean."

"Most people are not very nice, are they?"

"No. Most people are not very nice."

Then we were silent. We danced arm in arm across Central Park West and up the five steps of a very respectable brownstone, just as the siren, like a proclamation, announced twelve o'clock.

The girl's two-rooms-and-kitchenette was very clean. There were no cockroaches, rats, mice, no leeches, no tigers.

Softly feminine, the girl said, "Relax, baby."

Then she came over and tried to rip the button-down shirt from my body.

"Take it easy, baby," I said, biting her neck. "We have all the time in the world."

"I know, I know," she said contritely, "but I must have this release."

She elbowed me so hard that I fell backward onto a big brass bed, where she proceeded to remove my loafers, socks, and blue jeans. I wore no shorts because the chicken costume was very warm.

The girl kissed the soles of my feet.

"Come on up here," I said, feeling my kingly juices.

"You have beautiful strong legs."

I kicked her lightly on the chin, she fell back on the floor. I jumped off the bed. Ready, at attention. She whimpered. I mounted her right on the floor. She sighed and patted my forehead. I sighed. Irritable, I also frowned. "Let's cut the James Bond bit. Let's get this show on the road."

The girl sank her teeth into my right shoulder. I slapped her hard and carried her to the bed. She whimpered again. I fell on top of her. Her tongue was busy in my left ear. I whimpered. Her right hand, like a measuring tape, grabbed my penis.

With my right hand I cupped her chin and thrust my tongue into her throat.

The girl squirmed and tickled my ribs.

Lowering her head, I kissed her chin and the oyster opening of her neck where her bone structure *v*'d, until my face slid farther down, and came to rest in the soft luxury of her breast. More delicious than fruit, I thought, teasing the wishbone below her breasts.

Still going down, I stopped at her navel.

She said clearly, "Oh," and rose slowly.

Panting, I shoved her back down on the bed, and with my knees, opened her legs. They opened like a pretty, well-constructed fan, and then closed like a fan, engulfing my back.

"Mercy," I sighed, settling in.

She bit my lower lip but didn't say anything. I did not say anything either. But at the climax, I bit *her* lower lip. Her hands were mad on my back.

Now I was breathing deeply; my eyes kept closing. The girl sighed. Then her sharp teeth nipped my cheek with its day-old beard. Pleased, she went on to discover the delight of my nose, the treasure of my ears, my red but large eyeballs. And then, like one looking for truffles, she buried her face against my flat hairless chest.

"Baby," I whispered.

"Love," she said.

I looked tenderly into her smiling face, planted one resounding kiss on her nose. Then I fell against her, and the last thought I had before dozing off to sleep was, "I wonder what The Deb is doing?"

I was awakened by having my neck kissed.

"I've got love to give," the girl said, digging her fingernails into my backsides.

"Sweetcakes," I sighed, coming to life again.

"I just want to make you happy."

"And I want to make you happy," I said.

"Do you love me a little?"

I was feeling much too good to answer.

The first shadows of evening arrived. There was no moon, I noted through the sheer white curtains. And there were no stars. In the room, there was only the glow of the girl's shining hair and the glow of The Wig.

Silently, she anointed my body with Joy.

Yawning, I said, "I wanna Coke, and put some ice in it."

"Yes, love," she said.

Smiling in the darkness, I put my hands behind my head. I felt good. The frustrations of the day had been spent. The Wig, The Deb, and all those people I had encountered . . .

"Love," the girl called, breaking into my thoughts.

She sat down on the side of the bed and took me in her arms and held the glass of iced Coke as she would for an ill child. With her free hand, she gently stroked my brow.

"I want you to become my lover," she said quietly.

"We've just met," I protested. "We don't even know each other."

"You'll learn to love me. I'm a good woman. I've got money."

I bolted up from the bed. "Where's my jeans? I gotta run, cupcake. Perhaps I'll see you later."

"Please," the girl cried.

"Later," I said softly. I got into my clothes and made it to the door. Just as I shut it behind me, I thought I heard her cry, "I'm going to tell Mr. Fishback on you!"

Midnight found me on the Eighth Avenue A train for Harlem, wearing a pretty flower-printed plastic rainhood I'd luckily snatched up along with my clothes. It was raining out, and otherwise I'd have got The Wig wet. None of the passengers paid me the slightest attention. They had witnessed too many extraordinary happenings on subway trains: such as an old man getting stomped to death by a group of young punks because he didn't have life insurance; or someone getting sick and choking to death. Even statutory rapes had lost their appeal, they'd seen too many of them—so no one was likely to be impressed by a sad-faced, red-eyed young man wearing a plastic rainhood, shivering, biting his fingernails, staring at his reflection in the dirty window of the car.

I began to doze, thinking: when love waxes cold, said Paul in "The Third Coming . . ." then jerked up suddenly as the A train pulled into 125th Street.

I was the only passenger to get off. The platform was deserted. Workmen were spraying the platform with glue. Dazed and a little frightened, I ran up the sticky steps and out into the deserted street and hailed a taxi.

The driver, wearing a gas mask, stuck his head out the window.

"Oh, it's you," said Mr. Fishback, the funeral director. He

removed the gas mask, spat false teeth onto the sidewalk. Then he placed a fresh pair of false teeth in his mouth. "It's this goddam country. It's ruining my health. I can't complain, though. They're dying every second. But there won't be anybody around to beautify me when I kick off. Ain't that a bitch?"

I had a sudden urge to rip the taxi door off. "Why are you driving a Yellow Cab?"

"I was waiting for you, Lester Jefferson," Mr. Fishback said innocently. "Why, they brought this big fat mama in and I didn't even have a chance to bang her. Terrible to see them go into the ground before you get what you want. And I didn't wanna upset you by arriving in my hearse."

"Why should that upset me? I've been riding in your hearse all my life."

For reasons known only to him, Mr. Fishback replaced the gas mask. "When love waxes cold . . ."

"What?" I exclaimed. "You been experimenting again?"

"The Deb," Mr. Fishback began. "She got run over by a school bus this afternoon."

Numbed, I could only stare at Mr. Fishback. I took off the rainhood.

"No," Mr. Fishback said solemnly. "You know she had been taken up by café society and was staying high all the time. You had made her see things she had never seen before. Madame X said she called for an appointment but never showed. Under that tough, tart front, she was a sweet kid. An all-American girl. She left her rock 'n' roll record collection to charity. But I might be able to get you a couple of favorites."

"Mr. Fishback," I said, "it's strange, The Deb is dead but *my* heart's still beating, and I can't cry."

"It happens in all the best families and to the world's greatest lovers."

"Yes, that's true."

"Get in, son," Mr. Fishback said kindly. "Rest assured, The Deb is in the best of hands."

"I know," I said, "but I won't get in, thank you."

"She's a beautiful dead girl."

"Yes. Now please drive slow. I'll walk along beside you. That's the least I can do for her."

"Do you need my gas mask?"

"No."

"It's dangerous."

"I don't care," I said.

Mr. Fishback's mortuary was under the Triboro Bridge, at the edge of the polluted, muddy river. It was a one-story building of solid plate glass, with the roof also of glass, rising up dramatically like the wings of a butterfly. Mr. Fishback parked the taxi (which belonged to his brother-in-law, who was dying, he said) near the bridge and then walked down a lonely garbage-littered slope with me.

Side by side, we walked under a deep gray sky that was just beginning to break with the first light of day. The cool air was refreshing against my feverish face.

Once, for a brief moment, I panicked. "I can't go on."

"Now, son," Mr. Fishback said gently.

"What can I do now?"

"You know what you have to do."

"Yes," I nodded, clutching Mr. Fishback's arm for support.

We entered the glass building and walked like mourners to the direct center of the floor. Marble tiles slid back. Mr. Fishback removed his mask. He had a kind, dark, wrinkled face, the face of a genius, though being modest, he had always considered himself just God.

He escorted me down steps into a room the size of a standard bathroom. The room was mirrored and brightly lit, odorless. There was only a red bat-wing chair.

"I'm glad to get rid of these things," Mr. Fishback said, jerking out his false teeth and spitting blood on the floor. "Everything is so unsanitary!"

I flopped into the bat-wing chair: "The poor Deb!"

"Hush, now. You'll feel better after I cut off The Wig. Then one more act and you'll be happy for the rest of your life. While I was abroad, I kept in touch with Madam X. Remarkable woman."

Mr. Fishback pressed an invisible button in the mirrored wall and out popped a brand-new pair of sheep shears.

I closed my eyes. I felt no emotion. It was over. Everything. Love waxed cold. The Deb—dead.

"Watch out for my ears," I warned. "And hurry up. I'm hungry."

There were tears in Mr. Fishback's eyes as he expertly clipped The Wig in exactly one minute.

"It was so beautiful," he sniffed.

I kicked the magnificent burnished red-golden hair haloed around the wing chair. I smiled at my bald-headed reflection. "It's over. I can always do it again."

"It was so pretty," Mr. Fishback said. "Nobody had hair like that except Madam X, and that was before she became a saint."

"She's a funny woman. She gave me the creeps. I didn't stay for the first session."

"I know," Mr. Fishback said sharply. "Now stand up and take off your clothes."

"Why?"

"Just do as I say."

"You're always experimenting." I laughed weakly, but I stood up and stripped.

Mr. Fishback sighed. "You've lost weight. You look like a corpse. Think of something nasty and get an erection."

"Like what, for example?"

"Anything. Hell. This country is filled with nasty images."

"The Deb and I will never have children. Why are you torturing me!"

"Not so loud," Mr. Fishback said angrily. "Having children is the greatest sin in this country, according to Madam X. After a series of experiments, Madam X has concluded that having children is a *very* great sin. Hate is an evil disease."

"I've got an erection," I said.

"Fine," Mr. Fishback said happily. He pushed another invisible button in the mirrored wall and out popped a red-hot slender steel rod.

With a deadly serious expression on his face, Mr. Fishback jabbed the steel rod into the head of my penis.

He counted to ten and jerked it out.

Sighing hard, he asked, "How do you feel?"

"I'm beginning to feel better already," I said, smiling.

ABSOLUTELY NOTHING TO GET ALARMED ABOUT

....

*In memory of Langston Hughes,
Conrad Knickerbocker,
and Alfred Chester*

I had never before understood what "despair" meant, and I am not sure that I understand now, but I understood that year.

—Joan Didion

Life is worthwhile, for it is full of dreams and peace, gentleness and ecstasy, and faith that burns like a clear white flame on a grim dark altar.

—Nathanael West

IN THE HALF-WORLD of sleep where dreams and consciousness collide, I turned on the narrow, sticky plastic mattress. The brilliant ceiling light seemed to veer toward me. But with less than four hours' sleep, fourteen shots of vodka, six twelve-ounce bottles of beer, two speed pills, one marijuana cigarette—I chuckled in my pale, lemon-colored cubicle. The stone floor had a fresh coat of battleship-gray paint. After less than a week, the old terra-cotta paint was surfacing. The armless bentwood chair functioned as a night table. Narrower than a standard clothes hanger, the wardrobe was doorless. The new opaque window was jammed. Unlike other residents, I never came upon rats or snakes. What unnerved me were the goddamn arrogant cockroaches. Who cared? The cubicle was at least a roof, reasonably clean, reasonably safe and inexpensive, thanks to the charitable foresight of the Salvation Army's Bowery Memorial Hotel.

Now, the 6 A.M. voices of Sallie's men blended; became a litany of fear, frustration. Voices calling for ma, mama, and mother. Pleading: Stop and help—occasionally stamped with the moan of a dying male tiger. These nightmare voices were the twin of the daytime voices. These were weak men who no longer cared. Cheap wine chemicals had damaged their brains. As I listened, fear touched me. Would I become a soldier in their army? *Fool! Get yourself together. You've got to get out of here.*

Then my bowels roared. I bolted toward the bathroom. My timing was perfect. Afterward, pleased as a spoiled fat cat, I stood up and felt faint. Grabbed the door of the toilet booth. Too late, too late. I was falling, slowly, toward the tiled floor. Just another mini-blackout.

My heart was racing. Perspiring, breathing hard, I eased up from the floor.

"You all right?" a voice asked.

"Yeah." I grinned sheepishly.

A tall man with a weathered face like Robert Penn Warren was staring at my naked body.

"I can see your ribs," he said. "You don't eat. Me neither. Here, have a swig."

I took a healthy swig from his bourbon pint, thanked him.

"You better watch it," he warned.

"That's the trouble." I chuckled. "I have been watching it."

Solitary watchman. Lantern held high. Peering out at friends, strangers. Desperately trying to get a reassuring bird's-eye view of America. F. Scott Fitzgerald's sunny philosophy had always appealed to me. I believed in the future of the country. At four-teen, I had written: "I am the future." Twenty-six years later—all I want to do is excrete the past and share with you a few Black Studies.

I felt as if my testicles were packed in a bowl of dry ice. Things beyond my control had rimmed my brain, and it was strange to relax in Brownsville where the death of a boy had forced boys of his own age to riot in his and their name, and I who had been con-templating suicide for five days no longer a boy.

Now in the wake of his death, sporadic action nipped through these fucked-up streets. A new R & B—rage and brutality. Sirens of police cars and sirens of unmarked cars. Smoke drifted from Howard Avenue like the smoke of an autumn bonfire. A tall old woman hobbled down from a stoop, cackling, "I knew it. They is started."

A car pulls over to the curb, and a man says, "I'll let em pass, baby. They got their work cut out for them."

"You're right, brother," I replied. The P.R. bodegas were clos-ing or closed. In fact, P.R.'s were in the act of disappearing, although they crowded their windows, talked, and looked down into the almost deserted arena of the street. No P.R. men were lounging against cars tonight. A few of them sat on stoops or braced themselves against Victorian carved doors.

I had to buy a six-pack in a bar and returned to the flat, popped a few, talked with Tony. TV gave out *Take Her, She's Mine,* while the sound of shots, Molotov cocktails, angry voices drifted across the vacant back lot (filled with about twenty-five inches of rubbish and where at this very moment a slender middle-aged Negro man was studying the lot as if it were a mound of old gravestones) and into the flat's windows.

There was absolutely nothing to get alarmed about. Just another domestic scene in current American life. But they will use more sophisticated methods next summer. The kids will have matured by next summer.

Earlier a group of them had stopped me.

"Have you seen Joe?"

"No, man," I said. "I ain't seen Joe."

A mistaken identity. But I was with them—someone has to be on their side and I cursed their goddamn parents and this goddamn mother-sinking country that has forced them into the act of rioting. In the act of reaching the portals of the seemingly prosperous poor, their parents had lost them just as this country had forgotten the parents.

Certainly I felt these black kids had a legitimate right to break store windows and throw rocks and bottles. Recently, I had worked at a resort where bored, wealthy kids kept the security guard on the go as they ripped lobby sofas and broke into the underground lobby shops between midnight and dawn.

Meanwhile, the black children will continue to riot and die.

M. D. said, "There is a man that I want you to meet." We taxied over to Intermediate School, No. 201, 2005 Madison Avenue, and I met the man. I also saw, for the first time in my life, former Senator Paul H. Douglas of Illinois, chairman of the L.B.J. Commission on Urban Problems, and Senator Robert F. Kennedy and two of his handsome children.

We arrived late, and I could not hear what Senator Kennedy was saying. It did not matter. He seemed likable. And despite the rumor of the ruthless reputation, the cold blue eyes, I could picture him having a pint with the boys at McSorleys Ale House. Discussing politics, history, books, broads. I began to warm up to him and was rather pleased to think: This is our next President, '68 or '72. I might not have felt that way if I had listened to what he was actually saying.

Afterward, the crowd banked around Kennedy as if he were Jesus Christ or the son of Jesus Christ. I had never seen anything like it. Perhaps this was the op real-life version and I failed to realize it.

A few minutes later, the Senator's smiling daughter exited to a Cadillac. Father and son walked toward one of Detroit's modest models.

M. D. and I looked for a taxi. I heard an old black woman say, "Give me some meat. I don't want no bones."

You greedy meat eaters—this is where it is at.

We finished the typing session, rapped boredom out of the Vietnam war, raced minute cars, and had a wild game of cat and mouse around the dining-room table. Now it was almost midnight. An incredible moon outlined rooftops like a romantic proletarian stage set. But the voices of this tough territory were real and violent. Unflowery. Already that restlessness—peculiar to people with a remembrance of Mediterranean nights—had knifed me. Charlie Mingus was on the phonograph, and I went back into the dining room.

Clara Bow curls frame Anne's five-year-old face. "Sorry about that. You'd better buy some Beatles records," she said, her smile as refreshing as a slice of honeydew melon.

I began smoking filtered pot. There was a brief silence. Bruce, who is seven, jabbed me in the ribs. A charming clown of a little man, he neither smokes nor drinks. Surprisingly enough, the boys rarely curse and then mildly, like a tap on the shoulder.

Fire-engine-shirted Mick was drinking canned beer. He is nine years old. "We had to leave our father," he said, gesturing. His mannerisms, voice seem exaggerated. I believe these actions are nothing but excessive air from his vat of violence. "Man! He was stoned all the time and beat our mother."

Mick was interrupted by eight-year-old Ron. "That was in Jersey," he said, and then frowning, snatched the beer from his older brother.

Clasping her hands, Anne said, "I was born in Jersey."

"Shut your trap," Bruce said. "You don't know what you are talking about. You were born in New York. At Beth Israel."

"Charles," Mick said, "Ron and me was born in New Jersey, and the rest of them were born in Beth Israel. We moved after the apartment building caught on fire. There was a deaf-and-dumb boy who was always doing things. One day he set the building on fire and we moved."

"Doing his thing." Bruce laughed, twisting on the bar stool.

"Bruce," Ron warned. "Cool it. He couldn't help it. No one loved him."

"God loved him," Anne said.

"Yes," Ron agreed. "God loves everyone. I've got a picture of him. Do you wanna see it?"

"It's Jesus, stupid," Mick said when Ron returned with a color reproduction and another can of beer.

"Mama's dancing," Ron said.

Then I heard heavy footsteps and lusty masculine voices in the hall, and we all looked at each other.

"I hope she doesn't get drunk," Ron said.

"Man! She's already stoned," Mick told him.

I wanted to hear Bob Dorough sing "Baltimore Oriole" and went into the living room. I heard Bruce whisper, "I'm going over and see what's happening. I'm gonna get some loot."

"Git some for me," Mick told him.

I could see their mother sitting at the chromed table, wearing the perennial purple-splashed muumuu gown. A pleasant, plump woman with a wardrobe of hair pieces, Nellie's teeth look like ancient Spanish gold. A dark-haired young man was behind her chair, tonguing her left ear, his long slender hands racing up and down her bosoms as if trying to determine their length and quality. Between "No, oh no!" Nellie moaned.

Mick eased over and peeped through the crack in the door. Anne was looking, too. Beatle-maned Ron did not get up. Pierced with cut-crystal sensitivity, he sat at the table writing his name over and over again.

"It's time for you to go to bed!" Mick exclaimed, slapping Anne violently. She screamed, her little arms outstretched as if to curtsy.

"Mick," I said. "Watch it."

"It's gittin' late, man."

"Do you wanna go to bed?"

"No. I ain't sleepy."

Now Anne was rolling on the floor, sobbing. Bruce soft-shoed back in. "I got it." He grinned. I helped him count $1.37 worth of silver.

"You have to pay for the party tomorrow," I said.

"What time?" he asked, unable to conceal his delight.

"Late in the afternoon. Root beer, potato chips, and ice cream."

Ron looked up and smiled for the first time. He reminds me of the Mexican-Indian children I saw on the road to Boca del Rio. He is going through a bad time. The girl he likes is no longer allowed to play with him, although she sends him notes by messenger. Ron is a fine looking, healthy eight-year-old. Quiet, well-mannered, he looks like the type of boy you'd want your child to play with.

Nellie called him. He returned with her glazed mug, singing "Georgy Girl," and followed me into the living room.

"Charles. Don't give her too much whiskey. She's drunk."

Ron took the Scotch to his mother, who was pushing a bereted, tall man out the door.

"No," Nellie said. "Get out. You hurt me. You're dirty."

Ron took the mug into their apartment and wouldn't look at his mother. Three-year-old Glen and the two-year-old twins, Mal and Bobbie, followed him to my place. Mal is always without his pants, and his brothers tease him. He shook his thumb of a penis at them. Ron wanted to get Mal a pair of pants. I told him to get some records from the bedroom. I did not want him to see his mother.

The tall dirty man had her nailed against the wall of the hall. Hula-grinding, she had her arms around him.

I closed the door, and Ron announced, "I want some more beer."

"You won't drink my beer," I said.

"I'll git it," Mick said. "Mama lets us drink beer, and it's Saturday night."

The two-year-old twins were boxing when Mick returned.

"Man!" he said. "She's got the lights off."

"Oh God," I silently moaned to the moon. But I knew there were seven children in the room. I would have to make something of the night, regardless of what had happened or would happen.

I lit another filter and announced, "All right. Let's see if you remember how to type your name. Everyone will type except Mick and Ron. They're drinking beer, and I don't want them to spill it on the typewriter."

"Oh man." Mick frowned. Ron took a long sip of beer, ran over, and put it down on the cabinet.

Nellie called me. I went to the door and walked across the hall. The lights were still off. Nellie was naked.

"Here's a present," she said, offering a newspaper-wrapped package, half the size of a bank book. "The kids no trouble?"

"No," I said. "And thanks."

"Mama's naked." Anne giggled.

"Shut up," Bruce screamed, and then all of the brothers ganged up on their sister on the blue-tiled floor.

I pulled them apart and plotted the typing lesson. "All right. Knock it off. Anne is first. Everyone will have a chance to type. The twins will type too."

"Ah man," Mick said. "They're babies. They don't know nothing."

"Charles Wright," the young woman said, smiling. The young woman was a black reporter for a magazine. She was interviewing the writer for the magazine's forthcoming lead story, "The Real Black Experience."

I had had a couple of pills and enough drinks to make me feel warm toward almost anyone I might run into between 5 P.M. and dawn. Certainly I felt very warm toward the lady reporter. We both had, in a limited sense, climbed the black progressive ladder in white America. It was a difficult time for blacks to be truly black in a black reality. It was very easy to get bedecked in an ethnic showcase. But I had been black for a very long time. Before black was beautiful. Marcelled blacks gave me the cold eye ten years ago. I had an uncoiffeured, bushy Afro. I loved blues, collard greens ("pot liquor," as the collard juice was called), ham hocks before they became fashionable. And now I faced the young black reporter with lukewarm charm. I knew the magazine's editor had supplied the questions. I was going to be a gentleman about the whole damned thing.

By the time we reached the Cedar Tavern, despair said, "Good-evening, old sport. It's me."

We ordered vodka martinis. The young woman had dinner. I had more drinks and was prepared for war, while she promised a truce in her Brooklyn Heights apartment. The young woman talked about her Italian holiday. Oh yes, Italian men. I ordered another round of drinks, forced charm. I was almost tempted to tell her about the postal cards of supermammary-blessed Ethiopian women, about Italy's invasion of Ethiopia. With the Pope's blessing, they went to war with dreams of boobs. The young woman had a most respectable pair of mammaries. But I no longer wanted them or her. We had another round of drinks and left the Cedar Tavern. At Thirteenth and University I said, "Wait a minute, cunt. I have to take a piss." I went inside the wide door opening of an antique shop and urinated.

The black female reporter started running toward Fourteenth Street and hailed a taxi. I watched the taxi move off. I laughed and said aloud, "Thank God."

I moved near Chinatown to get away from you. Then moved *beyond* Chinatown. The seemingly casual arrangement of fruits and vegetables in Chinese store windows intrigues me. Memory paints another Asian display: Mrs. Han's flower stall in Seoul, Korea. A small woman, Mrs. Han was aloof. She had two sons. One was rumored to be a very important Communist in North Korea. The other son, aged ten, lived with Mrs. Han. He was a very large boy for his age, but he did not help his mother with the white mums, rose-red peonies, dwarf lemon trees. He stayed in back of the flower stall and painted watercolors. American and Allied soldiers were always pestering the boy. They wanted to take his picture, and they tried to bribe him. They wanted to take his picture and send it to the folks back home. The folks back home had never seen anything as funny as a star and cauliflower on a human face.

AT 10 P.M. ON AUGUST 7, the moon was full and the air had turned cool. Vincent Jew and Wing Ha Sze were returning from the movies, walking down Bayard Street, next to the Chinese Garden—a semi-official, peeling, red and white plaque says in English and Chinese, "Manhattan Bridge Park." José Ortez, his girlfriend, and another young couple were on the same side of the street. They had been to a social club and were going toward the subway, they said later.

Returning from the liquor store with a chilled bottle of vino, I could not see them from where I was on the opposite side of the Garden, walking down Forsyth Street, about fifteen or twenty feet from the corner of Division. On the opposite corner, I saw a stocky young man standing next to the parking lot. He had shoulder-length dark hair, wore a light-colored shirt of the T-shirt style, dark trousers. A leather type of shoulder bag was strapped against his barrel chest. He fumbled with the bag and looked around as if uncertain which way to go. Then suddenly turned under the bridge, and out of my vision.

Normally, I'm spaced out, move with the speed of a panther. But that night I was relaxed, my stride slow. Emerging from under the bridge, I started up Bayard and heard the first popping sound. Leftover firecrackers, I told myself.

The street curves here and is not very bright. Remember: the moon did not glow like a white light. I heard voices, the sound of fast footsteps on the pavement, heard the popping sound again, saw near the curb two streaks of red-blue-yellow light, two thin slanted lines like the halves of two V's. It was a fascinating, blinding light. On the far side of it, dark figures ran.

The first person I saw was the stocky man, first in the middle of the street, then a few feet east of that light, running. I knew someone had been shot. I saw no one but him. Head held high, looking as if it were extremely difficult to breathe, he clutched that shoulder bag and ran, very fast for a man of his size. I did not know if he had a gun and decided to let him get a few feet in front of me before chasing him. He did not run in a straight line and headed down Market Street, which leads into East Broadway. He ran under the bridge and did not turn in the direction of Forsyth, where he had come from ten or fifteen minutes before. He continued east on Division Street. A car blocked me, and I lost him in the dark, then returned to Bayard Street.

Wing Ha Sze lay on the sidewalk in front of the entrance to the Garden. His head was on the curb. A small, slender man, he appeared to be middle-aged. Still breathing at the time, his blood streamed down Bayard and glistened in that half-bright light. Dazed young Vincent Jew clutched his right side and stood a few feet from Sze. Now and then Vincent looked around, his face in shock or pain. Then he'd look down at his friend. Vincent was wounded slightly.

Baldwin, a man of the streets, arrived. "Don't touch him," he advised Vincent, "until the police get here. They're down the street."

But Vincent Jew went over to his friend. The experienced Baldwin said, "Don't touch him. He's dead."

At the sound of fast footsteps, I turned and saw a policeman. He asked me to stand against the Garden wall and questioned Baldwin and Vincent. A squad car pulled up sharply, and a young policeman got out and grabbed me. "Hey! Wait a minute," I protested. The first policeman came to my rescue (if he had suspected me, I doubt if he would have left me unhandcuffed, unguarded, about ten feet from him in the semi-darkness). Already you could hear voices and knew people were approaching.

The first policeman asked me to get in the squad car. I obeyed

and sat on his copy of Sunday's *Daily News*. Other squad cars
arrived. People began appearing as if God had snapped his fingers
and created them by the Garden wall. All of them were peering in
the car at me. I had that uncomfortable feeling which afflicts celebrated people: I was afraid the crowd would kill me. But I kept my
cool, lit a cigarette, and looked out at them and saw José Ortez for
the first time. Frequently the police park at Bayard and Chrystie
Streets. They were there when they heard the shots. They saw
Ortez running, they said, and added that although they fired six
warning shots, Ortez did not stop. He was finally apprehended on
Division Street.

A café-au-lait-colored man, his dark hair was kept in place
with a thin, old striped tie, and he wore a fancy knit shirt, the type
which is popular with blacks, Puerto Ricans, and Italians. His
trousers appeared to be less costly than the shirt. He was hand-
cuffed and had a serene, saintly expression.

Presently, Ortez, his girlfriend, and her friends, Baldwin, and I
were driven to the Elizabeth Street Station of the Fifth Precinct—a
slum of a station. A disgrace to the city and the men who work
there. All of us except Ortez were ushered into a large room.
Willard graffiti were printed all over the room. *Willard* the rat
horror movie.

Baldwin and I had a good rapport. Neither of us knew the
other people. José's petite girlfriend had an earthy sexuality, and
she cried and cried and cried. The other young woman had the
open face of a child. I might as well tell you: Charles Wright is a
distrustful son of a bitch. But the girlfriend, the young couple gave
off the aura of good blue-collar people out on a Saturday night. If
they were acting, their air of innocence was the world's greatest
triangle act.

We were asked our names and addresses. Then they brought in
Ortez and took him into a back room. The girlfriend started crying again. Around 11 P.M. we went up to the fourth floor. "Willars
hole," the wall read. That was the way it was spelled.

The five of us waited in the fingerprinting room for about
twenty minutes before being escorted into another room—the
large, depressing room of the detective squad. Bored, I began
drinking vino. The detectives did not seem interested in my stocky
young man or that he was white (later I would be asked if he were

Chinese). I was asked to return to the fingerprinting room, where I drew a rough sketch of the stocky hippie, whom I believed to be an ordinary young man with the veneer of a hippie. Then I went over to the desk, read Vincent Jew's testimony on page 36 of a small tablet. He and Wing Ha Sze were coming from the movies, walking by the bridge (they were walking on the sidewalk. The Chinese Garden was between them and the bridge). A man came between them, then started shooting. Vincent Jew ran across the street, then ran back to his friend. Wing Ha Sze was D.O.A. A bronze-colored book of matches, advertising Joe's barbershop in Ridgewood, New York, was on the desk. That was all. Without being asked, I returned to the other room, finished my vino.

Policemen, detectives surrounded José Ortez like desperate bees around the sweetest of summer flowers. The girlfriend was crying again. The other young woman picked blackheads from her husband's face. His close-cropped head was in her lap, and his eyes were closed. All of us were out of cigarettes, and I went out to get some.

On the first floor, I saw Vincent Jew and showed him my rough hippie sketch. Vincent did not remember seeing him or me. Puzzled, I left the station.

It was a quarter of two Sunday morning when I returned with the cigarettes. Policemen, detectives were in a jubilant mood like a group of men after the victory of their team. Ortez gave me a long, grateful stare. I was angry that the police had forgotten about the hippie. He was certainly a star witness. The alleged weapon had no fingerprints on it. The killer had supposedly had the foresight to wrap a handkerchief around it before firing, afterward it had been tossed on the sidewalk. It did not matter now. They had their man. Why should I get excited? It was only an ordinary Saturday night murder.

A week later, things changed. The police were not so sure about their man. My irrelevant statement was suddenly valuable. Now, there were frantic phone calls. Visits by detectives, a visit to the D.A.'s office. I await a lie-detector test. All I can think of is a couple of lines from Jorge Luis Borges: "The acts of madmen," said Farach, "exceed the previsions of the sane."

"These were no madmen," Abulcasim had to explain. "They were representing a story, a merchant told me."

* * *

By the time you read this, the celebrating will have cooled. The friendly neighborhood grocer will be paid, the common-law husband will have met his pusher, and the children will be stuffed with sweets. Perhaps there will be a visit to Busch's, the famed credit jewelers, or a sharp new leather coat. The old-age pensioners and the "mentally disturbed and misfits" will pay their bar tabs and get jackrolled. However, all welfare stories are not grim. There are the old, the lame, and the helpless poor. This is their only way of life. But for others it is a new lease on living, almost as easy as breathing. Now all that remains are the twelve days of survival, the next check. I want to tell you about some of these men and women.

Mary X. is "off." Temporarily off. Brave, long-haired girl in midi-dress, the smart suède shoulder bag, living here and there. Starving. Almost tempted to take a job in a boutique. And why should Mary X. suffer in the richest country in the world? She had to miss Dionne Warwick at the Apollo and Soul Sister Franklin at Lincoln Center. She had been receiving her check at a friend's pad. But the caseworker paid a routine visit. "Where's Mary?" The friend's old lady said, "She ain't been here in over a month."

"And I'm off," Mary, who is twenty-nine, lamented. "Lying bitch. She's mad because I won't ball with them anymore."

A few days later, Mary saw her social worker. Life is getting brighter. "Even if I have to go over there and throw a fit. Look, I haven't worked in four years. I could if I wanted to. But I think I need glasses, and I have to get my teeth fixed. And you know I have to take pills. I'm a nervous wreck." Speaking of a semi-drag queen who is almost at the top of the welfare-dollar ladder, Mary said, "That bitch. She gets $99.50 twice a month. And she's living in the street. I saw her trying to hustle over on the Apeside."

The Apeside is the East Village beyond Tompkins Square Park. In TSP I met Jojo. He was very uptight, his paranoia gave off sparks. "Man. They sent my check back. Got a cigarette?" Jojo, ex-garage mechanic. Blond, extremely bright, but frightened of touching his brain. He's spent three years in jail (robbery), dabbled in dope, and is now deep into a wine scene. He breathes like a man in deep pain. We stop off for a pint of Orange Rock. "Gotta steady my nerves, old sport." He smiles. We kill the pint, walk across town to the welfare haven on West Thirteenth Street, where the atmosphere is heady, hopeful like a theater where chorus gypsies are auditioning. I was surprised at the well-dressed welfare recipients. Radios, cassettes, everything was of the moment. A great many of them knew each other. Talked naturally of checks and who was off or trying to get back on. There were very few old people. *Mucho* preschool and school-age children, chasing each other between plastic, armless chairs. Like busy mothers everywhere, these paid very little attention to the children. They had plenty of time to gossip. Time to make love. And the well-lit, clean welfare haven was a pleasant place to kill time, wait for money, though a tense line shot through the undercurrent like a peak hour at the stock exchange. There might be some fucking hang-up, a cold cross-examination. Jojo sensed this. But we kept up a fast joking conversation, sliced with a few silences.

Almost three hours later, Jojo received a check for exactly $33. He would get more. He was properly modest. A serious Jojo faced the social worker. Welfare would arrange for a kitchenette pad. Jojo knew the ropes. After cashing the check, Jojo paid off a $7 loan, then invited me for beers, hard-boiled eggs. Later we switched to wine and watched the sports shoot pool. Life can be good for survivors.

Nellie will ball. Please accept my word: Helena will ball. "All I want to do is stay stoned every night," she once told me in lieu of an apology. There are few stoneless nights. Welfare money, booze, and beer from a platoon of male friends, sitting around the kitchen table, waiting on the free lay. Nellie has seven illegitimate children. Often they are hungry, thanks to their mother's careless life-style. Life in their mother's apartment has made them ferocious little warriors. Proud, the seven children are always on the defensive. It is only when they begin to trust you that they open up, play childish tricks, laugh. It is only then that, underneath it all, you feel as if melancholia is smothering them. I gave them candy, nickels, and dimes. I am tough, loving with them, and hope they understand.

But sometimes they avert their eyes. Melancholia becomes a

dagger. They are disappointed: I will not marry their mother and become their father. It is only because of the children that I have never bedded the mother. Although my childhood was quietly religious and happy, I, too, was briefly a child of welfare. After my grandfather died, and before my father's World War II allotment, there was nothing my grandmother could do but apply for public assistance for me. It was a pittance in every sense of the word. Sometimes she did daywork for white families (in the village of New Franklin, Missouri, not too many white families could afford part-time help, much less full-time servants).

I remember that in winter we became the local F.B.I. of the railroad tracks, looking for coal that had fallen from the open-bellied freight cars. Even today I can taste the delight of a Sunday supper: day-old bread in a bowl of milk sprinkled with cinnamon and sugar. I remember the Christmas we were too poor to buy a tree. But luck was with us, one cold, sunny afternoon a few days before Christmas. We found clumps of pine branches along the railroad tracks. My imaginative grandmother decided that we would make a tree. We found a small leafless young tree and tied the branches to it. It was a beautiful Christmas tree, the delight of the neighbors. And we did not even have multicolored lights for the tree. I frame this memory briefly to let you know that I understand the plight of welfare. I hold no bitterness against those days. It was a happening of that particular time.

Yet there is dark music in the towns, cities, about the welfare recipients. We have to pay taxes to take care of these lazy, good-for-nothing bums. Still, there are the happy Lawrence Welk voices who sing, and this works to our advantage in the end. This is where we want to keep them. We will give them enough so they'll be content and will cause us no trouble. Welfare is their addiction.

Anyway, for those of you who are interested in trying yet another new life-style, here are a few surefire suggestions I have compiled with the help of Green Eyes, who never had to use them:

1) Become an addict.
2) Become an alcoholic or fake it.
3) Get busted, a minor bust, though you could have a fairly cool winter in the Tombs.

4) Get hepatitis.
5) Have a real or fake nervous breakdown. Take the cure at Kings County or Central Islip.
6) It is extremely possible for females to get liberated from work and money worries by getting pregnant.

Warning: Above all, remember to stay on good working terms with doctors. Get a written statement from them.

Now you're on your own, ducks.

THE AFTERNOONS OFFER more than a sharecropper's bag of humidity and rain. But the lunar boys are exceptionally cool, as if the age of Aquarius had instilled in them a terrifying knowledge of silence. In groups of twos, threes, and fours, wearing brilliant-colored nylon T-shirts, jeans, John's Bargain Store khaki walking shorts, tennis shoes, and athletic socks with deep cuffs, they are not long-haired. Immaculate, one of them wants to become a trumpet player. Another, at the age of fourteen, has had faggot grooming. Five of them are school dropouts. The boy with the "hot" $35 knitted shirts is one of six illegitimate children, all of them under the age of sixteen and on welfare.

These budding lunar professionals will, say between two and three of an afternoon, stroll into the Old Dover Tavern (the very "in" Bowery bar). In the beginning, at the end of the school term, they stood outside, while the leader entered. Later, as confidence ripened, they entered and huddled near the door, near the cigarette and candy machines. Now they prowl up and down the bar like altar boys, seeking some rare chalice.

The leader of one gang will ask the bartender for change or order his usual grilled-cheese sandwich. They never buy cigarettes, and it was only last Saturday night that we discovered that they have been trying to jam the candy machine.

Then silent, their young eyes revolving, they walk out into the wet, narrow plain of the Bowery (affluent infant of artist studios, rock-and-roll craters, German police dogs, Doberman pinschers).

Sometimes, the budding professionals will stop and rap with the wine-drinking afternoon bums. But these are really rehearsals, you might say. Scouting trips for boys with faces like stockbroking thieves. Boys who wait quietly for the oncoming darkness.

It's dark now, and they've made it over from the side streets. From the tenements and the public-housing projects in their clean clothes, as if it were the first day of school. I remember that the famed gang of late May and early June marched like stoned killers past the gloomy bank at Spring and the Bowery (the bank that is now a famous artist complex). This gang has been replaced by a gang that shoots in from West Houston.

And these clean-cut boys, ladies and gentlemen, jackroll the wine-drinking citizens of the Bowery. The take is small or nothing. Still, there are legends of the fabulous scores, the fine old gold pocket watch, false teeth, a social-security card, and sweet, dirty old dollar bills. But these boys have watched their older brothers jackroll, have watched the real pros jackroll, and have the act down solid, and it's all so cool, so clean. A cold, passive sport.

As one winehead told me: "They said, 'Pops. Got any juice?' I said, 'Howdy boys.' I was just setting there, on the ground. Too drunk to stand up and take a piss, and they came at me without another word. Just went through my pockets and took all that was left of the $34 I got for selling blood, plus the bonus."

Violent vistas are part of their heritage. But they are seldom violent with the wineheads. It's all so painless, easy. You do not even sweat. Occasionally, a winehead will get kicked in the teeth if he tries to fight back or calls the gang a bad ethnic name. Occasionally, a knife rips a coat pocket and there's a little blood. Occasionally, an old man is doused with gasoline and set on fire. But this is another breed of urban and suburban teenager. Affluent teenagers or stoned kooks.

No, these lunar lads are nonviolent in our luxurious age of violence. But they do not make the Bowery scene on the fifteenth and first of the month. This is big time and usually a black time. Real professional jackrollers. Black migrant workers, mainlined with the cheating stop-and-go sign of urban American and Catskill life. Damaged brains pickled in wine or cool small-time Harlem thieves down for the bi-monthly take.

On August I, at seven in the evening, five blacks ganged up on one old white man at the corner of Prince and the Bowery.

Traffic jammed to a halt. The Bowery bar philosophers watched the happening. The white majority (Irish and Polish) were incensed by the bold black act. But they made no effort to do anything about it, except to spray two black regulars, two queens, with a water pistol of words. "Have I ever tried to rob you?" a hard-drinking black queen asked. "Shit. I could buy and sell all of you. Don't talk about my people."

Sitting four stools away, I suddenly laughed at the perverse reality of *this* sporting Bowery game.

The jackrolling blacks took from the old whites in the light of the day. At night the young whites drank freely of the old black queens and often stole from them, providing the queen bedded them.

Governor Rockefeller, campaigning for reelection, said yesterday that the addiction problem in the state had grown much bigger than he had expected four years ago.
The New York Times, August 4

"Young people today are being subjected to the most profound temptations and stresses—"
Robert Sargent Shriver,
The New York Times, August 6

"We didn't actually break in. The door was open so we just made ourselves at home."

"Hell. Charlie don't give a shit."

Sitting in the living room of a building marked for demolition, I wondered if I did care. After all, squatting out has become most fashionable. Earlier, I had been sitting in a bar, when an acquaintance had invited me to a party. In the past, I had offered Duk Up Soon a place to flop for the night, an occasional quarter, advice. This invitation was a thank-you gesture. And now we were in this living room, sitting on milk crates, a car seat, and the floor. Street lamps spotlighted the room. Votive candles created a ritualistic mood. The buffet: wine, pot, beer, and pills, plus the works. The kids were very polite, and I decided to sit in and see what would happen. Then Pepe came in. We were a little surprised to see each other; our smiles bordered on warmth. I had written about Pepe before, the summer jackrolling debut. Then Pepe's thing was pot, wine, beer, and glue. He was fourteen at the time. Now, almost seventeen, with a delicate dark mustache, sporting as always Italian knit shirts. Sneakers have replaced the $30 shoes. Sneakers are better for stealing, running. His welfare mother is now a redhead and still keeping the weekend lover. The other five children are in school and doing well. Pepe looks like a sharp vocational student as he takes the bags from the deep cuffs of his socks. Beaver has the works which until an hour ago were in a Frigidaire on Avenue A. Leon, who weighs about 120 pounds, bends a Coke can and looks a little frightened as he takes off his belt and turns on. Duk Up Soon and Beaver, who had been jiving like pill-high jockeys, silently watch Leon. Envy seems to touch their faces like rain. But they have their turn at the needle and begin rapping. Beaver, tall and very lean, is tensely cool. He shoots, then jumps into the middle of the floor, the needle still in his arm. "Man. Look. Look at that! Man. A fucking bull's eye. I hit it every time."

Presently, Pepe began to nod. Leon played with the expandable key chain attached to Duk Up Soon's trousers. There were eleven keys on the chain. Only one fit Duk's transient door. Beaver, cupping his hand over his nose and snorting, began his clean-up campaign. "Man. This pad looks like a pigpen. I gotta have a clean pad. You should see my sister's pad, a fucking dump." Watching him, I was listening to Frankie Crocker on WMCA. About an hour later, two teenage boys and a very pretty girl walked in, peering into the semidark room, a little uneasily. They brought knockwurst, beans, and bread.

"Shit," one of them said. "You said you had a pad, and man you ain't even got a pan."

"Fuck," the pretty girl said to no one in particular. She is fifteen and has a voice like a Bingo Bronx housewife. But her voice grew louder, and she began to put down her two friends.

"Fuck off, Tommie. You creep," the pretty girl said, just before she turned on.

The two friends had turned on and wanted to leave. "Bitch. I'm gonna git rid of you," Tommie said. "Git your fucking ass together."

But the pretty girl was high now, going through the dumb-blond bit. She sat down on a milk crate, crossed her fine, bare legs, opened her fringed suède handbag, and began making up her face. It took her almost twenty minutes to paint her lips. "Dumb bitch," the boyfriend taunted. The girl tried to put on false eyelashes with one hand and hold the mirror with the other.

"You ain't got no brains at all," the boyfriend said, snatching the mirror from the girl's hand. The girl was very quiet now as if she were alone. Our voices with the rock music were the sounds of people who were in hell and would never get out.

"Well," I said finally, "I've got to make it."

They were damn nice kids, despite the junk. The rapping had mainly been for my benefit. It was their way of showing that they were with it. Why didn't I call the cops or the narc people? Well, I had talked to these kids and kids like them for a very long time. I knew they had to do their own thing. That is unless they were busted.

Just the other night, I had an encounter with the cops. "Why don't you do something about the junkies and pushers?" I said.

"You should go back to Spanish Harlem," the cop told me.

"Sorry. I'm not Puerto Rican."

"Then go back up to Eighth Avenue and 125th Street."

I laughed.

Junkies like scavengers overturn litter baskets, looking for the heroin that has been stashed there, or they circle the full green-leafed trees looking for the bags, and no one cares as a slim junkie (using a master key) opens a car trunk, directly in front of Daytop Village on Chrystie Street, and makes off with a flashlight, a battery recharger in the Chinese Garden (officially named Manhattan Bridge Park in English and Chinese). The young Chinese boys play a new sport: baseball. The sun is high in the watery blue sky, and it is a quarter of two in the afternoon. Three junkies shoot up, while on the bridge a hard-hat construction worker looks on in amazement: Yes S. X. was gagging to death, and the others were high and giggled, but Beaver comes in, drags S. X. to the bathroom for a cold shower and ice cubes on his testicles. Dial 911 and watch two teenage boys steal a tire off a car at high noon. Later, I take a junkies count: two hours netted eighty-seven in a limited area, and I wasn't trying very hard. On Bleecker, a bearded hippie stops me with "Hey, baby. I need seven bags." Sorry, I say, and another cat comes up and asks what does that honky want, and I tell him, and the two of them make it to the corner, and one-twothreefourfivesixseveneightnineten they are busted by a hip-looking detective on St. Mark's. The kids are always stopping me: I am amused because I look so junk hip, and in the Chinese Garden I watch—are you ready—two young men walk over to a tree where two junkies had turned on twenty minutes before; the two young men have a camera, and the fat boy takes off his belt, kneels down, pretends to shoot up as his friend photographs him. Who knows, fake shooting could become a fad in the careless season of real shooting.

And here I sit popping pills, drinking wine, weighed down with twelve pounds of grief for you, Langston, remembering the reply to your hospital note that I forgot to mail.

Por favor . . . forgive the delay. I think of you often.

Now try to rest and think of what you are working on and your future work. That is all except a little good loving . . . now and then.

Flores, flores . . . from the heart.

And then . . . When? I can't remember. During some full-fledged moment of despair, I had written on that note: Just let me close my eyes and die.

I am dying and you are dead. The people are in mourning. The press has given you the full-dress treatment. They are caroling about your charm, vitality, your prodigious output. Your humor. You were a very logical man who would have been a better poet and writer if you had not been born black in America.

Ah! *The Weary Blues* . . . your first book, which you discussed with me last month, sitting in the Cedar Tavern, drinking black coffee and brandy. I had a vodka with beer chaser and listened to your advice. You were one of the few real people I had met during the last two years. I remember you saying: "*The Wig* disturbed me, and it's a pity you can't write another one like it. But don't. Write another little book like *The Messenger*. When I was starting out. Man . . ."

A good night. That last cold night.

Ah! *The Weary Blues* . . . no mothergrabber, he did not sell out to whitey with his simple tales. He did not even sell out to himself. He was born in another world. He created something that was real. One dares not mention that this was the only way for him to get published and that he had to eat and buy shoes. And none of it was easy. And it seems to me, Langston, that you knew what your literary black sons haven't learned: it's a closed game played on a one-way street.

Ah! The bitterness, some jiveass mothergrabber will say.

But we know better, don't we? The smile on your face in the white quilted coffin says so. The undertaker had a touch of genius, for the smile is nothing like your smile but the smile that was always underneath the surface smile. The smile that was in your voice and your laughter.

The serene mad smile of one who is trapped!

At the funeral home I heard a woman say, "Don't look like he suffered one bit."

No, no, no!

If you had lived, you would have been in Morocco now with the photographs and introductions I had given you. Florence, whom you met here, and Cadeau, the white Peke, were waiting for you. You spent four days in Tangier last year and liked it well enough to return and spend the summer there. That is, if you solved the money problem. And most of all you wanted to go to the folk festival in Marrakesh.

And it was strange that Tuesday morning, Langston. I hit the streets, slightly stoned, talk-singing that old Billie Holiday tune, "Good Morning, Heartaches . . . Here we go again . . ."

And there you were on the front page of *The New York Times,* dead.

I hated to leave you up on St. Nicholas Avenue . . . just when I had gotten to know you.

I hate to close this note, but I must put you out of my mind for the time being. And it is not your death that I'm mourning. It's the horror of it all. "Ah, Man!" you would chuckle sadly.

Poor black poet who died proper and smiling.

Langston Hughes was always concerned about my eating habits. Frequently, he invited me to dinner, restaurants or to his Harlem brownstone. I was always a smiling liar: "I have eaten, old sport. All I want is a double vodka on the rocks." But a few nights after his funeral, I returned to Harlem, buoyed with the memory of my black brother, the poet, who died proper and smiling. This buoyancy sunk as I walked through the streets of Harlem. It was like walking through the streets of Seoul, Korea, after the truce. Here the racial truce was a constant thing, almost as normal as the ultramarine evening sky, the tenements, the laughing voice of a woman describing the size of a rat ("a big cat without legs"), the expensive new cars, surreal against the backdrop of old decayed buildings. There were no stars, no breeze. The air was as potent as exhaust fumes. I walked around a long time that night, and the more I walked, pain and hunger increased like the folds of a fan. I went into a small clean "down home" café, ordered a double helping of barbecued spareribs, collard greens, potato salad, cornbread. I even ate two slices of sweet-potato pie. Good vibrations engulfed the café. The motherly owner, circles of thick braids wreathing her head, a bib apron fronting a sagging bosom, ample stomach, called me Sonny. I felt very much at home, savored the warmth, brought it back downtown like a doggie bag, then lost it.

A perfumed note from Paris.

Dear Charles:
I am staying in Anne T.'s flat on the Ile St. Louis. The poor thing had to go to Portugal for a holiday. So I'm alone and damned glad. Most of the Parisians are holidaying too, and I avoid the American tourists. Avoid quaint bistros where I'll be cheated anyway. I go out only to walk Bebe. Anne's Spanish maid is a jewel. My Costa del Sol Spanish comes in handy. I'm doing a little needlepoint, and yesterday I made a chocolate mousse. Hon, I'm simply laying low, working crossword puzzles, reading detective stories. I've even read *The Little Prince* again. I've gained a little weight and am almost my old self again. And you *know* what happened to me in the States. My goddamn family. A bunch of fucking rats! But don't be surprised if I should suddenly turn up, unannounced.
                              Take care. Bebe sends his love.
                                          Maggie

                    P.S. I FORGIVE YOU!

"Oh Jesus," I moaned, letting the wheat-colored note fall to the floor. "I forgive you," Maggie had written in caps. Maggie, it is a new season. I got up and discovered that I was out of Nembutals. Despite the succulent soul dinner, I did not have enough energy to masturbate. So I polished off a quart of Orange Rock wine, about a third of Chambray vermouth, chain-smoked, and tried not to think.

Around midnight, I hit the streets. No heralding trumpets greeted me. No royal streets led to the House of Orange. However, Hershey's Bowery bar became an orangerie, a smoky crimson stage where approximately thirty-five intoxicated men tried to upstage each other. Like ash-can whores, they tried to con each other and the bartender. A mangy, crippled dog sauntered in and bequeathed fleas. I ordered another wine, looked up at the mute television, which seemed to gradually rise toward the ceiling. Unlike the drinking men, the television apparently wanted to get closer to God.

That's when I turned, looked out the door, and saw the girl. I ran to the door and watched a black teenage girl walk down the Bowery. Walking as if it were day and the street, a pleasant, tree-lined country lane.

I caught up with the girl and remembered where I had first seen her, playing softball in Chrystie Street Park about a week before. She played very well and commanded every male's attention. What I'm sure most of us were admiring was not her pitcher's left arm but her ice-cream-cone tits, the wide womanly buttocks, although she appeared to be no older than sixteen.

"Hello," I said. "Where are you going?"

"Home," the girl replied, averting her eyes.

"You shouldn't be out this late alone."

"I was over at my girlfriend's on Houston. We were listening to Smokey Robinson and the Miracles, and I forgot what time it was."

"Where do you live?"

"Ludlow," the girl said, sounding like an eight-year-old.

"Do you want me to walk you home?"

"If you want to."

In the beginning, I had told myself that I wanted to protect her like a brother, like a father. But when we reached Delancey Street I had my arm around her. She rested very easily in my embrace. Innocent and sweet fantasies waltzed through my mind. But the Midwestern, Methodist country boy did not applaud the waltz.

"I don't have to go home yet," the girl told me, looking straight ahead.

We crossed Delancey and walked through the park, deserted

except for winos bedded on the pop-art-colored benches and a group of teenagers smoking marijuana. Their transistor gave out with the driving Jackson Five.

Once we stopped and kissed. The girl offered her lips willingly. There was desperation in her caress. I wanted to have her in bed, all night. I wanted to wake up with her in the morning. My hotel was out of the question. But at the far end of the park, beyond the recreational building, the land sloped. Large old trees formed a canopy, blocked the light. The wide ditch was cool and dark, and we went there and made love. The early-morning hours were delicious.

NOW I WAS MANAGING to write for *The Village Voice* every other week, supplementing that income with an occasional slop-jar job; washing dishes in penal delis, carrying one-hundred-pound bags of rice on my 129-pound shoulders. But I had my big toe in the door of my world again. The dusty black telephone which sat on the floor like a discarded toy and never rang except when management called bitching about the rent began ringing. There were letters, invitations to parties. I began seeing old friends again. One of the best was beautiful black Hilary, an artist-model.

After a pushcart hot-dog lunch, we decided to go into the Cedar Tavern and have a few drinks.

On the fourth Scotch and water, Hilary said, "You must be more social, Charles. Parties are where things happen."

"And don't happen. I'm tired of assholes and freaks and phonies."

"Now, baby," Hilary pleaded.

"Shit, Hilary," I exclaimed. "I wasted a whole weekend with those black middle-class cocksuckers on Long Island. Why? Because I was promised a job. And all they wanted to talk about was my experiences in Tangier and Mexico. Plus the hostess had 'always wanted to write.' Shit. Let's have another drink."

Hilary giggled. "At this rate, I'll be stoned before I get to the Art Students League."

"Won't be the first time, babe," I said, signaling to the waiter.

Hilary reached over and played the piano on my left hand. We got along damned well.

"Grit your teeth and curl your toenails," Hilary said absently.

"That's right, cupcake."

"T. C. Moses is having a party Friday night. And he asked me to see if I could get you to come."

"Is he still screwing that fat blonde?"

The waiter arrived with the drinks. Hilary's timing was perfect: "Do you think that nigger is gonna give up all that vanilla ice cream?"

"He might as well get it here. He sure as hell can't get it in Greensboro, North Carolina."

Joshing, Hilary cleared her throat and said grandly, "Baby, I'm waiting on your answer."

"I don't know." I sighed. "You know the last good party was the one that Bob Molock gave for me. That was nice. I like Bob. He's got balls."

"Are you coming?" Hilary wanted to know.

The night of T. C. Moses III's party was extremely warm. I had spent the day delivering circulars from door to door in Yonkers. Even an extremely fast Doberman pinscher could not catch fast Charlie. The weather, frustrations, the small circular check could not bring me down. I was laid back. With my cool. I even listened to a right-wing, country-western station. Relaxed, once I had bathed. I popped a couple of bennies, siphoned off the last of the vodka. It was almost 10 P.M. now, and I put on my party costume, which was nothing but a pair of clean blue jeans, a button-down drip-dry white shirt, a pair of second-hand imitation Gucci black shoes that I had bought on the Bowery for three dollars.

Once upon a time, Manhattan's Upper West Side was a slum except for the splendor of Central Park West, West End Avenue, and Riverside Drive. The police and underground knew it as the playground of drug addicts and flaming drag queens. But that seems a long time ago. A decade? Today it is known chiefly for Lincoln Center, expensive remodeled brownstones, and as the province of the literary and artistic Jewish Mafia. Yet another breed has staked out part of the West Side for its own. A strange black breed that was conceived in the idealistic Kennedy years, passed their youth in Johnson's Great Society, grew to maturity, prospered in the subtle South Africa of the United States of 1971. The majority of these young black men and women are clever, extremely intelligent. The majority of these young black men and women are only superficially militant. Of course, they give money to black causes and buy the Black Panther newspaper (how can they refuse with their manner and dress on a blue-sky Saturday afternoon?). All of them agree that New York's finest pigs are "terrible. Just terrible." And like skimming fat from milk, they are as bourgeois as a Republican Vice President. Y'all hear me? Riot all over the goddamn city, but don't bomb Macy's, Gimbels, or Bloomingdale's. Do not open a drug-addict center within five hundred miles of Tanglewood.

Some of these young black men and women are my acquaintances. I knew and liked T. C. Moses III. I was finger-popping as I rang his doorbell.

T. C., who went to Howard University, received his law degree from Columbia University, sported a conservative Afro. Dark-skinned, he wore an English suit, white shirt, and dark tie. Smiling warmly, he shifted one of his sixteen pipes from his right to his left hand.

"Charlie. My main man. We've been expecting you."

"Sorry I'm late." I smiled, hoping it was real.

Just then, Julie, the fat blonde in something long, flowing, and purple, squealed. "Angel, baby," she cried and gave me a solid hug, about a dozen wet, little kisses. She smelled of gin and perfume.

We went into the white-walled living room with its highly polished floor, garden of green plants, paintings, and drawings by black artists. As far as the eye could see, fake imported African artifacts took possession of walls, floor, tables. The most imposing had their own lucite pedestals (T. C. went to Africa last year and forced a protesting Julie to remain in Paris).

The lights were low, people milled about like museumgoers. Aretha Franklin was on the stereo, and I knew it was party time. Time for most of them to let their hair down about an inch. Earlier the music would have been a little Bach or a Mozart fanfare, and the talk would have been heavy: the fate of mankind, crime in the

street, and that man in the White House and how are you, my
dear, and Sybil is in the country for the weekend. "What you
drinking, sport?" T. C. asked.

"Double vodka on the rocks."

"Got it."

"Look who is running, running." Julie giggled.

Who else could it possibly be, dressed in silver from head to
foot. Hilary. She grabbed me, and we went off to a corner.

"Cupcake. Take it easy."

"Give me a kiss," Hilary said in a pouting little girl's voice.
"Party's a drag. Let's go somewhere and fuck."

"Be sweet," I warned.

"Be tweet," T. C. repeated. "Hilary, I want Charles to meet
Mr. and Mrs. Roosevelt Robinson."

"All right," Hilary was suddenly serious. "I'll be goody-good
if you get me another Scotch, love."

And off we went to meet Mr. and Mrs. Roosevelt Robinson.
Mr. and Mrs. Robinson were in their early thirties and stood
against the curtainless picture window that overlooked the Hudson River. They were an attractive couple and seemed slightly
uncomfortable. But we managed to make smooth small talk. I
found them pleasant. They had heard of me and were properly
thrilled. Neither of them had read my two books.

"Darling," Hilary cooed. "Charles is looking for a job, and I
know you have connections with that urban youth thing . . ."

"I'll give Mr. Wright . . . Charles, my card." Mr. Robinson
beamed, looking directly down into Hilary's Mount Rushmore
bosom. Mrs. Robinson looked first at Hilary, then back at Mr.
Robinson.

Hilary was wound up now. She squeezed my moist hand.
"Charles is so talented. And we wouldn't want him to have to
wash dishes forever, would we?"

I wanted to talk and comfort the attractive couple, Mr. and
Mrs. Roosevelt Robinson. But all I could say was, "Hilary's
stoned, and it was nice meeting you. Excuse us please." Escorting
Hilary toward the bar, I teased, "Oh, you bitch. You screwed that
deal."

"Fuck'm. Fuck'm. Phony shitheads."

"If I don't get a drink," I chuckled, "this new mass department-store culture will smother me."

Before we could reach the bar, a black voice commanded, "Charles Wright!"

"Oh, Charles," Hilary said. "It's A. X. and his gentleman friend, the poet." A. X.'s court consisted of two white men and one serious, plain young woman who looked as if she was a graduate of an expensive avant-garde girl's college and might at one time have considered joining the Peace Corps. A. X.'s poet was Afroed, bearded, serious, wore a rumpled suit and tie. He was searching. "Trying to get the feel, baby"—for a proper African name. Africa was where it was at. Poetry was where he was at.

"But is it art?" I wanted to know. "And why do the majority of black poets sound alike. I'm not talking about the kids from the street."

"But there's a war going on. We're at it with whitey," the poet said dramatically.

I looked at A. X. He nodded gravely. Was he thinking of his Irish doorman, who said, "Good evening, Mr. Coombs"?

"I wanna dance." Hilary pouted. "I wanna dance with my dress up over my head."

"Hilary," A. X. said, "there are ladies present. You are not in the Village."

"And, my dear, you are not in the subway john on your knees."

"Hilary," I exclaimed, pulling her away.

"Let's have a drink and drown all the schmuck faces. Am I really naughty?"

"Never," I said, bestowing a prize kiss on her unlined forehead.

A week later, a Monday, following the Newark riot, I was delivering circulars door to door in the Bronx. Now a good circular man is aware of dogs. Therefore, I stuck the supermarket throwaway in the iron gate, which was open. A healthy young dog came running from the side garden with his teeth bared. I managed to grab the gate; the dog, hunched like a quarterback, tried to chew my left foot through the fence.

"Don't kick him," a woman screamed. "This ain't Newark."

In the voice of a serene, opium-smoking saint, I replied, "I was not trying to kick your dog, madam. I was merely trying to close the gate. I didn't want him to bite my foot."

The fury had left the woman. "Oh, he won't bite you. He just don't like mailmen." My country 'tis of thee. Sweet land of old prejudices and new-old hates! A week before, a black co-worker and I had worked very hard to enjoy a long break. It was a very hot day and we were very thirsty. A neighborhood park was directly across the street. My man decided to go over and drink from the fountain. The scene didn't look kosher to me. Like some rare, two-legged bloodhound, I can scent a cracker neighborhood before you can snap your fingers.

There were teenagers in the park with that vibrant end-of-school-term air. I did not join my man at the drinking fountain. He returned, complaining, "They don't want you to even drink water. 'What is this neighborhood coming to?' one of them chicks said."

Naturally, I did not brood over what might happen to her neighborhood—a neighborhood where the majority of the people do not even read *The Reader's Digest*. Their mentality ran the gamut from the *Daily News* to the *National Enquirer*. The small old houses are kept in good condition. The lawns, the size of twin bed sheets, are green and mown. There are birdbaths, statues of the Virgin Mary, pink plastic flamingos, reindeer, climbing roses, interspersed with plastic turquoise roses (the famed Burpee flower growers would not be pleased). Many of the mothers look hard and tired and have voices like seasoned soldiers. This is hardly my idea of a neighborhood that I'd want to move into. My man, born in Harlem, wants to die there.

I want to die under a Moroccan blue sky. I want to die where I can get a drink of water. I want to die in a country where rioting will produce emotions other than boredom. It seems, despite the looting, the wounded, the dead—an extremely mild happening. The fact is, I was rather disappointed. What would have been marvelous is that the ugly old city should have burned to the ground. This shock and a minor little civil war would perhaps force us to face the cold cunt of reality. Blacks would lose the war. But we have nothing to lose but our lives, and that doesn't seem very important in the present climate.

That rude bitch of sweet dreams, Mama Nightmare, has hung me like a polka dot, like a black Star of David, below the fascist, Germanic clouds of South Africa, U.S.A.

She has been with me for a very long time, even before I could read and write. The guys at Smitty's gas station in Boonville, Missouri, called me dago. Aged five, I knew dago was not nigger. But they have remained stepbrothers to this day, forming an uncomfortable army with kike, Polack, poor white trash. But I had nigger, Negro, coon, black, colored, monkey, shit-colored bastard, yellow bastard. Perfect background music for nightmares. The uric sperm of those years has flooded my mind. Was I ever Charles Stevenson Wright? In private moments, I say aloud, my face igniting a sulphuric grin, "Your name is Charles Stevenson Wright." Occasionally, I applaud this honest sea dog facing me. Charles Stevenson Wright, the man. Face myself or else suffer the living horrors, the grind of a real fuck, guaranteed to keep you moaning until death.

Inherited bitterness, barriers, color nightmares. A rainbow then. Not Finian's "I've an elegant legacy waiting for ye," but a remembrance of you trying to rim the daylights out of me in the hope of producing another petrified black boy. My grandfather, Charles Hughes, was a boy at the age of seventy. It is remembering my grandfather and all the other boys who have been buggered through the years by that name.

Like a quarterly, ghostly visitor, one nightmare always returns. I am facing a Kafka judge (perhaps a god) and his court. Their skin and hair are as clear as rainwater. The quiet is frightening.

"But I always thought I was simply Charles Stevenson Wright," I protest desperately, then roar with mad laughter, knowing that whitey, too, has great problems, nightmares. At this stage of gamy, Racial American Events, it is impossible for whitey to produce good niggers. But he still is capable of producing Uncle Toms. But always remember: hoarded prejudices beget slaves who impale their masters on the arrow of time.

....

DAY AND NIGHT, night and day. An endless freight train chugging through memory, braking against the present. The enormous blast of the engine is a proclamation of exhaustion, a depressive motif of summer. Another summer on urban Hades. Pollution, Violence, and Corruption are the gods here. The young protest, riot. Their elders bite their lips, inhale anger, or flaunt their power. Nailed between two worlds, I try to stay stoned, clang like a bell in a small tower, comforted with the knowledge that I'm moving, moving on.

Get it! Get it! Get it!

I've moved again, moved near the financial district, two blocks from City Hall. The streets are always jammed. Jammed to the point of being stationary like a motion-picture still. Then, as if a powerful switch had clicked, the crowd becomes animated, moves on, goes through the repertoire of living, boogalooing between gray inertia and the red-hot scream of progress. They are as dedicated as a perverse Communist. Silent or vocal, the white and black American majority fills me with nausea and a suffocating sense of horror.

It is morning. My room is in the only hotel in the district. High ceilinged, half its former size, due to progress. The walls have a fresh coat of paint, Puerto-Rican-blue; small deep blue bottles highlight the paint. The large Victorian porcelain washbasin is a monument to another age of splendor. But the bentwood hatrack and chair, the vile painted furnishings dominate—a seedy stage for Tennessee Williams or Graham Greene (the stage is not waiting for me; I live here). But the mattress is clean, firm, and makes me feel good. Already I am debating whether I should christen it with the pretty black junkie girl. A daily visitor, Betty is always trying to "straighten up your pad, man," asking me to kiss her, or doing one of those brief junkie naps. I "respect" her; we get along damn well. But pride and the cold technician have always kept my emotion in check. At the end of each visit, Betty looks me straight in the eye and announces, "I will be back."

And Betty always leaves something. Things that females can't bear to part with in this age of liberation.

Bopping through a pauper period, I have nothing of value for Betty to steal. "Would you take money from me?" she asked.

"Nope," I replied.

"What about a little gift?"

Betty could steal a "boss" pair of sunglasses or an umbrella (it was raining that afternoon).

"Oh, Charles." Betty pouted, then laughed madly, displaying a solid gold wristwatch she had taken from a man in a West Side motel.

Depression knights my forehead. I cannot move.

Finished the wine. The lukewarm beer, a bummer. I go to the window. The gray street looks fresh and clean after the rain. Directly across the street, the city branch of Swiss Farm nurseries displays young green trees, plants, and flowers in red clay pots. I am seized with hunger for the country, the sea. Surrounded by the Hudson and East Rivers, the Atlantic Ocean, I second Eugene O'Neill's cry: "I would have been much happier as a fish." Yet like an addicted entomologist, I am drawn to people. Let them flutter, bask, rest, feed on my tree. Then fly, fly. Fly away. Goddamnit. Fly mother-fuckers.

In the afternoon, bless the solitude, salute it with vodka. Finished reading Henry Green's *Loving* and Muriel Spark's *Memento Mori*. Talk about a good high. Read a paragraph from an Imamu Amiri Baraka essay (no matter, no matter. I remember LeRoi Jones when he lived on Third Avenue and was married to Hattie Jones. It was the beat generation then).

"We own despair," Imamu writes. "And then some cracker sits in space with a part in his skull and lectures about what we need. What we need. What we need first is for him to cut out."

Turning on the black radio for a little afternoon jazz, a white Southern woman tells a radio reporter in a voice like bitter, congealed honey: "Governor Wallace? He's a gone man."

Voices of a hall argument penetrated the door like the blade of a power saw.

"Do you want my woman?" A black male asked.

The white male reply was cautious. "Addie's a friend."

Stoned, Addie seconded the reply: "Dickie, I've lived here a long time. Since way back in 1968. Jefferson, Dickie's young. Younger than I am. He just got back from Vietnam, the poor thing."

"Yeah," Dickie shouted. "Vietnam! And I'll—any man that fucks around with my woman. Do you wanna fight?"

"Do you wanna fight?"

"Dickie . . ."

"I said, by God, do you wanna fight?"

"No. There's nothing to fight about."

A long silence until Addie said, "Why don't you two grown men stop it. I never seen such carrying on. They won't even let me have a dog for protection."

"I just don't want no white motherfucker . . ." Dickie began.

"Dickie," Addie pleaded. "I've lived around white people for forty-eight years. But that white son of bitch down at the desk won't let me have even one little old dog."

No, it was not a *Daily News* robbery, a typical lower-echelon robbery (estimate of "goodies": $800–$1,000), powdered with the frost that occasionally makes living in the City of Dogs interesting.

The facts: At 10 A.M. one morning, a budding thief climbed up the fire escape of a building on East Eleventh Street, then, with the skill of an acrobat, raised an unlocked window and climbed into a front fifth-floor apartment. The thief, a thirteen-year-old boy, was familiar with the apartment, having visited many times. A chubby Tom Sawyer type, he lived two floors below in a rear apartment.

He had given one of the two occupants a perverse young female dog. The boy fed Blackie and unlocked the entrance door. But he exited by the fire escape, lugging a brand new tape recorder.

A cardiac man (a constant people watcher) saw the boy and called his wife. The couple lived directly across the street and watched our Tom try to hawk a "heavy, black case." Watched until the boy disappeared out of their view. Shortly after this, the boy returned, minus the tape recorder. The cardiac man did not have a phone, but vowed to tell the people in the fifth-floor apartment about the "heavy, black case." The Welfare Bonanza was nine days off, and it was a gritty time for the poor, especially for people who lived beyond the monetary welfare standard, for party people. But the couple across the street saw chubby Tom's mother dash out and return with "heavy goods" from the Pioneer supermarket.

Now it was almost 11 A.M. Eugene, one of the occupants of the apartment, returned and found the apartment in a shambles. He called his cousin Dash, who arrived an hour later. By this time, the police had arrived and departed. Dash waited for the detectives. Then it was time for Gene to go to work. Dash called me. I arrived at 3 P.M. and performed amateur spade-work. The locked American armoire was almost unhinged. The two doors were like two flags at half mast.

"Well," I said, "I doubt if it was a junkie. They didn't take clothes or record albums. And the phones are still plugged in. They could have taken Gene's stereo. It isn't that heavy."

Laughing sadly, Dash, an IBM man said, "But they took the tropical fish and the bird."

Blackie, the perverse little bitch, had eaten the other bird. "I have a funny feeling," Dash said. "I bet it was the little boy downstairs."

Tom's boyish charm seemed too smooth, like rich country butter, and I had been watching him for a long time.

"I've been thinking the same thing."

It was now around five, and the sky was an explosion of red, and we eased the pain with Gordon's gin and waited for the detectives.

"Call the detectives again," I said.

"Hell. I've called them three times. They said they'd be over."

"Well, call them again. What have you got to lose?"

The man on the phone at the Fifth Precinct had a happy-go-lucky voice. He wanted to know if anything of value had been taken. I gave him a rundown. Yes, he said—that's a little money. Did he have a rough idea when the detectives would be over? No—but rest, rest assured, they would be over. Yes, sooner or later, the detectives would be over.

Around midnight, we had definite proof that Tom was our man. The window-watching man and his wife would testify. In court! By this time, we all were a little high and laughed and joked and waited for the detectives. Blackie defecated on the bathroom floor and ate it.

Gene and Dash worked on Saturday, and I stayed in the apartment with young Blackie. Each time I went to the refrigerator for a beer, the little bitch tried to grind against my leg. Jesus. What a dog. But: this is the City of Dogs. Mongrelsville. Sanitary-minded people let unleashed dogs roam at will and defecate on the sidewalk. These people probably wash their hands before leaving the bathroom. But they seem to suffer from the Camelot illusion that the city is their urban estate.

Our Tom is a collector of dogs. He charms people into giving him dogs or steals them. He houses the dogs in the wrecked basement of the Eleventh Street building. Sometimes he will find a man or a woman or a young hippie couple and croon with raffish charm: "Mama won't let me keep Rover. Will you take him home, and may I visit him sometimes? I love him, and he is a good dog."

Our Tom will visit Rover or Susie and take a buyer's astute inventory of your flat or studio. Already, he knows your work schedule as well as you. And I knew a great deal about chubby Tom. Knew that he was one of five children, that his mother had been forced to move from East Sixth Street, that she was husbandless, that it was always party time in their apartment. I also knew that the thirteen-year-old boy took dogs and threw them off the roof. These dogs usually belonged to neighbors. He was the talk of the block. The police arrived a few times, but nothing ever happened. Something was always happening to Tom's sister: she was fourteen and whored.

Dash arrived at 4 P.M. and called the Fifth Precinct. About an hour later, two policemen arrived, and the four of us stood in the bedroom and went over the robbery again. One of the policemen was silent. He was chubby and might have been Tom's father. The other policeman was young, slender. A philosopher. He said, rather sadly, "There isn't much proof to go on."

"If you don't catch the boy with the goods, what other proof could you possibly have? Except a man and woman who saw the boy—and our willingness to testify."

Up to this point, the slender policeman had ignored me. Now he gave me his attention. We talked about crime in the street, kids. I wanted to go to the bathroom. Finally, we said good-bye, and the two men in tired blue departed. Once again Dash and I got high and waited for the detectives.

Sunday was sunny and pleasant after the rain. It was also a busy day for our Tom. Apparently he sensed that something was up, for he was in and out of the building about ten times. But we never saw him.

Later that morning, the detective who had been assigned to the case called. He warned us not to talk to the boy or harm him. And please, please, do not stage a personal raid on his mother's apartment. The detective would be over later in the day with a search warrant. He was an overworked, sympathetic man, who arrived on East Eleventh Street at exactly 6 P.M. that Sunday evening, almost three days after the robbery had taken place.

It was party time in Tom's mother's rear apartment. A toast to the delight of Miller High Life. Music, laughter created a stereophonic noise in the crowded, dimly lit four rooms. The detective had trouble getting in; people pushed and ran from room to room, at times creating the effect of a crazy, jet-paced counterdrill. There was almost no furniture in the apartment. All the detective could do was issue a summons to Tom's mother. They were requested to appear in Juvenile Court.

Dash and Gene arrived at Juvenile Court. It was 9 A.M. Their case came up at 2 P.M. Tom's mother would not accept legal aid. She would get her own lawyer. The judge warned her not to return without a lawyer. A new date was set for the trial.

But the sullen woman returned without a lawyer. She was alone and occasionally smiled at the judge.

Where was our Tom?

In a clear, today-the-sun-is-shining voice, Tom's mother told the judge, "He didn't feel like coming."

The brief silence in the courtroom was deadly. The judge was outraged and issued a summons for Tom's arrest. He would be placed in juvenile jail until the case came up again. Tom's mother made a quick exit from the courtroom. The sympathetic detective said, "I'll let you know when we pick up the boy."

That was almost five weeks ago. Sitting over a lazy Sunday-afternoon drink, I asked Dash about the case. But he changed the subject and talked about getting laid. We had another drink and listened to Richard Harris sing "Didn't We."

Then I remembered a UPI report: "Hove, England—The City Council has voted to build fourteen more public toilets for dogs, following experimental use of six fenced compounds equipped with dummy light posts."

Case dismissed. Dogs. Dog lovers.

ANOTHER CASE VIA AIRMAIL, another perfumed note from Paris, France.

Dear Charles:
 Anne T. returned from Portugal with a terrific suntan and bruises. Bruises, hon. The poor thing is black and blue, thanks to a fat, Princeton type of young man (he said he was working for the C.I.A. "Top-level stuff"). This young man stole a twenty-dollar bill off Anne's dressing table. She left it there deliberately. And now she's back, all bruised up, and wants to go to the south of France. But I haven't got a bathing suit. I haven't bought a thing all year except hose and a panty girdle. I'm so poor. George's alimony is a pittance, and I was such a fool. I should have taken that bastard to the cleaners. But I was thinking of the kids. *His* kids. I never could conceive, and I'm too old now, anyway. All I can do is play solitaire, work crossword puzzles, and read detective stories. Paris is terrible, terrible. The City of Lights doesn't mean a damn thing to me anymore. I'm seriously considering returning to the States. Ask Miss Feldman or Mr. Miller at the Albert or those nice people at the Hotel Van Rensselaer. I must live in the Village. Gone are the Barclay days! Have you seen Charles Robb or that bitch Hilary? I hope you are writing and everything is going well. I'm baking bread and drinking black-market Scotch. That's Paris for you. Bebe sends his love. He still thinks he can talk. Silly dog.

Love,
Maggie

Maggie, I say aloud. Someone on the sixth floor threw an empty beer can down into the courtyard. Maggie. The former country-club wife. The little match girl. A Chesterfield girl in World War II. It comes as a surprise to remember that she is white, that her eyes are blue. What surfaces first is Maggie in a yellow dress and dinner in a graveled court in Seville. Ma Griffe and Joy perfume, a chemist's supply of pills, booze. Maggie desperately trying to keep me from writing. Dear Dr. Joyce Brothers, have you seen Kafka lately?

Remembering, feeling black, I have a stiff vodka, hear heavy footsteps on the muddy brown floorboards of the hall. Footsteps like an aggressive soldier, then swift taps on my door, instantly telegraphing stoned horrors. The hoarse voice calling, "Charles, Charles," sounding like a man who was resigned to silence and closed doors.

I opened the door. Clancy swung in, shadowboxing. "Man. Goddamn."

"Hello, sport."

"Look." Clancy beamed. "A whole fucking gallon of pure grape wine. Pretty, ain't it?"

"You got money? Baby, we'll have a snowstorm in August."

"There you go. I made a little score. Do you want me to go out and get you a sandwich, cigarettes?"

"No, Clancy."

"Well, let's drink the juice and screw the moose. Hey, I like that. Screw the moose."

"What happened to Martha?"

"Man. That bitch is crazy. She starting fucking with my mind. I can't stand anyone fucking with my mind."

An occasional student of mainlining, a heavy drinker, thirty-year-old Clancy sat down and shook his head. There were tears in his eyes, but he looked up at me with the last of his altar-boy charm and laughed.

"Hey. How you keep yourself together? When you gonna crack up?"

"Tomorrow or never," I said, then poured two tumblers of wine.

"Ain't that something?"

"That's right, baby."

"No kidding, Charlie. You're together, and I had to see you."

"Here's to the vineyards and the people who toil in them," I said, thinking: At least he doesn't want to borrow money, doesn't need a place to flop for the night.

Clancy shook his head again. "I don't know, sport. I had this gig and was starting to get myself together. I bought some clothes. A TV. Then I start messing round with Martha. Shit. I'm gonna get me some dope."

"Well," I said, sitting down on the unmade bed, "you've had it before. And you're all screwed up. Why not a little dope? Maybe you'll get lucky and get hooked this time."

"Charles," Clancy pleaded. "Don't put the bad mouth on me."

"Did you call your brother?"

"No, but I will." Clancy sighed and filled the tumblers. "You know he's got a cabin up in the mountains, and this fall we could go up there and hunt. Do you good to get out of the city. Maybe you'd like it up there and could write."

Clancy and I did not hunt last fall, nor fish in the spring, but I said, "Yeah. I'd like that. I like the country. Anything to get out of this fucking city."

We had more wine, and Clancy began singing in a Rex Harrison voice, "California Dreaming," then bolted up and smashed his fist against the wall.

"That bitch. My fucking mother is in California. After Daddy died in prison, she left all of us kids and went to California with a shoe salesman. What kind of mother is that? Don't wanna bring you down, Charlie. Let's have some more wine."

"God said, Let there be light, and there was light," I said.

"You should have been a preacher or a teacher. You're good with kids."

"Yes, my son. Pass the jug."

"You can't destroy yourself, man. You just can't."

"Clancy, I think you've got a point."

"Goddamnit!" Clancy exclaimed, banging his hand on the table, spilling wine. "You can't destroy yourself."

I watched Clancy stagger to the bathroom, staggering like a man trying to avoid a great fire.

The afternoon wine flowed. Cigarette butts filled ashtrays,

became tiny smokeless igloos. The hotel was very quiet. The silence was strange, and it seemed to block our conversation as we continued to drink. Once, Clancy choked on wine and cried, "This shit is getting to me, and I'm gonna die. Die and burn in hell."

"Clancy. Take it easy. Feel sleepy?"

"No, man," Clancy said, frowning. "Can't sleep. Have all these terrible dreams. Priests and nuns are coming at me with bull whips, and I have no clothes on."

Sobbing and shaking, Clancy fell to the floor. Pounding his fist he shouted, "Everyone is against me, and they're trying to screw up my mind."

"Oh, shut it, Clancy. You're stoned."

"You nigger bastard. You think you're so fucking, fucking intelligent. So Goddamn cool."

What could I say? I laughed, stretched, yawned, had another wine. This name-calling game bored me. I can live without it. Whitey can't live without it. Without the "games," perhaps we would not be friends: equal in my eyes which you do not acknowledge. Therefore, I am always on my guard. I never know what son-of-bitching trick whitey might pull. My reaction is based on whitey's historical dealing with my people. If that's a poached egg, digest neckbones, chitlings. I know that sooner or later whitey will take a swing at the left nut of my psyche and shout "nigger," in anger, in jest, in sex. At the moment, whitey is trapped on an antique escalator in a building of the future. This is the level where whitey has sunk. With all his power and money.

I left the red-headed, former altar boy on the floor and went up to St. Marks to see what was happening, to bask in the zone of the departing, defeated army of hippies. There used to be a little magic on St. Marks. The black novelist Ishmael Reed calls it hoodoo magic, which means J. W. (jamming whitey). In the Village world of panhandling, the put-down, blacks jam whitey from the center of his emotions to nature's exit. On St. Marks, I met Larl. We had been out of touch and caught up on what had happened: the salt-pork taste of nothing. The mood on St. Marks was calm, almost like the Village in the old days. People sauntered through the speed zone. Up ahead, I spotted a young white man zeroing in on us. Pop-art print shirt, blue jeans. Larl did not see him until he said, "Baby, can you spare a little change?"

Larl turned swiftly, enraged. "Can't you see my face is black, boy! How the hell can I spare anything?"

The healthy boyish charm faded. The young man went away as if he had been punished.

Another small St. Marks encounter. The beggar is a wiry black man who bolted down from a stoop and began rapping with a young man whose face was a map of suburbia. The black man really rapped. Suburbian, Jr., would not release any coins. The black man put his arms around Junior and gave him a peace-movement kiss on the cheek. A few more words and Suburbian, Jr., reached in his pocket and gave the black man a quarter and a dime. The black man told me, "I wish America had another hundred thousand hippies. Then I could make a steady living."

But the fat black hairless queen does not have to worry about a steady living. He is a male nurse, has a sideline hustle. Waddling like a grand female duck, large brilliant eyes, going from left to right, he comes on like a Southern mammy. The queen specializes in young white beggars. "Oh Lord! So many homeless chickens. All they want is a little change or some pot and pills. So they put the make on mother. But I been round since the year one. I take'm to my penthouse on Avenue A. I got plenty of pills, pot, and poppers, and I turns them over faster than you can say eggs and grits. Sometimes they comes back and brings their little long-haired girlfriends. And they just all love mother. Oh, my word. Look at that boy crossing that street. What a basket. Well, I must rush off and tend to my chickens." The black queen's dimes, quarters, dollars are a good investment. If a black gives money to whitey, he will be the winner, regardless of what game is being played.

Like Shuffling Joe, who is determined, threatening. Union Square is his base. Union Square is filled with rats; Shuffling Joe has to find "fresh ground." One reason why Shuffling Joe is determined is that he will not drink La Boheme wine, which costs fifty-five cents a pint. "Gallo, man," he says. Gallo is seventy cents a pint. I watch Shuffling Joe hustle a bearded photographer and his lady friend. They are about twenty paces in front of him. The photographer shakes his head, gestures with his hand. His lady friend turns, looks serious; Shuffling Joe watches them move on, still rapping. He grabs the photographer's arm. Photographer grabs camera. Now Shuffling Joe is really rapping, gesturing dramatically. The lady friend has been watching gravely. Suddenly she opens her handbag. A good hustle. Five minutes netted one dollar. "Man," Shuffling Joe says, "I made that cat feel like a turd. I was rapping to him but watching his old lady. I told that cat I was tired. Tired. Tired of fighting whitey and never winning and now all I want to do is drink wine. I can't win 'cause I'm always losing."

This, of course, is a black panhandling truth. We know whitey is still violating our rights as men, as human beings. Whitey is still taking, taking. Even that stuffed rectum of a phrase, RIGHT ON, has reached the portals of the White House. Even the most angelic of white liberals fails to understand black anger, why we react as we do to the most ordinary happenings. Example: window shopping on West Eighth Street, trying to decide if my tight budget would okay an expensive shirt. A bearded white Jesus-type asked for a cigarette.

"Ask your mama," I shouted. In the early hours of morning, I had a pizza on St. Marks. Another white, bearded Jesus-type. This one wanted fifteen cents.

"Motherfucker," I screamed. "I need $5,000."

"Brother," Jesus said, "don't get so uptight."

"Cocksucker," I said, spitting pizza, "I ain't your brother."

I couldn't finish my pizza, suddenly remembering a Connecticut-New York bus trip. My seatmate was young, white, and drank wine. Good Spanish wine. The conversation turned to panhandling. My seatmate was an old St. Marks hand. He had given a black man $15 a few weeks before. I laughed. The boy assured me he would do it again. Indeed! That night the boy (who had made peace with his parents) would go to Kew Gardens, bathe, eat steak ("Ma said . . ."), take the old man's car, pick up his girl, and his buddy and his girl, and buy a pound of grass. Indeed.

But blacks putting the make on other blacks is a cold and colorless story. Even on the Bowery, even when they're sort of on the same wavelength. The "Hey, brother" bit is passé, suspect. The other night a black cat hails me with "Hey, brother. Got a minute to rap?"

"I ain't got shit," I said.

"How you know I want something?"

"Why the hell you stop me, motherfucker?" I asked.

A black and white combo, then? Sometimes this can be very effective, disarming, especially the West Village–St. Marks type.

Especially if they're clean and bright as daisies. But what I want to tell you about is a black and white team, a classic encounter. Larl was at Astor Place and Fourth Avenue. Two teenage girls, one black, the other white, skinny as jay birds in their hip department-store finery. The girls asked Larl for some spare change, Larl ignored them. In unison, the girls shouted, "Cheap cocksucker!"

Larl swung around, marched toward the girls. Then silently raised his hand and, with one powerful stroke, slapped both girls. A crowd gathered. Larl, very aloof, walked away and did not look back. He had to pay $40 to have his watch repaired. A costly street encounter. The games of affluent space-age children, I told a group of supposedly hip hustlers recently. They suggested that I'd make a great panhandler. But panhandling doesn't interest me, just as playing tennis or owning a string of polo ponies doesn't interest me.

LAST NIGHT OPENED tinned sardines. Frequently, opening sardines produces images of hallucinogenic power. It has the feel of a fast "Saturday-night special" (a cheap gun), zipping through that old blasé thing, reality. So I blessed the quart of domestic vodka, bedded on crushed ice in the large Victorian basin. Sardines in tomato sauce. A product of Poland. Sardines tasty, sauce thick, a recession bargain at twenty-nine cents. But do we have a trade agreement with Poland? Cold, iron countries thawing or what the hell, I think, blaming the bad pot. I must read *The News of the Week in Review* in the Sunday *New York Times* and not scan the damn thing.

The vodka is ice cold, delicious. All right then. Three stiff drinks. After working sixteen hours (washing dishes, cleaning up vomit and excrement), I need to unwind. Marat and Sade were the ancestors of my co-workers. The first, second, and third boss? What is there to say about one Jew, one Italian, and one black man? No doubt their mothers loved them. I know their wives do not play the old marriage game. Oh boy! Love is not a dunghill, Hemingway. Love is a 75-caliber machine gun. Another drink and I'll get carried away. In lieu of Beluga caviar (the caterers use supermarket caviar, *pasteurized* caviar, and spoon it out like misers). In lieu of Beluga cavvy, I'm opening another import: smoked sardines from Norway . . . a country that I know very little about except that there is a Lapp tribe in Karasjok. I have a crazy idea that Norway is like California's Orange County. In fact, the vodka just informed me that Norway is exactly like California's Orange County. So conservative that the barks of trees are covered with burlap bags. A country that produced Knut Hamsun, the novelist, and Henrik Ibsen, the playwright, has to be uptight.

The Norwegian sardines have a key opener, which means that I do not have to use my dime-store can opener. Except that I do have to use my opener. The key opener breaks under my muscle-man pressure. I even have difficulty using my own, the tin being soft, so soft that a child could bend it.

I try to make a long cut here and there. Finally, take the stem of my opener and pry the goddamn thing open. Mon Dieu! The tin is smaller than the average bar of soap. But what do you expect for twenty-five cents?

The smoked sardines are a perfect complement for the vodka. But I'm thinking about the cost of labor, the men or women who fished the sardines out of the sea, the people who packed them, the profits of the Norwegian businessman and the American importer and the Chinese owners of the store where I bought them, and how kind and smiling they are as if I were a new billionaire and had walked into their Knoedler's or Christie's or Parke-Bernet's and said, "Gimme twenty million dollars' worth of art."

Let me lay it on the line: I think progress is simply grand. The chilled vodka agrees. I believe in free enterprise, and hate indifference, cheap products, cheap people, careless people. Two nights ago at Numero Uno, the Pont Royale caterers, the steward, the pantry man forgot the parsley garnish for the prosciutto and melon. With the poise of third-rate comedians, the red-and-green-coated waiters wheeled the carts of prosciutto and melon into the main dining room, for the reception was breaking. Cursing like a nut-ward chorus, they returned to the kitchen with the carts. Dishwashers, bus boys, cooks frantically jerked plastic bags off the parsley, untied strings, snapped stems.

"The parsley hasn't been washed," I said, looking at my wet, dirty hands.

"The parsley hasn't been washed," I protested in a loud voice.

No one answered me. I became frightened and felt like a character in a Kafka novel. Dishwashers, bus boys, cooks, waiters, the steward, the pantry man worked silently and extremely fast. They were putting the final touches on a twenty-five-thousand-dollar wedding party.

The other day, weaving through the East Village, I was accosted by a small black boy about five years old.

"Hey, mister. You got two cents?"

Smiling, I looked down at the boy. "What are you gonna do with two cents?"

"Buy a cookie," the boy replied; his eyes danced darkly. He was very clean; perhaps his mother had just released him from the house.

"Here's a dime, sonny," I said, feeling good. I walked away, skipped a mound of dog excrement, regretting that I didn't have a son. I'd make a great father, friends are always telling me. Unwed mothers, divorcées, widows adjust their antennae of hope, and while I am very fond of these women and their children—they are not the women of future dreams. Maggie? Perhaps. But she is fifteen years older than I am; her womb was always barren. I have no knowledge of fathering children. A romantic rumor of a son in Mexico, that's all.

I looked back at the small black boy. He stood on the corner, counting coins, then approached another man.

I laughed. Clean and bright-eyed. Little black boy. Hustling in the city. Heir Apparent. Crown Prince of Con.

City children are special, seemingly endowed with a knowledge of life, endowed with the knowledge of surviving in the urban jungle while retaining the quicksand innocence and charm of childhood. Once, sitting in cutthroat Chrystie Park, I witnessed a little drama, a scene from a long first act, a lesson in surviving, a lesson for future street gangs. Actions that frequently lead to jail.

I wanted to smoke a joint and walked to the quiet section of the park. A high iron fence enclosed a special area for senior citizens. But that midnight, a group of prekindergarten-age boys had managed to get inside the senior area. They were having a dandy, cursing, rock, wine-bottle, and beer-can battle.

One little boy approached me. "Mister. You'd better watch out. My buddy is gonna throw a bottle over here."

I looked back and ducked in time. A white port-wine bottle zipped through the air, landed at the base of a young tree, where pushers dropped their three-dollar bags of scrambled eggs.

Children are great. Our future. Children are great. Charming little buggers. Especially at midnight. Always midnight. Especially if they are prekindergarten age. Especially if their parents aren't around.

Charles Wright was born in New York City and not New Franklin, Missouri. Charles Wright grew up in the ghetto, joined a gang, which staked out a piece of the turf and took possession of it. A cold Walter Mitty dream? But what takes place in the following dream? No doubt street money and politics would have been involved. A sharp pimp, pusher, addict? There is no doubt in my mind that I would have served time. Perhaps I'd be writing my lawyer, family, friends, asking for books, candy, and cigarettes—instead of writing an entry into a journal.

MOTHERS: California ain't Mississippi. New York ain't Georgia. All offer the same old racial climate. You do not have to go to the heartland of America—say, the Middle West—to take the pollen count of pro-George Wallace sentiments. Simply open the door that fronts on your own back yard. The death of George Jackson, one of the Soledad Brothers, made me realize that the Auschwitz gates are not closed. They are not awaiting instructions from their superiors. They are waiting to act on their own. Who will be next? Angela Davis? You, me? In Manhattan each day, blacks and Puerto Ricans are roughed up daily before they see a judge or jury. It happens every day to the little people from the urban jungle. Seldom do we hear or read about it.

Sometimes these happenings have the deceptive innocence of childhood, have absolutely nothing to do with drugs, mugging, or even disturbing the peace. It can be nothing more than a handwritten note: "Come for a drink around six. My aunt is coming down and there will be a few other people. Perhaps we'll have dinner. Anyway, please come. They want to meet you." Because I felt guilty for not calling friends, for accepting invitations and never showing, I went to the dinner party, wearing my best suit of depression. Before the hostess offered a drink, she invited me into the kitchen. "I'm so glad you could come. Randy's in the bedroom. I've got to get him out of here before my aunt comes. Could you help me?"

I had a couple of drinks, talked to several pleasant people, then went into the bedroom. Randy's always spaced out. But he was shooting for Zeroville. Since nothing was happening, I said, "Let's split and come back later." But like most schizos, Randy is extremely distrustful. I continued in my opium-saint voice, and we left. In the street, I suggested that we visit an old friend of his, a friend from vocational high school. Randy has a funny little habit of dropping to the floor or sidewalk when he is being advised to do something. He didn't want to see the old high-school buddy. So he fell to the sidewalk about twenty feet from where Wing Ha Sze had been murdered a couple of weeks before. I pleaded with Randy. People stopped, cars slowed. "Old sport," I said, "if you don't get up, I'll have to call the police."

Randy rose like Jesus on the third day. Then we walked down the street, and I bought a couple of Colt 45's. We sat on the stoop of a boarded-up tenement and talked. It was useless. Randy took a swing at me and missed. I took my half-empty can of beer and hit him hard in the corner of his mouth. He fell to the sidewalk.

"Get up," I screamed. "You're making me lose my cool. I'm taking you to Eddie's. I'm tired of trying to help romper-room weaklings."

By the time we reached Grand Street, darkness had set in. Once more, as if following stage directions, Randy fell, between two parked cars. His mouth was bloody. Several curious, long-haired cyclists stopped.

"He's all right." I sighed. "He's only acting."

The cyclists did not believe me. "Listen," I said angrily, "unless you know something about first aid, you're wasting your time."

Silently, they averted their eyes and drove off. About three minutes later, a tall pale-blond woman and a short dark-haired man with a Thomas Dewey or Hitler mustache stopped. I repeated the story for them. And you know—they didn't believe me. Like an expert rescue team, they picked Randy up and laid him on the sidewalk as I cursed them. Up ahead, two policemen were approaching. The dark-haired man ran to them and said, "Officer, this boy has been hurt."

The two policemen and I went over Randy, who went through his first-day Jesus act.

"What's wrong with him?" a cop asked.

"Nothing," I said. "He's stoned."

"Who hit him?"

"I did. He took a swing at me, and I hit him with a can of beer."

"A full can of beer?"

"Half full."

The policeman searched me, but I was clean as a whistle. And if I never, never had seen hatred before, I saw it in their eyes. Need I tell you, Randy is white and I am black.

The policemen went over to Randy. "Are you all right?" one of them asked.

Randy mumbled. I laughed at the absurdity of it all and was led toward a building with a nightstick in my back. The cop questioned Randy. He continued to mumble.

"Can't you see he's stoned?" I asked. "There's nothing wrong with him but his head. His old lady left him, and his mother moved and told the neighbors not to give him her new address."

The nightstick-lover of a policeman said, "If you don't shut up, I'm gonna beat you."

Just then a squad car pulled up to the curb. One of the street policemen went to the squad car. The two smiling men in the car had arrested Randy the night before; he had tried to attack a bum with a broken wine bottle. Then they drove off. The cop asked Randy if he wanted to press charges against me. Randy shook his head. The nightstick-loving cop was really angry now. He swung the stick like a demented drum majorette.

The four of us stood on the street corner silently for more than twenty minutes. Apparently the two policemen did not like the end of the happening. Finally, one of them came over to me. Pointing his nightstick down Grand Street, he said, "See those two guys coming this way? One of them has on a red shirt. I want you to start walking in that direction, and don't look back. I don't want to see you in this neighborhood again. I'll lock your ass up."

I walked away, inhaling the absurd Saturday-night air. Later that night, I saw Randy.

"Charles," he said, "I'm sorry. I need help."

I nodded but did not say anything. Mentally I was saying, Come on, feet. Let's make it.

* * *

Rain again. Dawn: gray but the light coming through slowly like mother-of-pearl blades on an old windmill. Against the grimy, windowless wall, rippling lines of rain water become an iridescent brick mosaic. Pigeons stir; yawn like grouchy old men. Early subway rumbles, six floors below in the earth, shake the old hotel. My feet want to dance or run.

The morning light expands. A haze evaporates in the room. I dress, go out for *The New York Times,* cigarettes. Return, make tea, eat a cream-cheese-filled bagel. I have decided to read and think about writing again.

Around 10 A.M., finished rereading two favorite Ernest Hemingway short stories: "A Clean Well-lit Place" and "Hills Like White Elephants." Then the phone rang. And although the sky was now fair—it had somehow become black. I will always remember it as a day of silent protest.

SEVENTH AVENUE, NORTH of Forty-second Street. Traffic flowing downtown. The streets are uncrowded at this hour. But the old gray buildings and the old shops with their face-lifted fronts are a staunch reminder of the materialistic present—the present of New Yorkers, Ltd. Three Japanese tourists photographed a florist shop, but I looked away and walked toward the Hotel Passover.

The first person I saw in the hotel was Abe Singer, a widowed accountant. He had his fifth-floor door open. An airline bag and camera case were on the bed. Seventy-year-old Abe Singer was in his underwear, drinking a water glass of bourbon as I passed.

"Jamaica, this time," he said, then added, still beaming, "I'm sorry."

The South Carolina maid was a large woman. She looked like an enormous lamp shade in her jungle-print cotton dress. She wore felt houseshoes and always complained of being cold. Age forty, the maid walked beside me, sighing.

"The poor thing," she said. "Sally wouldn't hurt a flea. The police were here, son. Don't touch a thing."

Sally Reinaldo's room was immaculate. A headless Hollywood bed, covered in dark blue satin, was the hub of the room. The turquoise walls were as bare as the gleaming wood floor, except for three white fur rugs. Silver-framed photographs of family and friends formed a semicircle on a round table by the bed. But I did not look at them. Green plants in red clay pots crowned a radiator shelf. The venetian blind was closed. I walked over to the dressing table, which had a mirrored top. Perfume, cologne, oils, powder. Bottles and jars—their contents foreign to me. All I knew was that they had something to do with the mystery and magnetism of a woman's face. A wicker tray overflowed with costume jewelry. I shook the tray, listened to the jangling metal sound, then sat down in a slipper chair and smoked a joint. That was when I discovered the overnight bag and the wig box, shiny as black patent leather. The lid had a thin layer of dust on it.

"You really put the icing on the cake this time, baby," I said aloud, and turned on again.

After a while, I could look over at the blue-covered bed, which had dark stains on it.

I could watch memory flash a kaleidoscopic report from the old world. I saw Sally on West Fifty-seventh Street in May. She had on a black skirt and a white blouse, and I had on a black shirt and white trousers, and we laughed and kissed on the street. Sally asked me to visit her at the Hotel Passover. I promised, but at the time, my social, sexual life was shared only with booze, pills, and pot. Ah, Splendid Solitude! The blessed hours. It is only now that I see the desperation in Sally's eyes, hear that sound in her voice. We had been lovers years ago in Hell's Kitchen. A divorcée, mother of four-year-old Nelson, Sally wanted to marry me. I was not even wedded to my own budding maturity. We got on damn well together. I remember that if money was tight, she insisted on Nelson and me eating the steak. I remember the Saturday she shopped on Ninth Avenue for food, bought material for a dress, cooked dinner, made the dress and wore it to the opening of Sergi King's Port Afrique on East Sixth Street, just off Second Avenue, in the zone that would become the East Village. Later that morning, Sally and I walked up Second Avenue with Sarmi (a Black Muslim before the great Black Muslim conversion). He had a hard-on for me because I reminded him of a young boy. Mona, a French poet, wanted to offer Sally lesbian love. Mona and Sarmi were friends, and the good-byes were warm, uncomplicated. But Sally cried before we made love, and in the afternoon, she leaned out the window screaming rape, pelleting a smiling, freckle-faced policeman with pecans. In June of that year, I returned to the Lowney Turner

Handy Writer's Colony in Marshall, Illinois. Sally made the Las Vegas–Hollywood *la ronde*. It was rumored that she was making $100 a day in Hollywood. No one knew why she returned to New York. No one would ever know. Sally Reinaldo committed suicide on the fifth floor of the Hotel Passover.

I walked all the way back downtown, oblivious to the teeming, early-afternoon streets. Grief, loneliness, self-pity never touched me during the long walk. I simply felt that I had lost something. I opened the door of my hotel room, turned on the radio, drank a beer, showered, and took a sleeping pill. But I couldn't sleep. So I whipped the memory of Sally Reinaldo, who danced a little, sang a little, modeled a little, whored a little, and who wanted to become a star or a housewife, into an olive-green towel and threw it across the room.

Stoned, walking through the early-morning streets, clutching a tumbler of despair. The bars closing. Gradually people appear in the early-morning streets, unsteady in their walk, uncertain of which way to go, what to do. The full white moon, stationary, like a manmade object flung into space, like a flag announcing, "We have arrived. We have set foot on the floor of your dead planet."

And it seemed to me that the street people were tourists on that dead planet. Against their will, they had detoured from the route of dreams. Frightening, oblique—loneliness became the fellow traveler. But there was nothing I could do about it. I felt that I had left part of my insides in Sally Reinaldo's fifth-floor room at the Hotel Passover. I considered myself extremely lucky. A practical man, I gave up Waterloo and concentrated on exile. New York. Hades-on-the-Hudson. It is time to take leave of it. But for the moment, I am comforted with nothing but the prospect of another sunrise, buried in my own mortality.

On the Bowery, bells do not toll. But cocks crow at the Shangwood Live Poultry Market, and sincere hymns blare from the two Bowery Salvation Army havens, pleading with the classless, transient army of men to come unto God. And it seems to me that they should try Him or seriously think about hitting the road. Urban renewal is upon them. A broom is all that is needed for these powerless, nonpolitical men. (Most of them believe they are part of the political scene, hard-hatted in their wine stupor.) "The Bowery will never change," one of them told me recently. "I should know. I've been here twenty-five years."

The Bowery has been changing for a very long time. And there was nothing subtle about the change. Three years ago, non-AIR residents were evicted from lofts, small businesses were forced to move. The raunchy bar called Number One, between the Bowery and Second Avenue, was the first to go, then the Blue Moon. Betty's became the chic circus-yellow front. The pissoir-rich old Palace bar is now Hilly's, where an old-timer rapped on the door one early dawn, like a Scott Fitzgerald ghost in "Babylon Revisited," and asked hoarsely, "Is Jimmie still here?" The legendary Horse Market restaurant folded, replaced by the Bowery Coffee Shop, which also folded. The hotels are going, gone. The Boston, the Clover, the Defender. But what soured hearts was the closing of Sammy's Bowery Follies, although few winos were Follies customers. It was a symbol like the White Horse, the Lion's Head, St. Adrian's, and Max's Kansas City.

Now live rock blares on the Bowery. There are elegant living lofts, waiting only for *House Beautiful*'s photographer or *Vogue* magazine and art galleries. Now local color is provided by the affluent children of Aquarius with their frizzed hair, dirty jeans, and expensive, scuffed boots, and their dolls with their frizzed hair and 1930s style of dressing and their talk of pot, peace, and pollution. They are as cold and capitalistic as the parents they fled. To them the bums are a nuisance. They lack the old bohemian feeling of togetherness. As one tall, bearded artist said to me, "Hell, I've told you about sitting on my stoop. I got an old lady and kids."

All the winos have is each other and the Capital of Pluck (wine). The Capital of Pluck is the Municipal Lodging House for Men on East Third Street, which throughout America's wine world is called "the Muney." Only in the city of New York are these men able to breathe. The Muney will secure free rooms at Bowery hotels, plus three decent meals a day. With the advent of the Nixon regime's phase-in, phase-out, the Muney is uptight. Even the annual Muney summer riots failed to materialize. (The parent group drifted away, got busted, went to the Catskills to work. The main man had severe drug hallucinations.)

On the Bowery, drugs are running a close second to wine.

Especially with young blacks and Puerto Ricans. Indeed, Eugene O'Neill's Iceman would come down to the Bowery looking for a fix.

Like New York night life, business is off in the bars, although men are sitting at the tables before the official 8 A.M. opening. But they sit all day, trying to hustle drinks like pitiful old whores, like shameless clowns.

Sitting and waiting for the silent mushroom in the sky, watching the desperate jackrollers, who in turn are watching them. Money is tight. A daytime robbery is a common happening. Most of the older men try to make it back to the hotels before darkness sets in or go in pairs, groups.

There are no black bars on the Bowery. The blacks prefer to drink on street corners, which is cheaper. There are hotels that will not rent rooms to blacks, and there are hotels which have separate but equal floors for blacks and whites, although both use the same bathrooms. The wine climate of the Bowery has always been racial. This has not changed. The majority of these weak drinking men come from the primeval American South. Wine has not shrunk their racial war; it has enlarged it to the point of fanaticism. Ethnic to the last pint of La Boheme white port (the most popular brand), the mix is roughly Irish and blacks running neck and neck, followed by Poles. There are few Italians, Jews, Chinese. But keeping pace with the national cultural explosion, increasing numbers of young men are nestling in the ruins. Most of them are very hip, according to the old-timer's social register.

The story goes that the police are tougher on white winos than on blacks. Whites are superior and shouldn't sink to that dark level. But it is only the old black men who retain the hairs of *machismo*. Before sunrise, black and white men are in the streets, walking up and down like women on market day, like desperate junkies. At that hour they are waiting for the early-morning "doctors," peddling illegal wine. Illegal wine is now $1.25 a pint. Yet the men who sleep in their own urine on the sidewalk and wipe car windows with dirty rags manage to pay the "doctor," just as more affluent Americans manage to have charge accounts.

For these Bowery men are American, too, with that great American dream. Tomorrow we will seek a new design for living, new territories, which is why the Bowery has expanded into little

Bowery zones. The main zone is the Greenwich Hotel on Bleecker and the Lady Jane West, both old zones. If it were not for the drugquake, the press, and law-and-order citizens, very few people would be aware of the zones. The Keystone Hotel in midtown, one block from Macy's, has been operating for a long time, and the winos have Herald Square, Bryant Park. Another group of winos operates exclusively on Forty-second Street. From the Port Authority, the junction being Grant's Cafeteria and the end of the rich line, Grand Central. Now they've made it down to Wall Street and up to Central Park and the chic East Side streets. Many of the new buildings have openings where a man can seek shelter from the rain or cold. Just for a night.

But then bums have always been transient, always on the move, returning to their home which has always been there, even if only in the mind. The artists will go, too, in time, just as the winos are going. And although Kate Millett may be liberated and celebrated, she, too, will go.

The Bowery is a cinema museum in hell where classic films play forever. Occasionally, selected shorts play, are spliced together, and become classics themselves. And although I still visit the Bowery, there is nothing more to learn. Ravished by their own weakness and the conditions of American life, Bowery men have their Grand Hotel and are content. But other men are attracted to the Bowery because of laziness. All they want to do is drink and shoot the breeze. I hope you realize that is the entire frame for the Bowery.

The Chinese say that the first step is the beginning of a ten-thousand-mile journey. But what is the first step?

At the end of the Bowery, there is Chinatown and the Chinese Garden.

Once almost as remote as a desert fortress, my Chinese Garden, my *bête noire*, is a symbol of the goose-stepping '70s. Sometimes I think nature, man, space-age progress are conspiring to build a terrible corrupt monument for the year 2001. Can this be true? Or have I been on the downward path as far as my fellow human beings are concerned? But once my garden was my church. Layered in concrete, the cesspool of greenery rises at its highest level about thirty feet where the Bowery and Canal meet to channel traffic to Brooklyn and elsewhere. Motorists consider it an unexpected, delightful slice-of-life landscape. Soon it will become a mini-tourist attraction.

Recently, a group of young black, white, Puerto Rican, and Chinese artists set up shop between the hours of eleven and three, painting pop designs on all surfaces except dirt and grass. Against the weathered gray of concrete, black silhouettes. A prisoner hanging from his cell. Two Afro heads in a heavy chess game. And from the old world, stencil designs of Chinese dragons. Although I applaud their slow, sincere efforts, this is of no value to me. All I know is my garden has been invaded by people who represent the blowup of New York. People arrive, perform, depart. Countless variations on an urban theme. These people make police reports, signal, Bellevue, Kings County, pay the bread man of drugs. These people confront policemen, merge with the winos and the goldbricking Department of Parks workers, the artistic elite from the neighboring lofts and the Chinese immigrants, who instantly, magically, accept the American middle-class outer garment. You see, I am the senior citizen of the garden. Six years, day and night, summer and winter—I have sat on that stone ledge, surrounded by thirty-nine trees, watching people arrive like ghosts in a real dream.

Except for the long stone ledges, there is nothing. The playground equipment has been removed. The toilets have been sealed for eternity in concrete. All that remains are the ledges, trees, and elegant lampposts. Most of the time, only a few lamps are lit. The other night, four teenage boys marched through the garden and surveyed the scene. Then three of the boys ran out of the garden. The fourth boy returned. He walked through the garden like a Midwestern basketball star before a county championship. But his turf was urban. Stone under those imitation French cycling shoes. His hand was steady as he shot out all the lights. And in the semi-darkness the boy looked over at me and smiled. I saluted him. Hadn't I reported him to the police (at their request) before? Once, surrounded by a gang, I cleverly signaled to a policeman. He knew that the boys were throwing bottles and rocks into the street, had hit a woman with a baby and had broken the window of a Ford station wagon.

And of course, there are the dogs. People unleash their dogs; smile proudly as if they had conceived them on some passionate, dark night. Their eyes never leave the dogs, even when they defecate on the grass where winos sleep, children play, young lovers love. It is very sad. The dog owners appear to be sane, intelligent, well dressed. The artistic types are fashionably disheveled.

The saddest scene that I encountered in the Chinese Garden was not the murder of Wing Ha Sze, nor a very masculine wino serving head at high noon. No, it was a fat, laughing Chinese girl about three years old. Even today, I can see the girl's parents' mood shift from pride to horror. Sunlight through the full-leafed trees, gleaming on the pale blue satin hair ribbons, the blue-and-white gingham dress. The laughing girl began running and fell to the ground. A rich image of dog excrement colored her bosom like a Jim Dine valentine.

I can also see three mothers and four children picnicking on the grass. It was late August. A humid afternoon. The pollution count was high, and traffic cried, crawled across Manhattan Bridge. I locked my mental camera at 5:10, according to the clock in the parking lot on Bayard Street. Opened another King Rheingold, content with the world around me and the world out there. That is, until a half-ass domestic French poodle tried to dry-fuck one of the children, a boy about four years old. The three mothers, elegantly balancing cigarettes and bottles of Miller High Life in their hands, might have been figures in a Bonnard landscape. But the screaming small boy's fear brought me back into the present. I finished my beer and watched the horny dog mount another child, a toddling tot, a boy still a little uneasy about what was underneath his feet. The excited dog knocked the boy to the ground. The dog's tongue flapped as if dying of thirst. The laughing mothers continued to smoke and drink beer.

I stood up, looked north through the arches of Manhattan Bridge, through the pollution screen toward the Empire State Building, then south toward the old buildings of Chinatown, sitting on a real-estate dish of excellent sweet pork. The cubistic Chatham Towers rise above them. With soot powdering their historic façades, municipal New York and Wall Street overpower them. However, new buildings such as the World Trade

Center rise above history, as if to embrace the sky. In Chatham Square, chained to a young tree, three metal chairs proclaim JESUS SAVES.

But there are eighteen broken parking meters in my garden, like the end of a rip-off happening of abstract sculpture. Drug addicts, functioning as human jack-hammers, carried them up from the streets between midnight and dawn. I arrived at 6 A.M. with coffee, the Sunday *New York Times,* and thought: Where are the police, the concerned citizens? Indifference might have a past. Am I right in assuming that it has a future?

Of late, small armies of policemen (usually Chinese, with a couple of novice Wasp detectives) march through my garden on a groping, fascist search. But there is no one except me, two young lovers, and the winos. Open, open! There is no place to hide. Frequently, New York's finest question me, their hands roughly moving from the top of my head to my feet. Then, apparently unsatisfied, they flash their brilliant flashlights in my face. This does nothing for them. So they turn the flashlights up into the thirty-nine trees. And as they walk toward the Bayard Street exit, I ask if I can help them. Their voices, like their eyes, are elsewhere. You see, New York's finest say they are simply on a routine patrol, which is a goddamn lie. I am the senior citizen of the Chinese Garden, the resident historian, the wild-grass accountant. I also do extra duty outside of the garden. Within a ten-block radius of the garden, I am familiar with crime and corruption. Therefore, I hope no one will be foolish enough to think the rise in crime has anything to do with the police's presence in my garden.

The sentry knows who patrols the desecrated island of concrete and trees. Just the other day, a daring group of British tourists marched into the garden. The excitement of discovery seemed to color their voices and eyes. A Byzantine ruin, or a secret Persian Garden? Here, marijuana, wine, baseball outrank young love and volleyball. Here, the sons of Chinese immigrants are becoming skilled American baseball players. Dressed in red, the Free Mason volleyball team plays an excellent game, lacking only American competitive drive. Their game is passive, as if volleyball were programmed and, chop—a programmed karate class, still working out at a quarter of nine in the evening.

The sky had not turned dark, and I watched the teacher and his male and female assistants. There was something uncomfortable about their voices and mannerisms. I tried not to think of the future of the mixed racial bag of ghetto students. No matter, no matter. Strange green thumbs are cultivating young plants here. I repeat: no matter, no matter—all of these people are in no way part of my garden. I do not regret their invasion. No, I regret America's invasion into the porous walls of their minds.

But the Cat Woman is the most radiant human being I encountered in the Chinese Garden. She arrived one afternoon in the summer of 1970, looking like a thrift-shop visionary, moving as if her yellow-shod ballerina feet were monitored by snails. The Cat Woman bowed toward the volleyball players in the former playground. Ah! She smiled—waltzed under the full-leafed trees that were like a roof. Presently I could see her lips move. Now and then, the Cat Woman held her hands above her eyes, then walked to the center of the garden. You could say the center is a cross. (The center has four squares of greenery.) Anyway, the Cat Woman prayed briefly, then stood between two trees and raised her arms toward the watercolor sky; then apparently passion seized her. She fell to the ground and began clawing in the dry earth with her hands, trying to dig up the beloved cat she had buried there the year before. More than a dozen people were in the garden that afternoon, and without talking to any of them, I discovered that the Cat Woman's father, and then her nine-year-old daughter, had failed to give her enough love. The dead cat, "He was so nice." Life was a soufflé without him.

Almost a year later, I thought I saw the Cat Woman. I was going home, taking the tourist route through Chinatown. I stopped at the clam house which is across the street from the garden. The moon was full. City lights glowed. The neon veneer of Chinatown created a rainbow haze. But the woman I saw was more than sixty feet from where I stood popping clams. Almost at the top of the second entrance's steps, where the trees began and where the light is dim. I ran toward the woman like a man possessed with a vision.

Indeed, it was the Cat Woman. She was blessed with a vision. She knew that someone would enter the deserted garden and ask her a question. Her young daughter was fine. But mothers and fathers were out this year, she said.

"The cat," she exclaimed, offering me a drink from a Hiram Walker pint. "You remember. Well, I've got good news for you. He came back to life, and I'm so happy."

Was there a time when a once dead, now live cat, or a child with a balloon, would have startled me in the Chinese Garden? Yes, there was a time. It was during the early stage of the Great Society.

LIKE MOST MEN, the Chinese prefer foreign sexual hors d'oeuvres, and there are many Occidental whores in Chinatown. But whorehouse hotels do not exist. Dollar-sign sex takes place in cars, in door entrances on dark, deserted business streets, or in hotels near the Bowery. Recently, encounters have taken place in the Chinese Garden. Miss Nell from Dallas, Texas, works here. An exceptionally large woman, Miss Nell appears to be powdered from head to foot with white chalk dust. She looks like a visitor from a country where there is no sunlight. Strawberry-blond ringlets circle her wide pleasant face. Her voice is like a tiny rusty bell. Extremely sensitive about her size and profession, Miss Nell will exit from a taxi as if taking the first steps to the funeral of a beloved friend. By the time she has planted her feet on the sidewalk, she has become the sultry, shrewd businesswoman and moves slowly, like a great, proud queen, her bell-like voice a litany of love for sale.

Shortly before 8 P.M. one night, Miss Nell arrived in the Chinese Garden with a customer. Standing under a Victorian lamppost, she surveyed the garden like a field marshal. Two young lovers sat with their dog near the former playground.

Miss Nell, wearing a sensational black-and-white mini dress and white sandals (a pair of 1940 Joan Crawford "fuck me" shoes), motioned to the nervous man to follow her. She held a large white handbag, white gloves, a clear plastic umbrella decorated with white flowers in her right hand. A perfect Fellini whore, she moved through the tall grass toward a large tree about fifteen feet from where I sat. The man, who had his hands in his pockets, followed at a fast pace.

Still clutching the white bag, gloves, umbrella, Miss Nell went through the ritual of going down on the man. She worked very hard. She worked with great feeling. She worked like a professional. Miss Nell worked for a very long time. Now and then, she'd look up at the man, and you could almost read her mind. Finally, she stood up, lifted her skirt, and offered her buttocks. This did not help the man, who was now working very hard. Miss Nell decided to try the door of life. Still clutching the bag, umbrella, gloves, she put her large arms around the man. She might have been a mother comforting a small child. But Miss Nell and the man moved with great passion. He was very relaxed and even smiled. He did not reach a climax.

Exhausted, Miss Nell led the man over to the ledge where I was sitting. The man smiled and joked. Miss Nell was angry. She looked down at me, opened the clear plastic umbrella with the pretty white flowers on it, and tried to block my view. It was like trying to cover the Empire State Building with a single bed sheet.

Once more the hard-working professional went down on her customer. And I thought they would make it this time. But Miss Nell jumped up and screamed, "My God! What's wrong with you? I ain't got all night. I've got to take care of business."

The man was still smiling and asked for a two dollar refund.

Miss Nell snapped open her white handbag and said, "With pleasure." Then she walked out of the garden swiftly, her head down like an unhappy queen. The man followed at a distance.

Then the young lovers, who are almost nightly visitors, rose and walked out of the Chinese Garden, the small auburn dog running ahead of them, his metal leash hitting the pavement dully, sounding as I imagined Miss Nell would sound with a very bad cold.

A profound statement from a country-club divorcée, age forty-two. A former secretary, the divorcée had also worked in advertising and public relations. It was almost midnight, and the tranquilizers and Scotch had failed to extinguish the lady's anger: "Hell. People think alimony is easy. I worked sixteen years for that money. And when it runs out, I'll become a whore. Men love whores. I know. Lennie married a bona fide whore."

The symposium, "Toward the Elimination of Prostitution," reminded me of—say—the Ku Klux Klan in Iceland: absurd. The Babbitt sisters of Salem, Massachusetts, or simply a confused but sincere movement of sisters? Even the together women writers such as Susan Brownmiller were caught in the breeze that whispered Joseph McCarthy. The good, "straight," middle-class white women should go underground like the Weathermen and produce an anti-prostitution pill, force chastity belts on the men they live with, or get married. Even an occasional lay would help. And although I'd vote for improving the female condition, I'm depressed by these hen-pecked solutions to the female-male misunderstanding. Depressed, depressed. It's like trying to ejaculate inside a vagina the size of the entrance to the Holland tunnel.

In a symbolical and a real sense, slavery hasn't been formally abolished in the United States. But the majority of women who become prostitutes do so of their own free will. It seems like easy work and fast money. I refuse to subscribe to the women's movement's use of prostitutes as a Salvation Army cause. The propaganda oozes emotional perfume. The shtick is a roadrunner of a masculine Madison Avenue campaign. How effective will such a campaign be in our time? The good women stated it beautifully: "The topic, if allowed to be openly discussed, would have reached to the roots of our sexual fears and fantasies . . ." Ours is a perilous voyage. There is the uneasy knowledge that it might be our last; the harbor hasn't been sighted. We could drown. How stupid of us! Why can't we redesign the lifeboats, take a good hard look at our male-and-female relationship? Perhaps redefine sin, morality, and corruption for our time on this earth.

The baptism of a whore is the acceptance of a pimp's psychological rap. After this ritual, the "straight" woman becomes a whore and the pimp's bank. If one rap fails to convince the "straight" woman, then the pimp will use another rap. Most pimps are not great lovers or handsome in the movie-star sense. I know a black, middle-aged pimp who is five feet tall and looks like a frog. Whores dig the man. They give him money, and he buys their clothes. All of them seem to be content with the arrangement. Recently I saw the pimp on Fourteenth Street. He had his arms around two of his girls, and all of them were smiling, and they might have been rehearsing for a 1980 television commercial.

"Would you whore?" I asked a young actress who had worked briefly at a whore bar.

"No."

"Why?"

"No moral reason. I just wouldn't enjoy the work." But like most women, the actress found the whore-pimp scene fascinating. "I can understand how straight women fall for it. Especially emotionally insecure women. The rap is beautiful. Reassuring. If straight men used the rap of a pimp, male and female relations would improve."

"Would you make me whore?" Kitty asked.

The words jammed against my Protestant shelter. But my male ego tripped. Kitty would whore for me. She would do anything for me. All in the name of love.

"If it were profitable for both of us." I laughed and took her to bed. Our relationship was warm, uncomplicated. We never mentioned whoring again. But a month later, Kitty told me that she had a dinner date at the Waldorf Astoria (Count Basie had just opened). The following afternoon, Kitty gave me $50 to buy food. She was an excellent cook. Mentally, the dinner that night lacked flavor. Of course, I could have got stoned, beat up on Kitty, and put her down or rapped about the fabulous Waldorf, then changed gears and, ever so sincere, rapped about a poor, uptight writer who loved her. That's it: there's nothing else to know. Kitty was an occasional whore, and it brought her little joy, although I believe she enjoyed it in a subconscious sense: it was degrading.

Last year, a twenty-year-old addict asked me if I would take money from her. I needed money, and she wanted to help me. I was for real. Hadn't I from the very beginning respected her? I had never put her down, *made her feel like dirt.*

There are a variety of trees in the prostitution forest. My friend's wife doesn't enjoy oral sex, but tries to go along with the program. My friend, the father of two children, loves his wife. They have been married for eight years. A mistress would definitely complicate their relationship. The husband, father, lover, friend has whores orally.

And oh, you earthshaking movement sisters! What about the boys in Vietnam? Your countrymen, husbands, brothers, lovers, and friends. As they wait to kill or be killed, would you deny them one of life's greatest pleasures? Would you want them to use five fingers? As a former army man, I want to tell you this: I put my young life on the line for you. I helped build roads, schools in Korea. I gave my time and money to those poor people. I hate to think of all the women and children who might have starved without some Korean woman selling her body for an hour, a night, or a month. To relieve the fear of the uneasy truce, boredom, and petty politics of barracks (tent) life, there was nothing else a man could do but get stoned and screw. Or use five fingers, abstain, or—a sign in an army john: FINCH WOULD DO IN A PINCH.

Prostitutes forever! Long live the golden girls of the streets!

I'm for legalizing prostitution. Suspicious of the women's movement's motives in their anti-prostitution drive. Afraid of competition? Outlawing prostitution gives "straight" women an advantage. But I doubt if it brings women and men together on an equal level of understanding, desire, and need.

THE EAST VILLAGE worms its way through a Ponce de León garden of drugs. But flowers dry, die. In the sun, in a musical cigarette box on a glass-top coffee table, in an oven, and, fenced in a newspaper blanket (limp as pizza dough), on a radiator. A *Reader's Digest* of scents, offering the fresh air of peace of mind or a hallucinating high.

Journeying into the interior of Welfare-Drugsville, where the last of the flowers were in the final stage of exile, I remember the sparse summer trees seemed unreal: models for Madame Tussaud's wax museum. In a ten-block area I encountered no police. The streets were monitored by junkies, thieves, pushers, a new breed of whores who sipped iced Cokes and coffee in the heat of afternoon. Domesticated hippies walked Doberman pinschers, German shepherds, or fashionable mongrels, while black and Puerto Rican teenagers, natives of "East Village" (the Lower East Side), motherfuck each other with words. The ancient tenements are monuments to the splendor of welfare. The poor, the uneducated are powerless against the government's yearly rape. Even whores get tired. Model tenements in Utopia! In lieu of flowers, garbage litters the pavement. Car arson is a big sport in the East Village (two cars in three days on East Eleventh Street between Avenues B and C). The fire department and police daily offer their services.

Social workers, VISTA (*vision*) workers, the Church offer services. Nothing changes. The old woman who laughs like an exhausted mare is still inspecting garbage cans, a Horn & Hardart shopping bag wreathed over her arm. A stringbean junkie, age twenty, has been stealing something almost daily for two years.

You see I am no stranger here. "You know all of those people over there," Shirley had said. "Please see if you can find Denise."

Denise had split from the pad on Ninth Street. The R.O.T.C. student had split. The last member of the party, a blonde, a chocolate-chip cookie of a girl, was alone and depressed; the rent was due. As I waited for the elevator, two junkies tried to sell me a pair of ice skates. Toto Thomas has worked many scenes: reform school, Golden Gloves, con artist, armed robbery, file clerk, messenger, truck driver. Then he blossomed into a blue-eyed flower and sat in Tompkins Square like a human rocket waiting for the countdown. Where was Denise? Well—

"Man. It's good to see you. And you know something? I'm gonna make it this time. I've got a good scene uptown. But I'm gonna make it down here once in a while."

We went over to the pad Toto Thomas had crashed and shared with four pleasant, apple-cheeked young men from suburbia. The pad was neat like a college dormitory. The young men were leaving. They were very careful with their garbage. I watched them force bulging paper bags into a garbage can and then replace the lid. Four well-mannered young men who for the moment controlled heroin like conservative stockbrokers.

"I don't shoot any more," Toto Thomas said. "Just baby shots. Water shots." Toto picked up wads of cotton which contained heroin dregs. Just before shooting up, he turned to me and grinned. "Now I'm ready to rap and go out and get a piece. Ball, baby. That's what I always say."

The same afternoon, I met Peter on Avenue B. "Where you been?" he asked. "You look bad. Are you still looking for that pet? Wanna couple of pills? I got pills, baby. Pills to go to bed with. I'm back with my old lady and *her* girlfriend."

A boy who appeared to be about sixteen years old walked up. Peter made a sale. Then the boy turned to me. Without blinking an eye, he asked, "You wanna get rimmed?"

"No," I said. "That bores me."

The three of us laughed. The boy started off, walking like an ambitious executive. At least the last of the flower children were interested in the pollen count. Anything goes! The New World's sexuality! Lord, sometimes I ask myself, Are they for real, are they free? Rimming, once a whispered desire of sexual swingers, is slowly surfacing from down under. And it seems somehow appropriate to mention human excrement and cannibalism as mankind prepares not to scale the summits but to take the downward path into the great valley of the void.

Thoughts pinballed through my mind; the questionnaire was almost blank, and I stopped off at Sam's; he lives in one of those medieval wrecks. The last of the communal flowers were limp in front of the building. They sat on the stoop, played guitars, sang on fire escapes, and got high on stairwells, seemingly placed there by a landscape architect, schooled in James Joyce's Nighttown.

Miss Ohio manned the second floor. Glowing with warmth, she had just returned from visiting her parents and giggled about her new silver-buckled shoes. Miss Ohio had been on the scene for almost a year. Nothing bad had happened to her—yet. Occasionally she gets high, talks about being "hung-up" on some "cat," spends most of her time with the neighborhood children. She seems so out of place in the East Village. She belongs to the world of babies, chintz-flowered bedrooms, country kitchens.

On the third floor, I had to step over a group of stoned children. Sam was talking with—let's call him Jerry. Sam works in Jerry's uncle's midtown office. We sat around listening to records, getting high. Then the white chick from upstairs arrived. She's got a Jones, a thing for black dudes. A hefty girl with a ban-the-bomb air. Her old man had split, and she wanted Sam to help her find him. "The bastard is probably in Washington Square because he knows I don't hang out there."

Meanwhile, long-haired Jerry had placed his booted feet on the lower shelf of the coffee table, his elbows rigid on his knees.

"I don't wanna cry," he whimpered. But he made no effort to check the tears. "I can't stand it. Last summer I was flipping out. Speed and every goddamn thing. Paranoid as a son of a bitch, and one night these punk kids tried to jump me. They were high, too. On pot and wine. I wasn't trying to cop a plea. I just didn't wanna fight. I started to run, and one of them comes after me. I gave him a belt in the stomach, and he fell back and hit his head against one of those old-fashioned stoops."

Jerry bolted up from the sofa. "I just can't stand it. I'm dreaming about it all the time. His mother—she was holding his head. 'You killed my son.' Now I don't take anything. Drink booze, smoke a little pot. I'm on probation, and the family and everyone treats me with kid gloves. But I don't feel free."

Later, suffering Death Valley Days of the mind, Jerry was crawling on the floor, crying, beating his fists against the floorboards.

I looked out the window. On the roof across the street, a sailor on leave drank a quart of Miller High Life and looked down at the street scene. A civilian last summer, he was always on the roof at dawn. Alone in the early summer quiet, then he drank cans of Rheingold, ranted and raved at the young people who balled and slept on the roof opposite him. His roof was one story higher than the Drugsville roof. I remember that he was like an angry Baptist preacher. A frustrated, beer-drinking, Saturday-night hard hat. Perhaps the navy had been very good for him. Perhaps he had matured and from the experience had become a man, had gained confidence and had had women. Perhaps his I-am-at-peace-with-the-world had crystallized because flowers no longer blossomed and balled on rooftops. I'll never know. I sensed he wanted to talk to me. But I turned from the window. It had been a long trip. Darkness was a long way off. The hip and beautiful flowers were dead, out of season, waiting to be reincarnated and given a new name, a new scene.

You know how it is. Memory quivers like a vibrating machine, and you smile. "Golly, Miss Molly."

I had been drinking in the White Horse with two of my more stable earthlings. A nine-to-five Literary Chap in a Chipp suit. His companion was a down-in East Village boutique girl. They wanted me to go with them to a Hotel Albert party. But I remembered too many roller-coaster days, nights, schlepping early-morning ghosts, hallucinating rock revivals at the priceless Albert. So I made it across town and went to the Old Dover in the Bowery. In this frantic bag of hell, I could be absolutely alone. The regulars, stoned on cheap wine, respected my privacy. I had trained myself against the babbling voices around me. I would play "Hey Jude" and "Revolution," knock down vodka, and make it. Sitting at my customary station at the bar, turned toward the street, I watched a chic *Harper's Bazaar* type of girl saunter in. She was Lady Brett Ashley, stoned on salvation.

"You weak bastards," she shouted. "Get back into the mainstream of life!"

The jukebox swung with "Can I Change My Mind and Start All Over Again?" The Bennington girl, masquerading as Lady Brett, wanted to dance. A real nigger type, carried away by the promise of the moment, asked me for a cigarette. "If you can't make it without a smoke, you're nowhere," I told him.

Meanwhile, the sotted sister threw her handbag on the bar and winked at me. A game, a happening, no matter, no matter. I knew her kind and gave her my Rover Boy smile. Lady Brett began dancing alone. A parody of a sensual grind. Surrounded by stoned but reserved men, she had for the moment forgotten her mission of soul saving. But the bartender, followed by his henchmen, threw Our Lady of the Bowery, kin of Hemingway and *Harper's Bazaar,* out the door. No one followed the lady's exit.

A dark, port-wine-drinking young man came up to the bar. Despite the warm night, he carried a leather jacket and had on black bell-bottoms, black T-shirt, and Swiss-hi shoes (in other words construction-worker high tops. Laces of tan leather, Dupont neoprene crepe soles. These shoes are extremely popular for comfort and durability, and offer the weight of a coffee cup's illusion of masculinity. In fact, knowledgeable people call them "fruit boots").

"Wanna smoke from a dead man?" Leather Jacket asked, offering a hand-rolled cigarette.

I accepted and discovered a man had died in the bar earlier. Men are always passing out, sleeping on the tables and floor, and the dead man was, well—on the floor. All Leather Jacket knew was that the cops went through the man's pockets, searching for identification. They laughed and joked with the regulars. A cop had given Leather Jacket the dead man's tobacco and cigarette papers.

Leather Jacket ordered two dark ports, before confession. Once again, I am working on my sainthood: I listen. A Catholic, another cross in the seemingly endless line of raunchy souls I've encountered recently: Czechs, Poles, Irish, Italians, and Puerto Ricans. Guilt works overtime for them. I'm not sure if they want help or simply want to recharge their emotional batteries. But Catholic youth is the victim of their passion, frustration, and hatred. Apparently family and Church have failed these weak men. Unable to recognize their latent disturbances, they simply hustle them down the medieval road of morality and guilt. Any intelligent child questions that road, especially if it detours from the reality around him.

"My old lady put me out," Leather Jacket was saying. "I lost my job and left Jersey City. I've been drinking since Easter."

"You seem to be doing all right," I said.

"Well, I got cleaned up. You should have seen me last week."

A small black queen, sitting ringside, graciously accepts the good nights of the courtly regulars. Makes it with a lean hillbilly escort.

"My old lady looks something like that." Leather Jacket laughed.

"Do you mean she's black and ugly, or a man?" I asked.

Leather Jacket looked directly at me and smiled. "I guess you got the scene figured out."

"I don't know," I said, ordering another vodka. Leather Jacket opened the cage of his past. An American Catholic Classic in some respects. Hard-working, hard-drinking father died when Leather Jacket was an altar boy. Mom ("A beautiful broad, I wanted to make it with her. I think she wanted to make it with me, too") put her two sons and three daughters in an orphanage and shopped around for a new husband. Mom eventually married a rich old man and moved to Montreal. The children remained in the orphanage. Leather Jacket rebelled against the sadistic fathers and nuns. "It fucked with my psyche, but I'm sort of together."

Enlisting in the army, Leather Jacket continued his personal revolt. "Nothing has ever been able to break me." After a medical discharge, he worked in factories, diners, gas stations. A black schoolteacher stopped for gas one day and propositioned Leather Jacket. "I remember following him up the steps. Man. He was big and ugly, but I sort of dug him. Weird man."

"And there were red lights in the pad, and he called you Daddy."

"You're a smart son of a bitch. You got the whole fucking scene figured out."

"I'm not putting you down," I said. "But I've heard the story before."

Leather Jacket's brain was at the bottom of the wine barrel. "I'm all fucked up," he said, breathing hard. "I get so goddamned tired and lonely, and it's not all sex, you know. Hell. I could have almost any broad I want, and you know about the queens."

I understood, thinking: Jesus. I hope he doesn't start the waterworks. Leather Jacket was more honest than most twenty-five-year-olds from his prison. I remembered a Spanish queen who lived nearby. Her old man had left for P.R. The queen was alone and lonely. Perhaps Leather Jacket and the Spanish queen could, at least for the night, quench their loneliness. As we departed, I wondered where was my saintly halo, my recluse's cabin by the sea.

Coco gave Leather Jacket her Park Avenue welcome. We went into the living room. All the major pieces of furniture were covered in custom plastic, including the fluffy 9-by-12 white cotton rug. The art objects were holy: gilt madonnas with rosebud halos. Jesus Christ was everywhere. Plastic, coppertone, brass plate, plaster of Paris. The room was heady with orange blossom refresher. Large votive candles created a mood appropriate for a wake, séance, or Mass. Coco and Leather Jacket made small talk while I looked over the record collection. Already, I could sense they would work something out and that it would go well for them. I put on an LP, smoked a joint, very happy about the whole scene. Then Pepe, the ex-husband, lumbered in from the bedroom, yawning. He greeted me warmly and shook hands with Leather Jacket, and I knew that they would be enemies.

But Coco was in his glory. An amused queen enthroned in a red Easy Boy lounge chair. Pepe showed me the long knife he had bought on Forty-second Street. Leather Jacket was an excellent knife thrower. Coco cooed and teased. Pepe and Leather Jacket fought for his favors. Then Coco invited me into his neat little kitchen. He thanked me, and I inhaled Avon's Fandango perfume.

"Forget it, doll."

"He came back and I took him back, but I'll show him tonight."

The night danced on and on. We got higher. Pepe and Leather

Jacket remained on guard. Coco remained on the throne. The three non-jazz lovers seemed to enjoy the records I played. Then something funny happened. Leather Jacket and Pepe became open enemies again.

Pepe, who had never worked for one day in the nineteen years he had been on this planet, called Leather Jacket a phony.

Leather Jacket, still breathing hard, said, "You little uncool Forty-second Street punk."

"Cut it out," I said. But I didn't get up and stop them.

Leather Jacket was ready to attack and ran his trembling hands through his long blond hair.

"You're a real little bitch," he told Pepe. "Did you know that?"

"I'm young, faggot," Pepe cried.

"Oh dear," Coco moaned. "Why do my husbands always turn out to be members of the sisterhood?"

FLASH! A CHICAGO POLL reports that segregation is flowering magnificently in America. Oh my God . . . interesting. Is John Wayne aware of the result of the Chicago poll? Once upon a time, John Wayne let Sammy Davis, Jr., wear that legendary hat in a Rat Pack western. John Wayne has given blacks two roles in films he has directed. One black was perfect for his role: he portrayed a slave. But American blacks are not responsible, according to Wayne. It was not surprising for him to announce in a May *Playboy* interview: "I believe in white supremacy."

Once upon a time, playing cowboy in an old wrecked house, imitating John Wayne, a nail zipped into my lower lip. I still have the memento today. But I want to tell you about Newport Beach, two years ago. Albert Pearl, my friend and tourist guide, pointed his finger in the direction of a palm-shrouded hill and said, "John Wayne lives over there." June Allyson also lives in Newport, I was told time and time again. I remembered her smile, husky intoxicating voice, the childhood MGM movies. But now I am a man; I know what kind of woman June Allyson is. Breathing the dry, clear air of Orange County, I always detected the scent of the far right. The only way I can describe the scent is to say: Inhale ether, or imagine facing a double-barreled shotgun ten feet from where you are presently standing or sitting.

Uncomfortable looking at the sterile, pretty pastel houses, the

Sears Roebuck landscaping. All I can think of is golf, insurance, and car agencies. *Reader's Digest,* the Republican Party, and watching Lawrence Welk on a Saturday or Sunday night. In my youth I visited California. I remember San Bernardino, Whittier (Nixon, the future President of the United States, was living there at the time. However, only family and friends were aware of it), Riverside, Pomona. All the streets linking towns. Even then, the place made me slightly uncomfortable. I certainly had never heard of the far right. Joan Didion was a little girl then. Today, the towns remain the same, the people remain the same—the custodians of San Gorgonio Mountain and Death Valley.

No, I do not want to tell you about Newport Beach today. I am in the East, waiting to fly or crack up. And before either happening takes place, let me say: Afroed, slender, Levi bell-bottoms, striped mock turtleneck shirt, and perhaps a book under my arm, I usually receive polite, guarded smiles in, say, Merrick, Long Island, if I ask directions. A visitor, or has one of *them* moved here?

Afroed, slender, Levi bell-bottoms, striped mock turtleneck shirt, and perhaps a couple of books under my arm, I am always the intruder, the rapist, the mugger on—say—Avenue J and Twenty-ninth Street in Brooklyn. Basically an Orthodox Jewish zone. I respect, am fascinated by their way of life. But men have landed on the moon, pollution is the common cold of science. We're running out of space, and I've been here for four hundred years, am no longer a stranger. I am only in their zones to wash dishes. I am underpaid. Almost all of them would cheat me if they could, and although I admire their women, it is at a distance. Their women would have to literally come crawling on their hands and knees before I would make love to them. But knowing my mood these days, I'd probably laugh, shout an obscenity, and walk away.

"Forest Hills, Forest Lawn," I joked in the smoker of a Long Island train. My two white co-workers were feigning sleep. Already, they had assured me that things were getting better. I hadn't asked them. The tone of their voices would make an agnostic quiver with belief.

The low-income Forest Hills project. The claim of nonracial motives and the political under-the-table blackjack game—no matter, no matter! The Forest Hills protest is a Forest Lawn monument to American racism. Would the good people of Forest Hills protest if five hundred of their own kind, five hundred of their black counterparts moved in, early one summer morning?

We'll shift scenes here. On the Bowery, the ex-blue-collar workers rage in their drunken or dry leather voices about the mugging blacks, welfare, and what they have done for this country, rage about the lack of police protection. Clean-cut, always with a demitasse of coins, and chain-smoking—their eyes are a seismograph of hate. Is it because of my money, clothes, cigarettes, my deceptive youthful aura, or my blackness? One or all?

Last night I visited an old friend, James Anthony Peoples, who lives just below the frontier of Harlem on Central Park West. We had been out of touch for a long time. Now it was midnight, and the goodies had vanished. There was nothing to do but get a six-pack of beer. I crossed 110th Street and Central Park West and thought: Is it any wonder blacks and whites are walking out on the black Broadway musical *Ain't Supposed to Die a Natural Death?* Eighth Avenue beyond 110th Street is a living death. The rat-infested tenements remain. Neon-lit bars are gripped with fear. Was I the Man, a new pusher, a new junkie? One bar locked its door because none of the patrons recognized me. There were subway junkies on both sides of the street. Desperation in their eyes, they resembled black ghosts. Dachau survivors. Wearing colorless rags, they were not junkie cool. They were in the caboose of the junkie train. These men and women did not cop and hock stereos, color televisions. Watching their desperate street bits, my heart broke. Life had ended for them. *But not for the people who had created them.*

I finally copped a six-pack in a superette on 115th Street. It was now almost two in the morning. The superette jammed with bobbing, bad-mouthed teenagers. Vibrancy exploded from them like fireworks. But did they realize that life had already ended for many of them? You can destroy the future's futile dream, your own frustration, your helplessness with drugs, acts of violence.

Stunned, angry, returned to Peoples' apartment and casually asked, "Did Frankenstein's monster kill his master?" Peoples said yes, and I said, Yes, oh my God, yes! What a nice ending for a story.

*   *   *

Bedded at 5 A.M., I woke up much too early. It was now a little after eight of the same morning. A bottle of beer, Scotch, gin, champagne, chartreuse had left no aftereffects. All I wanted or needed was juice, coffee, a cigarette. I stretched erotically on the yellow Danish sofa in the windowless, paneled Bridal Room.

The mirrored reception room reflected countless images of myself, chandeliers, reminiscent of the French Empire. The room fronted a courtyard, roughly 40 by 60 feet; a rock garden in the Japanese manner, while overhead seagulls seem to skate against a lapis-blue sky. I went into the Gold Room. Yummy, yummy: caviar on a bed of melting ice. Caviar, thin little crackers, hard-boiled eggs, and ginger ale would make a great breakfast—which I enjoyed, sitting in a steel chair, glazed like plywood, that I brought in from the school. I breakfasted facing another garden, offering Oriental serenity. But the quiet was broken by low-flying planes.

Where the hell am I?

In the catering section of a temple on Long Island. Last night I and four other "dish" men arrived. A fast, efficient worker, I was asked to stay over. This happens frequently. I go from temple to temple, hoping that my wages will equal my working ability. I would like to take a leave of absence from Jackson china and try writing again. Money and time. Time and money. A dish man spends a lot of time at Madame Sophie's employment agency. And time spent waiting in trains, buses, taxis. Nevertheless, the following morning, 7 A.M., I was busing across the Williamsburg Bridge, enjoying a splendid red-gold sunrise, headed for a short gig in the flatlands of Brooklyn. Herbie's International restaurant, a pleasant place to work. The pay is always decent. At 8:05, a hungover Harold arrived. It had been a wild party the night before. Harold had had very little sleep. "Chief . . . Charlie," he said. "Some guy made a mess in the men's room."

It started at the door, finger-painted the walls. The enclosed toilet was immaculate. The man's white boxer shorts looked like a psychedelic brown-and-white design and not really revolting—if you didn't inhale or think about it. The fresh-air ceiling fan had been on all night. A sweet, sickening odor lingered in the men's room. I looked at myself in the mirror. It seemed I had been stepping in human excrement for a long time. Bitterness, nausea became my epaulets. I considered America, the majority of people I encountered, dung mannequins wearing masks.

Harold and his wife, Lee, were unmasked. Harold and I had coffee and apple pie; then I went back to Madame Sophie's. At four that afternoon, ten men for "dish" (two Chinese students from Hong Kong), the race-track-addict chauffeur piled into a station wagon and drove to the celebrated Le Mansion in New Jersey. It's a mother of a place, a bad marriage between Greek Revival and New England colonial. Exquisite banquet rooms accommodate between twenty-five and three thousand people. And, ducks—total confusion. Parties breaking, parties beginning. Guests entering wrong reception rooms. They wore expensive clothes but lacked style. I suppose in their frantic race up the money-and-social ladder, they had forgotten good manners. Waiters, waitresses (the crudity of the waitresses is astonishing, especially a woman who looks like an apple-pie grandmother); the kitchen staff kissed, joked, and drank. "You ruddy-face old bastard. I'm gonna tell my husband!" Other crews arrived, then the young rabbi and *masgiach*.

The hired help ate in the gentile staff kitchen. I had chicken noodle soup and Dr. Brown's root beer, thinking, At least they feed you before the work shift begins—promising.

I don't remember the exact moment when things went bad. Our boss, Mary Louise, a plump vichyssoise black woman appeared, real, motherly. Her second, Uncle Tom's Shadow, was a dapper Dan, harmless. Our dish crew knocked out the previous party's dishes in no time. We were knighted with a cleanup detail in the Belmont Room, which was divided into two parts by a red satin curtain. Tables (set up for a wedding supper) were pushed against the wall of section I. The reception in section 2 was ending. But most of the guests did not want to leave. "Ladies and gentlemen," the band leader implored, "you are invited to attend the wedding ceremony." The well-dressed guests clamored for hors d'oeuvres, liquor. Waiters, waitresses appeared to be indifferent; they were partying too. A Puerto Rican of African ancestry said, "Everybody lapping up the booze but us. It's gonna be a long night, and I ain't got no grass. We'd better hit the whiskey sours. I know this place. It ain't no ball game."

The whiskey sours gave us courage to tote party paraphernalia up and down four flights of stairs (the service elevator had conked out before we arrived). Le Mansion's staff did not want the dish crew to eat the leftover smorgasbord. They watched us as if we were new floor waxers at Tiffany's. But we foxed them. We'd wheel a beautiful table out into the nineteenth-century incinerator room, rush back for another table like a swift relay team, and feast in the incinerator room, washing down the tidbits with whiskey sours.

By the time we returned to kitchen number I, bourbon-drinking mother Mary Louise had become Hula Mary. Dyed pale pale blue, carnations haloed her smooth dark hair. She split our dish crew into two groups. Eighteen men, two kitchens. It looked as if everything might run as smooth as a diesel train on a country road. The night dragged on, begat little disasters. Dishwashers disappeared. I questioned Mary. She offered me petits fours. My polite Hong Kong helper slowly, gingerly, unwrapped the non-breakable demi-tasse cups and saucers from Japan. The blasting kitchen radio was also from Japan, like Mary's sterilized rubber gloves.

God has opened the world's greatest stock exchange in Japan, I told myself. But the cut-glass cigarette holders were made in West Germany. The tea was American, Lipton's.

It was now almost midnight. Trying to do the work of three men, I was getting nowhere. Sotted, Uncle Tom's Shadow sauntered in, offering advice. The dish feeder said, "Man. Why don't you go somewhere and fuck yourself?" "Yeah," I added, "we've been working very well without you. Go and have another drink." "I don't know what's wrong with you guys," the sotted Shadow said and departed. A rack of soup bowls hit the red-tiled floor. From kitchen to kitchen to corridor—you could hear a four-letter Mass.

Mother Mary began going through her tough prison-matron bit. Uncle Tom's Shadow returned briefly. We threatened to break trays over his head. Then the kitchen staff began putting pressure on us. Watching the clock, the young rabbi in the gray silk suit wanted to know what was happening. I informed him that his kitchen staff was inefficient and stoned. I even mentioned the Bolshevik revolution, the Black Panthers. We were getting paid $1.85 an hour. (The majority of caterers paid $2.00 an hour on weekends. Le Mansion had a reputation and even advertised in New York newspapers.) Then, a silence engulfed the kitchen. We continued working until 3 A.M. No overtime. The grumbling kitchen staff took over.

After dressing, we lined up for pay. They took out seventy-five cents for some nonexistent tax. A tip? Tips filter out before the dishwashers have washed the last dish. However, the host and hostess, who usually come into the kitchen after dinner, displaying benevolent smiles, are unaware of the theft.

We waited in the early-morning darkness for our chauffeur to arrive. The sun was up when we arrived in Manhattan.

AT HOME (the Valencia Hotel overlooking St. Marks Place, conveying a chamber-of-commerce aura of decadence, affluence)—I usually avoid china and glassware. A paper container of iced tea, laced with brandy, a thin *Post,* a bar-mitzvah cigar. And *The New York Times.*

MILLIONS IN CITY POVERTY FUNDS LOST BY
FRAUD AND INEFFICIENCY

Knocking ash off my cigar, I sighed and crossed my legs. Serious too. Like sitting in a comfortable leather chair at the "club."

Multiple investigations of the city's $122 million-a-year anti-poverty program are disclosing chronic corruption and administrative chaos ...

Pouring a straight brandy, I said, "Shit. I could have told the cocksuckers that two years ago," and continued to read:

It's so bad that it will take ten years to find out what's really been going on inside the Human Resources Administration, said an unnamed assistant district attorney.

America is still painting a portrait of Van Gogh's "The Potato Eaters." To hell with arts and crafts, H.R.A.! Culture—cunnilingus! Self-serving sodomy! Work projects, lighthearted cleanup campaigns. Music in the streets, dancing in the streets. Perform for the poor. Three mini-vignettes of waste, money, time, inefficiency at a branch of H.R.A. are on the front lawn of my mind.

It's all there. Accounts in Swiss banks. A mysterious George José Mendoza Miller. An elderly man in a cubicle Wall Street office. The pulsating glamour of Las Vegas. Parked cars on a street in Los Angeles (straight out of a television detective series). A $52,000 check with Mary Tyler's private phone number on the back. Now, we'll switch to Amsterdam and it's not tulip time. H.R.A.'s money is so mobile—promiscuous dollars! Now, let's zoom in on the fabulous black "Durham Mob" from North Carolina. Out of sight! A rented car, the fuzz, and Forty-second Street.

Nina, a sensuous black divorcée, mother of three children, has appeared on the front lawn. She has an executive position at an antipoverty agency. Knowing of my financial hangup, she tried to secure a $ gig. I would write reports, Nina would school me. I had autographed copies of *The Messenger* and *The Wig* for her boss and went uptown on a fine, sunny morning.

"The switchboard service is lousy," I said, "and what are all those people doing in the lobby?"

Nina laughed. "Hustling, baby. Everybody wants a piece of Uncle Sam's money."

"But they're well dressed," I protested.

"I know. Only the poor suffer. Same old story."

"Enduring?"

"Yes," Nina agreed, then added: "Bad news, baby. Do you remember meeting a Mr. XX at a party on Riverside Drive?"

"Oh, him. I remember, and his pretentious old lady."

"He said you had a nasty mouth," Nina told me. "Bureaucrats don't like writers. The written word gets them uptight. All they know is numbers, percentages on charts."

"Now if only I was an out-of-work musician. A junkie or a jailbird," I fantasized. "Whitey and niggers dig them."

We laughed, saluted the gig good-bye. Nina sent out for coffee and doughnuts. While we waited, she talked about her program.

"Each time you come up with something that could help the poor, they veto it. I've been warned to cool it at meetings. Like the junkie program and the P.S. 201 thing."

The boy arrived with the coffee and doughnuts. Nina could

not wash her lovely hands in the office basin. It had been clogged up for a month. The American government paid a yearly rental of $25,000 for these three old creaky floors. It was not one of Harlem's better buildings.

Nina signed papers, talked on the phone, gave instructions to her secretary. Then she went down in the elevator with me. We talked on the sidewalk and watched the late-summer Harlem scene pass. Nina pressed two tens and a five in my hand.

"Get stoned or laid, baby," she said, then added: "See that sports car on the opposite side of the street? It belongs to an office boy. He's stealing the place blind."

Let's take a trip upstate. The one-way bus fare to South Falls-burg, New York, is almost six dollars. In August 1968, a branch of the Neighborhood Youth Corps spent almost thirty dollars of the government's money sending five young blacks to the Flagler Hotel (Catskill territory). I do not know who paid for their return (I was down at the lake, drinking wine). All I know is that four boys and one girl, well dressed and very clean, arrived one gray afternoon, under the impression that they would become coun-selors—according to the gospel of the Neighborhood Youth Corps. The boys did not like the living quarters. "Man, it's a barn," I remember one of them saying. But they were young, lived in another world, and did not know that stables, barns are com-fortable and sometimes chic.

The girl was signed on as a maid. The boys were to be part of the dish crew. But one boy, a suit-and-tie boy, wanted to work in the office. He said he could type forty-five words per minute. I remember the boy taking his pajamas from his luggage, arranging his shoes at the foot of his bed. I rapped with them in the former stable, then took them to meet the dish crew, who were Southern blacks. Always trying for the diplomat's degree, I tried to open the barrier between them: an impasse. After dinner that night, the hotel manager was perceptive enough to realize the teenagers would not groove in a Catskill scene, and they left the following morning.

Now, you know I am joshing. Is there any wonder why I love fiction? Dig: a friend, Larl Becham, had secured a gig at an antipoverty branch which was preparing a musical for the black community, and end-of-the-season gala. Becham was the chore-

ographer and assistant director. Considering his experience, reputation, the lavish poverty giveaway, he was paid nothing—$100
a week. The teenagers were paid $45 a week to study voice and
dance. Most of them were not interested in voice and dance. The
boys and girls who were interested in voice and dance were in the
Harlem tenements, the streets, sitting on stoops, standing on
street corners. The boys and girls I saw at rehearsal had booga-
looed under the wire with connections. I remember one girl, the
color of hand-rubbed teakwood. Awkward, sullen, she knocked
down $45 a week because one of the "big fish" was trying to
make her.

Becham gave me the script to read. Only the author (the director and brother of the agency chief) could relate to the script. It
was the type of musical MGM might have considered in 1886 and
turned down.

"Can you believe we are opening next week?" Becham asked.

Another brandy, Nathanael West? Let's buy Eartha Kitt Calan-
the harrissii orchids, jade, ropes of pearls. Let's listen to her rich,
bitter laughter . . .

Before 'Mericans heard of Our Lady of Beautification, Lady
Bird Johnson, and before all those black and white performers
brought alms to poor blacks, Eartha Kitt, in the late '50s, had her
own unpublicized antipoverty program at the Harlem Y.M.C.A.
Miss Kitt's first love was dance, and she had been a member of the
Katherine Dunham Dance Company. She sponsored the Eartha
Kitt Dance foundation. Larl Becham taught the classes. Any black
child could take free dance classes. You did not have to be a friend
of a friend or have someone get sweaty hands, thinking about how
you would be in bed with a couple of drinks, a little pot.

Revolting? I have an idea that one day black and white
bureaucrats will succeed in eating Uncle Sam's beard, balls, navel,
and the money itself.

Anyway, Birdie Greene, the maid, wants to clean my room,
and I have to take the train to Philly, to the City of Brotherly Love.

Shot down in Manhattan, my mood was like F. Scott Fitzgerald's
at Princeton. A lost writer in Philly, covering rock's elegant gypsies, Sly & The Family Stone. A taxi strike or what the hell?
Popped a couple of pills, encountered the Doubtful Mushroom

Company. Waited and waited for the Broad Street bus. Bolted into a Forty-second Street type of zone and found a cab at last.

The Second Quaker Rock Festival was held at the Spectrum Arena. An estimated 8,000 to 10,000 fans had made the pilgrimage. The ritual began at the upsetting hour of 7 P.M. Now, it was 9 P.M. and you couldn't get a beer, babe. The brandy pint was at half mast.

"Too many teenagers," a guard told me. "We don't want no riots out here." Popped another pill, sipped Coke, dug the crowd, promenading in their boutique and department store costumes. They were not as funky and fashionable as the Fillmore East crowd. I expected these earthlings to go home, change clothes, audition for a Crest commercial.

The Creedence Clearwater Revival had finished their set. The Grateful Dead were at the halfway mark, jiving for an audience connection. But the young earthlings were not into it. They prowled around the arena, clowning, taking pictures, searching and copping things such as other earthlings' empty seats. It was like Marat/Sade in Disneyland. They were trying to zap the moment, the night, as if, come morning, they'd be extremely old and wasted. But now, the Grateful Dead was getting next to them with a little theatrics. And suddenly it occurred to me that the swinging '60s will not be remembered for assassins, drugs, pseudo-revolutionary sweat, but for hair and costumes—façades obscuring Andy Hardy interiors and the Girl Next Door.

Between sets, popped the last pill. All those seats like blood ice cubes and red carpeting underneath. An endless collage of cigarette butts. Black faces are rare. There are no young blacks in Philly, I told myself. Perhaps they have gone to the country for the weekend. I counted five interracial couples. "Philly is the northern Atlanta, Georgia," a black told me, adding that a rhythm and blues radio station was now "acid rock" and owned by the University of Pennsylvania.

Another Coke. The Iron Butterfly. A drag, watching them move in and out with a van of electronic equipment—a space-age cortege. I am not a rock frontiersman, as my *Village Voice* readers know. A third-string convert, my interest goes down like Dow Jones. Now, Janis Joplin was one of the eight wonders of rock. She was the only artist capable of making unreality real. She pressed sincerity against her bosom like a contemporary Cleopatra with a humane asp.

Iron Butterfly gave a controlled performance. *Mucho* things working for them: a light show, fire, the drummer's hypnotic solo. Sly: a tough act to follow. One fact checked out: whatever followed had better offer more than peanut butter and jelly sandwiches and milk. The crowd's mood had changed. Let's-get-this-show-on-the-road! Little put-down remarks, peachy hands simulating megaphones. Twisting and turning in seats like the nursery-school set at a Saturday matinee. An orgy of fingernail biting. Two-fingered whistles. The gaiety of floating balloons cooled the action in my section.

Sly? I had watched the family arrive, single file. I caught a glimpse of Sly's father, little brother Sidney. Sly's aide-de-camp, loaded with cameras, directs the setup. Watching them drag out the electronic equipment, rock fans look bored. Young earthlings go on unorganized patrols. Then Sly & The Family Stone move through the semidarkness like secret agents boarding a ship at dawn. The spotlight doesn't hit Sly until he is at the edge of the revolving stage. Applause is polite. Guarded, as if the waiting, twenty little anticlimaxes had dried the applejack on the fans' hands.

Another delay. A cord, a connection, or some goddamn thing has been misplaced and the Family cannot perform without it. Two earthlings on my right look like the sons of prosperous farmers, but they have a good knowledge of rock. Resting their booted feet on the back of the chair in front of them, one says, "The fucking bastards are gonna take all night. Have you got the keys?"

The lost writer scans the lower arena. Primed with saliva, hoarded energy, they seem to rehearse sons-&-daughters-of-the-Lion's-Club retorts, handed down from generation to generation as the last heirloom in the American attic of—I am white and right and will not be kept waiting! Yes, a hard line separates this mood from that of a hard-drinking black crowd in an East St. Louis dive, or the silence of black balcony girls at the Apollo as blond Chris Connor comes onstage and scats, or the raunchy revolt of the Fillmore East audience. No, this unrest blew from the carved horns of legends, was removed from minds, lips by the second number. Sly & The Family Stone delivered. Through talent, a touch of sorcery, they grabbed the Spectrum fans. They did not have to crack whips, lock exit doors. In the top tiers, earthlings danced. Groovy, man, bravo, swinging; right on became a litany. In the row opposite me, a group of prep-school boys aped wrestling fans. "I hope Sly & The Family Stone makes more money than the other groups," one boy said. A very hip-looking Chinese couple turned around and laughed softly. Three over-thirty couples stood up and ritualistically let it all hang out. But they were dressed like swingers who go to bowling tournaments.

Sly & The Family Stone marched off and around the revolving stage. Hundreds of earthlings rushed to the main floor. Security guards were lost in the shuffle. Incredible. This was rock power, and it had left me exhausted. I did not stay for the last set, Steppenwolf. A good slice of the crowd left with me. It was almost one in the morning and we needed air, fair or foul.

Tuesday before Philly rock night, returned from gigging a fashion show luncheon. At 4 P.M. the last dish had been washed, and we were paid until 6 P.M. All right! Take me higher, as Sly would say.

But I'm waiting in the lady's pad to get laid; she hasn't showed.

"That is history," said Mae West, pointing toward the Hollywood bed, the headboard, tufted in lime-green plastic.

Hell, "That's history" is *my* line. Sprawled on the blue-tiled floor, higher than a blimp. But together, noting the blind-woman's knitted circle of a rug, folded in the corner like an apple turnover.

I was fingering my worry beads when the lady arrived from Manhattan labors and immediately passed out. She had had too many drinks. Heavy, radical conversation at the Cedar Tavern.

Down, boy. Pop, smoke, and drink.

Meanwhile, the floor had become the Straits of Gibraltar. I could almost hear Moroccan voices. But the voices below the window belonged to illegitimate Boy Scouts breaking whiskey and wine bottle. ¡Olé! Stoned images. The blue-tiled floor, the Mediterranean. Where are the ships at sea? The Algeciras ferry? Molly Bloom has disappeared on Gib. The rock, *a* rock. Fang? Phyllis Diller. A guest shot on tonight's telly? No. The Falangists, celebrating their thirty-fourth anniversary. The Spanish Civil War. Hemingway & company. Communism. The late Joseph McCarthy conducting the last or the first concerto since the Salem witch hunts? A 21-gun salute to that fantastic broad, Miss Virginia Hill. Dorothy Parker, Ayn Rand, James Poe, and the smiling, talkative Elia Kazan. The cold, righteous years. General Eisenhower pirouetting into Korea that winter. We sawed open the wooden floors of our tents and hid the White Horse (white lightning) gin, were forced to march in the rain because our officers were afraid to let us relax in our tents, and our latrine slid down into a ravine when the ground thawed. Hysterical, stoned, bored, frightened, some of us shot holes in the roofs of our tents, tried to shoot bullets at the stars, shot heroin, sniffed cocaine, and went to the whorehouses with the zeal of aspiring politicians. Death had spared us; America was begetting a nation of zombies, or so we thought. "Back home," "back in the world," our countrymen had heads shaped exactly like golf balls. Years passed. I remember a brief moment of splendor and hope. Fail and enter the age of assassination. J.F.K., Malcolm X, R.F.K., Martin Luther King. Men and women protest, march.

They are still marching, according to *The Village Voice*. I'm losing my high and look at the *Voice* photographs: the pseudo-Nazi: upchuck pop art, and below it the chilling, precise portrait of the white-Right, advising: FIGHT THE JEWISH-RED ANARCHY! (Collegiate and apparently serious, the minted middle class are unaware of the Ronald Reagan South African waltz and as upright as backwoods Baptists.)

Next, a group photograph, notable for a girl resembling Susan Sontag. MP's frontlining. Ditto: Black MP's. An accident, or did the Pentagon believe uniformed blacks could cool the liberal white temper?

Norman Mailer with a part in his hair. Robert Lowell, Sidney Lens, Dwight MacDonald—a group photograph, intellectually heavy. The last photograph: another crowd scene with a banner reading: NEGOTIATE WITH THE NLF.

Smell the hot bacon grease; or are you waiting for it to congeal? Try a side order of cole slaw, dished out to the masses at a box supper. I had roast pork, rice, and beans with the neighbor's nine-year-old son. We clowned over wine and beer, then I chased the barefoot boy out into the street: we ended our cops-and-robbers game. On our block, real bullets ripped the air. The nine-year-old and I witnessed a Saturday-night double murder, a near riot.

But by this time, we had become accustomed to the sound of bullets. They seemed unreal, a drag. We raced back into the lady's pad
and sipped lukewarm beer.

The next day, Sunday. *The New York Times* arrived (you can
never be sure in Brooklyn). Drinking my second cup of tea, I
thought about the man with the part in his hair. Norman knows
the whole fucking scene, I told myself, looking at his *Voice* photograph again. What the hell is he doing in Washington? Taking the
temperature of the Vietnam protest?

Honestly, I can't remember when the Vietnam War began. My
little police action had President Syngman Rhee of Korea. Drafted,
indifferent to the military, I wanted to emerge from the action,
blasé as Hemingway's stepson. Why, protesting, burning draft
cards was unheard of. In my time, regardless of personal beliefs,
young men did their thing. After all, Korea cut the familial cord.
The possibility of war offered escape, excitement. Death offered a
free tour, a trip. Fear curdled our Korea-bound ship. And there
were the Dr. Strangelove inspections. Standing on deck in the cold
and rain. Vomit peppering stairwells, baptizing heads. But we
were very religious and attended Protestant and Catholic services
with the same marvelous indifference. Old marine Phoenix ship
rocked at night, plus Bronx cheers from crap games, drunkenness,
arguments, fights, nightmares. Hallowed be Thy name and—
please let me sleep.

On the seaborne asylum, most of us tried to stay high. Fear
knighted many of us. Fear was alien to me, and although I loved
the sea—when was I going to see land and trees? Wading ashore at
Pusan, I was grabbed by something that would not let go. This
was not basic training, bivouac at Missouri's Fort Leonard Wood.
It was a bright autumn morning, and silent, efficient young soldiers advancing, wading through muddy water with M-I rifles held
high. Breathless, crawling up the sandpaper-colored beach. The
unreal knowledge of arriving. Homeward-bound GI's laughingly
telling us: "Joe Chink is waiting on your ass." "Buster, you'll be
dead before the sun sets."

But there was no fighting, only an uneasy truce. The majority
of us were fortunate young men in Korea. We soldiered, worked,
screwed, and got high. A nitty-gritty Cinemascope setting, the
script courtesy of middle America's veterans from World War II, a

script that had to be shot at Universal or Allied Artists. Without realizing it, the GI protégés, we were rehearsing for the '60s.

Ah . . . the moment has arrived. Vietnam, our cancer, or life's booster. A television corn flake commercial, or shall we hum an abstract hymn to the liberal's menopause?

Another angry glance at the *Voice* photographs: Jiveass motherfuckers. Faces I have encountered in person and on the printed page.

A few years ago their kind were marching for the blacks. But nonviolent marching produced sore feet, fear, and the suspicion that one might truly, truly die for the "cause," and, too, perhaps the movement lost its kick, and like those beautiful rich women, who riding sidesaddle creamingly ejaculate, the liberals had quite simply, ladies and gentlemen, found a new cause, fresh with the scent of discovery. A challenge, a map of a situation on which they could embroider *Peace & Love.*

What should the peace-loving earthlings do? Marshal their forces and elect a President in the forthcoming election who will guide them toward a peace-loving future. That is our only salvation. If they are able to mainline moral reality into the American way of life. If. If. If—

At the moment, mothers, nothing's shaking. From the Pentagon whirligig, right on down to you and you. We are freaking in and out, in and out of the reality around us. But oh, what a marvelous show!

THE GREAT DROUGHT has arrived. Dusty pollen falls like snow over Manhattan. Anxiety moans, obscures the sun; the sky seems tinted by a cheap detergent. Listless, suspended days, baked streets. An insane jungle of voices, day and night. *Le malaise* grips St. Marks Place. Earthlings seek not love, drugs, but a straitjacket for the mind, or at least an act of violence to release emotions. A legacy of sundry gifts has been handed down to them: war, pollution, corruption, hate, venereal disease. All of us are involved in the first four bequests. But it seems VD is the province of the young. Ah, Alice! The looking glass has microbes on it—an infected twelve-year-old girl.

You will find VDers in the morning (9 to 11 A.M.) and in the afternoons (1 to 3 P.M.), Mondays and Thursdays (4 to 6 P.M.), entering the public-health centers like members of a secret society. But I want to tell you about the Chelsea Health Center at 303 Ninth Avenue. At one time, I lived near the center. Viewed on a humid afternoon, the Chelsea Center is like a setting for a working-class *The Third Man*. Bureaucratic and faintly sinister. Situated between a public school, a warren of housing projects, and a devastated block that ends at Twelfth Avenue and the Hudson River—this small two-story brick building seems so asexual. One would think that men and women went there to relieve themselves, bathe, or sleep after a sexual quickie or a feast. Yet this small building is the salvation of that dandruff-like disease, gonor-rhea.

Mondays and Wednesdays are extremely busy, I was told, plus holiday aftermaths. S.R.O. But first you check in with the receptionist, avoid the children going to the dental clinic, the elderly waiting for X-rays. Male VDers go into a small, crowded waiting room with pale, pale green walls, almost the exact shade of gonor-rhea semen. No smoking, please. Bright-colored plastic chairs. Bogart and Marx Brothers posters. Before interrogation and tests, you read, sleep, or watch your fellow travelers. Tense young men who usually acknowledge each other with a sly/shy you-got-it-too grin. The promiscuous earthlings are cool. Conversation between a teenager and his slightly older friend.

"What we gonna do after you get straight?"

"I don't know," the VDer said. "Go to the movies, I guess."

"Are you gonna take Marcia?"

There was no answer. The teenagers were seized with boisterous laughter.

Clapped by the same prostitute, two young mailmen also joked and laughed, crossing and recrossing their legs. An occasional elderly man (looking as if he's on a permanent down), homosexual couples—their faces a portrait of togetherness like expectant parents—are given the nonchalant treatment. But what intrigues me are the young men who arrive with luggage, knapsacks, sleeping and shopping bags. Some of them are from out of town and give false names, addresses, as do Manhattan males. I overheard one longhair give a Washington, D.C., address, complete with apartment number, then ask if a friend could pick up the result of his blood test.

"No," the smiling health aide said.

"Could my sister pick it up? She lives in the city."

"I'm afraid not," the kind, smiling health aide told him, "but check with your doctor."

From my observation, the majority of longhairs are not the supply clerk and other nine-to-five types. Heavy radicals and Marx you I Ching.

I've been down, much too black about the Chelsea Health Center. In the narrow corridor, in the cubicles, occasional funny vignettes.

A male voice (like a recording device announcing time):
"What's wrong?"
"I don't know."
"Take it out."
"Here?"
"Yes" (wearily). Does it hurt . . . burn?"
"Yes, Doctor. It burns like hell."
A conversation in the back room.
"Well. What have we got here?"
The tall blond was silent.
"Jesus! Al, come over here and take a look at this." The penis inspector and Al made no further comment about the discovery, except to tell the blond to return to the waiting room.
Another cubicle conversation.
"Dark field, Miss Norse. Now, young man. Would you like to lie down or sit up?"
"Sit up."
"I think you'll be more comfortable lying down."
"I'll sit up, I think."
"Very well. Now take it out and turn it toward you."
"Toward me?"
"Turn the head of it toward you."
"Toward me?"
"Yes. Turn the head of it toward you. Sort of swivel it a little."
Heavy silence during the test. Then: "How long have you had it?"
"About a week, sir." (An ex-army man in the cube?)
"Does it hurt?"
Deep breathing, confiding tone, "Yes, sir."
"I'm sorry. Dark field, negative. We'll have to do it again."
"Again?"
"Yes," the voice of the doctor drones. "Now take it out so that it faces you. That's good. Hold still. Hold it . . ."
Indeed. Toward you. Indeed. It is in you. Gonorrhea, chancre (the primary stage of syphilis), or advanced syphilis with its nearer-my-God-to-Thee fear.
But the waiting room is bright, congenial. Fear: subtle as dust. After the blood test (strong-hearted men break into a cold sweat), the penicillin shot, VDers are in a holiday mood. But—wait. It's

not over. The social-worker interview. Everyone gets uptight. You are supposed to be very honest and name names and when and where. But there are the white lies, the loss of memory. Many VDers do not remember who they slept with and give the name of a foe/friend. You will never know the anonymous friend/foe who volunteered your name and address. Fake word-of-mouth also helps spread VD. And, too, it is much easier to detect VD in a man than in a woman. An ancient, misunderstood disease, often hereditary, VD is the thing this year. Our future. Aren't we promiscuous? Swingers in and out of bed? Aren't we top-of-the-morning Americans, seekers of fresh territories, and ever so mobile?

The drift? It continues. Frenzied days and nights. All I want to do is stay stoned; despair is the masochistic lover, chained to my feet as August spends itself slowly; time the miser with the eyedropper. Summer. Summer's end. Will the summer ever end? Will I escape this time?

Returning from another dish gig, I bought the Sunday *New York Times* and read the *Book Review*. You made the news today, boy. But that failed to ax despair. The frustration, the peasant's labor of the night before were still fresh in my mind. After showering, I feel less tense, prime myself with ice-cold beer. It's a mother of an afternoon. The sullen sky gives no promise of relief, rain. The murmurous St. Marks Place voices drift up as if begging for something which escapes them in this elusive city. But booze won't elude me. No. There's half a pint of vodka, and I made a pill connection on St. Marks Place, bought three pints of wine from a "doctor" on the Bowery.

And I sat in my room waiting, watching the sky turn dark, listening to radio rock, inhaling the Coney Island odors that wafted through the window from the nearby pizza parlors, hamburger luncheonettes. The night was a scorcher. Should I hit the streets? Visit air-conditioned friends/foes? Are you jiving, mothergrabber? What could they possibly do except accelerate the drift? So I showered again, opened the door, turned off the bed lamp. The Valencia is an anything-goes hotel.

Finger-popping, dance-marching around the room, wanting desperately to get higher; become incoherent, hallucinate, vomit, pass out. But that never happens. Once again, I was stoned in the hall of mirrors. It's brilliant, beautiful, but fear in the back of the mind bevels the edge. What am I frightened of? Death, aging, my fellow men, madness—frightened that one terrible morning or night I will no longer have the marvelous ability to drink, drink, knock it down, as they say: Yes! Mix it all up, pop a variety of pills, smoke grass and hashish—frightened of what might be my inability to love, although I am loving, generous, understanding with friends, strangers.

Shirley. Memory is a bitch, I think, hitting the cheap white wine. Maggie's latest perfumed note from Paris remains unopened. A difference in age. She had never been able to conceive and I had always wanted a son—

Little Richard rhythmically falsettoing on rock radio. Damnit. Should have married Anna Maria. But it ended badly, since I was having an affair with her sister. Anna Maria! Stoned, a little uneasy on the first tier of loneliness, self-pity . . .

"Oh, Mr. Wright, are you home?" Birdie Greene, the Valencia maid, asked. "Have you got a cig?"

"Birdie . . . wait till I get my pants or a towel."

"All right."

"Kinda hot tonight."

"Yeah," Birdie said in her Selma Diamond voice. "Damn machine broke again, and I just can't go out in the street. You know what I mean. And those people in 55. Just because they see me, don't mean I'm working."

"Take the whole pack," I said. "I've got more."

"Thanks, Mr. Wright." Birdie Greene smiled. "See you on Wednesday."

Midnight became the world's most uptight jackhammer. Jesus. When would the son of a bitch conk out?

"Hi," the girl said warmly, standing in my doorway. "Have you seen Joe and Helen?"

"Have I seen who?"

"Joe and Helen." The girl giggled. "They live down the hall, and I thought . . ."

"No, baby. I've been looking for Charles Wright."

Blond (why are they always blond?), Levis, pop-art T-shirt, no bra, no shoes, coquette repainting tomboy exterior, clutching a dollar's worth of white-yellow buttoned daisies. (On St. Marks Place with the peace, pot-smoking young, it's a single rose. The deflowered, hip, zipping middle-class Americans, off target, rico-cheting—back home.)

"What's happening?" the girl asked.

"What the hell do you think is happening?"

"Wow, man. How you come on."

"Wow, how you come on," I said. "Must all of you say every-thing that I expect you to say?"

"Aren't the flowers lovely? Peace, flowers, and love, brother."

"Come on in." I smiled and let it pass, flicking on the light. "Let's share a stick of peace."

The girl executed a mock curtsy. In the light I could see her decadent infanta gaze. The infanta, concealing jeweled daggers under the crinolines, a girl-woman with small, hard, cold eyes, fixed on my penis.

"Good grass, man," the girl confided.

"Yeah."

"Your eyes look funny. Glazed."

"A black devil."

The girl giggled again. "No, you're cool, brother. We've got to put the flowers in water or else they'll die."

"Well," I said rising, "we can put some of them in the beer bottle."

"That's cool," the girl exclaimed.

We arranged the daisies in the beer bottle. The girl bounced on the edge of the bed, keeping time with rock on the radio.

"Do you think you can get me off?"

Silence.

"Come on, cookie. If you want some bread or a place to crash for the night, okay. But don't play. I'm a superb gameplayer. I don't like monkey games."

"Do you think you could love me?" the girl whimpered.

"No," I said, turning off the light. "But let's ball."

The girl, a knowledgeable child, sexually proficient, was kicked out at noon. "Do you love me?" she had asked.

Still high, seeking solitude, yawning, I had turned toward the girl: "What? Get out of here. You're out of your league. A lot of black dudes on St. Marks will buy that jazz. So you'd better get out and find one."

"I've got one," the girl replied bitterly, "and thanks for nothing."

The heat had not diminished, and I went to the corner and bought ice, a half gallon of wine. Returned with my prime minister, *The Drift.* MJQ—the Modern Jazz Quartet was playing on the radio. It was a little after three in the afternoon, and I was knocking down white wine, chain-smoking. Then suddenly I knew what I was frightened of: the daisies in the beer bottle. Goddamn innocents, secretly smiling. Bastards knew I was frightened that something might happen, and I'd never be able to write the book I believed I was capable of writing.

Malcolm, Malcolm. Malcolm Lowry. Has the volcano been sighted?

Anyway, here's a bunch of daisies for the dead dog in the ravine.

AND ON THE FIFTH DAY, I left Manhattan, returned to the Catskills, my seasonal home away from home. I can always go to the Catskills and wash dishes. Real peasant wages, a peasant's caldron. Here—where it's green and serene—these flat, informal, manicured acres. The eye looks upward and sees dense treed mountains, a pearl-blue sky. Tall poplar trees ring the lakes and golf courses. Blacks and Jews may not share a passion for pork, but they do share a passion for Lincoln Continentals and Cadillacs. The Jews seem to prefer air-conditioned cars.

Early afternoon. The pool and cabanas are crowded. A bearded black tyro who will not speak to the black hotel employees plays light George Shearing jazz, which soars in the high wind. Far off, a woman sits alone and knits. Children play volleyball. A well-known Hollywood character actor frolics by the pool. This scene is visible from my window in the former children's dormitory. A pleasant vacation vista. The grind of Manhattan, Brooklyn, the Bronx is far away. Why move from the lounge chair? The entertainment director is trying to coax people to play games. The guests are indifferent. Perhaps they resent their vacation being regulated by a whistle. "And you're always complaining because there's nothing happening . . . Jesus," the director says into the floor mike.

The indifference flowers. A pleasant young man, a novice

politician, makes a brief speech. He has recently returned from
Israel. He is not soliciting funds; the young man works out of the
Lower East Side, which is a memory (or a business) for the guests.
The young man has a fine voice and, to use an old-fashioned,
unfashionable word, is sincere, mentioning briefly the June war.
Quotes from the Bible. Warns that peace is a long way off. Israel
needs support.

No one is listening, except to their companions; others promenade. The entertainment director is nervous. Finally, the young
novice politician thanks his apathetic audience, adding that this
might not be a proper place to talk but—

By 5:30 that afternoon, most of the guests had left the pool. It
had been a lazy afternoon. Israel was far away. The guests would
go to their rooms, bathe, rest, and dress for dinner. They had time
for an after-dinner walk in the clear mountain air. After all, they
gave to the United Jewish Appeal, and they were in the land of the
free.

I was free until midnight, moonlight as lobby porter. No hassle, though. The quiet, secure middle classes have quiet, secure
vacations, except for weekends. Occasionally something happens:
like the man who had brought a shotgun. It was not the hunting
season. Anyway, a houseman stole the shotgun. A kitchen man
stole the shotgun from the houseman.

"Fuck the hotel," the kitchen man said. "What has it done for
me? I've worked my ass off for nothing. I'm gonna drink wine for
a couple of weeks and sleep in the grass."

Up here, wine is king and beggar. A gallon of cheap wine can
destroy a $5,000 bar mitzvah. The hotel owners are aware of
this—and, well. But it is profitable to them, regardless, if crisis follows crisis.

Witness: The pot-and-pan man was alone and extremely well
for five days. After a fifth of must-I-tell (muscatel) wine, he's
packed his California suitcase (a California suitcase is a brown
paper bag, cardboard box, or shopping bag) and announces that
he is quitting. Pissed because he had to wash walls, a dishwasher
decides to quit also. The head dishwasher is on a drug safari.

A pantry man decides to hit the road with his buddies. Last
night, the nightclub porter pissed in the sink and got fired. Two
housemen went into town and never returned. Another has been

stoned in the dormitory for two days. The salad man swaggers in with a fifth of Scotch and is escorted out of the kitchen. A middle-aged kitchen man, a professional, chases the smart-aleck second cook with a meat cleaver. The baker, a former marine, is stoned as usual. Between offering bear hugs, he throws wads of dough. A day behind the scenes in a Catskill hotel; you take it as long as you have to, or split. The working and living conditions are terrible. No unions or overtime, which is why hotels fail to secure stable employees. You work long enough to get wine money or "talking back" money and move on. But—Monticello, the mountain Las Vegas, beckons; the police wait; and it is ten and ten: a ten-dollar fine or ten days in jail, or both. Now you are no longer required to see a judge, go to jail. You give the policeman ten dollars, and he drives you to another hotel, regardless of whether or not you want to work. Labor Day is near; the hotels are desperate. This year, the Bowery men are not making their annual Catskill expedition. A man might as well panhandle, eat at the Municipal Lodging House on East Third Street, and sleep in a doorway. Why should they work twelve hours and get paid for seven? And may I wish the Bowery men a happy holiday.

At this particular hotel, the only happy people are the guests and the young black men from Alabama who will work the summer season and hope to return home with $500 or $300. Like the Puerto Ricans, they work hard, save their money, and stick together. A natural-born citizen of the world's most prosperous country, I tremble to think of what life back home is like. But that's another story. A chapter of the story is in the beautiful, legendary Catskill Mountains, in the great and small hotels, bungalow colonies, where once Jewish workers came to relax from Manhattan sweatshops, gangsters came to play and kill. Now, small towns and cities bear ancient Indian names, and progress and builders have raped the wilderness, and money, anxiety, anger, greed dance through the clean mountain air like a chariot filled with lovers.

Indifferent, unchanging world—that's it in the final analysis, I remember thinking one night. There was a full moon. With coffee and cigarettes for company, I went down to the lake. I thought of F. Scott Fitzgerald's Dr. Dick Diver. Yes. Tender is the night. I became frightened and left the following morning.

*   *   *

Back home. Back in the summertime city, laying sevens against the nitty-gritty. Manhattan and the good life. The pace, the anonymity. A challenging, wondrous city. But do I want to stay here? In fact, do I want to stay in the United States of America? I have never felt at home here. Ah, memories of the old days! Obscured by green cornfields, I wanted to play seek and ye shall find. But the mothergrabbers felt more like a crude game of cro-quet; their mallets tried to split open my head with a golden eagle's beak. Pressing Onward in 1972, I fail to dip into that fondue of phrases, Right On, Brother or Right On, America, although the masses are ever so Aware and Hip, blessed with the technical reali-ties of the space age. I've got dt's in the rectum. "This world ain't my home," grandfather used to say. Ah yes! I'm coming from the edge of despair. Booze and pills fail to ax despair. I always get stoned on that frightening, cold level where everything is crystal clear. It's like looking at yourself too closely in a magnifying mirror.

Weighed down with my medals of merit from Catskill labors, a wailing Lourdes platoon tap-dancing in the center of my brain, I checked into the Valencia Hotel.

The pale blue room was immaculate. Surprise! No cockroach welcome. The parquet-patterned linoleum gleamed. But the floor was slightly uneven, and the linoleum squeaked like a man snor-ing. After showering, poured a stiff vodka, moved a straight-backed chair over to the window. In the middle of the afternoon, you could feel the heat rising around the sad, stunted trees of Third Avenue, dwarfed by the soot-caked, red-brick façade of Cooper Union. Traffic was a daisy chain of giant drunken crickets. Dressed in colorful summer finery, the teeming crowd, shuttling east and west, seemed exhausted, as if they were being manipu-lated by sadistic puppet masters. Was the pollution count unhealthy?

"Fair weather, fair weather," I said aloud, and began to doze.

What time was it? Where was I? In a post-sleeping-pill daze, the room was familiar. But I took another shower and recovered. It was five in the morning—that blessed hour. The streets were deserted, and with my quart of vodka, I walked under a starless, subtle electric-blue sky to the Chinese Garden. A solitary man slept on a cardboard mattress; half a loaf of Wonder Bread lay at his feet. The new lane of the Manhattan Bridge hadn't opened. Through the line of trees, I saw a squad car park on the lane. Two exhausted or goldbricking policemen sacked out. An old story. I had been coming here for a very long time.

I began knocking down drinks. When I looked up, a tall woman was coming toward me, moving with a slow, back-country woman's stride. Close-cropped gray hair, print cotton dress, and red-leather house shoes. She was like a curio, a ghost from Hell's Kitchen, a bit player from a Clifford Odets revival.

"Has a man passed through here?" the woman asked, her voice hoarse, hesitant, like a record played at the wrong speed.

"No. I've been here about an hour. I haven't seen anyone."

"I wonder where he went to. Some colored fellow has been following me all up and down the Bowery."

Jesus. One of *them*. Gritting my teeth, curling my toenails, I smilingly said, "Is that so?"

The tall woman nodded. She did not look at me. My vodka held her interest. "That's right. He just kept on following me and saying things. Every once in a while, he'd do something dirty."

"That's terrible. Why didn't you call the police?"

"What good are they?"

Chuckling, I offered the woman a drink.

She read the vodka label carefully. "This ain't wine."

"No," I sighed, "but it gets to you. One hundred proof."

When the woman finally released the bottle, she was panting. "Too strong. Wine's all right. Just like drinking soda pop, and you can get drunk, too."

"Cigarette?"

"You think I'll kiss it. But I won't."

"What?"

"You've got your goddamn hands between your legs."

"I've also got a cigarette in my hand. I have no intention of burning Junior."

"You can't make me do it," the tall woman said.

"Lady, have another drink and beat it. I'm getting a peaceful high, and I don't want you to zonk it."

Frowning, the woman reached for the vodka. "I won't do it.

You Spanish and colored men are always following me, trying to make me do things."

"Well," I began slowly, "I am a man of color, but there isn't a goddamn thing you can do for me." The woman shuddered. "Have I made myself clear, bitch?"

"I'll have another cigarette, then I'll go," she said quietly.

Now it was light, but the sun was still behind the tenements on the Lower East Side. It was a lovely dawn, quiet and cool. Early Saturday morning, and there was almost no traffic on the bridge. A few trucks going to and from Manhattan.

I forgot about the woman until she said, "That wasn't a nice way to talk to me."

"And it wasn't very nice of you to disturb me. Do I have to wear a goddamn sign that says I want to be alone?" I jumped down from the ledge and lunged at the woman. "Move, bitch!"

"All right," the woman said, starting off. "I ain't gonna ask you for another drink."

"Good-bye."

"I never said I wouldn't kiss it."

"Get out of here," I shouted.

The woman turned, hesitated, then came toward me. "Can I have another cigarette? That'll hold me till the bars open. That's all I want. One or two cigarettes. I ain't begging. You can't make me do it for no cheap-ass drink."

"Lady, take a couple of cigarettes and make it. I want to be alone. Can't you fucks understand that?"

The woman looked up at me with a hard, angry gaze and accepted four cigarettes. "You're a smart aleck. Well, I don't have to be bothered with your kind."

"You wanna kiss it?" I joked.

"You can't make me do it."

"Hell. Doesn't anyone fuck anymore?"

"Rotten bastard."

"Come here," I said.

"Oh, no, you don't," the woman screamed.

Forcing a Great Depression smile, I grabbed the woman's arm.

"You can't make me do it."

The woman didn't try to break from my grasp. I released my hold. "Well, mama?"

The tall woman with the back-country stride did not move. I looked at her tired, middle-aged face, reddened from wine, the cold gray eyes, watery like tarnished silver. It would have been impossible to kiss the thin, pale lips, and her chest was almost as flat as mine. The idea of dogging this woman, who was descended from thin-skinned rednecks, didn't appeal to me. Unlike many American black men—I have never had a super-charged, hard-on for white women. All I saw was a masochistic woman who wanted to serve Head.

Laughing playfully, I forced the woman's head downward to get a reaction.

The tall woman kissed the head of my penis delicately once, the second time with feeling. She went down with the obedient movements of a child. She was a passable Head server. I wanted her door of life and pushed her down into the grass.

"You can't make me do it," the woman cried. "I don't know what you think I am."

"Shut up."

"Rotten bastard."

I stood up and couldn't control my laughter. "Get out of here."

"I wasn't bothering you, and I never said I wouldn't kiss it," the woman cried. "Could I have another drink?"

ANOTHER LATE summer's morning with the humidity holding tight, no chance of rain. Angry traffic jammed. Silently people trot forward as if they were Communists. But I'm moving, moving fast, checking into the Kenton Hotel on the Bowery. I must stay skulled and get my head together, guard the mini-bank account. I must hold on, hold on, and wait for summer's end. Will the summer never end? The Kenton's mare's nest is cheap, fairly clean (this was before the junkie takeover, before the W.P.A. Off Broadway project moved next door). The hotel proper is on the second landing. You walk up steep marble steps, ancient, Baltimore-clean. You imagine that a Jim Dandy tripped up these steps after having a few with Eugene O'Neill's Iceman. But that was a long time ago. After high noon, you will be accosted by muggers, drunks, panhandlers. Those clean, cracked marble steps will be inhabited by sleeping, wounded, or dead men. You will inhale excrement, urine, vomit. Nausea builds; blast-off time is seconds away; and you are blinded by the bone-white brilliance of the steps and walls; and you have a sense of falling and become frightened. Where are you going? What are you doing here? What happened? "My God!" the self-pitying other voice cries. No matter, no matter.

So you grit your teeth, breathe carefully, take one step at a time. Ah! There is the great varnished door, the glass upper half a mosaic of fingerprints—but you've made it. Safe.

*   *   *

Skulled in the whitewashed cubicle, where the ceiling is high like in an old-fashioned mansion. Chicken-coop wire encloses the top of the cubicle. But there is no air. Only pine disinfectant, roach killer. Countless radios, two phonographs, and one television blast—this is the upper-class section of the hotel, and all the transient men are black.

The bed is lumpy with thin gray sheets, uncomfortable, like a bunk on a troop ship. No matter, no matter. There is a jug of mighty fine wine, a carton of cigarettes. I dismissed the voices, the music, the odors. I checked in to get my head together and write, but a few soldiers from the Army of Depression broke ranks. Now they brought up the rear. When would the bastards make it back to company headquarters?

Stoned, feeling surprisingly good, walking down Broadway, below Fourteenth Street. Less than a block away, I spot this dude on the opposite side of the street. There's something about his movements. Something isn't kosher, I'm thinking, as the dude crosses over to my side of the street and eases into a dark store entrance. It so happens this is where I turn the corner. Now, we're on the same side of the street. But he's in the store entrance of his corner, which faces Broadway, and I'm turning my corner, going west, picking up a little speed.

And who comes cruising along but "Carmencita in blue." Just tooling along like two men who are out for a good day's hunt in the country.

The squad car pulls over to the curb, and I go to meet them. The driver seems friendly. He's smiling. "Do you have any ID?"

"No. Some son of a bitch stole my passport, and I wish you'd find the schmuck."

"Where do you live?"

"Down the street. I'm sure I can find something that will verify who I am."

A brief silence. Calm as an opium head, I casually lean against the squad car.

"Are you the good guys or the bad guys? You see, I'm out to save the city from corruption like you guys. I'm working on my sainthood this year."

The cop sitting next to the driver takes off his cap and runs his hand through his straight, dark hair, which is combed back from his forehead. His nose is shaped exactly like a hawk's.

"He's too much," Hawk Nose said.

"Jesus," I lamented. "Are you guys stoned or am I stoned?"

The pleasant driver liked that one. He was getting his jollies off, and so was Charles Wright.

Then Hawk Nose came on with: "We're looking for somebody. We wanna bust somebody's balls."

There was a touch of cold reality in his voice.

Equally real, I replied, "Well, if you bust my balls, you'd better leave me on the sidewalk."

Still smiling, the driver made a playful lunge for his gun, or what I hoped was a playful lunge.

Hawk Nose, still in his tough, cop-shitting bag, was visibly irritated.

"There was a robbery a few minutes ago," he said, "and you fit the description of the guy. Height, weight, everything."

Everything meant color. And for a second I had a high fantasy of someone trying to masquerade as me. I started to tell them about the dude in the store entrance. But he didn't look like me and had probably disappeared anyway.

So I stood up straight and waited for the next line.

It was a long time coming; no doubt they were turning different endings over in their minds.

"You'd better not do anything," Hawk Nose warned, "or else we'll lock your ass up."

"Good morning," I said, smiling.

And two of New York's finest rode off into the lambent dawn.

The homosexual has come of age, displaying what he has always hidden, mentally, physically—testicles. Yet despite Gay Lib, there are enough unregistered closet cases to form a commonwealth about the size of Puerto Rico. But the types I'm concerned with here do not belong to either world, yet are as united as grass to earth. That third army of men. Buddies. Masturbating movie-goers, traditional shirt-and-tie men, images of father and grandfather. The ruddy-faced retired firemen, with the *Daily News* turned to the racing results. But hot lips wants to race down. Men who go to cheap movies and bars where three drinks will cost the price of one. Not much has been written about the Homosexual Bowery, where masculine sex outnumbers "girlie" sex.

In moments of grand depression, I think of myself as the Cholly Knickerbocker of the Bowery, writing about young and old men in the last act of life. Men who sit in the foyer of hell as they wait to be escorted into the ballroom of death. But it is always cocktail hour for the "girls" who are sometimes called garbage and ash-can queens. Their past lives and wine have pushed them beyond *The Boys in the Band.* I'm thinking of one queen in particular. Now what kind of female would wear a ratty fur jacket on a summer morning? But once he/she sort of had it together: white-framed dark glasses, jet-black dimestore wig, white halter, lime-green shorts (before the hot-pants vogue), plus a wad of dirty rags. This queen not only wipes off car windows at Houston and Second Avenue, but tries to engage motorists in conversation and, like a visiting celebrity, hops up on the hood of a car, announces: "I've just arrived from Hollywood." You may laugh or choke with disgust but the queen is for real. Sometimes 5 P.M. traffic is stalled: the queen is dancing, waving to her fans.

The closet cases are another story. Masculine, they open under the toll of whiskey and wine. Masculine gestures give. A grand lady is talking, inviting, and to hell with the buddies, the bartender, the crowd of regulars. No matter, no matter, the closet is open. Until tomorrow. But we've been to that country before, too, haven't we? At least we have read the travel folders, and our friends have visited that country. Well, now we're heading down the trail, deep into Marlboro country (before the appearance of James Jones's *From Here to Eternity* Pall Mall cigarettes were considered effete. Now Pall Mall is the "hard-hat" cigarette, the jail-house cigarette). The Marlboro men would be the first to admit it, sober or stoned. These men have been the backbone of our army, navy, and marine corps. Many of them were the heads of families. Most of them blame the opposite sex for their defeat. So they turned to whiskey, wine, and the company of men.

They do not hate women. They avidly watch and comment on the hippie girls and the blue-collar Puerto Rican and Italian women of the neighborhood. On payday and welfare day, most of them never get laid. But a surprising number of them have each other. Between the "weeds" (any place where the grass is high), jail, and prison, and the for-men-only hotels of the Bowery . . . something happened. Who lit the first flame and where? All I know is what I'm going to tell you.

In most cases, I do not even know their names. But I have seen them on the Bowery for a long time and have kept a mental file on them. I know the clean-shaven ex-army sergeant will be on the sidewalk come morning. About a month from now, he will look as he does this morning. I know the pipe-smoking old sailor has a photographic collection of nude teenage boys.

I know that at high noon, two winos entered the Chinese Garden. Each had a pint of La Boheme white port. They sat on the second entrance steps and talked and drank as men will do. Then one of them sprawled out, resting his head on the other's leg. He's passing out, I thought. But his friend looked down at him and caressed his face. The man turned his head and went down. At high noon. In full view of passing traffic.

The father and son are a Bowery legend.

"Oh, shut up," said the queenly father in a tough voice.

"Listen," the son told him. "I went out and worked to buy that wine. Don't tell me to shut up."

"Snotty-nosed bitch," the father said.

"You're just mad because I love John Wayne."

Now in my time I have observed quite a few men and women serving head. But the first prize has to go to a crew-cut man in his early thirties. There is a solid, Midwestern look about him. Even now he looks as if he owns a small successful business and can afford to take his family to New York for a holiday. If he is not self-employed, he is his boss's backbone. I suppose that is why he serves head with such passion. The other day, Crew Cut was going through a desperate scene in the Chinese Garden. His trick was a nervous little man who kept scanning the garden, while folding and unfolding a newspaper. He looked at me, crossed his legs, and pretended to read. It was very comical. I felt like saying: "Get with it and don't mind me. I am communing with my thirty-nine trees." Finally, Nervous Joe tried to block my view with the newspaper.

On another occasion, just before darkness set in, a young white man and a slightly older, slender black man were sitting about twenty feet from me, drinking dark port wine. They were sitting near the streetlight. But did I really see the black man place his head between the other man's legs? No, my eyes are tired, my mind is tired.

Presently the two men got up and walked over and sat down under a tree, almost directly in front of me, the sidewalk separating us. But I could not hear what they were saying. All I could do was watch the black man stretch out on the grass, then turn to the young white man, who sat with his back against the tree. Finally, he stood up, and I heard him say, "I'll see you around."

The slightly older black man decided to pay me a visit.

"What's happening?"

"Nothing," I said. "I don't have a goddamn thing."

"Wish I could help you."

"But you can't," I told the man.

He thought about this briefly, then spotted a tall, long-haired blond man walking through the garden. He took leave of me and ran after the tall young man, who ignored him. Nevertheless, the black continued to run down his game. He puts his arms around the blond man. Suddenly the blond swung at him, and one, two, three, the fight was on. The blond had the slender man pinned against a tree and cursed him. The slender black man rubbed the blond's buttocks. The blond bolted up from the ground and walked away silently with the black following. They stopped and began talking. The slender black man tipped up on his toes and kissed the blond's lips. The blond young man protested but relented, and then they moved over into the tall grass and made love.

And why are they more comfortable talking about baseball than about their sex lives?

Mail arrives as if programmed by a doomsday computer: P.E.N. dues, Xeroxed McGovern letters, Museum of Modern Art announcements and bills, a request to subscribe to a new *little* magazine for twelve dollars per year; they would also like me to write for them, gratis. Another one of Maggie's HELP notes from Paris.

Dear Charles:
What the hell is going on? Are you all right? You haven't invited me to the States. In fact, you said nothing. Should I return to the States? Well, the goddamn French are out of town. A holiday and I am grateful. Received a

goddamn letter from my brother. He's a square-headed, cheap son of a bitch.
I tore up the letter and went out and got stoned. But the following day, I
received a wonderful letter from Mother. I don't know how she does it. She's
in a wheelchair now but still advises the garden club, plays a mean game of
bridge, etc. I felt rather good after Mother's letter. But I've got to get out of
Paris. I've had the goddamn French. I was thinking about Spain. Shit. I'd
probably run into M., the bastard. He still owes me a bundle. I heard he was
on Gib, gambling. Mister Big-Time Spender. Why don't we meet somewhere? Do you have any money? Is the book finished yet? I will have to sort
of tuck in until the first of the year which means no new clothes.

But if I were back in the States, I could shop at Klein's, Orbach's. Take
care and write. WRITE. Remember: I am your friend.

Love
Maggie

Visited my broker, who has an office at First Street and the Bowery. Tony is familiar with junkies, artists, and writers. He remem-
bers Kate Millett from the old days. I pick up the portable typewriter, chat briefly with Tony, and make it up to the Kenton.

"I am a writer if I never write another line," Tess Schlesinger
wrote many years ago. No doubt it was a euphoric moment. But
I've lost that passion. Scott Fitzgerald and his dazzling green light!
His rich, hopeless dream: "Tomorrow we will run faster, stretch
out our arms farther."

But I'm knocking down wine, have swallowed my sixth Dexie
of the day. A goddamn tic has started under my right eye. I have
almost a dozen books that I've read and enjoyed. Then read, son
of a bitch.

I stare at the typewriter, mounted on a gray metal nightstand,
have a great fantasy: Miss Carolyn Kizer has jumped off the Washington Monument. Miss Kizer did not respond to my request for
an application from the National Council on the Arts. Even after I
got important people to intercede for me, it was another month
before the lady replied. Ah! She was sorry to hear of my financial
difficulties. The lady had recently read marvelous reviews of my
bête-noire novel The Wig. The novel had been published almost
four years ago, and government funds were tight, but would I be
interested in a job as writer-in-residence at a small black college in
the South?

Absurd truths, absurd lies. Drinking again and remembering

when—the United States Information Agency used certain passages from *The Messenger*. And one heard and read of writers who had received grants and hadn't published one book, or writers who had received grants and were reviewed on the back pages of the Sunday *New York Times Book Review*. One also heard of writers who received grants because they knew someone or had slept with someone.

Perhaps I should follow the advice that I've been given over the years: buy a tweed suit or whatever type of suit is fashionable at the moment and make the literary-cocktail *la ronde*. You know, even blacks do it.

And your father or my father might do it. I'll never do it: But I'll knock down more wine and go out on the fifth-floor fire escape of the Kenton Hotel.

From this distance the view is glorious. The pollution screen even filters the burning afternoon sun. There is no breeze. A sort of suspended quiet, although I can see traffic moving down Chrystie Street; children playing ball in the park; drunks in twos and threes, supporting buddies like wounded soldiers after the battle of defeat. Toward the east, a row of decayed buildings has the decadent beauty of Roman ruins. But only at a distance. Trained pigeons, chickens, and junkies inhabit those rooftops. Taking another drink, I think: I wish I could fly, fly, far away.

Here, there, again, and always, the Why of the last seven years. Skulled depression as I sit and watch the sun disappear. Aware of the muted, miscellaneous noises that drift up from the street, I am also aware of the loss of something. Thinking of all I've done and not done. Thinking and feeling a terrible loss.

"Man, they jumps," Sam exclaimed. "Didn't you know that?"

Sweet-potato brown, Sam has a Hitler, Jr., mustache. An ice-pick scar outlines his left cheek like a nervous question mark. His small bright black eyes seem to recede as if the sight of another pair of eyes was somehow indecent. We had worked together briefly in the Catskills, and I had helped him through several bad Manhattan scenes. His wife had taken the three children and gone to California with another woman. Sam's running buddy, "Two-Five," a thirty-three-year-old crippled Vietnam veteran, was beaten to death on the Bowery. But Sam was laid back now. He

had it together. A wide-brimmed, eggshell, plantation straw hat
raffishly knocked back on his head. The thin white body shirt was
new. He wore lilac bell-bottoms, trimmed in red. The Florsheim
patent-leather boots had a permanent shine.

"You can't even see the motherfuckers," Sam said.

"I thought you said you could."

"You can't see the babies, and even the big ones are like spies.
They good at hiding out."

"Oh shit, baby."

"Wait until they start walking," Sam laughed.

"Man, are you putting me on?"

"It ain't Mission Impossible. Now, do like I told you. I'll check
with you later. Gotta go to Brooklyn and see my sister. She's fighting with the landlord again."

Frequently, on the Bowery, I had seen dirty winos enter and
wipe off chair seats with their hands. I always marveled at this
small gesture: there was still a touch of human pride in the men. In
my novel *The Wig,* Mr. Sunflower Ashley-Smithe says, "I keep a
dozen milk bottles filled with lice so I won't be lonely." I had slept
around through the years, but I had never encountered lice. Small
wingless insects, parasitic on men, especially Bowery men, and the
sons and daughters of the Flower Generation.

They were in my hair, under my arms, in the jungle of pubic
hair. I itched and scratched day and night. You could take the
large ones in your hands and crush them; they made a crackling
sound, their blood was crimson. But the poor babies were interesting. Imagine a dozen white angora kittens about the size of pin-
heads, taking their first steps, crawling against the collar of your
brand-new black knit shirt. Genocide, baby. Burn the shirt,
shower, shower, shower. I anointed my body with so much oil that
I was under the delusion that I was the Sun King, reincarnated.

Toward 6 P.M. after the tic under my eye was sated and I could no
longer stand the bone-white cubicle, after I had controlled my
impulse to throw the typewriter out the window, I popped another
Dexie, desecrated the wine bottle, and later joined the residents in
the lobby to watch the news. This was the garrulous hour. Some of
the men had returned from work, others from panhandling and
dinner at the Municipal Lodging House around the corner. This

was the hour of camaraderie, con games, great lies, illegal drinking, loneliness, anxiety.

Always skulled, I made my way through the crowd, exchanging brief, social greetings. Then, sat on the windowsill, trying to concentrate on the six o'clock news or staring out the window.

Against the deep blue of early evening, they turned on the spotlight at the Holy Name Mission and church at Mott and Bleecker Streets and you could see the white-and-gold-draped statue of Jesus Christ. It was not a life-size statue. From a distance, with the lights playing on it, Jesus Christ was larger than life. Sometimes He appeared to move. Extend His hand, turn slightly. Desperate, I needed a lift. Take me higher. Ground the motors of the stockcars racing in my brain. But "God never worked very well with me," Hemingway's Lady Brett Ashley said. Somehow I can't get in step with the masses and their current religious phenomenon, seeking belladonna for the soul. Tricky business, too. For what is religion but the act of levitation?

It would be much better if I read Malcolm Lowry's *Under the Volcano*. Through his despair, I might be able to understand my despair, to cut the loss, elevate hope.

Of course, I was unable to do this. I did not even reread *Under the Volcano*.

The blank space is self-explanatory. There were a series of days and nights that I do not want to remember. Someday. Perhaps.

I lost love because the threat of insanity, suicide, and murder began to tango around the perimeter of that love.

Someone stole my passport.

I sold the typewriter, radio, and books.

I lost my grandmother's wedding band.

I kept my blackness.

I always felt like a refugee among foe/friends, friend/foes.

I lost my head at last. I watched my head boogaloo happily down the street. As Head desires.

However, one irrefutable truth remained: I could always return to the Catskills.

THIS CATSKILL SCENE is a Japanese watercolor: white poplar and pine trees command the fields; the mountains are shrouded in green. Serenity becomes a silent song. Then, suddenly, the sun is smothered by gray clouds. It's an Idaho sky, a pensive Hemingway sky, and you know you are in America. The eye travels out across the land: a buff-colored, shingled ranch house in a clearing of young trees. Fronting the house like emblems are two late-model cars, which spell money. Closer at hand, beer cans litter the wild grass like baubles from the moon. About a dozen butterball kittens are playing in the grass. Running, leaping, rigid before the moment of attack, their multicoloring becomes a shifting pattern in this unofficial season of death.

Originally this was hunting country. It still is, in a restricted sense, although No Hunting signs are everywhere. Vodka-mellow, I like to believe that Hemingway would have felt at home up here—Here where in summer young deer frolic like schizoid ballet dancers. But I wonder what Papa would think about the cats. "Any time you decide to shoot cats, it's the cat season," a man said yesterday. However, no one has said that it is the perfect season to hunt and harass men. Let me ease your mind: that, too, fuses in the clear air like the simultaneous orgasms of lovers.

The lower-echelon employees do not talk of love. It's always other hotels, booze, the Bowery, weapons. None of them own weapons as far as I know (should I write regretfully or gratefully?). Most of them are small-town men, accustomed to the hunting seasons and to being hunted in the ghettos of our towns and cities. Now all they have is this transient gig for a day, a week, a month. Loneliness is a mothergrabber for them.

I would not like to look into their eyes without the cats. In the evening, the cats silently sit on the porch of the kitchen-help house and wait for dinner. Sometimes the men steal tuna fish and tinned milk for their favorites. I am neither lonely nor a fanatical cat lover, but I buy cartons of milk for them. I find myself talking to them in the evening. Questioning them about their lineage, calling them every mother in the book, carefully pouring milk into the tuna tins.

Several ingenious men have built cat shelters out of cardboard boxes and remnants of carpeting. Some of them are violently jealous of the new kittens in the underground staff dining room— where at this very moment an argument has begun—and ends abruptly as one of the contestants exits with: "Fuck you. I'll see you in Monticello." A weekend employee turns toward me. He is eating Sacher cake and says, "Somebody is gonna break that son of a bitch's neck." This small man, who is very fond of sweets, is my dinner conversationalist, although we rarely sit at the same table.

Nodding, the small man smiles. "Yeah. Last week I bought a rifle for self-protection. Yeah. Up here you gotta be nice or they'll get you."

My dinner conversationalist is unaware of what I am writing and continues to rap, the Sherlock Holmes cap obscuring his eyebrows. A man's skull was fractured on the stone floor beneath my feet. A dishwasher was knifed to death two miles from here. And they never found out who killed the maid in————. Two motorcyclists killed a man, dumped his body in the waterfall, which is a fifteen-minute walk down the hill.

I question my friend about cats. "Yeah. They all right," he says. "I got two in Monticello. They nice."

Cats—common domestic mammals kept by man as pets or to catch rats and mice. Sometimes roasted over an open fire or the base of a succulent stew at Starvation Hour. But for the moment, the United States of America is the richest country in the world.

We do not have to worry about domestic cat on the menu—or do we?

Certainly, I wasn't thinking about cats when I went to visit Joey. In the sunflower brightness of a Thursday afternoon, I walked four miles to Joey's hotel, stopping off at a roadside café for a cold six-pack.

Joey offered vodka at ten in the morning. Why not, as we used to say in Tangier. We began drinking and exchanging local news. Then, shortly before twelve, the sound of bullets interrupted our conversation.

"Whenever a hotel has too many cats," Joey, an old Catskill hand, explained, "they shoot them." At lunch Joey pointed out the two men who had killed the cats. The "second," a transient mental-hospital patient, was Mr. Clean. His head was shaped and glowed like a choice eggplant. The main man was lean and rather placid. I watched as he placed his elbows on the white trestle table and hand-rolled a perfect cigarette. The second scooped up the dead cats with a shovel and threw them down the hill. Joey remembered a record by the DC-5 titled "Bits and Pieces."

Postscript: Exactly one week later, at my home away from home, the local fascisti shot more unwanted cats at dusk. House cats and favorites survived.

On my dishwasher's day off, I walked four miles into the village of Monticello, shopped around, paid my respects to several bars, and returned to my kosher hotel. I hoped to spend a quiet day reading, finding out what was going on in the world. But it was payday. The transient workers were doing their thing, celebrating their past and future, the low cost of labor. I drank with them. Skulled in the middle region of my mind, returned to my room, and began reading *Time* magazine. The black print kept slipping off the slick white page. Sleep came down like a knockout drop.

Morning arrived gray and disfigured. The afternoon was a merciless drag. Skulled again, I watched reality enter the kitchen. The bearded Puerto Rican "captain" (the dining-room porter) sat down on the floor and removed his shoes. A melodrama would end if someone moved a stack of plates twelve inches. Tottering old drunks put iced-tea glasses in the wrong plastic rack. A young black takes exactly twenty minutes to put on his apron. Fat Boy tells the fourth version of the woman he did not have on his day off.

On the lunch break, the dishwasher went to his room and tried to sleep. His mind double-timed. Perhaps he would stay in the Catskills forever. Too much, too much, I thought, while the building rocked with the beat of an army payday. I felt as if I had been riding a headless horse for a long time, and kept turning on the mattress. My penis rose as if to protest against the virginal fast. "You should masturbate," I said in a marzipan voice. Why was I always so sexually alert in the country, where the score was zero? New York City was impotent. Cold, corruption, hate had corroded the last vault of reality. Then I remembered *Time* magazine. It was quite by accident that I flipped to page 81—The Press. A magnificent photograph of Norman Mailer centered on the page. A tough, intelligent face outlined with compassion. The face of an urbane carpenter in a $200 suit. This emotion was enlarged by the dishwasher's respect for the man. They had met several times and had exchanged notes through the years. Certainly Mailer was the best writer in America. He was one of the few writers who could force the dishwasher's brain to waltz! I began to read "Mailer's America" with great interest. *Time* was inspired to reprint choice bits from *Miami and the Siege of Chicago*. Mailer's comments about Nixon and Humphrey (by the time you read this, the name of the next White Father Bird will be on the tip of your red, white, and blue tongue) were pretty good. His description of McCarthy's followers: "Their common denominator seemed to be found in some black area of the soul, a species of disinfected idealism which gave one the impression when among them of living in a lobotomized ward of Upper Utopia."

Like the overture of true love which will last until dawn or until you have brushed your teeth, Mailer's comments got better. Naturally, his comment on civil rights and blacks interested the dishwasher: ". . . he was getting tired of Negroes and their rights. It was a miserable recognition, and on many a count, for if he felt even a hint this way, then what immeasurable tides of rage must be loose in America itself? . . . But he was so heartily sick listening to the tyranny of soul music, so bored with Negroes triumphantly late for appointments, so depressed with Black inhumanity to Black in Biafra, so weary of being sounded in the subway by black

Absolutely Nothing to Get Alarmed About381

eyes, so despairing of the smell of booze and pot and used-up hope in bloodshot eyes of Negroes bombed at noon, so envious finally of that liberty to abdicate from the long year-end decade-drowning yokes of work and responsibility that he must have become in some secret part of his flesh a closet republican. . . ." Does personal despair, aging, the general mood of the times make a writer from the avant-garde uptight? Or was this "simple emotion" caused by the Reverend Abernathy's late appointment? Was Mailer looking for a fight? Years ago, he had written the famous *The White Negro*. He was the Father of Hip. He had almost single-handedly brought the world of Paul Bowles to the new frontier, exposing that world to thousands of middle-class youth and their elders. Certainly he had paid his slumming dues. Pot, pills, booze are old joys and nightmares to him—for he had touched the outer limits of despair in more than one instance. Even with his education, affluence, he went under in the dream, got flogged by the bats of hell. What could he possibly expect from American blacks in their situation? And now: "They had been a damned minority for too long, a huge indigestible boulder in the voluminous, ruminating government gut of every cowlike Democratic Administration. Perhaps the WASP had to come to power in order that he grow up, in order that he take the old primitive root of his life-giving philosophy—which required every man to go through battles, if the world would live, and every woman to bear a child—yes, take that root off the high attic shelf of some Prudie Parsely of a witch—ancestor, and plant it in the smashed glass and burned brick of the twentieth century's junkyard."

Prudie Parsely might have been incognito during the grass-green Eisenhower years. Indeed. But as I hunt and peck and go to press, Prudie has taken root and is trying to strangle anyone who opposes her. For years she has been the little sweet pea in the jolly green giant's pod; her small-town American heart (which is shaped exactly like a Norman Rockwell valentine) pulsed with security, a Dow Jones high of righteousness. Prudie was safe. Old Glory flew high, and God blessed the foreign descendants, and for a very long time they believed this was true. Heart of hearts! Vietnam, taxes, and black power made the beat irregular. Miss Parsely is aghast. She's a little afraid and is now working her army overtime. Anything goes. Why, the lady will take anything with two or four feet.

Indeed. The little uptight white Protestants and their non-Protestant followers are getting it together. Whips sing in the air; blacks beware. Genocide, masquerading as Law and Order awaits you. So be prepared, pray that you take one and, hopefully, a hundred with you.

Just about the time you think everything is breaking even—even-steven, mail arrives. There is no escape. A survey questionnaire: "Why You Did or Did Not Sell Out to the Establishment." Among the men and women listed: Norman Mailer, Paul Getty, Frank Sinatra, Nina Simone, and Charles Wright. The dishwasher was amused. What tony company. A shot glass of amusement, I thought, and then made it down the hill, down to Harrison's. The lower-echelon employees were not allowed to drink in the hotel bar. Harrison's was the only bar for miles around—a typical highway bar—these bars might well serve as a symbol of America; there was something magnificently expansive about them, yet they could suck in their breath, hold it, forever. Harrison's was located in the middle of the Catskills, and I had been mistaken for a Puerto Rican by a small-town Wasp who puked drunken black hatred. Another small-town Wasp offered to buy me drinks, then informed me that Governor Wallace would shortly appear on the television screen.

However, the mood of Harrison's that afternoon had the camaraderie of a late-summer afternoon. The television was turned off, and I ordered a double Scotch (I had received a small royalty check) which meant I would not have to signal the bartender-owner, who was reading John Updike's *Couples*.

"Chuck, my man," Chuck exclaimed. He was playing pool. Black, twenty-seven years old, he appeared to be extremely well adjusted. Chuck was the second cook at the hotel, and everyone liked him. Before making his last winning shot, he looked over at Miss Mary and winked. Miss Mary, as everyone called her, was a maid at the hotel and was something of a legend. Miss Mary owned a brand-new robin's-egg-blue Cadillac. Miss Mary was a moonlighter. I looked across at her, laughing over a Seagram and 7-Up with a couple of transient rednecks. Perhaps it was true, but I wouldn't fork over ten dollars or twenty dollars to Miss Mary. She was too much woman for me. But even after I turned away, the image of her tits under the white nylon uniform stayed with me. Those tits seemed capable of guiding an ocean liner into harbor. I wasn't interested in Miss Mary's face, although it was attractive, unlined. She must have been at least forty-five.

Chuck won, and there were a lot of bravos. He left with Miss Mary, left in his yellow Thunderbird.

The Thunderbird's motor was souped up, and I heard it as Chuck zoomed up the hill. I ordered another double, feeling a little down, wanting a little loving. Then I ordered a six-pack and made it.

About an hour later, there was a knock on my door.

"Chuck," Chuck said. "Busy, man?"

"No." I yawned through the door. "Come on in. The door's open."

Chuck entered in his dazzling cook's whites. His dazzling boyish smile was wide. We were never buddy-buddy but got along well.

"Oh, man. I'm sorry. You're reading. You gotta let me read some of your books."

"Any time," I said, sitting up. "Wanna beer?"

"Sure could use one. Hot as hell this afternoon. Must have put away two six-packs in the kitchen this afternoon."

"Yeah." I grinned. "That kitchen is a bitch."

"You read a lot," Chuck was saying, "and I'm sorry to disturb you, but I came up to ask if you wanted a piece of ass."

This is just too goddamn much, I told myself. What's the angle? But already Junior was standing tall, waiting for me to put on my racing shoes.

"It's just down the hill," Chuck said. He wasn't looking at me then with that dazzling smile.

I stood up. "Anybody I know?"

"Yeah, man. Great piece of ass."

"Let's make it, baby."

"Man, you're ready," Chuck said as we made it down the hill. I kept on putting Junior in place, but the son of a bitch wanted to stand up and cheer.

The low-slung maids' quarters was a former chicken coop. Remodeling gave it the appearance of a jerry-built post-World War II ranch house. Hundreds of stamping feet had killed the grass

around the quarters. But the hardy hollyhocks survived; they
grew tall; their riotous colors were like a torch against the surrounding countryside, and all was quiet except for the distant
sound of B. B. King on a phonograph or a radio within the quarters.

Chuck, grinning, unlocked number 7; there must have been at
least twenty keys on his chain, and they jingled like Oriental
chimes.

"Well," he said, "here we are."

We walked directly into the living room, wallpapered with an
intricate design of garden flowers. Crepe-paper flowers were
everywhere, plus the scent of lilac room refresher. For a moment, I
thought I would pass out.

Chuck offered me a drink. "Mary made all of the flowers," he
said with the sweet charm of an ambitious young mortician.

Muffling a laugh, I nodded. What was Chuck's game? Already,
I was getting a little uneasy. Boredom had touched me on the
shoulder.

"Want another drink?"

"Nope."

"Okay." Chuck sighed. "Mary's in the next room."

Miss Mary lay on the wide pastel-covered bed, her body (the
color of muddy water) was voluptuous. What appeared to be a
long curly wig outlined her pleasant face. She was wearing nothing
but a strong supporting white bra. I had never seen one like it,
except on models in magazines. All the women I knew used little
skinny bras.

Miss Mary had her eyes closed. A permanent smile colored her
lips. I had a funny idea that Miss Mary might scream, and that her
red lips might leap from her face and run out of the room.

"Hello, Chuck," Miss Mary said painfully.

"Hi," I chuckled. There was no door between the two rooms,
and I could see Chuck sitting on the sofa. But he was not staring
out the window. He was looking straight ahead at the floral
papered walls. Junior was at parade rest, Miss Mary weighed at
least 180. But what the hell! I stripped and sat down on the bed.
Even after my hot hands touched her thighs, Junior was still at
parade rest. I thought that Junior was retreating from the battle-
field and told myself, Baby, you got your work cut out for you.

Miss Mary opened her eyes briefly and touched my arm. "It's all right," she said.

I didn't answer her. My hot, greedy hands reached for the bra. Miss Mary's hand had engulfed Junior, who still seemed in the act of retreating.

Good God! There must have been twenty goddamn hooks on the bra. My short arms could not encircle Miss Mary. Besides, she was trying to rise and anoint Junior, who was beginning to march.

"Wait a minute," I said. Miss Mary appeared not to hear me. She had raised up, opened her mouth, was prepared to sing to Junior. He was at attention, and I had the bra off. Junior stood firmly at attention as Miss Mary lovingly caressed him, but depression touched my shoulder. I didn't particularly want to get blown. But I lay back on the bed and let Mary work out. There was nothing extraordinary about her tongue and lips. I raised up and grabbed her tits—mini-blimps; a man could fly high and safe between them or, buoyed by their softness, sleep the sleep of rapture. I pulled Miss Mary up toward me. Now she was crying softly. She held on to Junior as if she wanted to squeeze the breath out of him.

Miss Mary wanted to baptize Junior again in the name of desire; I wanted to get laid.

"Come on," I said.

Miss Mary was breathing very hard. She had a coughing spell, but I went ahead, while the woman who made crepe-paper flowers protested. Desire had reached its peak with me. All I wanted was to plow into those 180 pounds.

"Chuck—Chuckie, please. Oh, no—"

But it was pleasant with the pillow under her. Yes, lovely, for although she was a large woman, a baby cantaloupe couldn't fit into her vagina. It didn't take very long. Spent, happy, and grinning, I tried to pull away.

"No," Miss Mary cried. Her large sweating body shook, and the most terrible sounds I had ever heard, fast and painful, seemed to come from her stomach. Junior was getting uneasy, and Miss Mary's arms had me in a bind.

I took her again, took her slow and easy—this one was for her and the flowers. Those terrible sounds had stopped, and I could feel her pleasure as her body moved toward me.

Grind, slow and easy. Her face in my hands, her tongue in my mouth like a goldfish on a cake of ice, then suddenly she became rigid as her tongue sought mine and moans crept up from her throat.

"Don't get up," Miss Mary said.

I tried not to show my irritation. Leaning over, I kissed and caressed those fantastic tits. Oh! If Rubens were alive and I were a billionaire—I'd commission him to paint Miss Mary. The large, muddy-water-colored body against the pastel sheets and pillow-cases, trimmed with lace (no doubt Miss Mary's personal touch), and masses of crepe-paper flowers that never grew in Mother Nature's garden. Henry Moore could do the boobs in bronze— what a bedside trophy.

"Chuckie," Miss Mary whined.

"Love, I've got to go to the bathroom."

I passed Chuck in the living room. "Okay, man?" He grinned.

Returning the grin, I said, "Right on, man."

It was a very humid afternoon, and I had planned to shower. But I wanted to lay Miss Mary again, plow into those 180 pounds. I hosed down Junior and the surrounding hairy pond, made my swift exit, whistling—are you ready? whistling, "Wish I were in Dixie again." Miss Mary was a pretty good lay, and I felt good.

In the living room, I drank from the Seagram quart bottle, then started toward the bedroom.

Chuck, clothed in the cook's whites, was on the bed. I watched as he pulled Miss Mary's legs apart. She had her eyes closed and moaned like an old female cat. There was something ritualistic about their movements. Something familiar, and I didn't like it.

Chuck caressed the back-breaking large legs.

"Oh, Mama," he moaned. Then buried his head between Miss Mary's legs as if to sleep. Of course he did not sleep. A seemingly well-adjusted young man with a neat Afro crew cut, his medium-sized head became a spinning top. Several times he jerked his head back and stared into Miss Mary's door of life, before diving back down. Miss Mary's legs rested on Chuck's slender shoulders. There was something crude about her movements as she pressed Chuck's head tighter. But the young, black second cook was balling. Apparently, he preferred the leftover juices from our luncheon.

Nathanael West
First Comfort Station
Purgatorial Heights

Dear West:

Por favor—forgive the delay. True, it has been almost six years. Hope that it has been less than a day in your particular hell. It began in our New York and followed me through the small transient rooms of all your depressing hotels. Now Absurdity and Truth pave the parquet of my mind. The pain is akin to raw alcohol on the testicles. But I'm not complaining. Life's eyedropper is being sterilized with ant piss. Hallucinations? Joshing? West—I-Am-Not-Spaced-Out, despite the East and West Village rumors. Slightly skulled though. Celebrating the Day of the Dead.

I suppose the dead dog at the bottom of Malcolm Lowry's Mexican ravine is almost home now. But the yellow-button white daisies have taken root. I like that.

Take care and watch the shit.
Charles

P.S. Here's a little clipping from *The New York Times:* "Aosta, Italy (AP)—Cold, avalanches, and lack of food killed about 20 percent of the wild Alpine goats and chamois in Grand Paradise."